BOOK ONE

BOOKS OF
BEFORE & NOW

PAPA LUCY & THE BONEMAN

Jason Fischer

PAPA LUCY & THE BONEMAN:
THE BOOKS OF BEFORE AND NOW BOOK ONE
Copyright © 2021 Jason Fischer. All rights reserved.

Published by Outland Entertainment LLC
3119 Gillham Road
Kansas City, MO 64109

Founder/Creative Director: Jeremy D. Mohler
Editor-in-Chief: Alana Joli Abbott
Senior Editor: Gwendolyn Nix
Media: Tara Cloud Clark

ISBN: 978-1-954255-99-9
Worldwide Rights
Created in the United States of America

Editor: Gwendolyn N. Nix
Cover Illustration: Steve Firchow
Cover Design: Jeremy D. Mohler
Interior Layout: Mikael Brodu

Government
of South Australia

Arts South Australia

The first draft of Papa Lucy was funded by Arts
South Australia in 2011.

Printed and bound in the United States of America.

Visit **outlandentertainment.com** to see more, or follow us on our
Facebook Page **facebook.com/outlandentertainment/**

To Kate, Logan and Lottie,
you are my everything.

— PROLOGUE —

On the shore of a lake, a midden rose from the grit. A cairn of bone and shell could be seen for many miles, nothing more than a nameless curiosity to most. Over long centuries, travellers had added to this midden, stacking their sacrifices until the grave became a hill, the hill a shifting plain of death. Now, it only served as a landmark.

Over time, the purpose of this enormous shrine of bone was forgotten. Only the maddest or most fervent made the trip to this lonely place. Those who stayed reported bad dreams, an eerie feeling that the midden was calling to them, and always, the urge to climb into the grave, to burrow deep, deep into the bones.

Then the pilgrims stopped visiting altogether. Pilgrimages to Sad Plain became more popular, where the faithful gathered up shards of glass. They sliced at their feet and faces, wailing and petitioning the Family—Papa Lucy for protection, the Lady Bertha to curse an enemy.

Few came to call upon the Boneman.

So when the midden shifted, bones and rubble sliding and crashing into a cloud of fine white dust, there was no one to witness it. One whole side of the cairn collapsed, leaving the dome in ruins.

A naked man emerged from the midden, covered in centuries of filth. The woken sleeper clambered across the carpet of calcified shards. On shaky legs, he headed for the water's edge and waded out into the soupy murk, sluicing the brine along his face and arms, washing away the thick crust that clung to his flesh.

This lake had been fresh water once, fed by streams from the nearby Range, and clear all the way to the sandy bottom. The fish had been plentiful here. He'd known many friends in the fishing villages, spent several pleasant summers hidden here. It had been his favourite escape from the intrigues of Crosspoint.

Now it was a place of desolation, of death fully realised. The water was still and stank of sulphur, its basin ringed with dried scum. The thick grass on the dunes had died off, and the sand drifted now, blowing through the burnt ruins of the old villages, holiday spots where he'd loved and laughed and walked as a man.

That was all before Sad Plain. They had all been injured that day, but none were struck so badly as he. The fiery kiss of the enemy had melted the very flesh from his bones, but he could not die. His blackened skeleton had stood firm when the fires guttered and he had walked on, the visible frame of his bones held together by nothing but his own dark magics.

His mastery over death was no easy thing to set aside.

His brother fallen. His wife swallowed into madness. All of their forces scattered and broken. He'd fought on alone. Allies turned foes, a city turned to shards, the world itself turning on them. The Mother of Glass. Only his skeletal shape stood firm, destroying the enemy when things were at their darkest. This broken sorcerer had been many things before Sad Plain, but ever afterwards he was known as the Boneman.

"It worked, brother," he said out loud, his voice hoarse, his throat coated with a thick slime. The magic had taken centuries, and more death than he could imagine, but the flesh had grown back onto his body. He could feel the contours of his face, his shoulders and arms.

Smiling, he scrubbed furiously, the caked-on grot giving way to the vinegary brine, coating the still surface of the water with a spreading film of grease.

Then he saw it.

"No," the Boneman whispered, rubbing at his eyes. Was he going crazy? He'd been aware throughout his internment, a clever mind bound in a dark place, each thought a decade in the making.

What he saw was real enough, and not his imagination. His arm had the shape and feel of the old limb, but it didn't look right. The skin was see-through and rubbery, a translucent gelatine coating him from head to toe. Once he'd been olive-skinned, but now he was the colour of toffee.

Jellied organs, opaque muscles, all of his parts were present and working. But even now, after all this time, he remained an abomination. He was not fit to be seen walking the busy streets of Crosspoint.

He wept, and the tears were knives pushing through his eyes, long dormant tear ducts leaking across his face.

Is Crosspoint even there, still? he thought. *What if I've slept through everything?*

Wading through the lake, the Boneman pushed through the slick of scum he'd washed from himself. The lake water was too cloudy for the sunlight to penetrate, and once the ripples ceased, he could see his reflection quite clearly.

A skull stared up from the water. The bone was wrapped in the same smoky rubber as the rest of him, his jaw-bone and teeth clearly visible, a dark ladder of vertebrae feeding into the base of that terrifying visage. A jelly beak protruded from his nasal cavity, a nose perfect in every dimension save that it was see-through, as were his lips. His tongue was like a sea-slug, a clear thing darting out past his blackened teeth.

His eyes were the only parts of *him* that remained, soft and brown and witness to far too many horrors. It was all that had escaped the fires, perhaps the cruellest part of this curse.

Our enemy could not kill me, so she left me the means to see myself. To live as a monster forever, he thought.

So this is what it feels like to have won.

The Boneman shuffled back towards the shore. A chill wind blew across the lake's surface. The raised goosebumps felt obscene as they ran along his see-through arms.

He felt cold, after feeling nothing for so long. The Boneman took stock of his new body, feeling all his other processes revive. His lungs wheezed, his coiled bag of guts squirmed, and his heart squeezed out a flow of whatever passed for blood in this jellied flesh.

A cloud, heavy with moisture and the colour of mustard, passed across the sun. He walked towards the ruined village as the rain broke, fat drops that stank of iron and stung his eyes.

The Boneman stepped around a handful of boats drawn up to the ruins, wood rotting and bleached bone-white by centuries of sunlight. The bottoms of all the boats were staved in.

Passing through a sand-choked door, the Boneman entered one of the huts. As his eyes adjusted to the gloom, he saw a tangle of nets and long man-bones, fat clusters of trinkets, and other homemade magic nailed to every available surface.

He puzzled out the charms, the patterns of colourful beads and knotwork. They tingled with failed potential and soured hope.

The Boneman spent the night in that forgotten place, alone with the cracked pottery and the ephemera of the long-dead family. Although the roof leaked and the wind howled through gaps in the battered planking, it was better than being out in the open. He found a flint stone and a heavily scratched striker that was probably older than the village itself. It seemed appropriate for him, so he kept it, making a fire to warm himself from the broken bones of the boats.

The sparks from the striker terrified him, and he cringed from the first lick of flame. He fought down the fear, fought down the memory of his flesh melting, running from his bones. He was cold, and this wasn't just a fire, it was survival.

He did not sleep, having slept for far too long. He watched the play of shadows on the wall instead, and spent the stormy night with the company of ghosts and memories, anything to avoid thinking of what he was meant to do now.

The far doors were closed to him now, and so were the shadow roads. When the Boneman pushed at the fabric between the worlds, it felt...different. His will slid across the boundaries of the universe as though they were greased, and he could not get a grip upon them.

Other magics were harder to perform now. Moving a pebble a short distance with his mind left him weak and shaky. When he reached out to the rest of the Family, he heard nothing but the chill silence of the Aum, that mirror-land throwing back his words. It was the first act of an apprentice mage to bounce messages across that invisible realm, much like a child skips stones across water. By rights, he should have been able to easily reach into it, find word of his brother.

Something was keeping him out.

The sun climbed through the sky, baking the storm-soaked ground into humidity. The Boneman left the village and the dead lake forever. He looked back only once, to wonder at the scale of the midden his brother had built above him.

Cradling the flint and striker, the Boneman owned nothing else but his nudity and the growing hunger in his gut. He was terribly thirsty, but he was not foolish enough to drink from the poisoned lake water.

Be an ascetic, he scolded himself. *It's not like you actually need to eat or drink.*

As the thought came to him, he wasn't sure if this was true now. So many things had changed. Perhaps he had nothing left to him now but mortality, a second chance with a body that hadn't turned out right.

The old lake road was pitted and overgrown with weeds, and he followed it back to the tradeway. A wayhouse had once stood there, strategically located on the route between Crosspoint and Langenfell. He remembered the small cluster of shops that serviced the holidaymakers, the taverna that raged all hours of the night.

During his slumber, he'd heard the faint whispers of pilgrims in the town, felt their essences trickle towards the midden. For a while, the visitors believed they slept at a safe enough distance, but too many of them visited the cairn, slipping into the bones and breathing their last. Soon, the wayhouse was abandoned, and the Boneman left alone in his tomb.

He walked through the cracked clay buildings, saw the field of sagging poles where merchants had once tethered horses and the big lizards used for haulage work. The taverna was still standing, and he spent a few minutes inside, nudging through the broken bottles and plates. He remembered bringing his wife here, the grand nights of cards, of philosophies argued until dawn, of friendships sworn and toasted to.

All of those people were dead now. He left that place quickly, the memories sitting bitter on his mind.

The Boneman sat cross-legged in the market square, where only the scars of old peg holes remained to show where the stalls had been. The sun beat down upon his bizarre body while he cast his mind outwards, looking for anything: a sign of civilisation, even a lone traveller who could tell him where the places of men were in this age—if they did not flee in terror when they saw him.

He found nothing but the rats in the ruins and other creatures roaming the hills about, native beasts thriving in the absence of the settlers. He called to them and even gave summons to a great serpent lurking in its nest, but he was too weak to seize control. They easily shook off the strange tickle in their simple minds.

Lip curling, the Boneman called for the rats. Soon a pair came before him, pale and sleek, eyes glazed, small rib-cages heaving rapidly. He snapped their necks clumsily and wondered how he'd go about eating them.

Further searching revealed a knife half eaten by rust and a musty old rug that he turned into a poncho by cutting a hole for his head. While looking for more wood to feed his tiny cook fire, the Boneman saw something behind a stable that drew him up short.

A light horse cart, wearing the decay of decades, not centuries. The tyres were flat, the rubber tubing cracked, but there was plenty of junk in the wayhouse. He might be able to fix this. The cart was in good shape, and it wouldn't take much to get it rolling again.

A skeletal horse was still fitted to the harness, the long bones scattered, the broad bridge of its spine still held together by dried sinew. A faint stain on the paving stones showed where its throat had been cut.

A sacrifice, then.

"They left you here for me," he whispered. He stroked the long horse skull and felt the history of the bones, the dry marrow telling him that yes, the horse was obedient, that it had died in confusion and pain.

A further communion with the remains gave the Boneman a flicker of insight into the master's actions. He felt the kindness of the man, the love and regret that forced the knife blade so many years ago. He guessed the killer of this horse to be a devout man, intent on his final destiny. There'd been no malice meant to this animal, and he was simply destroying his means of escape should all courage fail.

"It's okay now," he told the large skeleton. "It's going to be okay."

In sleeping, the Boneman had lost most of his magic, but this one thing remained to him. Death was his, and in this strange second life, the sorcerer could still hear the whisper of life that ran in bones. The trick was in knowing how to speak to these off-casts of life and just what to say.

Always with compassion, he thought.

One of the dead rats had its nest in the rubble of a wheelwright's shed and offered up this knowledge to the Boneman, even as its tiny carcass roasted on the spit. *And only with the direst of need. They've earned their rest, and it's cruel of you to disturb it.*

Nobody was there to see when the Boneman set off from the abandoned outpost, the horse cart limping along on ruined wheels.

Between the shafts of the cart, still strapped into the mouldering harness, the horse skeleton ran tirelessly, hauling the Boneman along the old tradeway. The vertebrae flexed and rolled before him, the ribs swaying slightly as four ivory legs pounded the ground in a clumsy canter.

Each bone touched its neighbour, reminded by the Boneman's gentle insistence of the connections the pieces had held in life. The horse-form held true, even though the sinew and tissue were mostly gone. A scrap of mane fluttered from the long skull.

A spirit inhabited these bones, an essence brought back over from the Underfog, the realm on the edge of death. Either the horse itself had returned or something else that was willing to wear this frame, obedient and desperate to take one more step in the land of life.

Wrapped in rags, driving a monster down a forgotten road, the Boneman found his situation absurd. He needed to find his brother, the mightiest sorcerer this world had ever seen, but had no idea of where to look.

He pressed on, shaking the reins to urge more speed from the dead horse. *He won't be too hard to find,* the Boneman reasoned. *Papa Lucy has a way of standing out.*

PART ONE

— THE FAILED APPRENTICE —

– 1 –

Lanyard Everett was alone and halfway towards dead. He limped out of a dry sea, barely noticing when his boots stopped grinding against the crust of salt. He kicked up plumes of red dust with each step.

Behind him lay a vastness of white, stretching to the fuzz of horizon and beyond that for untold miles. The saltpan had become his entire world, blinding him with every pass of the sun, and the ground seemed to glow during the chill of night.

His tracks led back to murder, to the ruined seed of a town, to an enemy who taunted him in his dreams. His master would have stood resolute against that nest of monsters, but Bauer was long dead. Lanyard's education was half-finished at best.

He'd been overwhelmed, driven out.

Lanyard crossed into the Inland, leaving dead seas and defeat behind him. He hauled a wind-car, sails limp in the still air, the tube frame bent and buckled and its wheels no longer rolling true. He'd stripped the seized-up motor from its housing behind the driver's seat, dumping it to reduce weight, which made no difference if the wind didn't blow.

He'd lost count of how many days the air had been still. The sun did its best to bring him down, and a makeshift scarf, torn from a strip of sail, brought some relief to his face and neck.

A shirt worn to grey, a ragged pair of pants, and boots that wouldn't see another mile. Lanyard owned nothing else but the shotgun strapped to his back with a leather cord.

Every inch of the stock was carved until the etchings were halfway towards being a book. Pictures and words and marks that not even Lanyard understood. An iron base-plate was a later addition, fastened on with bolts, nails, and screws.

Both of the shotgun barrels were etched with words that went deep into the steel. Most of the script was filled with oil and dirt now, obscured or worn, but Lanyard knew enough of what they meant, enough to know that the gun was holy and very old.

What remained told the story of the bound man, of the Crossing, of promises made and things to come. These teachings were outlawed now, and the signs and marks brought death in all of the towns.

Lanyard Everett killed a Jesusman for this gun. One of the last. Bad luck had dogged him ever since, but he wouldn't lay down the brute of a shotgun…or perhaps it was bound to him now, forever his by blood and betrayal.

Still, a gun was a gun.

Barely surviving the crossing of the saltpan, he saw the Inland before him in all its sunburnt glory. Far ahead, a haze and maybe the shape of movement near that shimmer. Lanyard cursed his bleary eyes. He headed for what could be a mirage, praying for water, knowing what would happen if he was wrong.

Even here, at the edge of things, the maddest of the settlers kept their holdings miles back and on the other side of the Range. The moment he fell, he was done. His body might never be seen by human eyes, and the sun and moon would fight over his bones until they were splintered, buried in the Inland dust.

The front wheel of the skiff caught in a drift of powder, and Lanyard hauled it out and onto firm ground. Not for the first time, he considered abandoning the wind-car.

My luck, I'd die five miles on, and the winds would blow over my carcass just to mock me, he thought. Gritting his teeth, he plodded onwards.

The heat-haze turned into a soak, a patch of clay that ran with moisture. It had been freshly dug out, and a small group of people squatted by the waterhole, watching his approach.

Crooked folk, perhaps a dozen. Lanyard noticed their patched outfits, necklaces of finger-bones, vests of braided human hair. A bicycle lay sprawled and rusting on the ground nearby, and a pair of riding birds knelt by the soak, lapping at the trickle of water.

The crooked mobs ate man-flesh when they could get it, and Lanyard felt the weight of their stares. A woman spun a pair of clicker-sticks on a string. The birds ceased their guzzling, their legs unfolding to bring them up to their full height. Their bony crests brought them to almost ten feet tall.

"Man," one of the birds croaked. The other laughed at him, a sound that was somewhere between a kettle boiling dry and the hissing of a snake.

Eyeing the water, Lanyard stepped forward cautiously, leaving the skiff where it was. None of the crooked folk moved against him, yet, but he made note of the rusted gun leaning against a rock, of the crossbow made from truck springs and inner tubes resting across one man's lap. Homemade knives swung from every belt.

"It's ours," a man said, rising from his haunches and putting himself between Lanyard and the water. He was heavy with fat, patches of hair sticking out from a pate covered in scabs and scars. The grease-streaked remains of a suit jacket hung loose around his gut, the buttons long gone. He wore a kilt that might have once been sackcloth.

"A sip and I'll go," Lanyard croaked. The fat man shook his head. Lanyard noticed that the other crooked folk were circling around him, still keeping caution and distance, wary of the Jesus gun.

"Spent an hour digging that out," he told Lanyard. "I'm King Jollylot, and that water is on my land. Want a drink, you'll have to buy one."

Nodding once, Lanyard pointed to the skiff. Jollylot looked it over and shook his head.

"Buggy's so broken it's hardly worth fixing. How'd it get into such a state?"

"Ran into some bad people," Lanyard managed, and Jollylot smiled, showing a graveyard of teeth.

"That you did," the crooked man said. "Bad people everywhere these days. Gimme a look at the gun."

"No," Lanyard said.

"Seems to me you're carrying the kit of a Jesusman," Jollylot said. "Man carries that, makes you wonder how he came by it."

Keeping perfectly still, Lanyard sensed the crooked mob slowly pushing in on him, felt the moment just before the rush. He'd get one or two of them, sure, and this shabby pack of man-eaters knew that too. But numbers would always tell.

I was meant to die like this, Lanyard realised and held himself ready. For a moment, he considered jamming the god-cannon underneath his chin, evaporating his skull in a final act of defiance.

No.

In one movement, he slipped the leather cord over his shoulder and swung the shotgun up. Lanyard held the muzzle level with Jollylot's nose. Blinking into the double throat of the gun barrels, the big man stepped back, holding up his hands.

"Cut him up, Jol," the birdwoman cried. "Birds are hungry."

"Quiet," Jollylot said.

"Water," Lanyard demanded, the word cracked and desperate.

King Jollylot noticed the wavering of the shotgun, the way that Lanyard could barely stand. He scoffed, lowered his hands.

"You're dead already," he told Lanyard. "Take the trade, stranger, or Slopkettle here will whittle you up for the pot, one toe at a time. And we'll take your kit, anyways."

A whip of a girl crept forward, eyes mad and wide, tickling at the dozens of flensing knives that hung from her bandolier. A distraction. From the corner of his eye, Lanyard saw another cannibal, wrestling with the action of the pig-gun.

"You want this?" Lanyard said, and Jollylot nodded. Turning the gun over in his hands, he held it by the barrel and offered it to the crooked man. Jollylot bared his rot-tooth smile, and that was the moment Lanyard darted forward, swinging the gun like a club.

King Jollylot went down with his head stoved in, dying with a squeal and an almighty fart. Lanyard kept moving, clearing the body and splashing through the soak, dodging the beaks of the birds, driving them off with one round from the gun. The mob drew short as he broke through their closing circle, turning around to cover them all with the shooter.

"You're mine now," Lanyard Everett said. He fetched another shell from his pocket, quickly feeding it into the break action of the gun. Kneeling down in the mud, he scooped up a handful of the water, savouring that brackish muck. The outlaws watched him, sullen and fearful.

Then a wind began to blow, and he smiled.

Lanyard dreamt of the old man again. Perhaps the enemy was still close enough to touch his dreams. Perhaps he'd been out in the Waste for too long and had simply lost his mind.

In the dream he was younger, still the prentice of a man named Bauer. The grey traveller held court over their cookfire, and Lanyard looked down to see the jag of stone cradled in his hands, the same one he'd driven into the face opposite him, many years and miles ago.

"Can't escape what you are," Bauer said, and then Lanyard murdered him again, like he always did. He pried the holy gun out of that dead grip.

Lanyard held the god-cannon for a moment and it felt cold and mean. Then terrible things came out of the darkness and into the light of the fire, monsters beyond measure, and he realised that a Jesusman's gun made little difference.

He died a hundred deaths before he woke.

Lanyard saw beyond their savage façade and knew that Jollylot's mob were scared and hungry. So he made their lives a misery. He handed out beatings and insults, taking the best of their food.

They needed a bossman, someone more terrifying and brutal than they were. Lanyard decided that he fit the bill.

This mob had just lost a clan war, and a squad of bailiffs out from Price had their trail, hounding the outlaws until they ran. They'd given up any claim on their old turf, and newer, stronger mobs had taken over. There was nowhere left for them to go.

King Jollylot had been licking his wounds out on the very edges of the Inland, contemplating a push across the saltpan when Lanyard found them. This mob was as dead and lost as Lanyard was. They had a greypot but nothing to put in it, a barrow full of animal skins and shovels, and not much else. Everything else had been tossed or burnt in a desperate gamble to travel light and fast.

His new tribe, loyal only so long as they feared him. Strength was the only law in these in-between places, and mercy was a concept that never left the town-walls. Those who survived out here had forgotten all but the cruel religion of Papa Lucy and the Boneman, and everything else was meat.

The first attack came in the small hours of that first morning. They sent a boy with a fuzz of beard, creeping towards the fire that Lanyard claimed for his own. The wretch pulled out a knife, a sharpened jag pried from a car, handle wrapped in a strip of canvas.

He only had a moment to learn that the new bossman slept lightly and moved as fast as a snake. Lanyard snatched the boy's ankle, pulling his feet out from under him. A moment of struggle ended when Lanyard wrestled the knife from his hands. Terror in his young eyes, wide with the knowledge that he was at his end. Kneeling down on the boy's chest, Lanyard opened his throat in one slice.

"Put this in your pot if you want to eat." He snarled, knowing that those feigning sleep around the fire were watching intently. Eyes downcast, Slopkettle bent to her work, her flensing knives dancing across the body of the lad who'd drawn the short straw.

Bone knives, finger-lengths of old steel. Junk. Lanyard handed the dead boy's knife to the flenser, and she found a place for it on her bandolier.

"You hoped to be running your knives all over me," Lanyard said. Slopkettle did not try to deny it.

Lanyard never knew the dead boy's name and didn't ask. In the grey of the pre-dawn, the riding birds hovered over the leftovers, gnawing on the bones and offal that Slopkettle tossed over her shoulder.

Breakfast came later. When the sun rose, the greypot bubbled over the coals, sending the smell of people-meat across their rude camp. As bossman, Lanyard was offered the first bowl of stew, but he declined, chewing on a heel of bread as the crooked folk quietly ate one of their own.

The mob suffered his rule in silence, and none rose to challenge him after that night. *That will come later,* Lanyard decided. *When they are stronger, they will turn on me.*

Mutch and Dogwyfe were the bird-riders. The pair were heart-bound, scarified and marked for life, the closest thing to marriage under the old laws of Cruik, by those who followed that bastardised rite of Papa Lucy. They both wore a motley of badly tanned animal skins, with the occasional pale or tattooed square marking a man-kill. Mutch was older than his bride, and his hair was starting to go thin on top, with grey streaks running through the tangle of his beard.

On the promise of a bird and safety with King Jollylot's mob, Dogwyfe had long ago used her braid to strangle her first husband in his sleep. Divorce was not an option for the heart-bound.

Their birds were named Gog and Magog, a pair that Mutch had raised from stolen eggs. Lanyard had always thought the giant birds were equal parts hungry and stupid, there was no denying their usefulness. Their feathers formed a dusty coat of grey and brown, necks curving up to a honking crested head, scanning about with a permanent beady eyed stare. A bird was just as likely to tear out a man's throat as listen to him, and any bird rider worth his salt wore a map of many scars.

While these two birds would never amount to much on the racing circuits of Rosenthrall and Langenfell, Mutch did a reasonable job of breaking them in. He had repurposed a lot of scrap and rubbish, using it to craft harnesses and tack for their birds. It was ugly but functional, much like the bird master himself.

They would bear riders, obey most commands, and, most importantly, would go on the attack when prodded. They could disembowel an enemy with their talons and their beaks could take off a man's hand.

Dogwyfe taught Magog a few words, mostly profanities or the names of people who were now dead. Sometimes, Magog would hum to herself, the words of some nursery rhyme slipping from her beak, and Lanyard could picture the bird's mistress crooning over it as a hatchling. Dogwyfe held more love for her bird than for her man, and Lanyard marked this well.

Gog was the male of the pair and a much larger riding bird, Mutch's steed and a brute, who never took to the man-tongue. He understood the threats of his master well enough though, and his crest and neck were scarred from whip and knout.

Lanyard held a parley with the bird-riders. He offered them a third-share of any loot found by the mob, double what Jollylot had promised them. He needed the birds and they knew it. The deal was acceptable and a trade-stone from Jollylot's kit was brought out, kissed by the three of them to seal the trade.

"We'll all end up as rich as Neville, you'll see," and this brought Lanyard the smiles. *Those two were the only true threat here,* Lanyard thought and knew he would sleep safer that night.

Two birds, a bicycle, and a handful of savages as likely to kill him as anyone else. Lanyard knew he had enough to make a beginning.

At the edge of the Inland the pickings were lean. Badlands for miles in every direction, with little to see but red dust and flies, but even here a clever pair of hands could survive. Under his direction the mob gathered and laid away a store of bush tucker, grubs and roots, and bitter seeds to grind into flour for damper. The cannibals were slow students at foraging, better at stealing food than finding it. Lanyard persisted, beating those who worked too slowly or who came back to camp with too little food to show for their time.

If I hadn't come along, you lot would have eaten each other. One more month, there'd have been nothing but bones around a waterhole, Lanyard thought, stowing waterskins and sacks of provisions into the skiff. His ribs no longer showed and he felt strong enough to walk for miles.

"Enough hiding," Lanyard declared over supper that night. "We've enough food to do what needs doing."

He thought of the saltpan to the west, of his sworn enemy on the far side. He could lead this mob there, with the birds at the forefront, the rest all howling and rushing in with their crude weapons. He knew he could easily throw these people into a certain death. Their sacrifice might give him the grace to do what Bauer had taught him, in that place where the veil between worlds was thin, where the true monsters had stepped through.

It was his sworn duty, and now he had the guns that he'd prayed for, the means to go west and put things right.

You'll fail, he told himself. *You'll walk back into their lair, and they'll kill you, oh so slowly.*

"We go east," Lanyard said after a long moment, a stone twisting in his gut. "I'm taking back what Jollylot let slip through his fingers. We go roving."

They prowled the tradeways of the Inland, preying on travellers, raiding outposts and holdings. Bailiffs were sent to hunt down Lanyard's mob, first from Price and then the high walls of Quarterbrook spewed out a posse of coin-hunters, a mixed group of birdmen and bikers.

Lanyard had travelled these parts years ago and still remembered the hiding places his master knew, blind gullies and ruins that few had seen, ways of fused stone from Before that wouldn't hold a trail.

Each time he gave the hunters the slip and watched as the townsmen tore around the plains, their machines belching smoke and whining in the distance.

Travel became dangerous in the area, and the few who escaped the cookpot told of the growing gang led by a stranger who wasn't crooked at all. One rumour had it that the leader was actually a Jesusman, others that this Lanyard Everett had killed one and eaten his heart to gain that forbidden knowledge.

Other crooked mobs were being attacked by this new group, and the turf war between the outlaws was vicious enough to be noted with some worry by those huddled behind town walls. They could see the muzzle flashes in the distance, watch furrows of dust flying about as the cannibals warred amongst themselves.

Mere months after arriving from the west, Lanyard Everett looked upon a scene of destruction and nodded with some satisfaction. His mob now numbered over sixty strong, and old enemies of King Jollylot joined up for plunder or fled elsewhere for easier pickings.

The Inland was his.

Three motorcycles cobbled together from parts found in the bleed-throughs. A full brace of bird-riders and enough guns to give anyone pause. A skirmish with a lost posse of lawmen netted them a working buggy, which Lanyard claimed as his own, instantly falling in love with the wheels and the snarl of its engine.

One day his mob ransacked a compound, tearing down the tin barricade with chains and hooks. Pouring into the breach, the outlaws fell on the handful of farmers who had huddled together for protection. The sounds of slaughter were heard within, the only rebuttal to the attack was the pop of a pistol, and that soon ceased.

Lanyard guided the buggy through the carnage, past the stripping of sheep and pig carcasses, and did not blink at the horrors that his people inflicted on the farmers. *Life is hard and these people were fools to settle here,* he reasoned, watching Slopkettle perform her craft on the man she'd marked for the greypot.

If not us, somebody else would have done this.

Every swaggering step, every bullet fired, every inch of steel he had driven through other men, all of it based on that old comfortable lie. Still, a river of ghosts and blood could not lift him away from his biggest failure. He'd been given meaning once, but he'd lost his way. Underneath everything, he was a coward and a fraud. Worse than a fraud.

An apostate.

He climbed out of the buggy, poking through the buildings for plunder, gun at the ready in case a farmer lay in wait. Lanyard spotted an enamel bathtub in a hut, chipped and rusty, a bed of coals banked in the dirt underneath it.

It was full of warm water, and he picked up the bar of soap, pondering it for a long moment. Before the mob had arrived with guns and slaughter, someone had drawn a bath, someone who even now was likely dead or dying.

"No point wasting this," he said, peeling off his boots. Hollering out of the door, Lanyard called over Mutch. The birdman trotted over on Gog, the bird's face and beak splattered with blood.

"Don't give me that look," he said, noting Mutch's frustration at missing out on the looting. "You'll get your bloody share. Watch this door, I'm having a bath now."

Lanyard stripped off his clothes, easing into the warm water with a gasp of delight. In seconds a ring of filth appeared around the water's edge. Ignoring the distant screams, he scrubbed away what felt like years' worth of dirt and grime.

Lanyard had a tattoo on his chest, the washed out image of a bleeding man bound tightly to a tree, arms outstretched. The man's hands were clenched into fists but for the index fingers, pointing left and right. BEFORE and NOW were writ under each hand.

The Jesus.

He was always careful to hide this tattoo. It marked him as a Jesusman, and even the lowest crooked man would observe the law and enforce the old pogrom. Nothing but death awaited him should this secret be discovered. Once it was a noble calling, but now, the Jesusmen were outlaws, sorcerers, and heretics.

As far as Lanyard Everett knew, he was the last one.

— 2 —

There was nothing to the world but the howling of the sandstorm around them. To Lanyard's left, he saw a vague outline in the gloom, a loping shape, probably a bird. Over the wind he could just hear one of the bikes, whining and troubled as the sand invaded its innards.

Clutching at the dust veil across his face, he blinked again, cursing the dryness of his eyes. The sands of the Drift varied as much as the types of rain down south, and the powder got into every crease of his skin and scratched his lungs like the miner's death.

The camel lurched across a sand drift, and Lanyard snatched at the harness, heart racing. He'd junked the buggy half a day back; the motor dust-bound and finally silent. Snagging this riderless camel when it passed within arm's length was the only thing that had saved his life.

He despised camels and this one did little to melt his heart. It hissed, huffing out its feathers, and worried at Lanyard's hands with its sharp fangs. He swiftly jabbed it in the tender spot just north of the saddle horn, showing the animal that he'd ridden a camel before. With a mournful honk, the beast regarded its challenge as lost and plodded forward at his command.

On the Drift, anyone who got separated from his fellows was as good as dead. There were other things in there with them, dogging their caravan, feeding in the gloom. He'd heard the screams and did not need to urge the camel onward.

Lanyard knew that predators slept beneath these sands and were active only when the storms came. Yet still, he chanced on a crossing. He knew that people would die.

"The winds don't always blow," he'd told them.

Lanyard thought he was going to be as rich as the proverbial Neville. He'd scoffed at the towns that feared them enough to now employ them. They were a proper mob now, coin-riders that went where the pay was. There simply hadn't been enough time to go around the Drift, not if they wanted this job.

Now here he was, forced to admit the truth. It had been fear not profit that drove him east. He'd been slowly leading his mob away from his failure, and now they were choking in the dark.

I'm a damn fool and now we're all dead, Lanyard thought, sipping from the dead cameleer's water bladder. *We should have stuck to pouncing on caravans.*

Then he saw it, a light just visible through the whipping veils of grit. He drove the camel onwards, and to his relief he saw several shapes ahead of him, birds and bikes and man-shapes on foot.

Here at the Drift's edge, the windstorm began to falter, the bank of dust finally rolling back into the interior of the wasteland, as if it had lost interest in them.

Winds don't move like that, he thought with a shudder.

Lanyard pulled back his bandana, wiping dust from his face and hands. The camel's mane of feathers had turned aside most of the grit, and now that the danger had passed, it regarded its new master through slitted eyes, baring a row of fangs.

"Enough," Lanyard said, once more jabbing his fingers into the tender spot and again when the beast was too slow in dropping that snarl. Defeated, the camel walked on, bearing a man more stubborn than itself.

The glass spire that led them out of the sands was the work of the Taursi. Long before the time of the settlers, the natives crafted these by arts unknown, rough-edged beacons that littered all the lands, from Riverland to Inland and perhaps beyond. By day they drew in the sunlight, and when night fell they lit the old ways.

This structure was ancient, and as the sun sank into the sandstorm over their shoulders, the light intensified into an off-peach glow, flickering like an ember brought to heat.

"It's the bossman," someone muttered. He saw the remainder of his mob regrouping by the beacon and noticed the handful of riderless birds, as well as one of the bikes gone. A quick headcount showed that perhaps ten people were missing, gobbled up by the Drift.

His chosen lieutenants were among the living. Slopkettle rode behind Mutch, and Dogwyfe was on the ground watering Magog with the last of her waterskins.

Lanyard did not miss the glances between Mutch and the young flenser, the way her arms lingered across the old birdman's waist for a moment longer than necessary.

Trouble there, he thought, watching Dogwyfe coo over her animal, oblivious. He half expected to find the evidence of her second divorce in the morning and wondered which woman he would miss the most.

"That's Sully's camel," a gap-toothed biker said when he passed by. He slowly reached for the spear-gun on his hip.

"Sully is dead, and this is mine now," Lanyard said, staring the crooked man down until the biker found it more prudent to check on his machine. Standing up on the camel's harness, Lanyard whistled between his teeth. The mob gathered together, brooding and exhausted.

"We go," he said, pointing to a notch-toothed hill. "Waterhole about an hour that way. No point waiting here, there's no one else coming."

They spotted Carmel the following morning. The town squatted on top of a plateau with a commanding view of the plain in all directions. A telegraph wire stretched away on worm-rotted poles, the one thread connecting this town to the rest of civilisation.

The land surrounding the walled town was a bleedthrough field, picked over and sold off. Only the scars remained to show where a sprawl of buildings had sprouted from the ground.

"They've pried out every last brick," Slopkettle scoffed, cross-legged and relaxed on the harness behind Lanyard. "How do they mean to pay us, bossman?"

"From the treasures hid behind that nice thick wall," Lanyard said. "They'll pay."

As they crossed the plain, Lanyard could just make out the hundreds of statues set on the walls and roofs beyond. The Leicester: a watchful warrior that guided this strange people, the symbol of their prosperity.

"Listen," he told the flenser behind him. "I know you mark rote for the Papa Lucy, but keep your mouth shut. There's a different god in this place."

"No gods here, just bloody statues," Slopkettle muttered. "Heretics, and we're worse fools for treating with 'em. Whole place should be burnt to the ground."

"Watch your tongue or I'll take it out."

Her body tensed behind him, and she shifted around on the camel's harness. He wondered which knife she was reaching for and rested his hand on his leg, fingers almost touching the pistol hanging low on his belt.

She sat back, and he smiled.

"You're smart. Might just keep you alive."

"About to say the same thing, bossman."

Lanyard's mob drew up before the gates of Carmel. At his signal, the bikers revved their engines, kicking up dust and stones. Those on birds waved their clacker sticks and set them to screeching, and the camels acted up, too, cranky from all the racket. The crooked folk on foot began to wrestle and play knife games, blades flashing and arcing through the air.

Fifty mad cannibals camped on your doorstep, Lanyard thought, watching the bobbing of heads above, movement on top of the walls. *Give these townsfolk a bit of theatre. Keep them on their toes.*

Slopkettle slid down from the camel's back, joining in the knife rite, and Lanyard rode on alone as a bossman should. It was proper for him to treat on behalf of his mob. If this was a trap, a means to strike him down on the sly, he knew the crooked mobs would wage war on this place, regardless of their feelings for him.

He saw a fence of nervous guns bobbing in the air as bailiffs rushed behind the statues to line the walls. Lanyard knew he was as safe as a babe in arms. He ordered the camel to kneel and walked forward, waiting calmly before the gates. He took a moment to admire the slab of roof beams and steel girders.

"I've lost my tradestone, you'll have to bring one," he hollered through cupped hands. "Hurry up."

A minute later the gate cracked open, turning effortlessly on an unseen hinge, giving a gap few could squeeze through. The sliver of an opening revealed a phalanx of men with guns, kneeling behind a low barricade. Lanyard saw streets and buildings, cobbled together in the same piecemeal fashion as the outer wall.

One man emerged from the innards of Carmel, an older man in a Before suit. He moved slowly, arthritic, looking around for hidden cannibals. He wore a sash, blue ribbon swaying with a bob of melted tin, and a hat of rabbit skin, one brim upturned. The slouch hat was peculiar to the local religion.

"I had a hat like that once," Lanyard told the man, who clutched at the slouch when a strong gust of wind drove along the base of the wall, threatening to tear it off his head.

"No doubt it fell from the hands of someone godly and lost, to make its way into the possession of a man-eater," the Leicesterite said, tense and wary.

"I don't eat from the greypot like they do," Lanyard said, jerking his thumb to indicate the mad scene behind him. "And I got the hat from my old master. Not sure where he got it."

He supposed it had been camouflage for old Bauer and smart in its own way. The Leicesterites were disliked and seldom approached by those in good faith with Papa Lucy, the Boneman, and whatever was left of his rotten little Family.

A clever way for a Jesusman to move openly.

They stood for an awkward moment, the townsman and the warlord. Then the Leicesterite signalled to the gate behind him and a pair of boys came out at a trot bearing a large slate between them.

The tradestone of Carmel was more elaborate than the scratched rock Jollylot carted around, making deals with crude folk who could barely read. This stone was marked and embossed with the image of the Leicester, the white warrior overseeing a slab of neat text, laws and bylaws and all of the words that civilised folk tried to hide behind.

"The water barons have been at war, out there," the townsman said. He waved to the vast and unforgiving landscape, indicating everything beyond the safety of a town wall, the limit of his world.

"Used to be half a dozen carters to buy from, but only Vern the Half-Dann comes here now. His prices, he…the man has to be stopped."

Lanyard had heard of the man. Half-Dann was ruthless even for a water baron, the usurers who brought water to the parched Inland cities. He'd considered sending his mob for a raid on the water trains, but they were always ringed by coin-riders, a hard target.

Going after the Half-Dann's caravan he looked to lose at least half his mob. But there were always more crooked folk, living rough on the fringes of town law, and word got around. If he pulled off this job, others would travel for weeks to swell his ranks.

"This will cost you," Lanyard said and named a price. The townsman paled, frowning he shook his head.

"Feel free to kill Vern the Half-Dann yourself," Lanyard said. "Maybe we'll buy this load of water ourselves and drain the whole bloody lot right in front of your gates."

"You're just as bad as them," the townsman said, trembling with outrage and fear. Lanyard nodded and ushered the man towards the tradestone.

The deal was struck, and both men kissed the tradestone, giving their true names and the terms of the trade. Lanyard barked at the old townsman's title: Fos Carpidian, Lord Protector of Carmel. Shooting Lanyard a wounded glare, the man rose painfully from his knees, not once looking back as he returned to the safety of his stone curtain.

"Break a trade, eat a blade!" Lanyard called out, but Fos did not respond. This version of the trade banter was something that only happened in the low places.

Lanyard returned to his camp, wondering who would still be alive by sunset tomorrow. Overhead, the army of stone men watched, and he felt the full weight of their hollow eyes.

He dreamt that night, once more breaking open Bauer's head with a rock. Bauer did not resist and spoke throughout the murder, his eye fixed on Lanyard as the boy huffed from the weight of the bloody rock.

"Takes a long time," Bauer said. "Death."

"Shut up," Lanyard cried, bringing the stone down again. A heavy crack sounded as the thick forehead bone finally split, but Bauer's eye remained fixed on Lanyard, his lips moving.

"I don't mean to haunt you," Bauer said. "Feels like you're the ghost haunting me."

Crack! This time the crashing blow set Bauer's head into a sickening shape, fluid and gore oozing out and pooling underneath. Exhausted from swinging the rock, young Lanyard cradled his master's head in his hands, weeping over one more job he couldn't finish.

"Just walk away from this mob," Bauer said. "It's all going to run through your fingers." Bauer had just enough energy left to dig into the dust, sending out a drift with a jerky hand. The poetry of this moment drove Lanyard into a fury.

"Liar!" Lanyard said and this time the stone fell true ending the old Jesusman, leaving a bug-eyed smear on the clay. Lanyard pushed the bloody rock to one side and sat hunched next to the corpse.

"I will not go west," Lanyard said, reaching for the Jesus-gun, knowing that the monsters were coming. With a shrug, he put the shotgun under his chin, only to discover it would not fire.

"Stop putting me through this," he begged the corpse. "I've had enough."

The gun worked plenty well against the creatures that poured out of the dark. It was good for that, at least. Lanyard died badly in the dream, but even as the monstrosities overwhelmed him, he found one small measure of peace.

Compared to the monsters in his own skull, the water barons were nothing to fear.

It had all gone wrong.

Vern the Half-Dann begged for his life, sobbing, his face slick with snot. He offered Lanyard a share in the water business. As he scrambled away, feet skidding in the loose scree, he increased these terms to include the pick of his houses and finally all of his wealth.

Lanyard shook his head, not unkindly.

The Half-Dann was pitiful, a dwarf with a twist in his spine, one muscled arm grown out to the proportions of a full-grown man. Despite the promise of enough wealth to rival Neville, Lanyard killed the water baron all the same, giving him the kindness of a bullet through the temple.

He felt wetness on his neck and noticed that his shirt was slick with blood. Investigating the wound, he realised that Vern had scored his face and neck with his knife, a ragged cut that bled freely. The dwarf had missed his artery by a hair.

Lanyard walked through the dead and dying. One of his mob had been gutted by a coin-rider's bird, and he screamed as he gathered in the sprawl of his bowels. Lanyard eased the crooked man over with a moment of knife work and gave him a friendly wink as he bled out, his screams replaced by a final weak gurgle.

The water wagon was an enormous Before tanker, a steel cylinder on rubber wheels. Where a truck had once hauled the tanker, a pair of big stumpies lay in harness. One lizard lay dead, riddled with spears and bullets, now a meal for the survivor. The reins hung limp in the hands of the driver, a spear in his throat and the front of the tanker painted with his lifeblood.

Dead birds lay sprawled around the tanker, one pair tangled in a deathly embrace, claws and beaks still buried in feathered flesh. Pressing against the sting of his wound, Lanyard wondered if Gog or Magog were numbered among the dead but realised he couldn't tell one bird from another.

The plan had been for Lanyard's mob to round the walls while the Half-Dann waited at the gate, taking the water train by surprise and preventing its escape, while the Leicesterites gunned down the coin-riders from above.

There'd been no help from Carmel; the townsfolk didn't fire a single shot. Offering no help to either side, they sat behind their high wall and closed gate, watching their natural enemies kill each other.

Lanyard saw a couple of figures still moving. A waterman hooked a toe through his rifle and shot himself dead before anyone could seize him. Dogwyfe was straddling a wounded man's chest, driving a big rock into his face until he lay still, all the while shrieking her fury at the sky.

Magog was nowhere to be seen.

Lanyard felt dizzy. He wondered where he could find a needle and thread and poked at the long pucker of his wound so that the pain would keep him alert.

A noise, and Lanyard turned as if in a dream, gun up and tracking. It was a cockatoo, prying the eyes and now the tongue from a crooked woman, perched on the hand that still clutched to her chest as if that would keep her life in.

Not that. Rounding the tanker, behind the telegraph line, the pounding of feet, a bird coming for him. Holstering the pistol, he lifted the shotgun from his shoulder. He needed to make sure it would die from that first round before it drove a claw through him.

Turning, he nearly put a load of shot into Gog, who stopped short at the sight of Lanyard's shooter. With a groan, Mutch tumbled out of the saddle and fell at Lanyard's feet. His face was a bloody mess.

Lanyard wondered if King Jollylot was laughing at him, from wherever dead fat men ended up. A mob of fifty, all gone, and him with the life rapidly leaking from him.

"Bossman," someone shouted, and he realised it was Slopkettle. The flenser was kneeling behind a dead camel, her arms red up to the elbows and most of her knives gone. She held a rifle almost as big as herself, resting it across the feathered hump of her barricade.

The gates of Carmel were half open. A mass of men emerged from the town armed with guns and spears, their big half-native mutts straining against leashes.

"You're breaking the trade, Fos," Lanyard muttered and made for the water tanker, spatters of his life trailing behind him in the dust. The townsmen were close now, and any moment they'd let loose the dogs to wipe out anyone still standing.

"Slopkettle," he yelled, and she made sense of his intent, the pair running hard for the tanker. The townsmen found them standing by the valves under the tanker's belly, gun-butts raised, and they drew short to keep their distance. If Lanyard's men snapped the valves, all of the water would flood out, even by the time the townsmen dragged the tanker inside their walls.

"Fos! Deal's off!" Lanyard shouted.

Fos Carpidian knelt before Slopkettle. His hands were tied behind his back, and now she sat her rifle muzzle on the bridge of his nose, sending the old man cross-eyed as he looked from Lanyard to the gun and back again.

The negotiations were going well.

"We get what was agreed on, no less," Lanyard said, wincing as Dogwyfe hooked a bone needle through his neck. The crooked woman dragged a thread of sheepgut across his wound, stitching up the deep gash.

Dogwyfe was a dark-eyed automaton, numb in her ministrations, and hadn't said a word since a waterman's rifle had cut Magog out from beneath her. Mutch lay in the shade of the tanker, his face wrapped in rags torn from a dead man's shirt. He'd taken a hatchet to the face, and if the birdman lived, it would be with one eye.

"We're broke," Fos said, head slumped. "But we can pay you soon."

"No credit," Lanyard said, knocking his shotgun against the underside of the tanker, the rumble echoing against the town wall. He figured the hole from a gunblast would empty the tanker just as good should the pack of townsfolk quit negotiating and just rush them.

"Water thugs cleaned us out," the man continued, licking his lips nervously, sweat running down his nose. "But we've found another bleedthrough field, a big one. We need this water to get there."

"All of this water?" Lanyard asked, eyebrows raised.

"You don't understand, Mr. Everett," Fos continued. "We're packing up the whole town. By the time the Half-Dann's friends come for us, they'll find the doors open and the larder empty."

Lanyard looked over the townsmen lurking nearby, indecisive and pacing, and saw the shapes of people on the walls, dozens more peering through the open gate. He realised that Fos Carpidian spoke the truth. This gambit to seize a water tanker was desperation, a last resort.

If Lanyard had died like he was meant to, Fos and his flock would already be on the move.

"Tell me about the bleedthrough field," Lanyard said. "Where is it, how big, all the important stuff."

"I can't tell you that."

"Talk," Slopkettle said, moving the rifle so that the tip was resting a hair's width from Carpidian's eyeball. Fos blinked rapidly, holding himself perfectly still.

"I can't tell you, because I don't know. None of us does."

"Do you expect me to believe that?" Lanyard said. He scanned the mob of townsmen as they edged forward. One of the dogs set to snarling again, and he guessed that the owner was stirring it up, ready to let it off the leash.

"Stand back," he shouted, tapping a metallic rhythm into the tanker for emphasis. "You—explain yourself, or Slopkettle starts taking your fingers off."

"My girl's seen a Leicester. A strong one, too," Fos babbled. "Been twenty years since we last seen one, and never one this strong. A Waking City, just ripe for the picking. She'll lead us there, and we'll all be as rich as Neville, you'll see."

Lanyard knew a little of their belief, enough to puzzle it out. Sometimes, one of the faithful would be struck with the vision of a Leicester rising from the earth, a warrior in stone or bronze, and be drawn to it, waking and dreaming. The blessed would always find the statue, never deviating from the path. The path would always lead to another place where Before bled into Now.

The bleedthroughs brought all manner of treasure into this husk of a world. Machines, melted buildings, treasures and curiosities, books and booze. If this bleedthrough field was even larger than the vast scar surrounding Carmel, it meant wealth beyond all measure.

"Shut your damn mouth, Fos," one of the townsmen said, and the rest murmured in agreement. Lanyard doubted that his use as a hostage was going to last much longer.

"Here's the new deal," he shouted. "And forget your damn tradestone, I know what your word is worth."

"We take four of yours, and the lass who's sniffed out the Leicester. We travel fast and light, and the rest of you can follow our trail. Your people stake out the claim, and we take our payment. We'll be long gone by the time you arrive with this," he said, resting one hand on the cool surface of the metal water tank.

"Absolutely not," Fos said. "That's my daughter you're talking about."

"All the more reason for you to behave," Lanyard said. "Tell your kid to pack her bags. She'll be safer than you are right now."

Crooked folks weren't allowed into their holy city, so the townsfolk marked rite outside the gate, carting out a Leicester on a litter.

The statue was nearly perfect. The bleedthrough had only marred one of its marble cheeks. Lanyard had seen the bronze men on roadside shrines, half melted and grotesque. Those crafted from the milk stone bled through better, and these statues were considered the purest.

The stone man leaned upon his rifle, the muzzle resting between his feet, dressed in a stout tunic that seemed all pockets and ammo pouches. The very picture of a warrior, of someone prepared to defend the weak. Finder of treasures, seeker of secrets.

This Leicester was etched with the holy words, and a long list of names from the Before. Fos and his people had added newer etchings, names from the Now, but like anything crafted in this time, these seemed crude.

An attendant with hammer and chisel added one last name to the list: MATILDE CARPIDIAN.

A young girl knelt in the dust before the holy figure, head bowed while the entire population of Carmel worked through the rite. Tilly Carpidian, all of ten years old, was trembling.

"God of our fathers, known of old," a man in full regalia exhorted, garbed in a slouch hat and tunic of purest white. He was whatever passed for a priest in this faith. The man daubed at the girl's face and hands with white paste, until she was as pale as the statue above her.

"Look at that mob, praying and braying," Slopkettle scoffed, leaning all over Fos with a knife held casually against his throat.

"Shut your mouth," Lanyard said.

"What? If the town-bred don't stand for blasphemy in Crosspoint, why should I?"

"Still stands thy humble sacrifice, a humble and a contrite heart!" the priest shouted, laying the girl's head across a chopping block. An attendant brought an axe forward, and the priest rested the sharp edge on the nape of her neck. A moment's pause, and then he lifted the axe away, raised the girl to her feet. They placed a new slouch hat upon her head, and it was slightly too big, falling across her eyes.

"Mark my words, that girl will lead us into nothing but disaster," the flenser said. "We'll be lost and dead inside a week."

"Leicester-We-Forget!" the priest cried.

"Leicester-We-Forget!" came the ecstatic answer, a liturgy from a hundred throats.

— 3 —

The gates of Carmel spewed out families with handcarts and drays, piled high with the makings of civilisation. Lanyard privately dismissed these comforts as dead weight. Along the walls and into the high places wriggled children with hammers and chisels, sent to deface the holy statues that they could not carry with them.

The town burned, smoke twisting up into the clear sky. Lanyard understood, approved almost. He'd have done the same in their position.

The water tanker sat still, the lizard sagging in its harness and sulking on the ground. Teamsters beat the lizard with goads and whips until it lurched to its feet, snapping and hissing at the people. The lizard did the work of two, straining at the heavy watertanker, and it was clear that Carpidian's people would not be going anywhere fast. Lanyard wondered if Vern the Half-Dann's friends would catch them out in the open, crawling across the landscape. Following a girl with a statue in her head.

A wise man would find a way to contact the water barons, he thought.

"Let's go," Lanyard said, tapping his new camel with the switch so that its knobby legs unfolded. Behind him, Mutch was strapped into the harness, his head swathed in a mess of bandages. The man whimpered with the sudden movement.

Dogwyfe trotted by on Gog, having some trouble with the unfamiliar bird. Slopkettle kicked the remaining motorbike into life and though the engine rattled, the bike rolled forward.

A buggy kept pace with them, jammed full of Leicesterites, with Carpidian's terrified daughter somewhere in the middle. A hulk with a shaved head stared at Lanyard, his rifle resting against the wooden frame of the car. Lanyard had heard them call the big man as Spence, and from the cast of his face guessed him to be Tilly's cousin or uncle.

Lanyard offered a silent salute to the man, who spat and turned away.

Fos Carpidian stumbled along behind Lanyard's camel, a long rope binding him to the harness. Lanyard took care not to go too fast, not wanting to drag the old fool across the stones.

An hour's travel brought them to a stand of rocks, a crooked mesa that dog-legged out of the plain. Some forgotten generation had built a watchtower on top of this formation, but time had worn it down into a few layers of brick and stone.

"Here," Lanyard said, pulling Carpidian closer, reeling in the rope as if the exhausted man were a hooked fish. Leaning down from the camel's harness, Lanyard cut his bonds and the Lord Protector of Carmel stood there uncertainly, rubbing the circulation back into his wrists.

"Your people will come," Lanyard said, tossing the townsman a half-empty waterskin. This was the height of charity in the Now.

"You look after my Tilly," Carpidian said, miserable, defeated.

"It's in my best interests that she survives," Lanyard said. "We'll leave you markers to follow, as agreed. Fair trade and all."

They left Fos Carpidian beneath the overhang of the mesa, sheltering from the brutal sunlight. The man looked ridiculous from a distance, dwarfed by the stone above him.

"Should have left the old man his hat," Slopkettle shouted over her clattering engine. Smiling, Lanyard touched the brim of the slouch on his head and thought of the one he'd lost back west, the hat he'd taken from Bauer's corpse.

Hell if I know what the old Jesusman was doing with it, Lanyard mused. Fos Carpidian's hat was a perfect fit, and perhaps skulking eyes would think him a townrider, maybe even the leader of this expedition.

The odd group skirted the edges of the Inland, following the jags of the Range to north and east, along a path that only the girl could see. Soon they crossed the old tradeway between Price and Sad Plain, a track now marked with Taursi prints and scatters of glass and sheep shit.

A commotion in the buggy, and then the machine came to a shuddering stop, the townsfolk clambering out. Lanyard gave a signal and his mob drew close together, ready for grief.

"This it?" Lanyard asked. Everyone ignored him. The young girl walked deep into the dust and yucca, and there seemed nothing to her but skinny legs and a long smock, the holy hat sliding around on her head.

The girl held a twist of rag that she unwrapped, peered into. Within, a brilliant light leaked around the edges of her fingers and she squinted into the brightness for one long moment before she folded it all away, stuffing the pretty deep into her pocket.

Lanyard felt the lurch then, the flutter in his gut, the urge to retch right there in the saddle. He fought back his gorge, eyes blinking, watering. The gap between all worlds was thin here, nothing separating them from *elsewhere* but a film stretched taut to the point of breaking.

Something was coming through.

Swearing, he checked the action on the Jesusman's gun, hands beading with sweat. He'd been sniffed out by the ones he'd failed to kill, and now this stupid girl had led them all to a certain death.

One witch he could kill. Others, he might be able to keep at bay. More than a handful and he was as dead as the rest of these idiots.

I don't know enough, he thought, heart racing. *I never did.* Sweat ran down into his eyes, and he wiped it furiously on his sleeve.

Carpidian's daughter pointed to the earth, and the clay split apart, birthing a monster. The face was twisted, something out of his nightmares. Lanyard knew that others would follow, monsters he'd been sworn to slay that would know him for what he was, on sight.

A failed Jesusman, and a fool.

Spence and the others saw him raise his gun, and then they were pointing their own weapons at him, shouting. Lanyard ignored all of this, fixated on this intrusion from another world. Slopkettle slowly circled around on her bike, spiked chain at the ready, hand ready to squeeze on the throttle.

Lanyard lowered the gun, let out a shuddering breath. The moment that could have been a killing moment passed, replaced by curses and grumbling.

It was only a Leicester that pierced the earth, melted by the passage from Before to Now. Around the bronze statue, the tips of buildings began to push through like tiled pimples, the slag of lamp posts and other paraphernalia that those of the Now could only guess at.

A bleedthrough. As always, these thin spots held the hum of the land behind the veil, but nothing was watching them from that grey place. They were safe enough, so long as they didn't linger.

It was a modest site, perhaps a handful of buildings that weren't slag, but a motorcar appeared from the earth, poking up like a steel tombstone. It was whole, and only one pane of glass had bled through like toffee, the rest pure and clear.

"Your payment. Take it and go," Spence told Lanyard, pointing to the twist of buildings. There'd be good forage here, perhaps food in tins and machine parts, clothes and books if they were lucky.

"We should stay, bossman," Slopkettle said, coasting her bike to a stop beside his camel. "Let these damn idiots chase bullshit out in the Waste. There's loot enough here to be as rich as Neville."

She spoke sense. They'd kit out another mob soon enough from what they found here, and if they took the time to dig out the car, it would fetch a princely sum, working or no. He wanted to be quit of this doomed tribe, free to rebuild his empire. Everything he'd taken from King Jollylot had the stink of a curse on it, so this was a fresh start. Kill everyone here, including his own people. Take this wealth and browbeat some other mob. Perhaps even give up on the Inland and set up behind a town wall. *You can't outrun yourself, boy,* he heard in the long-vanished voice of Bauer. *Wherever you go, there you are.*

Then, Lanyard realised the Carpidians were trying to change the deal again. This wasn't the bleedthrough that they'd destroyed their town for and crossed the water barons to chase. Wealth here, but nothing like the Carpidians had spoken of. They were offering him a scrap, hoping to distract him from a proper meal. He shook his head, ignoring the protests of his women. Spence set his mouth in a grim line, even as the wealth of a dead world grew around them.

The outlaws and town-bred slept apart, two campfires smouldering upwind of the bleedthrough. As the sun fell behind the Range, Lanyard paced around their camp, setting what marks he knew. Making sure that none were watching, he quietly scratched out the symbols that would ward off lesser monsters from other worlds or wake him should something stronger blunder through his weak fence.

If those witches sniff me out, I'll have just enough warning to blow my own head off, he reasoned. He lay down on top of his swag, exhausted and sore from the long day's ride.

Mutch moaned in his sleep, thrashing about as Dogwyfe rubbed vinegar into his shattered face. Undressed, the wound stank out their little camp, a smell that spoke of a slow death and little hope of recovery.

"You need to do something," Dogwyfe said to Lanyard, her first words since Magog's death. "This is on you."

"I only know this," he said, patting the pistol on his hip. She scowled, stuffing rags into the hollow of Mutch's face. Lanyard thought he saw a glimpse of exposed bone in the firelight and kept quiet.

"Maybe yonder wall-huggers have a medicine bag," Slopkettle said, teeth gripping the stem of a pipe. Packing the pipe with kennelweed, she touched a match to the bowl. The flenser drew in the smoke with deep satisfaction.

"Go easy on that," he told her, and Slopkettle laughed. With a look at the dying birdman, Lanyard rose to his feet, groaning at the pain in his back. The camel he'd claimed was not long broken for riding and fought his every command. He wondered what Slopkettle would do if he took her bike in the morning, leaving her the unruly beast instead.

She would smile and let him take what he wanted and silently add this to the reasons for which she would one day kill him. He would never know the where and when, but he knew she'd already sized him up for the greypot.

If he tried to take Gog for his own, Dogwyfe would fly at him there and then, a dark but honest rage. He wondered which death he preferred and if he'd be better off just shooting them both.

He approached the town camp, making plenty of noise, his hands in clear sight. Spence and one of the others sized him up, and when they realised he was there to talk, they pointed him to a space by the fire.

"I need medicine for my man," Lanyard said. "Wound's gone bad."

None of the others said anything, and Spence went back to working on a joint of meat, sucking out the fat with loud wet noises.

Young Tilly was bundled up in rugs, her eyes bleary and near closed. She held her slouch hat in her lap, and a mess of mouse-brown fuzz spilled down past her collar. She'd probably never travelled this far from her home and watched Lanyard curiously.

"Are we going to help them?" Tilly asked. "You said they're guarding us, Uncle. Maybe we can make the sick man better."

"Be quiet," Spence said then grinned at Lanyard. "You, go look in your bleedthrough for help or cook your man or whatever it is that your lot do. I've got nothing for you."

"I'll remember this," Lanyard said.

Spence spat lamb juice onto the coals, the grease sparking into a brief flame.

Lanyard made a taper from wood and rags. Jesus-gun in hand, he poked through the bleedthrough, wary of distant eyes, hoping to find something that would keep Mutch in the land of light.

The torchlight showed melted and broken furniture. He kicked in doors too buckled to open, smashed windows with the butt of his gun. Everywhere the detritus of the Before. But there were no doctor's kits, no shelves of drugs and ointments. He found music discs, baby clothes, shattered crockery, and more books than he'd ever read.

Lanyard gave pause when he saw a plastic horse figurine, one leg twisted slightly from the passage between worlds. It had a mane and tail of real hair, and was forever frozen in mid canter. He'd heard stories about these mythical creatures when he was a boy, toys for the rich back when they bred true. After a long moment, he put the figurine into his pocket.

He returned to the camp empty-handed. Dogwyfe continued her vigil, worrying at her braid with her ragged fingernails. The occasional curse word reached Lanyard as she railed against the gods.

Slopkettle came to his bed at a strange hour, swaying slightly on her feet. Her shadow passed across his face, and adrenaline kicked him into instant awareness. Snatching up his pistol, he threw the blanket aside, ready for her knives.

The flenser was nude and laughed at Lanyard's reaction. She was whip-thin, with little feminine about her, the curves starved from her and worked into muscle. The dying fire cast deep shadows in her hip bones and ribs, and an elaborate whorl of scar tissue ran across her belly, the design spiralling from where a child had once been cut out of her.

She fell on him like water, and he responded. It had been far too long, and soon she was stripping his clothes off. She laid her hands on his shirt, but he gripped her wrists before she could tear open the buttons to reveal his Jesusman's tattoo to the firelight.

"What about Mutch?" he said, hoping to distract her. She shrugged, looking over her shoulder to see Dogwyfe wailing and scooping dust into the air, letting it fall across her tear-streaked face onto the body of her dying husband.

"What of him?" she said. "He was just meat."

The three outlaws gave the moon their cries of pleasure and grief. In the morning, Dogwyfe dragged Mutch's cooling body into the bleedthrough, breaking one of the car's windows and pushing the corpse inside the machine. She piled a cairn of bricks and junk over him, burying the car from sight.

"The meat's no good for the greypot," was all she said when she finished the grave, her hands dusty and rubbed raw. Slopkettle nodded at this breach of crooked law and helped set a fortune of books around the grave, dragging over lumber and fence palings. The women set fire to the whole lot to mark his passing and held each other while the smoke whipped into their faces.

"I'm sorry about your friend," Tilly said to Lanyard. He was lashing gear onto the camel's wicker saddle, including some small items he'd scavenged from the bleedthrough.

"He wasn't my friend," he said brusquely, regretting his tone when the girl frowned and turned away.

"Are we done with this savage's funeral?" Spence said. "You'll have signalled every outlaw in sight, lighting that pyre. We have to go."

Lanyard nodded. There was a fortune at the end of this road, more than this scattering of crumbs, and enough to tolerate this miserable company. He spent much of the day imagining just how he was going to kill Spence Carpidian.

The buggy turned north and west, heading directly into the Range that marked the edges of the Inland. If they kept this course, Tilly would lead them directly into the Waste, the horror which hugged the civilised lands.

A knot of uneasiness worked through Lanyard's gut. It was no fit place for people out there. Life was hard enough in the lands claimed by people, but this Range marked a boundary that few settlers were mad enough to push past.

Odd things lived out there, creatures beyond all sense of scale and even time. Beasts that had seen the settlers arrive and would see the last of them die under these unfriendly skies. Then there were the traps for the weak-minded. Waterholes that wouldn't let you leave, tiny airborne seeds that sprouted beneath your skin and turned you into a walking plant, standing stones that spoke to men's minds and drove them mad.

The sheer distance of the Waste was mind-numbing—more miles of badlands than anyone could hope to cross. And in far too many places, the veil between worlds was tissue thin. Lanyard did not want to go back out into the Waste.

Early one morning they stopped by the entrance to a pass, a narrow notch that led into the Range. There was a spring here, an island of fecundity in a barren scrub of yucca and kennelweed, and everyone filled their waterskins to bursting. There was no telling where the next lot of water was coming from.

Spence was arranging a marker of stones, the signal for their kin following with the water tanker. Lanyard sidled to the waterhole, empty skins draped over one shoulder. Tilly was there, splashing water onto her face. She'd pulled off her shoes and stockings and squelched her toes deep into the mud.

This close to her, he felt the itch of the witches' silver lands, their hidden realm that Bauer named as the Greygulf. He had no doubt the girl could sniff out the thin spots, but wondered if she knew what was on the other side, watching her, ready to step through.

"Be careful," Lanyard told the girl, pointing up. "Cockatoos."

She looked up to see a cluster of the birds, like a bunch of overripe plums dangling from the gum tree directly above her. She shuddered, stepping back quickly. One of the birds cackled, ending with a gleeful warble.

"They won't hurt you if you don't make any loud noises, but I wouldn't want to be here alone," Lanyard said. "I've seen a flock take apart a grown man. Stripped him down to bone in under an hour."

The girl looked at him with wide eyes. Lanyard failed in his attempt to crack a friendly smile.

"Just a joke," he said. "They only eat dead things. Cockatoos are too stupid to hunt anything themselves."

"That wasn't very funny," Tilly said quietly.

"Sorry," Lanyard said, dipping his waterskin into the spring when he saw that one of the townsmen was watching him. "I don't talk to many kids."

Tilly waited while Lanyard filled his skins, sloshing the mud from her toes at a respectful distance. When he finished, he slung the full skins over one shoulder. As he passed by the girl, he fished the plastic horse out of his pocket and offered it to her.

"Here. I found this in the bleedthrough. You can have it."

"Oh, I love it," she said with a grin, plucking it from his grasp. She turned the toy over in her hands and quietly popped it into the front pocket of her smock before any of her companions could see.

Lanyard wondered at the other thing in her pocket, the shiny pretty wrapped up in the rag. It could be a bauble or keepsake, but she seemed scared of it back at the bleedthrough, stuffing the bundle back into her pinafore like it was a hot coal.

"You're smart, kid. See you," Lanyard said, passing by Spence as he returned to his group. The big man made to stand in Lanyard's path, but Lanyard brushed past, touching the brim of his stolen hat in a mocking salute.

"Don't you bloody talk to her, you crooked mongrel," Spence shouted, but Lanyard kept walking, the ghost of a smile tugging at his lips.

"Making friends?" Slopkettle said back at their camp. Her face was tight as she trimmed her nails forcefully with a short blade.

"Just enemies," Lanyard said. "Mind your fingers there," and sure enough she took off a sliver of skin. Lanyard took Slopkettle's hand, and a smile fought its way onto her face as he gently kissed away the trickle of blood.

— 4 —

The pass was still cold, the sun yet to cook away the shadows from last night. The small caravan negotiated the tight turns, motors growling and echoing along the hollows and hidden places.

Gog had little trouble with the tangled path, overgrown and blocked with rocks in places. Lanyard's sure-footed camel trudged forward undeterred by the rough terrain. The buggy bounced over the low-lying rubble as nimbly as Slopkettle's motorbike, but more than once they were thwarted by fallen slabs of stone cracked from extreme heat and cold. The Leicesterites were forced to halt, cursing as they cleared a path with picks and shovels.

"Bend a back," Spence snarled, but Lanyard ignored the man, watching the pass instead. As the sun crested the eastern lip of the pass, the walls began to pop. Somewhere behind them yet another sheet of rock gave way and crashed.

A noise to the left and a thin dribble of loose stone pattering against the canyon floor. His pistol already up and tracking, Lanyard drew a bead on a lone Taursi. The creature was watching their passage from a high shelf of slate.

Standing taller than a man, the Taursi wore a coat of clacking spines, sweeping back from its forehead and dangling past the small of its back.

A word he might have used was *echidna*, but he'd only heard it in Before-Time dreams, and so he kept the name tight.

It had the long drooping snout running down its wrinkled face, the one that made the half-tame town lurkers look vaguely ridiculous, wearing man pants, snuffling at grog and cigarettes with their long alien mouth.

This Taursi was wild though, a nude hunter with a small animal in one hand, limp and half-skinned. It leaned on a spear with a thick glass head, brilliant in the rising sunlight.

In the face of a drawn gun, it suddenly drew its quills, puffing up to near double its size, a threat display that could become a real threat in less than a heartbeat.

The Taursi had a second gut that held only sand, and the workings within it to turn this into glass, sharp and sure. The Taursi's quills glowed red-hot by drawing the heat away from the Taursi's body as it brewed up a batch of glass. Jags pushed out through the scarred glands along its forearms.

In a previous life, Lanyard had been a grog-runner and a slaver, and knew that even one Taursi could cut up a bunch of people in moments. He remembered many tense encounters on the river delta, watching the treelines next to people he didn't trust, waiting for the whistle of battle glass slicing through the air from these creatures indigenous to this land of Now. Keeping an eye on the angry Taursi above, Lanyard slowly holstered his pistol, keeping his hands out and empty.

Slopkettle took Lanyard's lead, reaching forward to switch off her rattling motorbike and keeping perfectly still. Dogwyfe kept one hand to Gog's bridle. The bird became skittish when it caught scent of the Taursi, who were the ancient hunters and bridlers of its kind.

Spence swore when he noticed the Taursi. At his urging, the townsfolk dropped their tools and grabbed for their rifles. Tilly looked up, wonder and fear on her face.

"Shoot the damn thing!" Spence shouted, but the spiky creature was already gone. After a long moment of scanning the top of the pass, the townsfolk renewed their efforts in clearing the path, frantically prying stone and shale out of the way.

"Don't rush," Lanyard told the men, easing his camel forward. "At least a dozen Taursi are watching us right now. You won't see them, so don't look. If they meant us dead, we'd be dead."

"We die, your fortune dies." The Leicesterite blustered as he directed his fury into splintering a large slab with a crow bar. "Keep a better watch, man-eater."

Lanyard dipped into his nearly empty tobacco pouch and rolled a thin cigarette. Allowing Gog to slump to a rest beside the bike, Dogwyfe clutched at her braid with white knuckles and said something quietly. Slopkettle talked with her briefly, low words that made the birdwoman chuckle. They looked at the town men for a long moment, and the flenser absently brushed at her sash of knives.

"Enough whispers." Lanyard barked and the two women jumped apart.

"If you've got time for chitter-chatter, you've got time to bend your backs."

They muttered at the instruction but did not defy his rule. From camelback he watched Slopkettle and Dogwyfe straining at their task, cigarette smoke slowly wreathing his head. When he saw Tilly watching him from the buggy, running the toy horse along her arm, he threw her a droll wink.

The pass opened onto bleakness without end, with nothing before the tiny group but open land and an egg-white sky. The Waste.

They halted here, ate a muted lunch in the face of this impossible distance. Lanyard tethered the camel near the mouth of the pass, and it tipped over rocks with its feet, pouncing on a pale Rangewyrm when it found one hissing and coiled.

Spence and Tilly walked a short distance from the group. The big man gripped her by the elbow, shaking her about as he told her something. The girl did not fight his grip, and shuffled to keep up, her head low. Lanyard felt his hackles rise at the sight and was surprised by his reaction.

She's not your problem, he told himself and tried to believe it. He wondered how any kid could still be so pure when this rotten, hungry world demanded nothing but survival and strength.

Tilly doesn't belong here, and neither do I, he decided. *If I have to kill her, I'll make it quick.*

Tilly crouched on the ground, peering into the little parcel from her pocket. Lanyard felt it again, a pinprick through the world veil, the barest hint of chatter from the other side.

And then, silence. Gathering up the scrunched rag and dousing that weird glimmer, Tilly pointed in a direction, then pointed again after Spence turned her around a few times.

"Kid's sniffed out that bleedthrough like a meat-mutt," Slopkettle said at Lanyard's elbow, watching the girl's slender arm point like a compass needle, unwavering in the direction. Lanyard had become so absorbed in Tilly's connection with the Greygulf that he hadn't heard the flenser approach and sidle up to him like a ghost.

I deserve a knife in the back, he thought.

"Papa Lucy does not smile upon this place," the flenser continued. "Nor upon the company we keep. We eat with this lot long enough, the Papa will think we've become statue lovers too."

"Money makes a lot of sins go away," Lanyard said.

"Says the man in the heretic's hat."

Slopkettle followed Lanyard back to the camp, their footprints the only thing marking the dust on the clay. Lanyard wondered if the flenser would ever consider a heart-binding and whether being her groom would keep him alive a bit longer.

He looked to where Dogwyfe was struggling to feed and water the unruly Gog and decided that brides still had braids. It was only a matter of time before the truth came out, and if he continued his tryst with Slopkettle, she would spot his inkings sooner or later.

If the flenser was insulted by the followers of Leicester-We-Forget, she'd certainly carve out the eyes of a Jesusman.

She has to die.

The flenser laughed as the camel plucked another Rangewyrm from its nest. The serpent hissed and struck at that leathery face to no effect.

Spence hollered at them to break their camp and move. One of the townsfolk set to laying another marker for Fos Carpidian, this one with a broad arrow of stones, perhaps ninety degrees west of their true heading.

"Clever," said Slopkettle, dragging her bike next to the sign. When the buggy pulled ahead, she quickly scuffed out the stones with her feet, kicking the marker into a meaningless scatter.

"Slop and I been talking, bossman," Dogwyfe said, Gog dancing alongside the camel and hissing. "We don't need them statue-kissers now."

"No one out here but us and that lot," Slopkettle added. "They'll make their move soon, you know they will. We kill 'em first, right now, and we take the girl for ourselves."

The buggy slowed and stopped, and Spence was leaning over the back, hollering obscenities at their crooked escort. Their hesitation was being noted.

"So you've been talking," Lanyard said, face thunderous as he chewed over the words.

The crooked women were silent, but Dogwyfe's face spoke volumes. The moment of his overthrow was coming, and soon. But right now he was ready for them, and the sorcerer's gun lay across his saddle horn with its promise of thunder.

"I'm still your bossman," he told them. "If we're going to do this, we do it my way. We'll need everyone out on the Waste, you'll see."

Soon the ruddy line of hills was swallowed by the horizon, and there was nothing but Waste in every direction. The bare landscape was peppered with curiosities, and Spence steered them clear of each one.

"Don't look at anything, don't touch anything, and if something talks to you, you run and run," the big man bellowed. Spence wore his own slouch hat now, and the Leicesterites shared around a pot of white face paint, perhaps hoping for divine protection in this strange land.

Ambitious homesteads dotted the Waste this close to the border. All ruins now, but some had been partially rebuilt into the suggestions of dwellings, empty frames of cattle-bone and clay. The yawning gaps of doors and windows stared at the intruders from the south. Lanyard could not shake the feeling that these abandoned houses resembled skulls with something sinister lurking inside each one, willing them to enter as they passed.

They gave a wide berth to a ring of what resembled people, preserved in weathered sandstone, that stood around the crumbling remains of an enormous sandstone horse, as if in supplication and worship.

As the whispers of these stone people reached the convoy, Lanyard felt the strength of their entreaties, the suggestion that he should drop everything and go stand in the circle with them, just for a moment.

The horse spoke then in a voice that was half the clapping of a great bell, half the breaking of crockery, and the entire party was drawn in, beasts and all. Spence fought it and failed, sweat running down his face as his hands moved on their own, steering the buggy towards that alien voice.

As a prentice Jesusman, Lanyard had encountered one of these spirits with Bauer, who taught him that these interlopers were stuck between the Now and the Greygulf, and were desperately hungry.

With the last of his willpower, Lanyard clumsily made the sign that stilled the stone horse's tongue and whispered the word that made the binding stick. With their willpower restored, the motley group fled north, engines whining, running the beasts as fast as they could bear.

There'd best be Neville's fortune at the end of this road, Lanyard thought. That small use of sorcery had left him shaky and a little nauseous. Every encounter like this reminded him that he was only half a Jesusman, one who knew just enough to get himself killed one day.

The further north they went into the Waste, the weirder the light got. The sun was now a pinpoint barely penetrating the blanket of cloud cover. Though they kept a true path guided by the girl's internal compass, the light shifted, playing a little to left and right. When Lanyard wasn't noticing, it was over his right shoulder, shuddering across the sky.

If they got lost out here, the sun would only navigate them to their deaths. Looking back, the scar of their passage was already erased by wind, as if the Waste had already forgotten them.

Slopkettle's bike was low on fuel and began to falter. Signalling a halt near the warped twist of a lone traffic light whose misshapen globes still blinked, Lanyard haggled a tin can of grain liquor out of Spence. The price he demanded was a fistful of rifle bullets. Slopkettle handed over the greasy kerchief reluctantly, fists clenched as the skinhead tipped them out to count in front of her.

"My bullets should be in his heart, not his hand," Slopkettle whispered as she passed Lanyard. "Make it soon."

Spence made camp on the rise of a broken bridge. A coat hanger of steel and cement missed its central span and arched over nothing but clay. For once, the Leicesterite did not object to Lanyard joining their camp. As the sun slid towards false west and night, they made a fire with the last of their wood. Lanyard added some camel dung he'd saved.

Poked into one of the dried nuggets, Lanyard had secretly hidden a scrap of paper, marked with some writ he remembered from Bauer. Safeguards, sigils of protection, the names of known Waste devils—the fire was as holy as he could make it, which was little comfort.

"Do you hear the people of this place, man-eater?" Spence asked, looking over the broken edge of the lost bridge. "My dead wife... men I killed...they're all whispering, up here." He tapped his temple with a fat finger.

"That means the Waste comes for you, tonight," Lanyard said, as he sat down on the buckled asphalt to wait, his back to the fire to preserve his night sight. He made a neat stack of guns at his feet, sharing out what was left of Mutch's kit with the crooked women.

He was cleaning Bauer's old gun when Tilly arrived with a ladleful of weak broth, fresh from feeding her nervous protectors.

"Be careful, it's hot," the girl said, holding the ladle steady as Lanyard sipped at the soup. He coughed as a chunk of scalding meat slid down his throat the wrong way, and Tilly's hand shook, dropping the rest of the broth onto the Jesusman gun.

"I'm so sorry," she said as she made to mop up the mess with the edge of her smock. Lanyard quickly pulled the gun out of her reach.

"Don't touch this," he warned. "Guns are dangerous."

She stared at the old gun, taking in the eye-twisting mess of pictographs and writings, forbidden marks. Lanyard laid the shotgun to one side and draped the cleaning rag over the stock.

"Where did you get that?" she asked.

"I had to kill the man who owned this, Tilly," Lanyard said. "He was a bad person, or perhaps he was too good to live. A gun's a gun, so I took it."

"Are you a Jesusman?" Tilly asked warily.

"No," he replied. This was truth enough for a child's ears.

There was one final squeeze of light from the sun and then darkness fell at once. There were no stars out here, and the moon was a wasted thing, defeated by the unmoving bank of clouds. The only light in the universe was the weak sputter of their campfire.

The group huddled nervously within the circle, clutching at rifles like talismans, looking outwards. As Spence stacked masonry and junk into a barricade, Tilly sat close to Lanyard, arms clenched around her knees, her tired eyes staring into the murk.

Lanyard's mind drifted away from the island of frightened humanity. He cast around in the dark for any sniff of that which did not belong, any sign that the world veil was torn.

"You can feel them too," Tilly whispered. His teeth ached, a faint hum in his ears grew into a painful buzz like a dozen mosquitoes trapped inside his ear, burrowing into his brain.

Joints aching, Lanyard fought the urge to vomit and rose to his feet. The world veil stretched into a sharp point working at the fabric of the universe. This far into the Waste, it was so thin that it gave way almost instantly. Murder slipped through the rip in the cosmos, close enough to raise the hackles on his neck.

"They're here!" Lanyard shouted, his gun barking into the night.

The gloom spat out horrors, nameless grinning things that circled the edge of the campfire's light, faces shifting and greasy. These intruders were nightmares made of scale and horn and limbs sheathed in tin and barbed wire. One creature had a marble bust installed as a head, the stone features flexing and mouth gibbering. Another was a cluster of slimy limbs erupting from a rusted refrigerator, trampling over a snake with a television for a face.

Junkers, Lanyard realised. They were bleedthroughs gone wrong. The Greygulf caught the objects somewhere between Before and Now and churned them into an unnatural life.

Lanyard's flimsy scrap of protection held. The junkers roared and tested the boundary, but they were unable to advance on the terrified people within.

He remembered a time when Bauer held firm against a roving horde of junkers. That sharpshot paladin hollered out all the words of unmaking, then sent a barrage of lead for those junkers too stubborn to hear him. As a prentice Jesusman, Lanyard could do nothing but reload his master's guns. At some stage during the onslaught, he had wet himself.

He was no Bauer.

Lanyard Everett unleashed the thunder of his holy gun at the fridge beast that shrieked as a round of shot punched out its life. Spence and the other townsfolk responded with a flimsy defence, peppering the hostile detritus with rifle shot, but their bullets were unmarked and made little difference.

The scrap of protection held the junkers back for another moment, but the fire flared into a blast of magnesium brightness as Lanyard's journeyman sorcery finally failed.

The shotgun offered another almighty kick, and Lanyard saw the junker before him fall into a splintered heap, a dining setting melded together like a wooden cockroach. The sharp chair legs twitched once and were still. Lanyard's camel wasn't so lucky. The animal's horrified honking was all the warning Lanyard had before a small pack of junkers tore it apart like a chicken.

Slopkettle snagged a monstrosity of umbrellas and TV antennae with her spiked chain, dragged it down, and stomped the life out of it. Gog darted about like a bloodied fighting cock, his talons ripping apart any junker that dared to face him. Dogwyfe clung to her husband's bird, eyes wide, the speargun in her fist forgotten.

Lanyard heard the alien cries of the junkers, words never uttered by a human tongue, and the sickening crunch as an engine-block hand fell onto a man, turning him into red paste. As Lanyard quickly reloaded from his dwindling supply of shells, he beat back junker arms with the gunstock when they got too close. He swung that smoking hot hammer, driving the iron butt-plate into anything with a false face.

He was down to his last two shells.

A sound, and he turned to see a junker bearing down on him. It wore a marble bust as its own face, someone with a hawk nose from the Before-Times. Its body was lumpy cement punctuated with brick, wrapped around an old safe.

The statue mouth curved into a hateful smile, and the fist rose, an engine-block smeared with gore. Lanyard let off a round into the trunk of the demon. This did little more than drive it backward a half-step and gouge out a fist-sized chunk of cement.

One shell left, he realised. He aimed high and took out that hateful face, leaving nothing but a marble stump. The junker wobbled and reached up with its off-hand—one that ended as a blender—to gingerly touch the damage.

It rolled forward, its cement arms throwing a flurry of wild blows. Lanyard danced backwards until he slipped in the spilled guts of his dead camel. Unable to rise, he held up his empty gun like a sword to block the downward chop of the blender arm. The effort jarred his arms and shoulders.

The engine-block fist rose, and Lanyard looked up helplessly at the brutal instrument of his death. Then he spoke a forbidden phrase he'd heard a lifetime ago, a guttural tongue that made little sense to him.

Lanyard's voice wavered, but the effect was unmistakeable. The junker teetered above him as the sorcery binding the bleedthrough parts failed. The building materials caved in on the safe that served as the beast's heart, and the engine-block dropped from the sagging cement arm, narrowly missing Lanyard's head.

The words of unmaking. There were words strong enough to bring down your enemy's walls and words to part dark parasites from the bodies they'd stolen, but Lanyard remembered only the barest handful of the Jesusman's rote.

In the face of this magic, the remaining junkers darted for safety, a few even leapt off the edges of the bridge. Lanyard could see them in his mind's eye galloping across the dark plain and braying with fear. These errant bleedthroughs would terrorise the Waste until something stronger crushed the false life from them.

He turned to look at the chaos where the campsite had been. The fire was trampled and close to going out. By its dim light, he could see the bodies of the junkers and the broken remains of two of Spence's crew. Underneath the buggy, Tilly Carpidian huddled untouched but weeping.

Good. Our treasure map is safe, he tried to convince himself. He was relieved that Tilly was safe but felt nothing for anyone else on that bridge.

Dogwyfe was busy tending to Gog's wounds with pitch and a hot coal. Slopkettle stood above the ruin of the big junker, poking at the separated parts with her boot. She made no offer to help Lanyard to his feet.

Did she hear me say the Jesus words?

"What are you?" Slopkettle demanded but backed away with hands raised, not interested in anything he had to say.

There was only one explanation, and it ended in blood.

— 5 —

Dawn. That perfect darkness gave way to a blazing fury of light, the clouds gone somewhere else in the final hours of night. The sun was as hot as anywhere in the Inland and jerked across the dark blue sky like a greased coal.

Those who'd survived kept the morning fire going with the flesh of dead junkers, wood being wood. While the others slept or cooked what might be a pitiful last meal, Lanyard laid his pistol bullets across a rock. Barely a dozen rounds.

With his bowie knife, he scored the lead tips of each bullet with the mark of the Jesus—a simple cross flanked with the letters B and N, Before and Now. He hoped this would be enough to give any demon the true death, and he rued the useless weight of the empty shotgun on his back.

Slopkettle and Dogwyfe were busy carving up the fallen camel for meat, plucking out the yard-length ruddy feathers, taking care to cut around any of the bite-marks. Lanyard spent a minute or two picking through the large stack of his gear figuring out what he could do without.

With a heavy sigh, he left most of the gear foraged from the last bleedthrough but kept one packet of cigarettes for himself. The rest he traded with Spence for fuel and ammo. The bald Leicesterite drove a hard bargain.

"You ride with me, bossman," Dogwyfe said as she charred camel steaks for quick transport. "Slop won't have you on her bike."

I bet she won't, he thought but nodded in agreement. After Spence doused the fire, the dwindling caravan continued onwards, today's north somewhere closer to south if the sun was anything to go by.

"Everything is a lie out here," he told the birdwoman, who said nothing as she urged the reluctant Gog onward with the weight of two on his back.

Tilly rode with her uncle and the remaining Leicesterite, a timid townie with a name like Bevan or Darren. The buggy misfired more often than not as the roughgut fuel slowly scoured the insides of the motor. The machine might make it to Fos Carpidian's miracle bleedthrough, but there was no way it was getting home.

"Idiots. They're already dead," Lanyard said. He clutched Dogwyfe's bony waist as Gog lurched across a vast field of shattered gravestones stacked two or three deep. The woman said nothing, whirling the clacker stick and whistling through her teeth to drive the great bird up and over the mess. The bike and buggy picked a slower path through this cemetery litter. The names of the dead were too faded to make out.

"If they build a new town, set to digging out here in the Waste, those folks will be dead within the month. Or turned monster themselves."

"Never going to be a town. No dig neither," Dogwyfe said. "Just their bones, and us."

"Only when I say so," Lanyard said. "We need them still."

"It's not up to you now," the birdwoman said.

Quicker than thought, Lanyard had his gun out and poked into her ribs. He yanked down her braid so hard that her head tipped back.

"Your smart mouth just got you killed," he said.

They saw the buggy clear the hill of headstones. Spence was running the wounded engine hard, swerving and sliding sideways down the last slope.

A crack of a desperate rifle shot from the buggy, and then Slopkettle jumped that apex of tombstones on her bike, throttle back and whining. She had the hook and chain out and she was swinging it good.

The crooked women had set up an ambush.

"You pair of bitches. We're in this now." Lanyard swore. Dogwyfe smiled as he withdrew the pistol from her ribs, lining it up on the approaching buggy instead.

Spence shouted when he saw the bird. He cursed them as he fought the bucking of the steering wheel, rifle over the dash as he tried to aim at them. Tilly sat beside him wide-eyed and screaming.

When the bike drew level with the buggy, Slopkettle released the chain so it tangled around the nameless Leicesterite, its fat hook jagging deep into the side of his neck. The flenser jumped from the bike, slid down the stones on her backside, and hauled back on the chain. The man tumbled from the car, shrieking, twitching like a hooked fish.

The buggy was so close now that Lanyard could see the knives protruding from Spence's chest and the glaze in his eyes as his life ran out of him. Tilly was the picture of fear, white-faced and crying.

"He's going to ram us," Lanyard said as he released his grip on the birdwoman's braid. Smirking, Dogwyfe tapped her knout lightly against Gog's scarred neck, and the bird danced on the spot, muscles quivering as the machine bore down on them.

In that final moment, Spence Carpidian steered into them, hoping to take out the bird with speed and metal. His rifle cracked once, the muzzle low and shaking. Gog leapt up into the air and landed on top of the moving car as it passed through the space where he had stood a second before. The bird became a flurry of claws and beak, stabbing downwards at the bald man.

The buggy coasted along until the motor belched and went silent. A moaning gurgle escaped from Spence as Gog feasted on him, claws squeezing the life and juice out of that belly. Dogwyfe tapped a command onto the bird's neck, and he climbed out of the buggy dragging the dying man with his beak.

Lanyard dropped from the saddle and walked over to the buggy. Tilly was crouched low on the seat, whimpering and staring at the bird's grisly feast, rapid sobs shaking through her small body.

He leaned into the car and picked her up. Rather than fight this, the girl hung limp in his arms like a rabbit weighing almost nothing. The back of her dress was wet from both her bladder and the life blood of her uncle.

"Your uncle Spence was a stupid man, Tilly, but you're safe enough," Lanyard told her. "I won't let anything happen to you."

"It ate him," she kept saying, babbling and sobbing.

"This wasn't my doing," he told her. Now she fought him, little fists pounding into his chest, feet kicking into his belly with no consequence.

"I'm going to put you down now," he said, depositing the girl onto the clay. She stood back, fists clenched, and looked around helplessly. There was nowhere to run.

"Your people are dead, and that's just how it is," Lanyard said. "Your Pa and all those people following, they're not going to make it out here either."

"No!" she yelled. "You're lying."

"You've seen how it is here," he said, kneeling to her eye level. "This place is going to kill them. But you're still alive."

She stared at him in silence, rubbed away the tears and snot until her face was a dirty slimy mess. Lanyard saw an inner strength to her, fists bunched as she sized up a grown man twice her size.

Her childhood ended today, he realised.

"I'm your people now, girl. You lead us to your Leicester-We-Forget, and I'll see that you're taken care of."

"Mister," Tilly said, "you can fuck off."

Lanyard took the buggy and ran it gently to conserve the dying motor. Tilly was trussed up in the back seat after having jumped out of the moving vehicle once already. Slopkettle wanted to carve the insolence out of her, but Lanyard drove the flenser off with a pistol butt to the side of the face.

Everyone else was dead, and everything around them was melting weirdness.

The only thing visible for miles was a lone bottle tree standing near the shattered finger of a cement pipe. A trickle of water from the pipe lent the tree just enough life to survive. Lanyard called for a halt, wondering if Before-Time water was safe to drink.

"Maybe we boil it," Dogwyfe suggested, as the crooked folk considered the unusual sight. Lanyard dipped an empty can into the shallow pond and sniffed the water suspiciously.

It had a rotten egg whiff to it and seemed almost yellow. He tipped it out and watched the tainted water soak into the cracked earth.

"Nothing for us here," he said and headed back to his vehicle. He leant over the side and hauled Tilly upright.

"Will you behave now?" he asked, knife in hand. She nodded and he sliced her bonds.

"Take a good look at those other two. I hope you realise that I'm your best friend now," he said. "Give me a direction to the bleed-through. No more fooling."

Biting her lip, she scanned the horizon unsure. She looked down at her lap.

"Go on, talk to whatever it is you keep in your pocket," he whispered. "I know you're scared of it, but you should be more scared of Slopkettle there."

Tilly pulled the rag bundle out of her pocket and carefully unfolded it on her lap to reveal a sliver of dark green glass the size of an arrowhead and knapped like flint. Lanyard thought it might be Taursi work, but it seemed older and different from the cutters and pretties that the spiky folk favoured.

The glass drank the sunlight, and there was instantly a deep voice, an alien babble in Lanyard's skull. He staggered back, gripping the side of the car. He fought against this incomprehensible intelligence. A force pressed against his mind seeking access.

He saw it then, a great glow on the horizon and other pinpoints dotting that bleak vista like searchlights, small breaks in the world veil. But these were nothing to the great column of smoke behind them, a beacon somewhere near the edge of the Inland.

"Jesusman," the thing said into his ear. Lanyard's feet shifted in the direction of the towering smoke. He took one step and then another before Tilly threw the rag over the glass to starve it of light. The presence was gone, reduced to a faint babble coming from Tilly's hands.

"Turtwurdigan likes you," she said. She offered the bundle to Lanyard. He retreated, shaking his head.

"That should be buried in a deep dark hole. No, I won't take your glass from you."

A sharp screech behind him, and then another. Gog drew up to his full height staring at something in the distance, feathers puffed up in a threat display. The bird scratched at the clay with his murderous claws, and then hopped from foot to foot, beak raised to the sky, throat vibrating with a long, pitiful whine.

"What's wrong with your bird?" he asked Dogwyfe.

"I don't know!" Dogwyfe said, hauling on a hanging rein until the bird was still. Even then it hissed and burbled at an unseen threat. Shaken, the birdwoman quickly repacked their supplies into the bird's netting. After his strange experience with the glass, Lanyard was all too ready to leave this place.

Lanyard threw himself into the buggy. He was reaching for the ripcord when Slopkettle called him over. She was madly pumping on the starting pedal, but the bike only emitted a tired chug.

"Bossman, there's something wrong with the bike!" Slopkettle cried out. She hadn't called him that in days, and he frowned at this suspicious show of respect.

"Leave it here. You ride in the buggy," he said.

"We'll be pushing that bloody thing tomorrow. We can't leave the bike, not out here!"

Pushing her out of the way, Lanyard gave it a try, grinding down on the starter pedal with no result. There was a lick of fuel left in the tank and everything else seemed okay. Kneeling, he saw that the sparkplugs were hanging loose, and that was the moment that Slopkettle slammed the spanner against his temple.

Lanyard awoke bound to the bottle tree, his skull a firepit of pain.

He hung from an old pair of handcuffs, a long chain running between the manacles that stretched up and over a high branch in a triple loop. The hook bit deep into the flesh of the branch, a tear of piss-coloured sap running from the wound but never quite falling. There'd be no shaking that loose. The chain gave him just enough slack to slump against the great bulb of the tree but not enough that he could lie down.

"You've tied people up before," he managed. Seeing that he was awake, Slopkettle beat him with a fury, breaking one of his teeth. He laughed ruefully and spat it out with a dribble of blood.

"Tickle me some more," he said.

Slopkettle drew a sharp craft knife held together with duct tape and pushed out an inch of rusting blade. Tugging off his boots, she slowly sliced away his trousers, the seam parting easily for the keen little blade.

"I like to take my time with the special ones," the flenser told Lanyard. She nicked him when cutting away the inside leg and licked at the spot of blood, madness in her eyes.

"Make your bird dance again, my sweet," she said to Dogwyfe, who hauled a little bone whistle out from under her leather jerkin. She emptied her lungs into it, and while it made no sound, it drove Gog crazy. Once more the bird capered and shrieked, feathers puffed out. The perfect threat display trained into the bird as a party trick.

"Your rooster is smarter than you," he said to Dogwyfe. "At least he knows that someone is blowing on his whistle."

"Shut up," Dogwyfe said and spat on the ground. She snatched up a dirty pile of rags and rope that turned out to be Tilly, trussed up tightly and gagged with an old sock. As Dogwyfe tied her to the bird, the young girl shared a look of tired defeat with Lanyard and there was no fear in her eyes.

Yet.

Poor girl, left alone with this pair, Lanyard mused. The girl was one more failure for his list, perhaps his last.

Slopkettle neatly sliced away the buttons on his shirt but recoiled with a cry of alarm at his Jesusman tattoo finally revealed. The flenser stared at the forbidden ink, her face suddenly pale.

"You-you damn sorcerer. You have defiled me!"

Slopkettle stepped back and threw the knife to the ground. She walked away rubbing at her forearms and muttering. She held a hurried conference with Dogwyfe, who stared at Lanyard with shock.

"Hey Slop, how about one more for the road?" He laughed then broke into a coughing fit. The flenser stormed around the tree, howling up into the weird sky and cutting at her own arms with a short knife. Dogwyfe stood over him with her crossbow shaking nervously as she cranked back the string.

"Bad luck to spill the blood of a Jesusman," she said as she pocketed the quarrel and released the tension from the string. "I won't have this on me, I won't."

Forearms weeping blood, Slopkettle slumped down on the earth before Lanyard and pointed her bloody blade at him. A spatter of tears ran down the ritual scars on her young face. "I am sworn to cut skin for Papa Lucy. Now the Family will turn from me, but you? You are a dead man."

For long moments the hot wind blew and the sun darted about like a slow firefly, but neither of the crooked women made a move to harm him. Then Dogwyfe gently lifted Slopkettle to her feet and made to lead the weeping flenser away.

"He's not worth it, Slop," the birdwoman said, an eye to the blistering heat rising from the plains. "Let this bloody Jesusman die in his chains."

Slopkettle shook off Dogwyfe's tender ministrations and approached Lanyard. She wiped her blood across his face and drew a sign on his forehead with the sharp edge of a fingernail.

"By the laws of Papa Lucy and the old rite of Cruik, I accuse and affirm you of heresy," Slopkettle said. "Lanyard Everett, I sentence you to life imprisonment."

She looked to the sky, to the Waste around, and gave a gruesome smile.

"I give you a day at best."

Dogwyfe set the buggy on fire and threw the scraps of Lanyard's clothing and kit into the flames. Tilly was a limp bundle lashed to the bird. She was next to the Jesusman gun that was wrapped in canvas and rope. A weapon too valuable to junk, too dangerous to leave.

"I'll come get you, Tilly," he cried out, and the women laughed. Tilly's mouse-brown head rose for a moment, but flopped against the bird's flanks, all strength and will gone from Carpidian's child.

The crooked women left Lanyard chained to the bottle tree and did not spare him a backwards glance. Bird and bike became a distant speck, then a heat mirage somewhere near the horizon, and then nothing.

Lanyard woke from dreams of Bauer to see a Taursi standing over him and leaning on its glass-tipped spear. A female, her twin row of teats atrophied and scarred from an old litter. The giant startled when Lanyard moved, her coat of spines clacking and rustling.

The sun had already cooked Lanyard a bright red, and his throat was parched. The spiky native blocked the sunlight, and he peered up at her gratefully.

"Good hunting?" he asked, voice dry and failing.

"No," she said. She squatted down, her crooked dog legs folding gracefully underneath her.

"Long way from your land," he managed.

She shrugged as she idly scooped a handful of crumbling clay from around the roots of the tree. Her long snout danced about in her hand and drew the sand into her second stomach for future glass firing. Lanyard had cut enough Taursi throats to know that they had a second throat hidden in there, a neat little valve that sent the food one way and the grit another.

"Does it have a second arsehole?" one of his old bosses had asked over a slit throat, a moment before Lanyard put the same blade into the man. A job was a job, but respect was always important.

Respect wasn't exactly friendship. You could respect a venomous snake, a deadly sandstorm, a Taursi at an execution.

"What are you doing here?" he asked. Each breath was more difficult, and his eyeballs were cooking in their sockets.

"You done my auntie's mob a favour, many years ago," the Taursi said, clearly uncomfortable with the man-tongue. "Drove off a witching fella what was killing them."

"I'm calling in that favour," Lanyard said, rattling at his chains. "Set me loose."

"No. We're not to interfere with your man laws. Not ever."

"Why did you come?"

"I came to honour you, Lanyard Hesusman," the Taursi said, using the much older title. "I will wait with you while you die."

Lanyard knew that this Taursi would do as she said. She would not harm him, would not help him, and merely meant to observe his imminent passing.

He made a lunge for the spear, which the spiky native simply moved out of his reach. "Get stuffed," Lanyard croaked.

The heat made the foul trickle from the pipe look good, even knowing it was bleedthrough and not safe to drink. His chains wouldn't quite let him reach, so he did not even have the dignity of dying with the bloat from bad water.

"Drink," he begged the Taursi, but his honour guard would not share a drop with him. A near-full waterbag sat at the top of her clay and reed basket, but she moved it underneath a flour stone, out of sight. A small kindness to not mock him with its closeness.

"Man laws," was all she said and settled back to watching him die. He wondered how the creature had travelled here, how she knew where to find him. The Taursi rarely braved the madness of the Waste but had been known to travel fast when needed, to go missing when slavers or bailiffs hunted them.

Only grog and greed had destroyed this people. They were the superiors of the settlers in every way but for that of cruelty.

"The Taursi have a special relationship with the Greygulf, and it wouldn't surprise me if they knew some of the shadow roads," Bauer once told a young Lanyard. "Now, they're a broken lot. Their great civilisation was on its last legs when we came here, but you wouldn't know it now. We stole bloody everything."

The prentice Lanyard pressed his master on the topic of Sad Plain, but the old man never spoke of it.

Dusk brought a little relief from the brutal kiss of the sun, but Lanyard wondered if he would survive the night, nude and chained. The Taursi set to drawing out a star-glass, honking and groaning as she forced a curlicue of molten glass from the glands on her arms, working it rapidly with scarred grey fingers. Her quills puffed out, white-hot as they drew the heat away from her body, and then the work was done.

"No stars, no moon here," the Taursi said. "This will help."

Lanyard watched through failing eyes as the little sculpture drew in the last of the sunlight, and when the sun gasped its last, the star-glass shone clearly, the only wink of light on the dark plain.

Beyond that moon-bright circle, Lanyard heard the sounds of visitors, a dozen tiny breaches in the world veil, creatures passing back and forth and feeding from each other in the darkness.

With his toes, he scratched out what wards he knew, but nothing came close that night. The Waste seemed to know he was defeated and left him to his grisly demise.

The deadly chill of the night was a pleasant warmth now, and he drifted, lost in memory, disconnected from the pain of his dying body. This was his reward, the end of a life lived hard, and very soon it would all be over.

"You don't die today," Bauer said into his ear, and Lanyard flinched, awake and hurting. His Taursi guardian was leaning close to check his breathing, a kindly sadness in her eyes.

He struck, snatching at her wrist, pulling himself to his feet with the last of his strength. Even as the spines pierced his skin, he wrapped the slack of his chain around the creature's throat, and her curses became a phlegmy gurgle.

He sat down, fast, and the chain became taut, his weight an immovable anchor on that iron noose. The Taursi sliced at him with glass, kicked at him with her spurs, but soon enough she was still, the black needle of her tongue sagging from her snout.

Lanyard snagged her spear with his feet, the weapon dropped and forgotten by the surprised Taursi. He clumsily brought it up to his bound hands and jammed the broad glass spearhead into the handcuffs where the small key was meant to go.

He pushed hard, and something gave way. One more push and the cuffs sprang open, the mechanism destroyed.

Lanyard stood shakily then pushed the dead Taursi out of his way. He left her there and wondered if the Waste would send something to feed on her corpse. He gathered up the spear and staggered to the native's travelling basket, fumbling for the waterskin with hands that didn't seem to belong to him.

He forced himself to stop drinking while his brain screamed for more. He'd heard of men swapping one death for another, drinking more water than their gut could fit, and far too quickly. He picked up the star-glass and made a slow circuit of the campsite in the hope that Slopkettle and Dogwyfe had left something behind, some scrap he could wear to ward off the cold.

Spence's buggy was still smouldering so he warmed himself by the hot metal for a moment, poking through the ashes with the spear. Everything was burnt. All he found was the scrap of a boot that was leather cracked and blackened.

There, by the trickling pipe, snagged on a rusty tangle of rebar, fluttering in the night breezes, was Fos Carpidian's slouch. Wheezing with laughter, Lanyard wore it for all the good it would do him and wondered at the picture he presented, bloody and naked but for a hat.

Casting about for tracks, he found the place where Dogwyfe had pounced upon Tilly, the churn of dust where little feet scuffed and dragged against the pull of the larger woman. Nearby, Lanyard found the plastic horse he'd given the girl, ignored as the junk it was. With a heavy sigh, he knelt to pick it up, and stopped.

She'd propped the toy against the rag bundle, and the glass within whispered weakly to him. Turtwurdigan begged him for daylight, for blood and rote. By the melted horse, Tilly had used a stick to scratch into the clay the letters B + N.

The mark of the Jesus. The girl had left him a gift.

— 6 —

Lanyard crept into the ashes of the burnt-out buggy, soaking up the last scrap of warmth left from the fire. Breaking his fast on the Taursi's stock of meat and mealie bread, he waited for the sun to rise. The star-glass failed close to dawn, and he threw the dim trinket into the pitch black, the pads of many small feet fleeing from the loud crash as it broke.

Sunlight. He rose to greet it with stiff joints, every inch of him cold to the touch. No tracks remained for him to follow, as if no one had ever passed this spot.

"I will find you, Tilly," he swore as he reached into the basket to touch the plastic horse.

After marking a circle of protective signs, Lanyard carefully sat within its boundary. Leaning out over the sigils, he unfolded the scrap of cloth with his spear tip. Instantly, the cacophony boomed in his mind, a skull-splitting static as the ancient shard of glass drank at the sunlight.

His protective circle nearly useless, it took all of Lanyard's willpower to fight off the spirit that dwelt within the glass. Once more he looked upon the small nicks in the world veil, the glow of the bleedthrough, and the smoking column behind him, where the glass insisted he go.

Obey! it whispered, probing into the deepest parts of his mind, searching for a way to wear him as a puppet. *Obey Turtwurdigan!*

"No," he said as he threw the cloth back over the glass, starving it of light and reducing it to a whispering menace. He knew where Tilly was heading now, if she could keep the direction in her head without the glass. That was enough.

Climbing to his feet, he took up spear and basket, and he trudged naked through the day. He could be dead by sunset, but at least he was alive and free. Futile as it was, he meant to track his treacherous comrades, walk away a rich man. Free that poor kid before she ended up in a cookpot.

He made it barely a mile down the road when he felt the signs, so strong that he almost passed out. Something was coming. Before him, the air stretched taut, the tell-tale shimmer like a heat haze. He could see the outline of a pair of hands grabbing at the world veil and ripping it apart like a flimsy shirt. A tear began to open that hovered above the slithering bike tracks and the trail of the bird.

"No, you dirty bastards," Lanyard moaned. He'd put thousands of miles between him and his hunters, but they'd finally found him, naked and broken in an endless stretch of nothing.

A witch slid out of the hole, wax-fleshed and grinning. Then another wearing a Leicester form as a jape. A third, lesser witch shifted between the shapes of a dog and a little boy.

"No," Lanyard whispered. He contorted his hand into the witch ward and spat out the first words Bauer taught him, swift glottals of banishment and undoing. As he did this, he dashed forward and thrust the spear into the first witch's chest where a heart should be—though it often wasn't.

The sharp glass tip punched through the chest as if piercing butter, but the witch pulled Lanyard into its runny embrace. It smiled as it patted him on the back like he were a babe.

The witches dragged Lanyard into the Greygulf, and he screamed the whole way.

The Greygulf sat between Before and Now, and other worlds and times. It was a thin world, cast in murk and silver; the only light a faint leaden glimmer that ran through everything. Shadow roads ran in and out of this mirrorland, and the fluid landscape shifted often, an exaggerated reflection of the realms it pressed up against.

From this side, the world veil looked like smoky glass, easy enough to push through if you knew the trick. You could go anywhere if you didn't mind the cost.

Few other than the Jesusmen knew of this place or could survive a passage through it without being struck mindless and dumb. Lanyard had been here twice: once with his master, once as the prisoner of a witch he'd hunted to its nest.

This time, he was not sure he would ever leave. He screamed until a band of waxy flesh ran across his mouth sealing off the sound. The three witches melted and ran together into a new shape, a collective of arms and legs that thundered along at a great pace.

Although Lanyard could still feel the presence of Turtwurdigan nearby, Tilly's glass could not feed from this grey light. The insistent chatter was gone and replaced by a morose grumbling.

Part captor and part litter, the witches hustled him along the shadow road. The path wound like a silver ribbon up into the grey sky, weaving through countless others, stretching from the entry point into the Waste to parts unknown.

Terrified, Lanyard tried to see where they were taking him. Slow shapes travelled across the distant road, reaching out through the world veil with impossibly long arms. Feeding. Most witches kept their nests in here, too, the better to world-hop through that smoky glass. Others found a place like the Now and made their homes near a food source.

Supposedly, the Jesus was still in here somewhere, bound and suffering. Guardian of the Crossing, master of a doomed order. His disciples were dead or missing, or had taken one too many trips to this place and tasted the pleasures of the other side. Jesusmen, turned to witching.

They'll keep me in here forever, Lanyard thought, nostrils flaring as he drew in short, panicked breaths. *The last damn fool to ride with mark and word.*

This won't end well.

The shadow road entered a rickety spire, a structure that was half shadow and half brick. Rusted Before-Time antennae bristled along its flanks that were peppered with satellite dishes and other growths that Lanyard did not know the names for. A fat tangle of shadow roads entered through archways and modified windows, dozens of roads converging at impossible angles.

"A terminus, Jesusman," a greasy pair of lips whispered into his ear. "My way, we'd leave you here."

"Yes, yes," said another voice, a broad grin rising from the white bulk in front of his little boy eyes. "We'd pass you around, Jesusfool, let the whole place have a lick of you."

"But the master says fetch, so we fetch," the waxy dog snout declared. The witches bickered then dissolved into their singular selves. One formed itself into an upright sarcophagus on legs and swallowed Lanyard completely save for his face. The dog witch trotted ahead with its ears swivelling and head erect, while the other appeared as a two-headed Leicester, the heads arguing comically over the ownership of Lanyard's slouch hat.

The inside of the terminus resembled a great cathedral, a hall of stone and ancient beams. Flickering TVs covered the walls, while stock market tickers fought with neon signs for remaining space.

"He likes to be up to date," one of the witches said. They stepped from one road to another, a grey ribbon sloping towards a downward angled window.

Below them, a fortune of junk gathered and stacked high: cars and boats, banks of electrical equipment, museums' worth of artworks and statuary.

Under the converging paths, the interior of a faux house was kept in the midst of this mess, a display from a Before-Time store. Settees, a bedroom setting, and a kitchen with an electric stove. Pots bubbled away on the red-hot cooktop, tended to by a trio of waxy arms.

In the middle was a vast white shape like a fat candle half-melted and running all over the furniture. The face in the middle was stretched out, broad mouth filthy with juice and grease. Arms and limbs danced around the massive glob, constantly ferrying pots of food into that wide gullet.

"Morning, Neville," the dog barked cheerfully. The only response was a deep burbling mumble, the twitch of limbs as the bloated witch reached out for them. Fingers as wide as a man brushed the shadow road that they walked along, swaying it slightly.

"Rich man, him," the false Leicester said to Lanyard. "Rich as you like."

The witches left the terminus tower and followed the shadow road down towards the ground. Every horror from Lanyard's dreams walked here. An aeroplane lay twisted and burning on a silver mountain while a team of witches plucked out the terrified passengers and stripped them for the greypot—a church bell with its clapper removed and perched upside-down over a roaring bonfire.

In places, the world veil sagged, broken to the point of insta-bility. Junk tumbled through, and just as often tumbled back out, bleedthroughs in the making. A lawnmower turned rogue, roaring about joyfully until two witches pinned it down and tore it apart with their bare hands.

The worst sign of wear in the world veil was an enormous bulge, a pulsating boil that threatened to burst. Lanyard wondered if this was the bleedthrough that Tilly was searching for. He was frustrated by its nearness.

If I were to slip back into the Now with all those fridgerators and mattresses, wouldn't that be a nice surprise for Slopkettle? Lanyard thought mournfully.

A big walker followed their path, its impossibly long arms dragging through the world veil as if drift fishing. It pulled a house through and settled around it to grind away the eaves with its peg teeth. Lanyard shivered when he looked at the blunt face, the stretched features that had once been human.

"Well, it's been fun, but here we are," the dog witch said, pointing ahead of them as if sighting a duck. "Through you go."

The shadow road ended in a door, a dark pucker like a sphincter, knotted tight. The two-headed Leicester tapped around its edges, pressing against something that caused it to spiral open.

On the other side of the door was a neat circle of daylight, eye-watering against the silver gloom. Lanyard saw the burnt teeth where buildings had once stood and the maddening tangle where another witch-nest grew, a thing of shadow and scraps.

The broad white of the salt flat that almost killed him.

They were taking him back to face their justice, as if he'd never fled from this place, beaten and broken. He thrashed around in his bonds, bit into the witch's sour flesh for all the good it did.

He was going to die here, and he was going to die hard.

The sarcophagus witch turned back into a man-shape and ejected the prisoner from its innards. Choking and gagging, Lanyard retched, his gut heaving violently as he fell to his knees.

As always, the passage from the Greygulf churned his insides, but his mind was still intact. The mark of a true guardian of the Crossing: the ability to pierce the world veil and still have a thought in his head.

"He was sick inside of me," the first witch moaned, squeezing the chunks of Lanyard's vomit out of his pale flesh like pimples. Its companions laughed, and the creature suffered their jibes with a wide smile, from lips that wrapped almost all the way around its head.

"Here mate, can't have you meeting the bossman completely starkers," another one said, a wax tentacle depositing the slouch hat on his head. More laughter, half of it silent and bouncing around inside his head. The static of their mind-talk gave him a throbbing headache, and the proximity to so many witches made his bones ache.

At their prodding, he walked forward.

The nest rose before him, an alien architecture of spires and jutting bungalows, clad in tin and shadow, wired to power-panels that drank the sunlight like a Taursi glass. A handful of witches climbed around on the structure like white spiders, spitting goopy threads into the gaps, running electrical lines into the innards of the structure.

One wrestled with what looked like a miniature bank of dark cloud, pushing it into a buttress and securing it with spit. It began to spread like a vine, dark fingers holding the disparate pieces together, forming a wall that a cannon would be hard pressed to shatter.

Below the nest, a man crouched by a low fire, poking at the coals with a stick. A writhing mass of white snakes vacated the fireside as the witches came to warm themselves by the banked coals.

Here the witches frogmarched Lanyard and hurled him down into the ash and dust.

Coughing and his body a litany of abuse, Lanyard got to his hands and knees. He slowly scooped up a handful of ash. *I'll go down the same way I lived—fighting dirty.* Raising his head, he stared across the fire in shock, speechless as a familiar figure knocked the coals away from a fresh-cooked roll of damper.

"It's been a long time, Lanyard," Bauer said, the old Jesusman smiling as he broke open the steaming loaf. "Hungry?"

— INTERLUDE —

The Boneman drove the skeleton horse onwards, keeping to backroads as he crossed the Overland. Having met the miserable men of this age, he feared they would shoot him on sight, a jelly-fleshed freak with a visible skeleton.

The first person to see him was a young shepherd watering his sheep by the banks of the Niven. The boy wailed in terror, abandoned his crook and his flock, and plunged into the water to swim for safety.

Although the Boneman never said a word, he realised that his steed and his reflection said more than enough. He would not be able to get close to a town, not looking like this.

Another time he was driven off by a travelling tinkerman who had set his birds on the Boneman the moment he showed himself. No one would give directions to a walking monster, and he knew he'd get no help in finding the whereabouts of his brother.

Spending a nervous day lurking around a small logger's village, the Boneman crept in like a thief by night. A dog set to barking as he passed by a cabin, but its owner merely grumbled at the beast to shut up.

How far I have fallen, the Boneman mused, pilfering clothing from a wash line. An old man slumbered next to his hearth, feet bare and warmed by the fire. The Boneman crept inside and snatched his shoes. He stood up to find the man awake, wide-eyed and gasping.

"Shh," he said, holding a finger to his clear lips. The old man screamed fit to bring the entire village out. The Boneman ran to his cart and tumbled into it. He shook the reins and urged the dead horse into a swift canter as the villagers came for him with braces of dogs and hefting torch and axe.

He remembered his house in Crosspoint, the fine clothes and servants, and sighed heavily. This was not the reception a god deserved.

Everywhere was the work of his foolish kin. The Overland was a ravaged mess with great swathes of earth blistered and drained of vitality. Most of the old public wells were capped and sealed with crude signs warning that the water had gone bad.

The Boneman remembered setting up the great irrigation scheme. He'd been pleased when this opened up cropland as far as the dust of the Inland. Now, the canals were empty and crumbled. The Niven was less than half the river he remembered. Apart from the narrow strip of farms hugging the river, little grew.

You idiots. You really screwed the pooch while I was away.

There were towns along the tradeway that he didn't remember, and ruins where he'd expected towns. Halfway to Crosspoint, he came across a small wayhouse, a handful of buildings in a stockade. The taverna held no interest for him, but he soon found what he was searching for.

The hard-eyed young woman looked up from her washpot to see the shadow in her doorway, and with a sigh she reached for her buttons. But when she saw the monstrous hand that gripped her by the wrist, she went pale, and then another hand clasped her over her mouth even as she drew breath to cry out.

"Please, don't scream," the Boneman said to the whore. "I need you. No, not for that."

He took her to the dresser. The mirror showed him as a parody of a man. His stolen clothes did nothing to hide his face and hands. Confronted by his hideous reflection, the Boneman sobbed, tears splashing down onto the girl's face and cleavage. She stopped fighting and looked at his reflection, more curious than scared now.

"I-I have a problem," the Boneman said. "Give me your creams and paints, whatever you use to hide the bruises. Please, give me a face."

She nodded and he let her go and sat down on her foul mattress. With trembling fingers, she applied the makeup, dabbing at his water-clear skin until a face slowly appeared. Filling in the crevices of his nose and eyes, she worked swiftly and evenly.

"Wear these," she said as she fished a pair of satin gloves from her drawer. He pulled them on and wriggled his fingers. Now that his finger bones were out of sight, he felt almost normal.

She unpacked a box of wigs, fine work from the world of Before. *Ah, so there's still a Crossing, a way to get goods here,* he thought. *Someone must be around to keep the shadow roads working.*

Looks like I'm that much closer to finding you, brother.

The woman selected a short wig, a brown mop. She put it on his bald scalp and trimmed the fringe a little, and rubbed sheep fat into the hair to make it look less clean, more like a man's hair.

When he looked at his reflection, for the first time he smiled. At a distance, he could pass for a man. He would be able to enter Crosspoint and ask questions in the temples.

"Thank you," he told the whore, digging out an old purse of cracked leather from around his neck, a cache from a ruined river-shrine of Lucy's. He pressed gold on her, fat coins from his own time. Eyes wide, she quickly secreted the money.

"Don't mention it," she said, handing him the pots of makeup, the brushes, a small mirror. "We're all monsters, love."

The Boneman walked the streets of Crosspoint for the first time in hundreds of years, and he wanted to weep. The broad plazas and squares were filthy and neglected. The public parks he'd marked out with his own hands were now given over to slum housing.

A quick trip through the marketplaces revealed that Crosspoint was the centre of a scrap-driven economy. The Boneman wondered why everyone made do with junk and scavenged goods. The only working machines he could see were cobbled together affairs kept running by the woefully ignorant tinkermen of this age.

You've really dropped the ball on this, Lucy.

The Moot was now the private house of a rich slaver, who had partially demolished the adjoining Petitioner's Court to fit his menagerie. Only the outer walls of Chorister's Hall remained, gutted by a fire sometime beyond living memory and rebuilt into an open air market.

The Lodge of the Jesusmen lay in ruins, as the Boneman had expected, and no one had rebuilt on this tainted land. He watched as hobbled goats grazed on the weeds in between fallen stone columns. Pigeons perching on the defaced statuary added to centuries' worth of shit.

Where did we go wrong, my friend? he thought, sitting on the steps as he munched on a pennyloaf. *Centuries of friendship, tossed aside over a misunderstanding.*

"You deliberately endangered us all!" Hesus yelled that fateful day. "There were so many better worlds to settle. We found them easily once we learnt your method. And why the Cruik? Why such an interest in the Taursi relics?"

"I do not answer to you!" Papa Lucy thundered.

"You must explain yourself!" Hesus demanded. Then, Sad Plain happened. *Well, I warned you, Hesus, but you wouldn't listen. And now look at us.*

Papa Lucy's temple thronged with worshippers, but the main atrium now doubled as a fighting pit. The worship was some mad amalgam of Cruik rote and a low version of the Family story, often retold and much changed by the centuries. He left there saddened, finding only junk possessions of Lucy's passed off as relics. There was no sign of his brother's whereabouts, and even more worrying, there was no sign of the actual Cruik itself.

I hope he destroyed his favourite toy. No one can master the Cruik.

The Boneman's temple was a crumb of itself. Most of the complex was sold off and knocked down, rebuilt as tenement housing for labourers and unemployed drovers. They'd kept only the priory, which seemed to function as an undertaker. His handful of priests were little more than public embalmers now.

Lucy's palace was in much the same shape as he remembered it, now the home of the current Overseer. Lingering in a poorly equipped public archive, the Boneman learnt of the revolution: bailiffs had thrown down the Moot some centuries back, replacing reason with a hierarchy of tyrants.

Bertha's light and airy manse was now a lunatic asylum. This was more than fitting.

The greatest tragedy was his own palace, which was converted into the town barracks. Bailiffs drilled in the courtyard, and he did not get far before crude men with rusted guns turned him away. He saw the gardens converted into a bird-pen, his gorgeous marble stair trampled and muddied by centuries of feet, carpets and tapestries long gone.

Get out of my house! he wanted to scream at them. *Look what you've done to the place!*

But he smiled, holding up his hands diffidently. As he left in a hurry, he hoped the furious runnels of sweat weren't washing away his makeup.

Unwilling to spend another minute inside those walls, the Boneman made a camp on the hill overlooking the First Town. With a wearied soul, he watched the crude flicker of gas lamps and Taursi glass and heard the howls and laughter as the night scum preyed on each other. He wondered how his noble experiment could have failed so badly.

The Boneman made a little fire next to the site of the original Crossing, a scar of fused rock and glass. This was the place, the beginning of things, a holy site that was unremarked now and forgotten by the savages of today. The Greygulf was close, but he couldn't force a way through the world veil.

Something is keeping me out.

The Boneman remembered the day of the Crossing well. A band of sorcerers had achieved the impossible by leading the exodus from a dying world. It was their greatest work. They tore a road through the Greygulf, battling the creatures of that sour realm. Many of his comrades died, and only five made it to the other side. There they opened a shaky door to a barren place, to survival.

Five fierce friends, the sorcerers were bound with ties of blood and the guilt of survival. In those days, the Boneman had called Hesus a friend and confidant.

Their faithful followed them through the door, a blank-faced crowd numbering in the thousands. The Greygulf wiped their minds, as Lucy suspected it would, but "better to be a dummy than dead." It was chaos. Knots of humanity wandered, mindless and bawling, the livestock running loose and no one to round them up. Only the disciples of Hesus kept their wits, as they were trained to do, and it was left to them to keep it all together, to enforce order, to reteach all of the forgotten things.

It was far from perfect, but the sorcerers had their new world and their second chance. It was a noble venture, and they were both scared and excited. Laws were discussed, and systems of governance. Hesus was against a mageocracy of dictators, citing the final wars and everything that resulted in the exodus, the mad gamble. It had been tried, and it failed.

"Well, that was before, but this is now," Lucy had said, and the names stuck, the concept easier to explain to their afflicted flock. Before and Now, the old and the new.

Hesus had eventually proven the truth of his argument, even though he was the one who went native, who lost his way.

Reliving the memories of war, failed friendships, and now this, the ruins of an empire, the Boneman spent the rest of the night curled around a flask of rotgut booze, surly and defeated.

He found the answer while poring through the current version of Family scripture and rote, once he had discerned the truth from the rhetoric and lies. Papa Lucy's passing from the mortal plain was mentioned as "through the roots of Cavecanem, there to await his brother's rebirth."

"Cave Canem," the Boneman chuckled, breaking the phrase into an old scholar's tongue from Before: "Beware of the Dog."

Lucy always enjoyed word bastardry, the twisting of old phrases into something new and absurd, and delighted in the art of the awful pun. It did not take much for the Boneman to realise the final resting place of Papa Lucy.

A few days later, a misfiring car dropped him off at the side of the tradeway, midway between Crosspoint and Gladhands. The gap-toothed driver lugged his baggage out of the vehicle's trunk and dumped several sacks at the Boneman's feet.

"What's in these?" the man huffed, wiping a streak of earth onto his pants. The bags were dirty and clacked like they were full of sticks.

"Camping gear," the Boneman said as he paid out the last of his gold. The man pocketed the coins then quickly tipped another flask of rotgut into the fuel tank, cursing as he spilled a trickle down the side.

"It doesn't sit right, leaving you out here," the driver grumbled. "Dangerous parts. You have any sense, you'll climb back in and come with me."

"I'll be safe enough," the Boneman replied. He took in the rolling red hills of the Harkaways. "My thanks."

With a wary eye to the hills, the driver leapt into his machine and took off, leaving the Boneman in a shower of dust and small stones. Wrinkling his nose at the blue cloud of exhaust, the Boneman began tipping out bags and arranging bones.

Within minutes, the horse skeleton was following him along an old trail through the hills, the rest of the baggage strapped to its clacking frame. A dark cloud clung to the tips of the Harkaways, and soon rain came as a persistent drizzle that soaked every stitch.

"This place used to be full of hikers," he told the horse as they huffed up the muddy path. "Families here with picnics, the Riders of Cruik out on exercise. Now, nothing."

The trails were overgrown, and time had completely erased the food stands. A cement pad marked the ablution block, the only sign that people had ever visited.

The Boneman felt it then, a chill in his skin, the idea that something bad was watching him. Shadows flitted about on the red hills, long-limbed shapes that vanished when he looked directly at them. Panic tickled at his gut and grew with every step along that path, until he took a deep breath to clear his mind. He recognised the sorcery straight away, realised that it was Lucy's work.

I am close, he exulted.

Digging into the trickle of sorcery remaining to him, he found the first ward on a high ledge, marks of repulsion carved deep into a stone. The runes were still strong, inlaid with molten gold and only partially covered with moss. The conditions for the illusion were spelled out quite clearly, and the Boneman was impressed at the clarity of this magic. Laying his head along the flat rock, he sighted the next mark, on the hill opposite, and another further down the valley.

Seems Lucy had built himself a fence to keep out the nice families and the hikers. Small wonder the folk of this mean age thought the Harkaways were haunted.

The Boneman led the dead horse up a winding path. The wind and rain were powerful. Blinking as the makeup started to run into his eyes, he smeared it away with his sleeve so he could spy out the narrow path ahead.

Twice the horse staggered, its ivory legs thrashing for purchase in the mud. The Boneman rested a hand on its quivering face, wondering if he should dissolve the poor beast before it suffered a nasty fall.

"Sorry, old boy. We're almost there, I promise you."

The trail switched back across one of the taller hills, a crag that might as well be called a mountain. Finally, they stood on the apex, a lichen-strewn curve of rock with sheets of rain washing across it.

A rock formation was the only feature here, a shape roughly reminiscent of a dog's muzzle. Where mouth and throat should be, a low cave wound down into the hill itself.

"Cave Canem." The Boneman chuckled. "Dog Cave."

It took some effort to untangle Lucy's final defence, marks of pain and paralysis carved into the overbite of the "dog." There had been an actual guardian here once, a vicious killer brought in through the Greygulf. But the rune was surrounded by an old scorch mark tapped of any energy.

Seems someone or something had broken in long ago.

He led the skeletal horse in from the weather, a pointless charity, and retrieved a blanket to dry his own skin. He removed the last of the makeup, leaving a flesh-coloured smear on the cloth. He threw the soggy wig onto a rock. It looked like a miserable rat, and he was glad to be rid of it.

Instructing the horse to wait there for him, he removed his belongings from the panniers and loaded up a stout backpack. He shone the flickering torch into the depths of the cave. It had cost him a fortune in the market, but the batteries seemed good.

The Boneman remembered his first trip to the Harkaways, the first time he and Lucy had walked into this cave. It was during the great survey, the mapping of this new homeland, and when they learned of this place, the sorcerers enjoyed the chance to do some amateur caving. The Boneman remembered searching for Taursi relics and finding nothing.

"If politics gets too much, we could live down here," Lucy joked, as little witchlights darted about their heads to light the way.

"The ladies would never visit," he who would become the Boneman told his brother, flashing the easy smile he wore so often in those confident days. Later, there was war, and they forgot all about pottering around in caves and smiling.

Roused from memory, the Boneman descended through the curlicue of stone, weaving through the forest of stalagmites. The roof of the main cathedral was far above, but his torchlight did little to pierce the gloom.

Exploring every nook and all of the side passages, he found nothing else to suggest that Dog Cave was inhabited. Then he spotted the shimmer of a wall that seemed to move slightly depending on his perspective.

"You and your illusions," the Boneman said as he passed easily through the stone that wasn't there.

A passageway punched through the rock. The rough edge of the tunnel soon became a smooth walkway, the walls and floor stretched out and rubbed smooth by sorcerous hands.

A row of glowstones were fixed into the stone ceiling, dim and long dead. As the passage wormed its way into the depths of the hill, he found more marks of protection, all of which had failed now. He stepped over a dark scorch mark in the floor. Nothing was left of the intruder but dust.

I just need one bone, the Boneman said. *That will tell me all I need to know.*

He soon got his wish. The tunnel ended in an iron grille that was twisted and buckled from an old explosion. Beyond that one room was a single narrow chamber littered with treasure, statues, urns, and artwork. A carpet of bones lay underfoot, peppered with shattered skulls.

Everywhere were the mirrors that Lucy had mastered: gilt-edged, plain bathroom fittings, ornate hand mirrors of ivory and mother-of-pearl. Most were frames of jagged glass now, ruptured by the intruder's explosive entry into the tomb. A single mirror remained whole, wedged behind the remains of a propane barbecue.

On a dais lay a garish sarcophagus, the relief face unmistakeably Lucy's. The artisans had remembered him with a broad, shit-eating smile and a phallus that coiled around one leg, ending somewhere by his feet.

"You idiot," the Boneman said, smiling sadly. There was no life in here, nothing he could sniff out. He'd come far too late. Papa Lucy was dead.

He climbed over the broken grille and his feet crunched on bone. Instantly he was buffeted by a series of invisible blows, a swift flurry that he could barely feel. It was like being beaten by a child with pillows.

"There's no vinegar left in your guardian," the Boneman said, flexing his will to dismantle the old spirit. Sorcery was becoming easier to do, and in moments the creation dissipated with a soft sigh.

That's when the remaining mirror glowed with a bright inner light, bathing the chamber in a television glow. The Boneman slid the gilt-edged looking glass out from behind the pile of loot and held it up carefully.

"You look just how I feel," Papa Lucy said from his glass prison, nothing but a head floating in a black abyss. "What took you so long, brother?"

"Quick, I want to look at my handsome arse," Lucy said from his mirror, his disembodied head leaping about in the glass and grinning. The Boneman hooked his fingers under the lid of the ridiculous sarcophagus and pushed against the weight of stone.

The lid crashed to the floor, sending up a cloud of bone dust and filth. Waving away the haze, the Boneman lifted his torch and looked into the coffin. He shook his head sadly.

"What is it? Give us a look," Papa Lucy said. Without a word, the Boneman picked up the mirror and held it up above the coffin.

"Damn it. Here I was hoping to just hop in and take it for a drive," Lucy grumbled. The coffin was filled to the brim with honey that glowed golden in the torchlight. Beneath the surface, as if trapped in amber, lay the mortal remains of Papa Lucy, Master of the Cruik, First Watch of the Moot, slayer of men.

The most loyal of brothers.

His body was wreathed in hair, great coils of it floating around in the goop like a brown fleece. His beard reached past his navel, granting him modesty, but even this wasn't enough to hide the damage. He'd been shot several times and his left leg was almost completely severed, attached to the body by several strands of reaching sinew. Three of his fingers were missing, but the healing had gone wrong. The tiny finger growths were melted together like a toasted sandwich.

"It almost worked," Lucy said mournfully. "Some of those bullet holes have closed right up. Another fifty years, the leg would have been back on, and I would be good to go."

The true dilemma remained unspoken between the brothers; without a living body to climb into, Lucy would never be able to leave the mirror. He was trapped forever.

"I'm sorry," the Boneman said.

"It was Jesusmen did this," the disembodied voice said bitterly. "The last handful of those lay-low bastards, come gunning for revenge."

"Were these Jesusmen, too?" the Boneman said, scuffing the femurs with his foot. He could get a quick answer from the bone, but refrained, knowing that his brother frowned upon the corpse arts.

"Just robbers," Lucy said. "There's nothing left to this world but the low men, animals picking through rubbish. Our age has passed."

Sighing heavily, the Boneman sat on the steps of the dais and cradled the mirror on his lap.

"Here, then, is our glorious awakening," Lucy said. "A man in a mirror and a walking bone bag. No offence."

"I'm not offended," the Boneman said. "You did your best to help me."

"I should have done more," Lucy said. "I should never have woken you and let you see yourself like this."

"You woke me?"

"I need you, Sol." Lucy used his old name, the one he'd worn in the Before. "It's Turtwurdigan, that sour old rattleface. She needs to be dealt with, again."

"We beat her at Sad Plain," the Boneman said, numb. "I killed Turtwurdigan. She's gone."

"Beaten, but not killed. The Mother of Glass is waking up," Lucy said, head swimming around in the mirror like a tadpole. "We need to find Bertha, and fast."

Trapped as he was in the Aum, the shadow roads and far-doors were firmly shut against Papa Lucy, no matter what he tried. Wherever Lady Bertha was, the Boneman would be walking there.

He led his dead horse carefully down the switchback trail. The foul weather was gone, replaced by the calm still of a spring morning. Strapped to the horse's spine, his mirror half wrapped in a mouldy old rug, Papa Lucy saw daylight for the first time in centuries. He laughed and darted about in the glass and drank in the rays.

"You?" the Boneman said, indicating the clear sky.

"Yes," Lucy said, and the Boneman felt the final threads of a great weather working to dissipate as his brother tugged away the final thread holding it all together. With typical Lucy panache, his brother had kept the Harkaways wrapped in a permanent storm, just to keep the hikers out.

"Nice. But you've lost your touch. Can't even get yourself out of here." The Boneman drummed at the glass with his gloved fingers.

"Don't tap my glass. Haven't you ever owned a fish, Sol?" the bobbing head scorned. "It's just rude."

"You must have been bored," the Boneman said. "Hundreds of years in there and no one to hear your terrible jokes but you."

"Not so, brother. Sometimes I can peek out of a whore's handglass and whisper in certain ears," Papa Lucy said. "In fact, I've spent a lot of time talking to this one particular girl…"

PART TWO

— THE SELECTOR'S DAUGHTER —

— 7 —

I'll hang this Lanyard Everett and every damn Carpidian I come across. They're all gonna pay."

Quentin Dann paced around the private audience room, a gigantic man in a murderous fury. He towered above the guards— riverfolk, dressed in the sombre grey that their master favoured. The water baron's own retinue lounged against the far wall, seasoned thugs tanned from roaming the Inland.

A waterman stood with head bowed. There was a bandaged stump where an arm had been. This was the only survivor of Fos Carpidian's betrayal. An eyewitness to murder, and most importantly, the brazen theft of an entire water consignment.

Horace Rider, the Selector of Mawson, let the water baron rage. There was no fear in his rheumy old eyes, nothing but quiet contempt. He was dying of riverlung, and today was a bad day. The puff-faced lord drew deeply from a kennelweed pipe while he soaked his bloated feet in a steam tub.

"He killed my boy, Horace," said Quentin. "Vern was there on business, nothing more. This is an outrage."

"You trade in misery," Horace said. "You rob the north and complain when they snap at your greedy fingers. Enough. Mawson will have no part of this."

"Speak carefully, Selector," the Dann said. "There's agreement between our towns. A posse leaves Graham's Wash tomorrow, and your men had best be with it."

"My agreement is with your Magistrate, not you," Horace said, breaking into a coughing fit. "Get out."

The water baron and his retinue left the room. The big man slammed the door so hard that one of the hinges cracked. Horace Rider shook his head and packed another pinch of kennelweed into the pipe.

"No such thing as a happy petitioner, Jen," the Selector said to his grown daughter, who slouched on a chaise lounge, scattering little chips of wood as she worked a whittling knife. "It's all threats and begging, day in, day out."

"I won't mourn Vern the Half-Dann," Jenny Rider said. She blew a loose speck from the woodwork on a new pipe for her father. "The world is a better place without that creepy little freak."

"True, but see to the heart of this if you can," Horace said. "That man who just left is the vilest creature imaginable. He's bought his way into polite society with water money. He has the Magistrate of Graham's Wash in his pocket. But beneath all that, he's a grieving father."

"So, we should help him?"

"Absolutely not. Young Vern deserved that death one hundred times over. The lesson here is: vengeance makes people stupid. Quentin should have left this to the Magistrate, let the bailiffs bring in Fos Carpidian and his coin-rider, this Lanyard."

"Quentin has showed his hand," Jenny guessed, and Horace nodded, smiling weakly.

"The water barons are hurting from this, more than they're letting on. If the Inlanders stop being scared of those thieves, they're finished."

Finishing her work, Jenny stood and dusted the woodchips from her shirt. She didn't give a second glance to the mess on the floor as she gave the pipe to her father.

"Beautiful," he said, admiring the dolphin set in wood, the stem its twisting tail. Flashing a lopsided grin, she refrained from hugging her father, knowing this would only pain him. As a servant brought his lunch, she slipped out of the room, waving off his insistence that she join him.

Not bloody likely, she thought. She grabbed a cold meat pie from the kitchens on her way out. The thought of the rank kelp soup and boiled offal that the physicians pressed upon her father made her stomach flip.

The Selector's Tower was a glorious Before-Time building, almost completely intact. It was still in good condition some three hundred years later, and as near as anyone could figure, it was a vertical warren of homes from the Before, or what passed for a wayhouse in that golden age. The scale of the place boggled her mind, an imposing structure with nothing but slap shacks and piece-meal tenements to compete with its glory.

Each Selector added to the Tower. Her father replaced all of the fouled window panes with fine Taursi work. In his greatest triumph, his engineers pumped up enough water to fill what had once been an immense public bath, several stair-flights above the ground.

When I'm Selector, she thought, pushing out through the freshly greased revolving door, *I will bring in a team of tinkermen and get the furnace working again. Or get them to find a way to make all the pipes and taps work. Those poor lads shouldn't have to lug water kegs up the stairs.*

Jenny stepped out into the muggy streets of Mawson, fanning her shirt as she picked her way through the slow mass of bicycles and birds and stumpy-teams hauling logs and cartloads of river slate. Barges loaded with grain lined the banks. Farmers from up and down the Niven waited to deposit their crops in the town silo.

Money made its way downriver, and Mawson sat in the mouth of the delta, catching all of this stray coin. Caravans left daily to take Riverland goods to the Overland and further, and to bring back the pickings of Inland bleedthroughs. Those sick of drought and the bandits arrived daily to trade freedom for a place in the crowded city.

As Mawson grew, so did the treasury of the Selector. When Horace Rider died, as he soon would, Jenny was going to be as rich as the proverbial Neville. The thought of her father's fatal illness cast a pall on her good mood, and the hectic pace of Mawson didn't make her smile as it usually did.

She would give it all away, everything, for one more year with her father.

Jenny climbed into a rickshaw and asked the pedalman to take her to the Temple. He recognised her and refused all payment.

"You should not be out here, miss, not without your guards and such," he said, his accent giving him away as an Overlander. "There's a lot of robbings, lot of new folk too."

"This is my home," Jenny said. "I'm not scared of anyone, and I certainly don't need anyone to hold my hand. So let's go."

Pedals whirring, he weaved the contraption through the busy docks, avoiding the poor neighbourhoods full of recent immigrants and shoddy buildings. Lounging across the broad rear seat of the rickshaw, Jenny looked down at the city. She admired the view as the pedalman huffed his way up the great hill, frequently flicking a mosquito whisk against his sweaty back.

The Tower dominated everything, of course, but the size of the city was still impressive. Teams of workers hacked the mangroves back, and she saw more housing and infrastructure sites in the newly cleared land.

The town sprawled across the delta like an alien idea, nature itself resisting the works of the riverfolk. Beyond the press of buildings, the terminus of the Niven was still a wild place, a maze of waterways and peaty islets, with a handful of Taursi tribes still living there in the old way. Grog runners and slavers were known to trawl the delta, quick and quiet, wise to the ways of town patrols.

Out beyond the brown flow of the Niven was the shining sea. The river gave way to the bay, which was peppered with islands. Wild places, braved only by those keen to avoid the Selector and his laws.

If they're mad enough to brave the sea and the things that swim in it, they're welcome to their peace and quiet, Jenny thought. *I know I won't bother them.*

The Temple was a broad-shelled library from the Before, its dome only slightly warped from the bleedthrough. Marble columns held up a lofty roof. Words in some dead language were barely visible along the lip of the portico: the gilding had worn away and the inscriptions were dull from centuries of monsoonal weather.

"I will wait for you here, miss," her pedalman said as he pulled into the ranks of rickshaws and bird carts. "These other folks will rob you blind."

"Thank you," she said and pressed a scrip note into his protesting hands. "No, no charity, I saw you pedal up that bloody hill. Take my damn money."

She joined the throng of worshippers milling about in the entrance and was glad of the spring shower that washed over her face, cooling her down in the press of people. One of the attendants recognised her on the steps, and despite her protests over any special treatment, he hustled her in through a side entrance as the service began.

The interior glowed from a hundred well-placed skylights, but the bookshelves were gone now, replaced with seats. One whole wing was given over to dense blocks of elaborate mausoleums, an undercover necropolis littered with candles and shuffling mourners.

The interior of the cupola was painted with several scenes from the faith, depictions of Papa Lucy and Bertha, stories of the old war. Jenny loved the fine details of this large frieze the most: Jesus, the foul betrayer, trampled underfoot at Sad Plain; the Boneman lurking on the battlefield, giving solace for the fallen; Bertha exhorting her Mad Millies, a tide of shrieking women charging into the fray.

Certain figures had been painted out of the frieze, clumsily replaced with other artwork or blended into the background. Her father told her the truth of this: Leicester-We-Forget had once figured prominently in the Family canon, until a schism in the faith occurred some years back. Those who prayed to the white statues were not quite heretics but more a weird splinter cult, tolerated only for their ability to sniff out bleedthroughs.

In the centre of the Temple floor, the original mezzanine was expanded into the fighting pit of rote, dug deep and lined with sand. The mundane fights had been on earlier, pure gladiatorial meets with no religious significance, but now the sand was freshly dressed, combed into perfection.

Down the steps and out onto the sand came the Eminents Three. These high priests dressed and spoke as the Family. Their oversized masks reflected the jolly laughter of the Papa, the deep scowl of Lady Bertha, and the Boneman, who did not speak in this ritual but aped about, a skull-faced figure that got underfoot and drew laughter from the congregation.

"Long bound be the Jesus," Jenny chanted, along with those around her. "Death to the bitch of Sad Plain, cutter of feet, mother of lies. All glory to the Family, who trod Third-Word-Again into glass."

Jenny left sometime during the blood rite, not wanting to see the condemned criminals dressed in the fashion of the old Jesusmen and bled out in the name of the Family. Leaving the congregation, the Selector's daughter found a quiet corner where she sat with her arms around her knees on the stoop of an elaborate sepulchre.

Her eyes raised to the painted dome, Jenny prayed fervently. She asked the Family for something, anything to keep her father alive. She heard the squeals of the suckling pig, the modern substitute for the boy child of rite. The Eminents gave grim pronouncements in the name of the Cruik as they tore a finely tailored set of man-clothes from the squirming beast. Finally, there was an awful shrieking as the High Flenser peeled the life from the pig.

She smelled the sizzle of the cooking flesh. Communion was almost ready.

Once more, the gods gave her no word. Perhaps their voices were small, drowned out by the howling congregation. Perhaps Jenny Rider wasn't worthy enough to be graced with an answer. She left the Temple in tears. The pedalman kept his silence as he returned her to a world of privilege, to the tall house of a dying man.

The Over-Bailiff paid her father a visit. The moustachioed lawman delivered a fat sheaf of papers to the Privy Moot. The long table was empty but for the two men and Jenny, Selector in all but name now. At the head of the table was the mirror-backed chair of the Papa, an empty seat for an absent god, who oversaw all the decisions of his servants.

The old chair always unsettled Jenny. She had once sat in Papa Lucy's seat on a dare when she was a young tomboy running wild with the sons of guards and cooks. That night, young Jenny had experienced the Bad Dream for the first time, a smiling man whispering to her from a dark place.

Jenny had awoken near dawn, dressed, and poled a barge across the harbour. A fisherman had pulled up alongside her and shook her by the shoulder. She had no memory of leaving her bed or sneaking out of the Tower. The next night, she woke to discover herself in an alley halfway across town, a squirming rat in her hands. She had been about to bite into its neck.

As time passed, just looking into a mirror was enough to set her off. On waking, she would find herself in a different place with no memory of how she got there. In the Bad Dream, she was always party to a long and involved conversation, the words of which drifted into fuzz when she opened her eyes.

It was an awful childhood, full of secrets and terror.

She became very religious. Jenny resolved that when she came to her rule, she would have the mirror chair covered with a cloth. She once stood in front of it with a hammer, but fear stayed her hand. Fear of the thing behind the glass.

If I break the mirror chair, will I let it loose?

The whispering dreams had stopped in her adolescence, but she had feared mirrors ever since.

The Over-Bailiff was still discussing the problem of the Half-Dann's murder, and she made herself pay attention to the matter at hand. Ever conscious of the way the mirror chair tried to attract her eyes, she looked to her father instead, drawing strength from his presence. He was a wise man, locked inside a failing body, and soon she would have to face the mirrors on her own.

"The Dann is sure to cause us grief. Best learn what we can of his son's killer," Horace said. With an eye to the Selector's incredibly swollen fingers, the Over-Bailiff peeled the pages apart for him, laying them out in a tarot of infamy.

"Lanyard Everett, late of Quarterbrook. Inland scum. Came to our notice nine years ago. We strung up the rest of his mob, but he must have been tipped off. Left Mawson with the coin-riders snapping at his heels."

"He lived here?" Jenny asked.

"Briefly, miss. Grog-running, slaving, general mayhem. He did a spot of toe-cutting for Gareth March, until that mean old dog swung from a rope."

"I remember March," Horace said. "Bad man. I pulled the lever myself."

The next page the Over-Bailiff laid out was a sketch, a purple mimeograph of an old wanted poster. Lanyard Everett had a thin face, hard mouth downturned at the edges, thick stubble and a lank lick of hair on his forehead. His cold eyes stared out of the page. Jenny shivered.

"Everett is known to lug around the kit of a Jesusman," the Over-Bailiff said. "Witnesses spoke of his shooter, big old gun crawling with Jesus marks. Makes no sense for a scoff-law to carry a gun like that."

"Is he a Jesusman?" Jenny asked, pushing the paper away from her with the point of a finger.

"Apparently he killed the Jesusman who owned it, one of the last. But a man doesn't bear that mark without a reason. We've still got a standing order to shoot this man on sight."

"He's a fool if he steps anywhere near a town," Horace said. "The law is the law, and carrying this mark means death."

One fat finger brushed against the forbidden mark, writ large below the wanted man's face: B + N. A heretic's mantra, Before and Now.

"If he had any sense, he'll melt back into the bush and that will be the end of it," the Over-Bailiff said. "The Dann will never find him, and I won't waste my men on this farce."

"As for Fos Carpidian, he'll be dead within a week," the lawman continued, scooping up the sheaf of yellowed documents. "The water barons will bleed that town to get their water money, drop for drop. Best we stay out of it, Selector."

"I agree, Ronnald," Horace wheezed. "This whole thing is bad news. Jesusmen!"

Jenny could not get the image of the Half-Dann's killer out of her head. She knew that grim purple face would haunt her dreams.

She looked up at the mirrored chair and felt the hairs rising on the back of her neck.

Someone's watching me.

Jenny kept a suite of rooms at the very top of the Tower. They were her father's, once, but he had not been able to climb the stairs in many years. The elevator had worked as recently as seventy years ago, with a team of lizards hauling on a rope to lift the box, but now the mechanism was seized up. The elevator car would not budge, no matter how the tinkermen greased the gears and stripped them apart.

She could do all fifty floors in less than twenty minutes, half of them at a run. The Selector's daughter was lean and fit from years of stairwork, and she knew every inch of the air ducts, the little crawl spaces behind the amenities, even the elevator shafts, navigating the oily ladders by feel alone.

None of this compared to her love for the penthouse. At the Tower's tip, she was higher than anything else in Mawson. Jenny could see the gas lights and star-glass lanterns laid out, neat squares in the messy sprawl of the new neighbourhoods.

Best of all, no one came up here to bother her, unless it was actually important.

When she had taken the penthouse as her own, the servants puffed and sweated as they lugged all of her favourite furniture up here in stages. An obscenely massive four-poster bed dominated the suite, ringed by record players and silent televisions, the best items scavenged from the bleedthroughs. Her mother's old dressing table was covered with stacks of dirty dishes. There was a hoop where a mirror had once sat, but she put a poker through it one morning.

Mirrors bring whispers.

Rummaging through the detritus of a spoiled childhood, Jenny pulled out the items she needed for high prayer. A bag of ox-tail bones for rolling. A ceremonial stiletto with a howling woman inset in ivory. A bowl for water, in place of a looking-glass. Her well-thumbed volume of scripture, margins jotted with her own thoughts and theories.

The fly-leaf was covered with sketches of the whispering man, as best as she could remember on waking. *Knowledge is armour,* her younger self had written in a sure hand.

The doorway to the roof was sticking, the wooden frame buckled from centuries of rain and humidity. With the application of a boot, the hatch squealed open, and she climbed up into the night. With only the moon and stars for company, Jenny laid out the accoutrements of faith then sat cross-legged before them.

Stuffing a pipe with a mixture of kennelweed and tobacco, she lit it from the low flame of her oil lamp. She drew back on the mellow blend and let the smoke feed into her lungs, bringing on a tickling cough that left her light-headed.

She began by emptying the bag of bones. Each was meant to represent a human knuckle, the old rote. Apparently in the Inland, man-bones were still used by the savages and scoff-laws. Jenny had made this set herself by etching the symbols deep into the cow bone.

"Boneman, show me the wisdom of the dead," she intoned. Pricking her thumb with the stiletto, she smeared the bones with blood, making them dark in the low lamp light.

"Lady Bertha, show me the truth of hearts, my own and others."

She passed the bones through the water bowl to wash off the blood. A dark swirl formed in the water, the beginnings of a clot, dancing and turning.

"Papa Lucy," she said reverently, "show me the wisdom of the Greygulf. Show me how to keep my father alive."

With one hand to the curling pages of her scripture book, Jenny cast the bones. She saw symbols of travel, duty, and hunting. Another cast presented vengeance, glory, and the death of another. Her third cast gave fire, the finding of something lost, and the knave's cross, an incomplete mark meant to represent the Jesus without honouring him.

Always, she got the Cruik as the fourth bone: the mark of a hooked stave, symbol of an old order. Her family had sworn with the Riders of Cruik, an uninterrupted chain going back almost to the Crossing. Her father had said the words as a boy but hadn't ridden a bird in years.

Horace never pushed the family tradition onto his only daughter, and they had an understanding. He was going to be the last one to bear that weight, and she would be a Rider in name only.

The scripture gave her nothing useful. These combinations were ambiguous at best. She looked deeply into the bowl of water, wondering if she should try the rote again. She felt her gaze drawn into the depths, the sensation that her mind was being dragged out of her body.

Jenny gasped as she was pulled down into a dark valley, water towering around her on all sides, and then she was through the water, through a barrier between the world she knew and a world of darkness, black and complete.

It was the half-remembered place of her nightmares.

A smile on a blurry face bobbed towards her in the gloom. Jenny felt her bladder give way back in the world of flesh, but here she could do nothing, not even turn away.

"I miss our talks, girl," the smiling man said, broad lips drawn wide, tongue curling against those perfect teeth. His face was that of a man with a garrulous booming voice, but something about this place muffled him. His words travelled the darkness as whispers.

"Let me go, spirit," Jenny stammered. "In the name of the Family, I command you to let me go."

"But this is what you wanted," the blur-faced man whispered, smile broadening. "You followed rote and you wanted an answer. Well, I am here with your answer."

The face changed shape, flesh growing purple, until the mimeographed image of Lanyard Everett hung before Jenny, the shabby villain looming larger, his cold eyes boring straight into her soul.

The face drew closer as it seemed to grow, until she felt like a gnat, paused before a gnashing wall of teeth. The whisper was strong now, the volume reaching the sound of a normal voice.

"Take up the Cruik, girl. Ride in my name. You sniff out this Jesusman, and you kill him."

8

I 'm taking up the Cruik," Jenny repeated. Her father was still shaking his head, fat jowls wobbling. "Then I'm hunting down this Jesusman."

"Absolutely not! You would ride out on the strength of a-a hallucination?"

"It was Papa Lucy," she said, eyes shining fervently. "He spoke to me, told me that this will cure you. I must go."

"The Cruik stays here," the old man protested. "The Riders lost their way, a long time ago. Cannibals, bandits, and now you? I forbid this."

"I'll be back with this monster's head, or not at all."

"You don't know the first thing about that world, girl," he said. "You'll be peeled and cooking in a greypot within a week. Let my men find this Lanyard. I'll send everyone off on Quentin's damned crusade, but please, you stay here with me."

The Selector looked helplessly at Jenny, who was dressed in travelling gear of thick leathers and stout boots with a sleek pistol dangling from her hip. She weathered his protests with a stony face.

"I'll have the bailiffs stop you." He gasped. "Your place is here. I don't have long, and Mawson needs you. Jen, I need you."

"You're the Selector. So select someone else," she said softly and withdrew from the solar.

"This is madness. I'll cut you off. You'll have nothing!" he cried. She flinched as she gently closed the doors behind her. She knew he would make good on his threats with the bailiffs and knew that the Over-Bailiff would hunt her himself.

In the garage underneath the Tower, her father had collected a small fleet of cars. The machines were cobbled into working order by the tinkermen. Most had been built from the combined remains of several vehicles.

Her favourite buggy was down here, a stripped down affair, more wood than steel, lightweight. She loaded canisters of fuel into the trunk, food and water, a box of precious ammunition she'd pilfered from the bailiff's armoury.

She strapped a rifle to the dashboard. It was a working .303 that would put a hole through anything. Jenny was out the front, frantically hand-cranking the engine, when a shadow fell across her.

She turned to see a relaxed-looking Ronnald. The buggy was completely surrounded by armed lawmen. One of the men kicked the chocks back under the wheels. Another young bailiff climbed into the car, turned the steering wheel towards the wall, and pressed down on the brakes.

"Jen, don't be foolish," Ronnald said, reaching for her. She quickly drew her pistol and aimed it at his chest. She had kept the chrome plating buffed into a shine, and now in the dim light of the lone gas lamp it shone.

"Pretty gun," he said. Quicker than thought, the lawman turned into her aim and twisted the pistol out of her hands.

"Now, your father would like a word," the Over-Bailiff said. Jenny darted forward and felled the lawman with a swift knee to the crotch. Slipping through a ring of reaching hands, she made for the outer doors of the garage, running light and fast.

One of the bailiffs had his gun out and tracking, but the gasping Ronnald howled for him to stop.

"We're not meant to kill her, you idiots," he said, still wincing. He set his men to unpacking the car, marvelling at how much she had looted from the Tower.

"Don't worry, she won't get far now," he said, rubbing at his long moustache. "That silly girl will be home in time for tea, mark my words."

Jenny ran through the morning streets, cursing her own stupidity. Once, she heard the sputtering of a bike and hid inside a coal box, fighting the urge to sneeze.

I should have just left Father a note, she thought. *I could have been halfway to Crosspoint by now. You idiot, Jen!*

She took a circuitous route through Mawson to avoid the main thoroughfares and market squares. Ronnald would have people out looking for her now and watching the caravanserai and the harbour. She'd never be able to leave the town on foot.

Jenny had only the clothes on her back and the determination of her quest. A god had spoken to her. She had always been Papa Lucy's instrument, ever since she sat in his mirror chair.

A handful of bailiffs won't stop me, she thought.

Hungry and footsore, Jenny padded towards the Selector's Orchard. Rounding the corner, she was nearly spotted by a lone bailiff sitting on a motorcycle in front of the locked gates.

Nice try, Ronnald, she thought. She took off her leather coat and draped it over the high wall. The mortar was embedded with broken glass to deter intruders, but despite Jenny's best efforts she still managed to cut her hands.

She quietly dropped to the ground. Slipping from tree to tree, she kept a look out for any other guards. Judging by the smoking chimney at the gateman's hut, everyone was still at their breakfast.

Snagging a low-lying apple, Jenny munched on its woody flesh as she stole through the trees.

There. In the middle of the orchard lay a small cluster of buildings, a bird yard converted to another purpose. There were fodder sheds, a fenced-in exercise yard, and beyond that a block of newly raised stables.

A small hut stood just behind all of this. Jenny saw the curl of smoke in the chimney and heard the faint snores from within. She rapped on the door, rousing the occupant.

Barris was the stablehand, an old birdman with the scars to prove it. Cracking open the door, he blinked at her blearily. He stank of booze.

"Young Jen," he rasped. "Bit early for a ride, isn't it?"

"Good a time as any," she said calmly. *He doesn't know.* "Come on, let's get him saddled up then."

Barris led Jenny to the stables, a leather bridle dangling from one hand. He whistled through his teeth and out of the stall bounced the rarest of all creatures—a young horse, perfect and healthy.

"Melts my heart every time," the stablehand said. "There won't be any more after him, more's the shame."

Seph. The last of the true horses, and her father's greatest treasure. If a foal lived these days, it came out feathered and fanged, and most of these mutant half-breeds died before their first year.

Seph was the final example of the horse-breeder's art, his dam and sire now dead from grazing on pattercurse. The breeders at True Horse Plain had not let Seph go cheaply, but Horace Rider paid the price gladly.

He also surrounded the world's last horse with these high walls, every gate guarded by an armed man. Barris might be a hapless drunk, but he didn't need to be vigilant, not in the middle of all that.

"Here you go," he said as he led the saddled horse to the girl. "Put your foot in there like I showed you and just swing your other leg over."

Jenny hoisted herself up into Seph's newly stitched saddle and smiled. The horse smelled good. It quivered underneath her, a warm machine of muscles and hair.

"Do you have a sack or something?" she asked Barris. "I feel like going fruit-picking while I ride him around."

"Should have one in the shack," he said. He rooted around in the rubbish and empty bottles until he produced a hessian bag. She took it from him with a smile, then kicked Seph into a gentle trot, pleased with how quickly she'd learnt the dying art of horse riding over the last few months.

She paused underneath the apple trees to pluck several of the stunted fruit. No matter how they tried, no one could grow them right anymore, and orchards everywhere were failing. In recent years, they were lucky if one in three apples grew to full size.

Good enough for me, she thought as she quickly filled the bottom third of the sack. She rode to the far gate, the one that led out onto the Temple road. The rhythm of Seph's pounding hooves roused the guard. Stretching lazily, he emerged from his hut to watch the horse at play. She realised that the bailiffs hadn't yet reached this side of the Orchard.

"Morning, Miss Rider," the man said, smiling as Jenny trotted the horse towards him. The smile became a panicked grimace as Seph bore down on him, a tonne of muscle. As he dodged to get out of the way Jenny swung the bag of apples. The sack connected with a satisfying crunch, and the man fell senseless to the ground.

Climbing down from the saddle, she checked the man's pulse. He was alive but battered. He wore the key to the gate on a chain around his neck and kept a snub-nosed revolver in his coat pocket, an old bleedthrough spotted with rust. She took the gun, not even knowing if it worked, hoping it wouldn't come to that.

Jenny unlocked the gate and rode Seph through it at a swift canter. People in the streets of Mawson stared as she clattered past them on the near-extinct animal. Seph's custom-built shoes rang against the cobble stones. Jenny smiled, weaving through the morning trickle of merchants and the last of the evening shit carts.

A brace of hitched riding birds flapped themselves into a mad panic when they saw the horse heading towards them. One of them snapped free of its harness, swearing in a booming voice, lashing out with its legs, and busting up a grog stall as it escaped.

A stumpy lizard snapped hungrily at the horse, and it was Seph's turn to shy away, nearly throwing Jenny from the saddle as he bucked and danced sideways. People cursed her, and the distant sound of a whining motor was joined by another.

Bikes. She didn't think she could stand out more if she tried. No doubt someone had flagged down a passing bailiff and pointed them in her direction. Not even the Selector's daughter had the right to take the last true horse out of the Orchard.

Not sure what horse thieves get these days, she thought, rubbing her throat nervously.

No traffic covered Temple Road so early in the day, and she made better time. Urging the horse up the steep incline, Jenny looked back to see the first whining bike emerge from the tight streets of Mawson. A trio of bailiffs dogged her path up the hill.

"C'mon, boy," she said as she dug her heels into Seph's flanks, the way Barris had shown her. The horse responded with a surge of speed, eagerly leaping up the road, strong and sure.

Jenny risked a glance backwards and saw that the nearest bike was halfway up the road. One of the bikes was rolling backwards, black smoke boiling up from its failed engine. Two bailiffs left.

"Quickly, Seph," she urged, shaking the reins. This was the first time she attempted a gallop, and she slid around in the saddle like a sack of rivermud. She gripped tightly with her knees, scared that she was going to fall off.

The Temple was before her now and she made for the broad marble steps. A terrified woman who was sweeping away the rubbish from last night's congregation froze at Jenny's approach. Seph climbed the stairs, and the cleaner squeezed her eyes tight, clutching her broom as the horse brushed past her.

Seph walked into the Temple through the large double doors, his sides heaving, slick with sweat. The sound of his hooves rattling against the flagstones echoed from the painted dome. Jenny dug the pistol out of her pocket and gripped the plastic handle tightly.

Jen, you're being really stupid, she thought. But she remembered her vision, and knew she had no choice. When the first priest came running to investigate the noise, she levelled the weapon on the man. The hefty Berthite stopped short and raised a pair of trembling hands.

"Take me to the Cruik. Now," she demanded. Hearing a footfall, she turned to see the cleaner lurking just outside the doors. "You. Close those doors and bar them. Quickly, please."

She clumsily dismounted and led Seph around the killing pit on foot. She pointed the gun towards anyone who looked at her. Acolytes and attendants hid behind statuary and stared with fear and confusion as the Selector's daughter took the Temple hostage. Jenny paused to let the horse guzzle greedily from a baptismal font. She looked up nervously as the bailiffs started pounding on the outer doors demanding entry.

"If anyone touches that door, I will shoot them dead," she yelled, brandishing the revolver as if she meant it. *I've never even fired a gun in anger,* she thought. *Jen, you've lost your bloody mind.*

Once Seph had drunk his fill, she prodded the Berthite priest towards the inner sanctum. There was a crashing sound, and she realised that the bailiffs had given up on the main doors and were trying to force their way in through the vestry.

The inner sanctum of the Family lay almost directly underneath the highest point of the dome, an open-roofed structure the size of a large villa. As Jenny led Seph inside, her guts did a nervous dance as the Eminent Three emerged from their apartments.

The high priests didn't need masks to be intimidating, and Jenny realised just how much trouble she was in now. She herded the earthly equivalents of Lucy, Bertha, and the Boneman into a ragged line.

"Bar the doors," she ordered one of the acolytes. "Put statues and heavy things in front of them. Hurry."

"Miss Rider, you are being incredibly foolish," said one of the Eminents, a hawk-faced woman in the black and white of the Boneman. "The penalty for trespassing here is death."

"Shut up," she said. "I'm here for the Cruik."

A noise, and she turned to see the High Flenser rushing her, long curved knives in each hand, open robe flapping. Jenny brought the pistol to bear. As she drew the trigger, she observed the maze of scars across the High Flenser's face and body, the sash of knives that bounced upon his chest as he ran.

Then, the crack of the gun, and Papa Lucy's holy skinner lay sprawled at her feet, his knives still reaching for her as he breathed his last.

I'll hang for that, she thought, numbed by what she'd done, pistol shaking in her hand. The holy knifeman wasn't moving. Then Jenny remembered Papa Lucy, the promise of her father's recovery and what her god demanded of her.

Standing over the dead High Flenser, she once more demanded the Cruik. This time, no one questioned her. She followed the Eminents to the centre of the sanctum that presented a stout door with three keyholes. Each of them brought out a key from underneath their robes and broke the final seal.

"It's here," they told her. She led the horse into a large reliquary, its walls lined with treasures—the confirmed belongings of the Family—and some good old-fashioned loot.

The far wall was decorated with a frieze depicting the Family at Sad Plain. Lucy cradled the mortally wounded Boneman. Bertha was strangling some nameless Jesusman with her braid. A fourth prominent figure on the far left had been defaced, chiselled back into rough stone, but enough details remained to show this was Leicester-We-Forget.

One of Papa Lucy's hands extended from the frieze, held out as if warding off some unseen enemy far to the right of the scene. His stone grip curled around an ancient staff of wood, bound with brass, the hooked pole of a shepherd. The Cruik, holiest relic that the Temple of Mawson possessed.

"It's perfect," she whispered.

Seph chose that moment to drop a load of dung, followed with a heroic stream of piss that flooded the floor. Smiling, Jenny fastened his reins to a willowy nude of the Lady Bertha, then turned her attention to the staff of Papa Lucy.

She leaned forward and twisted the stave loose, snapping several of Papa Lucy's stone fingers. Holding the Cruik high, she felt her skin crawl and the sense that something was watching her. It was greasy to the touch, as if the wood were pliable. It felt as heavy as an iron rod, even though she lifted it with ease.

This wasn't a replica. In her hands, Jenny held the evidence of a god, and this scared her.

Nearby, she heard the banging as the bailiffs tried to force the sanctum doors. She ordered the Eminent Lucy to strap the Cruik to Seph's saddle, then looked around the reliquary, poking at the floor and testing the walls.

"You," she asked the red-robed Eminent Bertha. "Where's the way out?"

"The–the door back there," the priestess stammered. She licked her lips nervously as Jenny poked her in the belly with the barrel of the gun.

"Try again. My father told me that this hill is riddled with tunnels, hidey holes that you've had hundreds of years to dig. I want the secret way out of here, and I want it now. Do you want to end up like the flenser?"

The priestess shook her head.

"Well, open the damn hatch. Then get out of my way."

9

Seph ate up the miles, legs flashing as he tore across the open road. The horse seemed to relish the chance to stretch its legs, and once more Jenny was grateful for the tunnels and catacombs, high walled and wide enough for the animal to escape the Family Temple with her.

"I could never have left you back there," she said, patting the horse's neck. "You're not meant to be hidden behind a wall."

The hoofed animal was much faster than a bird and much easier to ride. She tried to remember everything that Barris had shown her, and rode Seph for only short stretches, dismounting and walking him frequently.

Mawson lay a half day behind her, but it might as well be a world away. If she didn't come back with the head of Lanyard Everett, she would never be able to return.

"I had to kill that man, Seph," she said quietly. She walked him into a sprouting seed crop to graze. "I didn't want to, but I had to."

The horse's reply was to rip voraciously into the green shoots. A great line of hoofprints and destruction trailed through the river-fed farm.

Jenny owned nothing but the clothes on her back, the gun in her pocket, and the Cruik, the creepy relic strapped to the side of the saddle like a catch-pole. There'd been no time to scrounge for supplies or even grab some coin, not with Ronnald's men on her heels and a holy man dead by her hand.

"Enjoy it while you can," Jenny said, watching Seph grind at the tender shoots with his peg teeth. "I don't know what I'm meant to feed you when we head north."

It was a long trip to Carmel, that dust-locked scavenger's town hidden deep in the Inland. The last known location of Lanyard Everett, the place where the Half-Dann had breathed his last.

"Got to beat the Dann there and turn up before all of his coin-riders and killers," Jenny said. "Rest time's over, horse."

It was dangerous to stay on the tradeway. Much as the delay irked her, Jenny was forced to take the farmers' causeways and wade across the paddies, cursing the irrigators. Seph took to the water with grace, his long brown legs chopping through the islands of rice.

The fertile delta land soon gave way to abandoned holdings, the irrigation channels collapsed and filled in. Soaked through, Jenny climbed back into the saddle and let the horse push through the dead farmlands.

She had asked her father why so many people left the land, but he wouldn't answer, perhaps he couldn't. These days, farmers clung to the Niven, and every year the yield was that little bit smaller, the fruit trees failing, crops soured and rotting in the field. Starving animals cropped on the native grasses and got sick. Lambing season brought horrors more often than lambs.

"One, two generations left, then we're done," her father said over his pipe when the kennelweed loosened his tongue and none else were around to hear. "People come to the Tower for answers that I don't have, and they'll come to you too. Mawson will go the way of the Inland, and then the last of the Cruik's tribe will have become crooked. Man-eaters in our streets, a greypot on every corner."

The bush was already reclaiming these old farms, the native plants smothering everything the settlers had brought into the Now. Once, Jenny was sure she spotted a Taursi in the scrub, but the spiky giant melted away, the treeline once more still, far too quiet. The silence of this place was beginning to scare her.

She was completely alone.

Jenny found the ruin of an old humpy, three daub-and-wattle walls still standing, chimney intact. There was a dead dog just outside of the doorway, a pack of cockatoos feasting on the carcass. She threw stones at them until they wheeled away screeching and vengeful. They were said to be cowards, but she held the pistol ready and shivered when she thought of them nibbling on the dog's eyes.

Most of her matches were soggy from the trip across the paddies, but one precious flame caught the mess of leaves and twigs that soon crackled away in the exposed hearth.

Jenny spent the night there, lying in dirt in front of the fire. The saddle blanket was damp from horse sweat, but it was all she had to keep off the bitter cold. Seph shuffled around in the ruin, sleeping on his hobbled feet. Hunger gripped her stomach. She'd never gone without a meal in her life.

She had started her morning as the Selector's daughter. Now she was a penniless criminal, an exile. A murderer. Clutching at her holy knuckle bones for comfort, Jenny cried until exhaustion took her, a dreamless slumber that was the only small kindness of her day.

She woke at dawn, half-frozen and sore from sleeping on the ground. Cracking her bleary eyes, she looked up to the roofless walls and started when she saw a pair of cockatoos perched there, quietly watching her sleep.

"Get lost!" she shouted, picking up a stick to scare off the scrawny birds. They took off in a flurry of feathers and screeching, sounding like a mocking laughter.

That was when she realised that she held the Cruik in her hand, that she'd been clutching onto it the whole night. Before burrowing in to try and get some sleep, she remembered leaning it against the far wall, as far from the door as possible. In the firelight, it seemed almost sinister, the hook of the ancient staff like the twisting neck of a serpent.

She remembered it had cast a shadow in the firelight that made her eyes swim, a watery ripple that didn't match up to the shape of the staff. Jenny was still lying in the dusty depression marked out by her hips and legs, and hadn't stirred once during her deep sleep. Sometime during the night, the Cruik moved into her hand by itself.

"Sweet Family save me," she whispered.

She felt a slight humming in her hand, like the Cruik was hollow and filled with flies. With a shudder, she lay it on the ground and quickly backed away from it. She saddled Seph as fast as she could manage, keeping one eye on the relic. When she fiddled with the girth strap, the Cruik shifted in the corner of her vision, as if a snake slithered and coiled in front of the fireplace.

"Stop that," she said shakily, looking once more on the hooked pole. For one long moment she was tempted to leave the thing behind, to stoke the fire once more and feed the Cruik to the flames.

Remembering the whispers of Papa Lucy, Jenny strapped the holy staff to the saddle. Seph did not seem to fear the touch of the Cruik, but it scared her on a deep primal level. She only hoped that it would be of use when she found the Jesusman.

The sun was already baking the moisture out of the ground, and a cloud of flies buzzed around the dead dog. Jenny remembered the look on the High Flenser's face when she shot him and thought she was going to be sick. She couldn't shake the image from her head and knew it would haunt her for all of her days.

"How am I supposed to kill another man, Seph?" she asked the horse as she led him along a faint track into the rainforest. "How does this save my father?"

Questions of theology and divine intervention were lost on the last true horse. Seph was more interested in snuffling at a stand of grass slick with dew. Jenny thought of hauling him away from the grass, worried about the horse's belly. Some native grasses caused colic or brought on the foaming death.

"Ah, fill up then. It's not like I brought your breakfast along." At the mention of food, her own stomach grumbled painfully. She felt dizzy now, almost weak. Kneeling next to Seph, she ran her hands through the grass then licked the dew from her fingers.

"Father was right," she told the horse. "I'm going to be dead inside of a week."

The dew did nothing but wake her thirst. As they pushed into the rainforest, she kept her eyes out for a stream or a spring. She'd read about the crooked gangs of the Inland and how they dowsed for soaks. They sometimes dug up hibernating frogs from the clay, decade-long sleepers bloated with water.

It seemed ridiculous to be within a day's ride of the Niven and be so parched. Jenny hated to think how thirsty the horse was. She wondered if he'd see the day out if they couldn't find something to drink. She felt panic rise up in her chest, followed by a sense of injustice that a future Selector should die in the wilderness.

Even worse, she'd doomed this beautiful horse. How was she going to keep feeding poor Seph? Tears ran down her face at the thought of his bones bleaching in the sun. She was a privileged idiot, who had never so much as planned a long journey.

"I was never good enough to be the Selector." She whimpered. "Can't even run away properly."

When the Cruik slid into her hand like the questing snout of a dog, Jenny was only a little surprised. The staff had wormed its way free of its bindings, but when she looked down at it, it was only a wooden pole, inflexible and firm.

Frowning, she pointed the staff forward, more out of instinct than art. Suddenly, she felt a presence in her head, a sense of direction that reminded her of how she'd navigated the darkest corners of the Tower, always knowing which way to go.

It was a spring, somewhere to the right of the faint trail. She could smell the chill iron of the water, see the tannic depths littered with leaves and debris. Jenny urged Seph into the undergrowth, and the horse soon picked up speed, nostrils quivering as it smelled water nearby.

The Cruik trembled in her hand, a pointing compass needle. It corrected their course whenever the horse stepped around one of the big trees or picked its way over runnels of shifting rock. As Seph clambered through a blind gully, she saw the faint trickle of water pushing through the slimy undergrowth and knew that they were close. Up ahead, there was an uncanny light that rippled against the rainforest canopy.

"Well, I'll be," Jenny said. A spring ran over the edges of a natural depression, and it was everything the Cruik had shown her. A glass spire jutted out of a cleft of rocks next to the water, glowing softly in the shade like a tall candle. Taursi work and incredibly old.

The water was clear and sweet as girl and horse drank deeply. After drawing in gallons of water, Seph wandered off to graze on the plants around the site, reins trailing as he sniffed for something good to eat.

Jenny lay the Cruik across a flat shelf of rock and looked into the spring. As the ripples ceased, she saw a layer of leaves and the tickle of sunlight from above coloured the water like weak tea. There was a deeper darkness that drew her eyes. Probably the roots of the spring for some underground river that ran through there.

Then, just as before, Jenny was pulled into the water, the spring rising around her vertically, and she passed through the membrane of reality. There was nothing but darkness and silence around her. Papa Lucy drifted out of the shadows, all smiles and whispers.

"You have the Cruik," he said softly. "I was right to trust in you. Clever girl."

She was speechless and terrified. Back in the daylight world, she felt her body tremble. Once more she was face to face with the bogeyman of her childhood. Now, Papa Lucy was her master.

"This," and here the image of the Cruik floated between them, "this will guide you to the Jesusman. You've seen how."

She saw flashes of light in the dark place, images that appeared like lightning and were gone as quickly. The patchwork walls of Carmel, its stout gate wide open. A saltpan, broad and blinding. Two crooked women and a girl, standing in a nightmare landscape, a city growing around them.

"Visions I have gleaned from the Greygulf," Papa Lucy explained. "Three places bound to Lanyard's fate, and we know of one. Go to Carmel, and then the Cruik will lead you to your enemy."

"Please. I don't want the Cruik anymore," Jenny said, pushing away at the image of the holy staff. It faded before her hands like smoke.

"This was my staff during the war," Papa Lucy said, frowning. "I gave it to my Riders when my time was done, the greatest tool of sorcery ever entrusted by me. And what did they do with it? They stuck it in a great big statue and turned to farming and fucking. So, when I say that you will take up my Cruik," and here Papa Lucy brought the smoky image of the object back, "I'm not asking. You will bear it."

"My–my lord," Jenny stammered. "I cannot do this for you. I'm not worthy. I killed the High Flenser in the middle of the Temple!"

"I'm glad you did." Lucy laughed. "Children, aping the old ways, twisting our words, our instructions. None of them are my servants. None of them but you."

She was filled with a sense of well-being. The fear fell away. Jenny felt Lucy in her head, moving things around and pulling out things the way a tinkerman worked on an engine. Back in the real world, she felt the Cruik wrap around her arm like a snake, the tip brushing against her face.

Jenny Rider let Lucy in and did not resist. Where there'd been hesitation, she now felt resolve and ruthlessness. She saw scenes of warfare flicker behind her eyes and saw herself wearing the hands of others long dead. All the knowledge she would need filtered into her, deep into her muscle memory. The Cruik pulsed as it changed her.

She felt competent, ready.

"You were right to kill that false priest. He got in your way," Lucy said. She had the sensation of the god pulling out of her mind. "My champion, my Rider. Now go, and kill the last of the Jesusmen. I firmly believe in the tying up of loose ends."

She woke beside the spring and decided that it was time she found herself a mirror.

Jenny rode the tradeway openly, resting the Cruik across the saddlehorn. The sense of supreme confidence she'd felt by the spring was slowly wearing off, but she no longer feared discovery.

A thousand voices danced in her mind, their whispers bubbling up from her subconscious. They whispered about the Before and the earliest days of the Now, and she saw their lives in flashes, their memories terrifying and strange. She knew they were there to teach her, and at first, she did not think to resist the passengers in her skull. Already, she sat straighter in the saddle and knew more about horsemanship than Barris could ever teach.

An hour of forage brought her enough bush-tucker to break her long fast, and she instantly knew what foods were safe and what were deadly. Examining her pistol, she saw the minor defects and knew that it desperately needed to be cleaned with a file and brush.

With every hour the voices quieted, until once more she was alone in her skull. Exhaustion replaced vigour, and she had a slight headache from Papa Lucy's tinkering. Although the voices were silent now, she felt a collective presence pushing into her mind, a thousand weak hands beating against her will.

What happens if one of them breaks through? she thought. *Does that dead person get a second life, get to wear me like a puppet?*

Will I become a pestering whisper in the back of someone else's mind?

This faint worry took the edge off her resolve, and Jenny wondered if Papa Lucy's tinkerings were a temporary fix. She'd woken as a superwoman, but this bravado was fading by the hour.

On the third day of riding, the rainforest thinned to become scrubby plains. The Riverland gave way to the Overland, home to drovers and miners. For the first time in her life, Jenny looked upon the last band of good land, the stubborn growth that bordered the dust of the interior.

The road was strangely familiar, the landscape expected with every turn. She found herself expecting towns and wayhouses in certain places, only to find ruins or nothing at all. A new wayhouse stood by the burnt remains of another, the replacement a miserable looking place of bleedthrough planks and tin. A pair of filthy children stood by the tradeway watching Jenny approach, slack-jawed at the sight of the horse.

"You can pat him if you like," she told them, and they approached cautiously. Seph suffered their enthusiastic touches with quiet grace as he lapped away at the bird trough. Jenny slid out of the saddle and took a short wander to stretch her legs.

I wonder what I can trade these people for something to eat, she thought, looking at the mean little wayhouse. *They'll send me packing or try to buy the horse. Fat chance.*

Overhanging the tradeway, a dead gum tree served as the local message post. Letters and bills hung from nails, some of them weathered and faded. Town law punished the theft of mail with a broken hand, and the second offence meant the loss of that hand. Message posts were often corseted with letters for the dead or the absent, and these hung in place until the paper rotted.

Jenny saw the notice driven into the tree with a fresh copper nail, and her heart sank.

Now she was the one with a mimeographed picture, a purple sketch on a wanted poster. They'd done a reasonable job of depicting her, the bailiff's artist no doubt copying from one of her recent portraits.

WANTED FOR MURDER, HORSE-STEALING, SACRILEGE, it read across the top. Below her picture, the block text continued. JENNIFER RIDER, SELECTOR'S DAUGHTER. KILLED THE HIGH FLENSER, STOLE THE CRUIK. RODE NORTH ON BUCEPHALUS, THE LAST TRUE HORSE.

ARMED AND DANGEROUS.

It then named a staggering figure for her capture, which made her purse her lips.

There was movement from within the stockade, and a trio of men stood just inside the gateway, one holding a wood axe by his side. They muttered darkly, as if daring themselves to approach the woman on horseback.

There'd be no hot meals here.

"Time to go," Jenny said, climbing into the saddle. The kids moaned their disappointment. Hauling on the reins, she dug her heels into Seph's flanks and left the wayhouse behind her, a dozen sets of eyes watching the passage of the rare animal.

A telegraph line flanked the tradeway, a sagging wire that connected Crosspoint with the Riverland towns. Her poster was nailed to every tenth pole, condemning her to anyone passing this way.

An hour's hard ride brought her to the bill poster, one of her father's men wearing his Mawson greys. He was tacking up another poster when he heard the thunder of Seph's hooves, and his eyes went wide when he recognised the Selector's daughter. He scrabbled into the saddle of his bird and whipped it into a run. Posters flew out of his open satchel, littering the tradeway with a dozen images of her face.

"Faster, boy," she said to Seph. She pictured bailiffs on the hunt and herself in a hangman's noose. These posters could not be allowed to reach Crosspoint.

Horse and bird pounded along the tradeway, and the riverman looked over his shoulder fearfully. He aimed a speargun at her, an inner tube stretched over a wooden stock, and sent a barbed quill singing past her ear.

The old Jenny might have felt terror, but the passengers in her skull were no strangers to being shot at, and so she was only annoyed instead. Closing in on the loping bird, she passed over the revolver to haul out the Cruik instead. This man was only doing his duty, and she didn't want his blood. She just wanted to pull him out of the saddle and tie him up on the wayside. Then burn all of the posters.

The one-sided race was over in moments, the horse easily outstripping the bird. As Seph pulled alongside, the bird wove across the road, screeching with panic in the face of such an alien creature.

The riverman was trying to reload the speargun when Jenny reached out with the Cruik, hoping to snag an arm or loop it around his waist. A slight shifting in her head made her feel the rising presence of one of Lucy's ghosts, the sensation that she was wearing another pair of hands.

The Cruik hummed in her grip. It felt like a natural extension of her arms, a curved finger that weighed almost nothing. She struck out like she was snagging a fish with a gaff pole, and the hook caught the man by the throat.

She saw the Cruik shift slightly as the wood closed most of the way around the man's neck. Choking, he dropped the speargun and clutched at the band of wood with both hands.

"No," she cried out, even as her hands gave an expert twist. There was a loud snap, and the riverman fell from the saddle, a floppy rabbit with a broken neck. The Cruik straightened, releasing the man, and an anonymous killer withdrew into the depths of Jenny's mind.

She reined in Seph and leaned over the saddle, sending a spray of vomit over the horse's flank. Jenny shook with sobs, tears and sick sliding down her face. She'd killed that poor man as easily as swatting a fly.

"What is this?" she howled. "What am I now?"

10

The caravanserai was almost a mile from the thick sandstone walls of Crosspoint, a messy sprawl of shanties and tents so big that it was a twin of the First Town. Most of the tradeways met here, and Crosspoint was the natural centre of commerce. Here, goods scavenged from bleedthroughs drifted south, the food and water went north, and the cattle and Overland coal went everywhere.

In the Overland, they practiced the slavery frowned upon in the Riverland. Crosspoint pointedly ignored an acre of slave pits that were erected within sight of its walls. Lives were haggled over, and debtors and criminals were distributed to the miners if they were lucky, to crooked mobs flush with coin if they weren't. Broken Taursi were kept pliable with grog, the chained natives sold off for glass-crafting or for guides, though they rarely showed the water-holes and secret ways of the Inland.

Even crooked folk were tolerated here if they had fair trade and kept the peace. Jenny saw several packs of the man-eaters, raucous folk covered with outfits of skin and bone, hawking bleed-through gadgets and the leavings of those too dead to care about ownership.

This place had the same bustle and hectic pace as Mawson, but the people were pushy and loud. Jenny found it intimidating. As a young girl riding a horse alone, she was attracting a lot of stares. She kept one hand on her pistol as she watched for bailiffs, wondering if a description of her had been sent by telegraph.

Less than a week ago, the Overseer would have received her in his palace, a grand manse rumoured to once have been the house of Papa Lucy himself. She would have wanted for nothing and could have spent hours poking through the historical buildings of Crosspoint. She would have been given anything she asked for, the price be damned.

Now, she didn't dare approach the town gates.

Her father had visited Crosspoint as a young man sworn in as a Rider of Cruik. Often he'd spoken of the historic sites and promised he would take Jenny there one day. At the thought of her father, her chest seized up in anguish.

It's not too late, she thought. *I can go home. Throw myself on his mercy.*

It was a comfortable lie and she knew it. Mawson meant nothing but a noose for her now, if she was lucky.

Fool! You'll eat the Bastard's Bacon! one of the spirits in her head crowed.

In her mind, she saw a horrific scene. For killing the High Flenser, they'd peel her in the pit, rub her raw flesh in salt while she still drew breath, and she'd be forced to cook and eat her own skin, while the priests dissected her from the feet up.

They wouldn't do that to me! Jenny thought, as her unwanted guests mocked her from the depths of her mind. It had been done before, and this would be her fate.

Fighting the torment within her mind, Jenny made her way through the caravanserai, ignoring the catcalls and vigorous touting. She kept her eyes forward, hauling on the long rope. The dead riverman's bird trotted behind Seph, its beak bound to keep

Seph safe. As she approached the bird yards, the animals went crazy, screeching and snapping their beaks at the horse.

I should have left you somewhere safe, she thought, then laughed. There was nowhere safe to store the last true horse, no one she trusted the reins to. *Do your business and get the hell out of here.*

She found the chief bird wrangler, a heavily scarred man missing an eye and a hand. Pointing to the bird, she tried to talk calmly over the squawking and began the age-old ritual of the haggle.

"I'm more interested in your horse, missy," the bird wrangler said. "Haven't seen one of those in a few years, now. If that were mine, I'd have a dozen guards around it. Hell, I wouldn't ride it either."

"They're bred to be ridden," she said. "The horse isn't for sale."

"Pity," he said, with an appreciative eye to Seph's form. He gave her an insultingly low bid for the bird, but she caved in quickly. *I don't have time for this,* she thought as she took the pittance the man offered.

She felt his eyes on her as she rode away on Seph, then chanced a glimpse backwards. He was talking to a crooked man, pointing at her animatedly. The scofflaw was watching her intently. He gave her a file-toothed smile when their eyes met.

With a shudder, she urged the horse on and gathered provisions. A broad-brimmed hat to keep off the sun and a kerchief to hide her face. A pouchful of cheap bullets, shells refilled, the tips uneven. Through the savvy eyes of someone long dead, Jenny picked out the bullets most likely to fire, tipping the rest back into the box of seconds and scraps.

A hawker sold her a hand mirror with a large crack in it. She tried not to look into the glass as she haggled. She pointed out his half-hidden greypot as a bargaining point and threatened to bring a bailiff. The hawker slid the dead man's mirror across the counter with a curse.

The ragmen sold her a length of tatty cloth that she used to disguise the Cruik. Hiding beside a water trough, she strapped the hook so that it resembled a crutch, then covered the sections of brass cladding with more rags and mud. The last of the rags became false bandages, covering all sorts of imaginary sores. She rubbed dirt into her face, though she was already filthy from a week on the road.

Pointless. It's not like I can disguise the world's last true horse, she thought. Perhaps she should have sold Seph to the bird yard, just to leave a dead trail for the bailiffs.

No. He's mine.

She loaded up on food and bought Seph a large sack of oats meant for sowing. The road to Carmel was long, and she hoped this would be enough to keep the horse going. Nothing grew in the Inland except for bones.

Finally, she needed water. She'd been putting it off for last, the moment when someone in the Dann's pocket may spot her. Prudence dictated that she hide the horse, but this left her at a loss. *This whole place is full of thieves.*

She didn't trust anyone to hold the horse for her. Father had bought Seph six months ago, but as recently as two years ago, a handful of true horses still lived. Jenny hoped word of this hadn't travelled north, that these people saw Seph as rare instead of unique, the last of his kind. Even so, he was worth an absolute fortune.

All worship of the Family was done in Crosspoint itself, with only a handful of overlooked shrines servicing the caravanserai. The followers of Leicester-We-Forget kept a large pavilion here, since the religion was frowned upon in the towns. Jenny led Seph into the large tent, noting the guy ropes bolted to blocks of cement, the walls shored up with tin and planking. A permanent structure.

Inside, the shrine was dim, the only light was the bank of candles surrounding a white Leicester. A handful of shapes crept around in the gloom. As her eyes adjusted, Jenny made out the shapes of stacked crates, a buggy, even a line of motorcycles.

She made for the fearsome white warrior and knelt as if in worship. Presently, the priest appeared at her side, his painted face ghastly in the candlelight. He wore the same strange hat as his god, the brim tipped up on one side.

"Good travel, little sister," the priest said, his eyes straying to the horse and lingering for a long moment. "What road brought you here?"

"A hard one," was all Jenny offered. She'd learnt from her father the wisdom of brevity, of leaving spaces for others to fill. The man waited for further information, but this wasn't forthcoming. Jenny knew next to nothing about the statue-lover's faith. She'd expose herself as an outsider if pressed for detail.

"From Carmel?" the priest whispered and took Jenny's silence as affirmation. He laid a proprietary hand on her arm and patted her like a dog. "Fos Carpidian is a fool," he confided. "He made enemies that day, enemies for all of the faithful. But don't worry child, you're safe enough here."

"I've seen a bleedthrough," Jenny blurted. The people lurking nearby gasped and whispered. The priest said nothing, but the greed in his eyes said plenty.

"Hold my horse here. I go to treat with the water barons," she said. The priest took the reins, and she knew that Seph was as safe here as if he were locked in a vault.

Jenny took the disguised Cruik and checked that her little pistol lay within reach. With her hat pulled low and affecting a limp, she made her way through the caravanserai, leaning heavily on the staff.

She cut through a row of shanties, stepping around naked toddlers playing in the dirt, and kicked at the dog pack that barrelled into her, brawling and snapping over a camel bone.

Hard eyes watched her from within the slap shacks. The watchers endured a poverty she couldn't begin to imagine.

Jenny walked around a corner and almost collided with a pair of bailiffs. The sight of their peaked caps made her stomach flip, and for a split second she was sure they'd be reaching for their knockabouts, ready to strike her down and drag her back to Mawson in chains.

"Pardon, miss," one of them said.

In her mind, a killer shifted around ready to seize Jenny's hands like a puppeteer. But the lawmen walked straight past the fugitive without a second glance. They didn't notice the Cruik right under their noses.

Too lucky, Jenny thought, hobbling along. *They're looking for a Selector's daughter, someone with the stink of Neville, a stupid rich girl on the run.*

I left her back in Mawson. That person is dead.

The water lot was up ahead, carts and tankers ringed by guards with dogs and guns. Factors set up in stalls ready to cut usurious deals with the Inland towns, while small amounts of water could be purchased by waiting in a long line.

The water barons were fiercely competitive, and they hoisted more flags and placards than any of the other merchants in the caravanserai. Jenny recognised the trading mark of Quentin Dann fluttering on several pennants. If the Dann was here in person, he might recognise her and grab the bounty for himself. Even better, this would humiliate her father and he would never save face, not even with her bloody execution.

If she waited in that line for an hour or more, someone might see through her flimsy disguise and recognise her from a poster. As she wondered how to get a trouble-free supply of water, the Cruik throbbed in her hand with a jolt running up her arm. Her teeth twinged.

That means I'm in danger. Sure enough, she turned to see a trio of crooked men approaching her through the slum. She recognised the man from the bird yard and remembered his hand-crafted fangs. A quick flash of that awful smile was enough to send her heart hammering.

Hidden from the busy market lanes by the shacks, they openly came for her. Jenny saw the flicker of knives held low, and though she felt panic, calmer hands than hers drew her pistol and held it steady.

The gun changed everything, and the crooked men scattered. She dropped two of the men in two heartbeats. Crack shots punctured vital organs, with a coup de grace precisely in between a cannibal's eyes.

She heard the rattle of tin behind her, and turned to see the file-toothed man swinging a crowbar at her. He knocked the revolver from her grip then advanced on her.

"Where's the horse?" the crooked man demanded. He took an unexpected swing at Jenny's head, even as she opened her mouth to retort.

The next bit happened so fast that she barely understood what was happening. The Cruik was up in a blur, blocking the attack. Then her hands swung the stick incredibly fast, driving the man back onto the defensive. Wood crashed into the crowbar and his forearm, sweeping aside his legs, staving in his face when he was on the ground. Then, one sharp blow to the heart that stopped everything.

Jenny stood over the dead body, panting, her pulse hammering in her ears. Lucy's ghosts exulted in triumph, chattering with excitement at this grisly victory. Only Jenny had the sense to be scared. She turned and ran when she heard the whistles and shouting of the bailiffs.

It was the Leicesterites who graced her with a small fortune in water for the expedition. They returned Seph to her, fed and watered. Their dim tent bustled with preparations from a caravan of the faithful ready to escort her to the bleedthrough. Jenny quickly scrambled up into the saddle and dug in her heels. They cursed when Seph leapt forward and knocked over someone stupid enough to stand in the way.

No one shot at her for fear of damaging the expensive animal. She heard the whine of a bike misfiring, the cough as a buggy kicked into life.

Emerging into daylight, she gave the horse its head and it forced its way through the heavy foot traffic. Most of the people simply gazed at the creature in awe, although one man who snatched at the bridle was promptly punished by the Cruik lashing out and breaking his wrist.

Jenny saw a buggyload of Leicesterites nosing along behind her, the drivers shouting for the way to be cleared. Merchants and crooked folk alike jeered at the statue-lovers, and soon the cramped laneway devolved into an all-out brawl. She saw the bobbing hats of bailiffs and kept low to the horse until they'd reached a corner.

Her passage through the press of merchants and slavers was nightmarish, treacle slow. Any moment she expected to be hauled down from the saddle, slapped into chains, or simply stabbed for the horse she rode upon. She did not know how far this strange protection of Papa Lucy's reached, how many foes the Cruik could break before she was broken herself.

And then, she was past the slave pens, trotting alongside a caravan of grocers headed for Quarterbrook. The stink of the caravanserai fell away, replaced by the warm winds of the plains and the smooth motion of Seph's body as he pulsed along the tradeway. Both she and the horse were glad to leave that loud place. The coin-riders ringing the caravan eyed her horse a little too closely, and Jenny prudently booted Seph into a canter that quickly outstripped their birds.

She would never walk the streets of Crosspoint with her kind and gentle father. Never see him again, unless it was as a witness to her brutal death. With one last wistful glimpse at the sandstone walls of Crosspoint, she made north for the brutal interior.

Two days travel brought her to the edge of the Inland, an almost divisible line between the scrubby flats and the lifeless red clay. Making a lonely camp that evening, Jenny doled out a portion of oats to Seph, and the horse emptied an entire waterskin in moments.

"Go easy," she said, a little worried. "Nothing to drink where we're going."

Swallowing nervously, she fetched the broken mirror and watched her reflection in the firelight. But tonight, the mirror was just a mirror, and Papa Lucy left her questions unanswered.

When the Jesusman is dead, will you take away these voices and ghosts? she thought, too tired for tears. *Or am I your champion forever? Your roving murderer?*

She felt her faith slipping away as she stared into the glass. All of that confidence Papa Lucy gave her back at the spring felt false now, like a drug. She reached back to her learning and the rite book she knew by heart. There'd been parables of those tested by the gods and found wanting, but now that she needed help, it was hard to hold onto that lesson.

When will you let me go?

No smiles and no whispers for her, save the quiet murmur of ghosts in her mind. She slept little that night, and when she walked in dream, she walked as these lost people. Their Before-Time lives made no sense to her.

There was nothing to go back to, no option but the dusty track that lay ahead. Success meant redemption, both for her and her father. Jenny could not bear to think of the alternative, of her death or capture. When she dozed in the saddle, she sometimes saw the face of the Jesusman leering in purple and startling her awake.

The mind-numbing landscape stretched on. She saw no one else on the tradeway to Carmel. There was nothing for anyone there now, just one more town swallowed up by the Inland.

She saw devil winds on the horizon and recognised the Drift from her geography lessons. She wondered if Fos Carpidian had crossed it in a panic, if the bones of an entire town lay stripped and forgotten in the sand. Did Lanyard Everett lurk in that deadly place, abiding with the monsters and devils?

He's just a man, she told herself. *No one could survive in that.*

Finally, she stood before the walls of Carmel, dusty and weary. This was exactly the image that Papa Lucy had shown her: patchwork walls squatting on top of a plateau, impregnable gates thrown wide open.

"This whole place just up and walked away," she told the horse.

She found evidence of the ambush before the gates, dozens of bodies left to rot in the sun. The smell was horrendous. The bloated corpses crawled with maggots and flies. Gagging, Jenny wheeled Seph around and made for the open gates. She did not bother to search for the Half-Dann's body.

That's Quentin's problem. I need to find evidence, something to point to where Lanyard went next. Passing beneath the mutilated stares of a dozen Leicesters, Jenny entered the gates of Carmel, the Cruik stripped of rags and held up high.

The hooked staff was as silent as the abandoned town. There was no voice from beyond, no instruction from her master. The mirror gave her nothing but the reflection of her dirty face. With a sigh, she slid it back into the saddlebag.

Everywhere, she saw the signs of a panicked evacuation. The streets were littered with abandoned bleedthrough goods, broken maliciously to cheat the water barons out of any profit. A broken wagon lay on its side, stripped of wheels, and nearby the remains of an enormous bonfire, books curled and blackened, valuable Before-Time furniture completely destroyed.

Anything wooden had been burned.

She wept at the sight of several dead pets, strung up on clotheslines like a row of tiny criminals. Many of the doorways had been smeared with what looked to be faeces or blood, the white-washed walls painted with insults to Quentin Dann.

"When these people leave, they really leave," Jenny said.

Most of the Leicester statues were vandalised, faces chiselled into oblivion, hands snapped off. In some instances, the heads had been removed. The little hairs stood up on the back of Jenny's neck. The clicking of Seph's metal shoes against the flagstones echoed too loudly for her liking.

Only one building remained intact. It looked to be a large house of worship with a spire and a belltower. A high row of windows were bleedthroughs, clear and true, where all other glass had been smashed. The doors were thick beams from the Before-Time, carved with a deep image of the Leicester-We-Forget.

Jenny tied Seph to a bird rail and climbed the steps, pistol in hand. She pushed against the door with the Cruik and it opened effortlessly on oiled hinges. She stepped inside and scanned the shadows for any signs of movement.

The church was well-lit and reminded her of a scaled-down Family Temple, but there was no killing pit, no friezes or murals. Nothing but rows of plain bench seats facing onto a raised platform on which stood some sort of altar.

On the altar, a white stone Leicester stood vigil, brooding over a stone trough. The stone man was mounted on a strange litter, long handles slotted through recently fitted iron rings. A portable statue, left in a permanent structure.

"Why break all the others but leave this one here?" Jenny muttered. She found the austerity of this scene more disturbing than anything out in the streets. The sunlight through the windows cast a reflection of the water in the trough against the back wall, and it seemed like the white warrior was underwater.

This close, the water trough stank. *A pity*, she thought. *We could have used the water.*

A horse trough, another voice told her quietly, as if such things were as common as horses themselves.

Gripping the Cruik tightly, she walked forward with her boot-heels clicking loudly on the tiled floor. The stone man watched her approach, glaring sternly at this trespass. Climbing the first steps of the altar, Jenny saw a long list of Before-Time names at the base of the statue under the title "In Remembrance Of."

At the bottom of this list, someone had crudely chiselled the words "MATILDE CARPIDIAN." These marks were very recent, with the exposed bronze of the plaque still fresh and bright.

Then, Jenny looked down into the water trough and gagged. A body floated face down in the water, bloated and pasty from weeks of damp decay. An old woman, flower-print dress split open by the rotten expansion of her waterlogged torso.

As Jenny fought the rebellion in her stomach, the Cruik shivered faintly. When she prodded the body with the foot of the staff, a scene flooded into her head, vivid and terrifying.

She looked upon the same location, but the seats were lined with the faithful, slouch-hatted and daubed in white. A priest exhorted the statue, holding up a silver tray as an offering. Something lay upon that tray that glinted in the sunlight, impossibly bright.

Beside this, a small girl leaned over the water trough, crying hysterically. She held down a thrashing body with her tiny arms, pushed the head back down whenever it breached the surface.

Jenny guessed this sacrificial victim had gone into the waters willingly, but at the end of things, the old woman fought for survival, scratching at the girl with her nails, her struggles getting weaker and weaker until the body lay still in the trough.

The crying girl looked up and stared directly at Jenny. She recognised the child then from the scene that Papa Lucy showed her, the one where the twisted city grew from the earth.

The shining of the relic grew in intensity, until Jenny could no longer bear to look at it. She cried out and was once more in the empty church alone with the corpse.

A week ago, she'd never seen a dead body. Now, she'd killed five men and seen more corpses than anyone deserved to see. Her charmed life was behind her. Now she was Papa Lucy's monster, a killer on a cold trail.

Think, Jen, she thought. *All you've got is this town, this place to track down the Jesusman. Find the answer here or you might as well march back home and peel off your skin yourself.*

You might be lost now, but you can still save Father, still serve the Papa, and hope for mercy. Forgiveness. A miracle to point to when the bailiffs finally track you down.

There, in the depths of the killing trough, barely visible through the tangle of drifting white hair, a glint of something metallic. Grimacing, she put her hand into the chill water and felt past the cold flesh and the slimy ropes of hair. Her fingers brushed against a small chain, so snug around that swollen neck that it was sawing into the flesh. Digging her fingernails into dead meat, she got a grip on the chain and quickly snapped it loose.

She retched, then pulled the necklace out of the fouled water, a thin silver chain with a locket spinning on its end. After wiping the muck from her hand, she leant the Cruik against the trough and popped the locket open.

Two small portraits nestled within. One was an older woman with silver hair and a kindly smile, opposite was a young girl with mouse-brown hair with a crooked half smile. It was the girl from her visions, the weeping killer, one of three who walked the Waking City.

"NONA JOAN" read an inscription under the older woman. Under the young girl's face was one word: "TILLY."

"Oh no," Jenny realised sadly. "They made you kill your grandma. Those mad bastards."

Jenny's tutors had often praised her as a quick study. She re-read the list of inscriptions on the statue, both the names from the Before-Time and those added in the Now. She noted that two final names had been carved into the plaque. They'd taken their time with the first inscription, fitting the letters as closely to the original as possible. The last addition was a rush job, the letters larger and uneven.

These two names were JOAN CARPIDIAN and MATILDE CARPIDIAN. It all fell into place. This was a list of sacrificial victims, people given to their grim-faced god.

"Tilly," she said, thinking of the vision Lucy had shown her. Two crooked women who were clearly her captors were dragging the girl into the nightmare city. "They've thrown you to the wolves, love. You're meant to be dead."

Jenny left the church of Leicester-We-Forget, fixing the necklace around her own neck. She was picking the stones from Seph's hooves, the way Barris had shown her, when she heard the sound of nearby voices and the squawk of two birds squabbling.

No sooner had she got into the saddle than Quentin Dann turned the corner, accompanied by a full brace of birdmen. The big man saw her, and his look of surprise turned into a very nasty smile.

— 11 —

Well, fancy meeting you here, Jenny Rider," the water baron called out. He was mounted on the biggest riding bird she'd ever seen, half again the size of those around him.

Coin-riders filled the street, blocking her passage to the gate. The only way she'd be leaving Carmel was through them. She cursed as she turned Seph this way and that.

They came, through all the gaps and over the burnt buildings, birds and camels and even a lizard with a pagoda on its back. Ten gunmen at least, and even a mounted machine gun resting on a pivot. Mercenaries flush with water money, brought north to destroy Fos Carpidian.

"I've been seeing lots of pictures of you," the Dann continued. He walked his bird slowly forward. "You've been a naughty girl, young Jenny."

It can't end like this, she thought. She dug into her saddle-bags and brought out the mirror. Once more, the glass was silent, Papa Lucy unable or unwilling to answer her.

"Turns out you're worth a lot of money," the Dann said. "You come quietly, and I'll see you home, back to whatever your father calls justice."

"Back to the reward money, you mean."

"Ha! I won't even ask for a lick of Neville's left nut," the Dann scoffed. "I'll hand you in for free, just to see the look on your old man's face."

Jenny felt exposed. There was nowhere to hide, nowhere but the church behind her. If she went inside, they'd simply bar the doors or set the place on fire and smoke her out.

The bird-riders started to surround her, blocking any escape from the town square. Mean-faced men and women looked down from their high saddles, unconcerned by the tiny pistol that Jenny drew. The birds shied at the scent of the horse, but their masters brought out the goads and whips to urge the birds forward.

Don't let them put a ring around you! one of her ghosts cried. *Take the fight to them!*

"Just you try it," she shouted, hoisting the Cruik like a lance. "You'll be as dead as your dwarf."

"Enough! Get her!" the Dann roared.

Jenny jammed her heels into Seph's flanks, sending him into a mad gallop, bearing straight for the Dann and the gate behind him. Birds scattered at the approach of the horse.

She heard the whining of the machine gun, the chatter as it hurled a hail of bullets across the square. The gunman swept the big gun to track the horse, but Seph had already plunged into the midst of the birds, kicking and wild-eyed. One of the panicked birds wandered into the line of fire. Beast and rider were instantly chewed apart by a hail of lead.

"Stop your shooting!" the Dann yelled. "Take her alive, you morons!"

Guiding Seph with her knees, Jenny forced her way through the blockade by swatting aside the braver birds with the business end of the staff. She traded blows with the bird-riders, shrugging off the licks of their whips, cracking heads, and pulling people out of their saddle with the hook. She felt a sting, and a detached part of her saw the spear-gun bolt protruding from her leg, but she barely noticed the pain.

"You're mine!" she said through clenched teeth, ever closer to the Dann. She lined up her revolver on the water baron as he lifted his own gun, using the thick neck of his bird as cover.

Then the lizard charged into the fray, scattering the birds like fluttering chickens. The giant reptile pounced on the horse and seized Seph's neck between its enormous jaws. It lifted the horse off the ground and shook it like a dog with a rabbit. Jenny fell from the saddle, landing awkwardly. Her pistol was gone somewhere amid the dust and dancing bird feet.

"No!" she screamed, rising painfully from the ground. Ignoring the frantic cries of its crew, the lizard hauled the horse away, squeezing the life out of Seph with its powerful jaws.

The last she saw of Seph was the twitching of his hooves. The lizard settled down to begin its expensive feast, its teeth and claws making short work of the dying beast. It plucked one of Seph's forelegs like a drumstick, exposing bone and muscle.

"I'll kill all of you bastards," Jenny sobbed. Someone was reaching for her, a rope in his hands, and she broke his nose with the Cruik, although she couldn't remember picking it up.

She fought with all of her fury. By the time they brought her down, three men and one bird lay dead. Not even the murderous arts of Papa Lucy's ghosts could keep so many enemies at bay. When they finally plucked the Cruik from her hands, it was no more useful than a stick.

Quentin wanted a pyre for the Half-Dann, but the people of Carmel had left him little wood to burn. He settled for a cairn instead and interred his ill-born son right underneath the open gate.

"Pile the rocks high," he said, tears running down his cliff of a face. "Block the gate. This whole damn place can be Vern's marker."

Jenny lay slumped against a rock, observing the water baron's grief through the one eye that still opened. She was a mess of bruises and cuts, bound hand and foot, but they needn't have bothered. She didn't think she'd ever move again. A birdwoman with a stitching kit and a hot iron had drawn the bolt from her leg and cauterised the wound, doing the bare minimum she could to keep Jenny alive.

"Now we hunt these two-faced dogs," said the Dann. The enormous man walked over to Jenny and scooped her up with one hand. He threw her protesting body over his shoulder. The coin-riders had a second lizard hauling a wagon full of supplies. It was into this wagon that he dumped her among the water barrels and sacks of jerky.

He posted a guard to watch her, but once the mercenary realised that Jenny was no threat, he spent most of his time chatting with the wagon driver. The ropes were tight, and she couldn't feel her hands behind her, let alone pick at the knots.

Jenny managed to work herself into a sitting position by propping herself up against a sack of flour. The guard noticed the movement, but when she became still, he relaxed and returned to his bawdy conversation.

Look at you. She watched the Dann trot up and down the line. *You don't even know what you're hunting. I hope the Jesusman cuts your throat.*

The Dann was no fool. He made much of his fortune from the lazy assumptions of others who thought him slow. The man was sharp and meticulous to a fault, checking everything with his own eyes, constantly berating his employees over small infractions. The water baron rode to the rear of the goods wagon every hour to look in on Jenny. She noticed the Cruik lashed to his riding harness. He obviously did not trust the precious relic with anyone else. At one point the big man stroked the curved head of the staff, smiling vacantly to himself.

You bastard bloody thing, she thought, the feeling of jealousy sudden and overwhelming. *Finding a new friend?*

When the Dann saw the guardsman chatting with the driver, he cracked the man over the head with his riding knout.

"You've got one job. Do it," he said coldly.

The guard climbed into the back of the wagon with Jenny. For hours on end he stared at her glumly. The swarthy gunman began to feed her scraps of information, out of boredom perhaps, but she pressed him too hard and he eventually kept his own counsel.

She learnt that small groups of birdmen had circled Carmel and eventually picked up a trail. The Carpidians had made pains to hide their tracks, but they were townfolk and made stupid mistakes. There were diggings for toilet pits, scrapings where they'd buried their fires. A broken handcart surrounded by jetti-soned belongings confirmed they were on the right track as the fugitives were becoming careless.

"Fos thinks he's safe now," Jenny heard the Dann rumble. "I'll feed him to my bird, one slice at a time."

If the strangers in her head had anything to say, they kept it to themselves. The pressure of their presence was still there, but faint, as if they'd retreated to the furthest corners of her mind. For days she'd been both scared and annoyed by the ghosts, but she found herself missing their strange chatter.

The Dann set camp in a chalky gorge, where a trio of Taursi spires glowed softly in the dusk. Jenny was let out of her ropes and pressed into service with the waggoneer who doubled as the camp cook.

"If I see you spit into any of the food, I'll close your other eye," he warned. He set her to peeling a sack of potatoes. She worked the plastic vegetable peeler sullenly, wishing they'd trust her with a knife. They weren't complete fools though, and a fresh guard squatted nearby, shotgun across his knees as he watched her closely.

The cook was hard but fair, and after everyone else had eaten, he gave her a large helping of stew and damper that she wolfed down. She was allowed to attend to her toilet, but she burned with embarrassment as a man stood only a few feet away, gun trained on her in case she attempted to run.

Then it was back into the ropes and bundled into the goods wagon, every muscle aching as she slumped onto the wooden planks. The cook threw a thin blanket across her, more to prevent exposure than out of kindness.

Sleep came instantly, as did the dream. She walked through the passages of a big house. It might have been the Overseer's house in Crosspoint, but freshly built, an idealised pleasure manse drenched with sunlight. She shared the house with hundreds of others, figures that moved through the colonnades and lingered by the fountains. They seemed familiar. She approached the nearest, a man who sat stroking a sleeping dog's belly.

"This house is not safe," the man said. When he looked up, he had no face, his features smoothed away as if by sandpaper. Nothing remained but the suggestion of a nose and a slit for a mouth.

"Ask yourself this," he said. "If the Cruik is so powerful, so useful, why did the wisest of the wise bury it in a gaudy statue?"

Jenny saw that most of the people were faceless, blank-faced mannequins that played at quoits and boardgames. There were others yet who lingered in the shadows and who seemed much less, little more than outlines. Her fingers flew up to her own face, and she could not feel her nose or lips. Her ears were nothing but holes, slowly sealing over.

"Did they lock away Papa Lucy's staff to keep it safe? Or to keep *you* safe?"

She woke instantly when the scratchy blanket began to slide down her shoulder. The blanket jerked some more, an inch at a time. Jenny's mouth went dry, heart racing. Was it the cook creeping in to molest a rich man's brat?

She bunched herself up tight, ready to thrash around with her head to bite at anything that came near her. Then she stopped and held herself perfectly still. A slight weight rested across her legs and moved slowly over her hip, cascading around to her back.

Not a man. A snake or something worse. She didn't dare scream. If she startled the creature, it might bite. The venom of a Rangewyrm could kill a man in hours, but the lesser Inland snakes brought a painful death in just minutes.

Please no, she thought, trying not to whimper as she felt something cold rubbing against her bound hands and nudging into her wrists. Was it getting ready to drink from her veins?

She heard a tearing sound behind her and then another. But she felt nothing pierce her skin, nothing but the creature jerking around on her back, tugging viciously on something.

Then her ropes gave way and her arms were free. The circulation painfully pulsing back into her hands. Shocked, she felt the creature wriggling down her legs, and only then did she chance a glimpse of it.

It was the Cruik, only now it resembled a wooden worm, sawing away at her bonds with a splintery tooth. Eyes wide with disbelief, she slowly sat up, rubbing at her wrists. The man posted with guarding her sleep was slumped across a flour sack, head leaning at an unnatural angle.

The work of freeing its mistress finished, the Cruik wrapped gently around her forearm until it was like a wooden sleeve. The relic shivered like a terrified puppy, and she could not coax it loose. Jenny crept toward the dead guard and prised the shotgun out of his grip. There was nothing in his pockets, no more ammo, nothing but tucker and fleas.

The cook lay still upon his bench, his bedding scattered, his black tongue protruding. The Cruik had strangled him here, a messier kill than the guard. She mourned the foul-mouthed cook for a moment, a man guilty of nothing more than throwing together plain fare for ruthless men.

Not that guilt or innocence bothers my pet, she thought, contemplating the alien shape that writhed on her arm. She leaned out from the wagon, but quickly lay down flat on top of the dead cook. There was the silhouette of a man cast against the glass mounds.

Guards continued their rounds of the camp. She'd half hoped that the Cruik had choked everyone in the Dann's employ, but from what she'd seen, it couldn't do much under its own steam. It had wriggled free from its strappings and had just enough life to sniff her out and free her from immediate danger.

I'll have to do this myself, she thought. One or two voices began to murmur in the back of her mind, then the whole chorus of dead memories roused itself, ready for her to call upon.

She saw the birds snoozing along their line, pegged and hooded for the night. The Dann's huge bird had a peg of its own and slept beneath a warm quilt. Three men watched over the birds, mumbling over a gas lantern, and eyeing the main fire with envy.

Too tricky. Jenny's riding skills weren't too bad, but she always felt awkward in a bird saddle. She bounced around, out-witted by the animal at every turn. In comparison, she'd mastered the lost art of horse riding. Jenny felt the ache of loss in her chest.

Poor Seph, she thought, wiping away an errant tear. *Get it together, Jen, you've got no time for this.*

A trio of camels brooded by the fire, slit-eyed and mean. They were as likely to take an arm off as let her ride, and they weren't fully asleep anyway. One honking cry and the coin-riders would investigate, then she'd be done.

That left her the lizard, a long bank of rippling scales, just visible at the edge of the glasslight. She hated the creature for eating Seph, but she needed to escape. Survival trumped loyalty.

She needed to steal this monster, and most of all, she needed the priceless machine-gun on its back. With that, she could take on anything, up to and including a Jesusman.

Stroking the Cruik, she managed to coax it from her arm. A rope ladder hung from the gunner's hut, and up above, she saw a faint ember, perhaps a cigarette or someone on the kennelweed. The crew were no doubt over by the fires, boozing and playing cards, but at least one man sat watch over their valuable equipment.

She touched the tip of the Cruik to the ladder, and watched as the hooked staff ran like damp clay, wriggling up the rope like a serpent.

Quickly now, she thought, nervously watching for coin-riders. The shotgun was heavy in her grip. She heard movement above, a muffled curse, then the drumming of feet on the floorboards drowned out by a loud grinding sound as the lizard shifted in its sleep, scales rubbing against the chalky ground.

One hand on the ladder, Jenny made to climb, but she heard a soft footfall. A large shadow fell across her. She barely had time to dance to one side when the Dann was upon her, swinging a blood-stained cricket bat with great velocity.

She ducked below the haymaker and jammed the shotgun into his gut. She pulled the trigger. Nothing. Cursing the dud shell, she rapidly worked the pump mechanism, trying to eject the faulty round. The Dann brought the cricket bat down again and jarred the gun from her sore wrists. Then he caught her in the stomach with his boot. The wind knocked out of her, she fell onto her backside, gasping for breath.

"You stupid little shit," the water baron swore, raising the bat up high. At that moment, a dark shape fell onto his head, a floppy mess that draped down to his shoulders.

It was the Cruik, but something was wrong with it. Although the staff was pliable, it barely moved, unable to constrict the giant man with any noticeable result. Ignoring the beaten girl, the water baron struggled with this disturbing new attacker, his efforts stretching it out like warm toffee.

Go, a strident voice urged her off the ground. Adrenaline lent speed to her hands and feet, and she climbed across the ribs of the lizard up into the pagoda.

The remains of a man hung over the side of the pagoda. It was a broken shape reaching for the open air, for any sort of escape, neck and arms broken, head bent into a strange oblong. The Cruik had done this, at her bidding. She shivered.

The machine gun lay in its housing, a complicated device with belts of bullets feeding into it and a series of tanks and hoses to cool it down. Jenny barely understood the use of basic firearms, but as she examined the weapon, a nameless gunner from her mind took over her hands to grip the handles with warm familiarity.

The Dann clutched the side of the pagoda, and as he pulled himself up and over, Jenny Rider swung the gun around and calmly squeezed the triggers. She saw the blank terror in his face as he registered the churning barrels. Suddenly he wasn't the bully dominating the Moot, the sneering tyrant of the water trade. He was just a scared man facing his own mortality. A split second later, his head evaporated into a bloody mist.

The chattering thunder of the weapon startled the lizard out of sleep. It leapt forward, snapping the chain tether on its foreleg, confused and darting in all directions. Jenny heard the panicked cries from the main campfire and saw the silhouettes of coin-riders running and reaching for their weapons.

She swept the gun across them, the belt feeding round after round into that terrifying weapon, water trickling over the hot spinning barrels as they stuttered death. Her lead hornets sawed men in half at the waist, and she did not stop until she had driven the life out of everything that stood.

Jenny looked down to observe the butchery from somewhere in the back of her mind, and she felt nothing.

— 12 —

After she gave the mercy of a bullet to those who needed it, she released all of the coin-riders' birds. They chattered and shared their pilfered man-words then loped across the gorge and out into the Inland flats to freedom.

She picked through the belongings of the dead, and for a moment she felt like a cockatoo, like a ghoul. She pushed away the guilt and got on with the business of survival.

For all that he resembled a mountain on legs, Quentin Dann had pursued the vanities of the newly rich. She found a shaving kit in his bag along with a small folding mirror.

Jenny settled down by the fire. Every inch of her was in pain. Once more she was the captain of her own mind, but this time, her useful ghosts gave up control with great reluctance.

"No more," she mumbled. "I'm not letting you lot take over ever again. No way."

The voices chattered defiance but murmured in the background, exhausted from their brief excursion into her body. It might take all of them to bring her down, but she couldn't hold them off forever.

You've gotta sleep sometime, Jen, she thought. *What then?*

The Dann's mirror was a clean bleedthrough, marred only by a slight scratch in one corner. She peered into her reflection, taking in the horror that was her brutalised face. Instantly, she was through the glass. The sensation was of pushing forward, not being pulled through. She wondered how she'd learnt to do that.

She was alone in the dark place.

"Hello?" she cried. There was no answer, no way to get herself out. She panicked and thrashed around, but there was nothing underneath her feet, no purchase to push against.

Nothing here but a silly girl, bobbing around in the dark. For eternity.

She screamed, then hollered for help. The whispering man appeared at some distance as a glimmer of white in the darkness. He seemed to have trouble approaching.

"You shouldn't be here," she heard Papa Lucy say faintly, no longer smiling. The effort seemed to cost him. His face flickered once like a lamp in danger of blowing out.

"Where were you?" she asked petulantly. "I needed you, but you left me."

"There's been trouble," Lucy said. The next few words were garbled even though his mouth continued to move. "...can't even use the Aum. Mirrors aren't safe."

"Please. I don't know what I'm meant to do."

"...the Cruik," he managed, his words cutting in and out like a badly scratched record. "...glass...Jesusman."

Once more the images appeared before her: the wall, the salt flat, the Waking City. The pictures were faint like tissue paper. If she hadn't seen them already, she doubted she'd make out what they were. Lucy cast aside two of the images like discarding playing cards until only the nightmare metropolis remained.

She felt him reach out across the distance, a pressure in the middle of her forehead like a fingernail scraping the skin. An alien hieroglyph wormed into her mind, something that felt like a code.

"...Cruik will make sense of that," Lucy said. The head looked to one side as if scared of discovery.

"It's hurt," Jenny said. "How do I fix the Cruik?"

"Blood," he said. "Now go."

"Wait. Is the Cruik safe?"

Papa Lucy would not answer. She felt him pushing her away and the mirror-world give. Then, she saw an enormous hand swimming through the darkness, reaching out for her. A grey slab of flesh dominated that black sky with fingers like mountains.

In the centre of that palm was a great bloody hole that seemed to serve as an eye as well as a mouth. Jenny felt it drink in every contour of her face. Beneath this wound, a word in darkness was carved into the skin in letters as tall as her father's Tower.

"BEFORE."

As the fingers closed around her, she stirred from the mirror-world. She was once more surrounded by dead coin-riders. The shaving mirror splintered into a thousand tiny pieces. Glass shards spilled out of the frame as fine as sand.

She sat there shaken for many long moments. That hand had come for her like a gigantic squid on the hunt, and even Papa Lucy was afraid of it. There were no more of the sly smiles or insistent whispers that had ruled her dreams for so long.

Nothing but a scared man alone in the dark.

"What can frighten a god?" she whispered. It had almost touched her, almost dragged her into that awful ragged hole. She didn't know what was on the other side, but if it scared Papa Lucy, it terrified her.

I need blood, she thought. Picking up the Cruik was like lifting an armful of melted toffee as it ran over her arms and drooped to the ground. She fetched a shovel from the supply wagon then scooped up the slimy mess and dumped it onto the nearest dead man.

"Well go on, eat him," she told the Cruik, but it burbled as it slid off the dead man's chest. She experimented with the other corpses, but the Cruik did not appear to feed or recover from its malady.

"Okay, maybe it needs to be living blood."

She guided her captured lizard across the campsite where the cook's lizard grazed on its dead master. The mini-gun flared in a brief cacophony, tearing open the flank of the giant, startling it into flight.

Instantly her own lizard jerked forward as its predatory instinct activated at the sight of his cousin's blood. The two beasts grappled, biting and tearing at each other with their claws. Jenny did her best to hang on.

"Here you go," she said, tossing the Cruik to the pagoda's side and onto the bloodied shoulder of her lizard. But the Cruik would not feed, and she was forced to put the other lizard down by shredding its head into pulp with the mini-gun. Jenny's lizard feasted long into the afternoon, and she felt a little better. *At least I'll fatten him up for the long trip.*

Her last resort was pricking her own thumb to release a gentle dribble of blood onto the goopy mess. Finally, the Cruik responded favourably. It grew firmer until she could pick it up. One end of the staff gently lapped at her thumb like a lamb on the suckle.

Only a moment seemed to pass, but when she stirred, the sun was much further across the sky. She felt weak and dizzy. The Cruik was like a serpent's head, drawing out her blood. A second strand of goop had fastened around her index finger, her flesh tingling and sore where a tooth had pierced the skin. Rather than suckling, it felt like it was pushing something *into her.*

"Enough!" she gasped and extricated herself from the Cruik with some difficulty. It reached for her, but she pushed the mass away with her boot.

"I will give you more tomorrow. But you have to do this for me," she said and pointed to her forehead. "Your master hid something here and made a mark. Show me his message. And no funny business."

The Cruik extended a faint tendril towards her, and she let it touch her on the forehead. The world dropped away, and she was soaring across the Inland like a cockatoo on the wing. She crossed the Range that marked the edge of all claimed land, and then she was over the Waste, looking down upon all manner of strangeness.

She passed the trio: one biker, one woman on a bird, and Tilly Carpidian, bound and gagged on the back. Then her invisible eye went past them, struggling to keep a straight path as it fought the twisted logic of the Waste.

Finally, she reached the place where the Waking City was rising. Jenny saw this potential through Papa Lucy's eyes and felt the enormity of the bleedthrough just waiting to burst. But there was nothing here yet, no Leicester-We-Forget to mark the spot, no riches from Before.

Alone on the plain, Lanyard Everett stood, naked and bloody. The Jesusman held something in his hand, and as she approached him, he uncurled his fingers and let the light touch what lay on his palm. He smirked at her.

She saw the glass shard and recognised it from the church at Carmel, the bright offering over a drowned woman. It sparkled brightly as it drank in the sunlight, then it became a sun all by itself, burning away Lanyard's flesh and the vision. All the while, an alien voice hammered at her, demanding that she submit and that she kneel before Turtwurdigan.

Then, silence, the only light was the burning orb of the sun baking the Inland. She was back in the campsite, back in the ache of her own body. Jenny stirred from the vision to see that the Cruik was once more stealing her blood and replacing it with something else.

"You stop that!" she said, fighting her way loose. She decided to leave the relic behind, but even this resolution seemed fuzzy. As she paced the camp, fretting and confused, she still felt the pull of the Waking City no matter where she stood. With eyes closed, she could still point to it in a direction far north and east of here.

Papa Lucy had found the Waking City and planted the directions in her head. In the Waste, she would find her enemy, save her father, and redeem herself.

Jen, you are practical to a fault, Horace often said. She decided that she would need everything at her disposal, even the tools that scared her. Gashing her palm with a knife, she let the Cruik lap at her blood. She stopped fighting the ghosts and let them take over whenever she needed help.

Thus, she crossed from the lands of people into the landscape of the strange, the Waste drawing her on, her journey near its end. There was nothing to the world but herself, the sullen dragon beneath her, and a terrifying monster at her bared breast, now suckling directly from her in the most intimate of ways.

She had imagined herself at this moment, a noble warrior on the last true horse riding down a villain. Now, poor Seph was dead, and she didn't even know what she was anymore. There were no more Riders of legend, no heroes, nothing but monsters, and she was fallen and lost. She tried to roll the knucklebone rite, but it felt like a child's toy now. One by one she threw the bones away from the pagoda, cursing the day she'd sworn herself to Lucy's cause.

It was only her love for the staff keeping her going now.

She spent many miles nursing the Cruik, barely remembering to eat or drink. Each time she saw the wash of her own blood slowly leaking out, it seemed more brown than red—the creature was giving back just as much as it took.

Jenny dreamt.

Once more she walked in the airy palace. This time the faceless men and women welcomed her into their games and showed her every wonder in the galleries and the gardens. She was almost one of them now. In the bustle, she gleaned that she'd passed a type of probation or a rite of passage.

Only the mournful man who still scratched his dog gave her pause. He shook his head and pointed towards the sun-framed doors.

"It's not too late for you," he said. "Leave the Cruik."

"No," Jenny said, her mouth little more than a slit, her eyes pinpricks. "It needs me."

"Oh, it will tell you that," the man said. "It pretended to need all of us too. Look."

He pointed to his own shadow and those of the guests playing badminton nearby. Each shadow was a skinny length with a hook end, a dancing reflection of the Cruik itself.

"Not too late for you," he repeated. He pointed to Jenny's shadow, which was thinner, but she could still see her arms and legs. Her shadow's head was starting to pinch and turn, slowly turning into a hook.

"For now, you are a guest," the man said. "Soon, you'll be a prisoner without even knowing it. Then, a whispering voice in the halls, and then you are nothing, just like them."

He looked to the colonnades where the almost vanished guests lingered. She shivered and awoke.

The Cruik still suckled from her, coiled about her ribs like a constricting snake. The tail end poked into the crook of her elbow where it fed its leavings directly into her veins.

It was strong now, stronger than when she'd ripped it out of the statue's hands. When she looked upon it, she knew love and regret that she'd ever considered leaving it behind.

Jenny knew she'd done the right thing. The Cruik was beautiful. The Cruik was perfect.

She'd loaded the pagoda with supplies, weapons and ammunition, and enough water to keep herself and the giant lizard alive. It had been tricky operating the winch and pulley by herself, but more experienced hands than hers took over to throw together a rig much more efficient than the one the Dann's people had used.

Then, she'd left the dead to rot and went where her master told her to go. The Jesusman was going to the Waking City, and so was she.

One of her restless ghosts had been a lizard wrangler, so she handled the reins with expertise, driving the creature across the weird landscape. The Waste. She had a direction now, a point on the bare horizon that she could find with her eyes closed.

There were dangers here, creeping things that preyed on travellers and fools, but Jenny did not fear them. She shot them down from her vantage point, and the lizard snapped up the small night creatures.

She walked among the demons with the Cruik held high, and nothing could touch her. The staff was whole. She marvelled at its perfection, the grace of its curve, the heft of its shaft. The more sinister among the locals attempted to trap her mind, but she'd already been claimed by something much more powerful than they. Barely realising that she did it, she broke these old whisperers and drew them into the Cruik itself to feed them into its false house.

The staff relished being in the Waste and drank deeply from the thin spots in the world veil. What was left of Jenny noted with some bemusement the changes in the lizard, the way the gun became a permanent part of the creature, its ammunition belts now stretching out of a valve in the animal's back.

The gun spat a hail of bones and sharp teeth at any who threatened them, and the creature grew with every mile and every meal. It had almost doubled in size.

Jenny Rider could still be mistaken for an olive-skinned Riverlander at a distance, but up close her skin was coarse, a dry sheath resembling bark. Now when the Cruik bled her, it was an amber sap that ran from her skin, not that it needed to feed from her often nor feed into her.

She was almost complete. Jenny faced the glare of the misbehaving sun undeterred and focused only on her prize. Whenever she saw Lanyard Everett in her mind's eye, he was only an inconvenience, an interruption.

The Cruik hungered for the glass, for Turtwurdigan. For just a moment, Jenny's fingers pressed together, her hands curving out as long wooden hooks. The staff itself was nowhere to be seen.

There was no time, no day or night, nothing but the relentless march towards the Waking City. She was so close to the edge of all things that the world seemed like a skillet, greased and steaming, light and form sliding around her.

Then, she found clarity in the madness. A cityscape lay before her, like she'd only seen in books. The Waking City, growing from the ground like a cement garden, its roots deep in the world veil, stretching from Now to Before and perhaps even further back.

Her eyes were keener than an eagle's, transformed by the Cruik into perfection. She saw the Carpidian girl on a rooftop waving frantically.

Her nose was the nose of the Cruik, and she could smell Turtwurdigan: this great alien presence that demanded her obedience. It was old, and it had once been very powerful. But instead of fear, she felt a great hunger and the urge to suck at the buildings like bones, to draw out the marrow where surely the glass chatterbox thing was hiding.

Only then could she return home. Jenny was no longer sure if this meant Mawson or some other place that only the Cruik knew. The idea of home was close, so close that she ached for it.

Oh, my Father, she thought, and in her confusion, she was no longer sure if she meant the dying man by the river or Papa hidden in mirrors. They felt the same now, a promise to two father figures from a scared little girl.

"I will kill this bad man," she muttered, clutching to that one goal, knowing that both home and faith were lost to her. "I will not fail you."

Then she saw the Leicester-We-Forget, the white statue that marked out the bleedthroughs, always the first thing to come over. She saw another Leicester, and then another. They were moving, running for her, and then a tide of white figures was flooding out of the twisted metropolis, hundreds of white warriors coming to intercept her.

She aimed the big gun, now a thing of cartilage and steel, and the weapon sprayed a hail of bone and razor-sharp gristle, scouring away the outer rank of statues, grinding them into dust. And then there were more Leicesters, and the lizard barrelled through them, snapping them in half with metal-tipped teeth, sweeping them aside with cement-sheathed claws.

Jenny growled as slouch-hatted statues climbed all over the lizard and caught the edges of her pagoda. She cast them aside with her hook hands, plucking off stone heads and shattering marble limbs, and always howling, howling at the closeness of her prize.

— INTERLUDE —

Make no mistake, Lanyard. You killed me," Bauer said, drizzling pan grease onto the split damper. "I am dead."

"Do dead men eat?" Lanyard asked.

"An old habit," he conceded, working on the bread with his stained teeth. The two men sat in an awkward silence, as if prentice had never killed master and this was just the latest of many cookfires.

The witches retreated to some distance, but even as they pretended to work on the nest, they watched and waited for a signal. It was strange that a pack of witches would defer to their sworn enemy, but not as strange as a man returned from death itself.

Bauer handed Lanyard the rest of the loaf. He bolted it down like a starved dog. The old Jesusman offered his naked apprentice a half bottle of scotch, good Before-Time stock. Lanyard snatched it out of his hands and drank it like water. He coughed, nearly gagging up his food.

"Go easy," Bauer said. "You never could handle your booze."

"Shut your mouth," Lanyard said. Bauer shrugged and kept his own counsel while the younger man drank the rest of the scotch.

He threw the empty bottle, and it smashed against the side of the witches' eye-twisting nest.

"Still got that temper, lad," Bauer said.

"Shut up!" Lanyard shouted. "You're meant to be dead."

"Yet here we are," Bauer replied calmly. "Maybe we should talk about that."

"Maybe I should kill you again."

"Try, if you like," Bauer said, preparing a billy kettle and completely unconcerned. Lanyard sat sullen, scowling as his master set about brewing a pot of tea.

All of his schemes, everything he'd tried to make of himself, it all came undone as that grey veteran once more sat across from him. Bauer paid him no mind, letting him sulk, as he tapped out an even measure of tea leaves into the water.

"Do you remember what I told you about the land of the dead?" Bauer said sternly, passing a hot tin of tea across the fire. Lanyard nodded. The drink burned his tongue.

"A sad place, where the souls go," Bauer said. "Some linger a while, watching the goings on up here, but most don't. It's easier to let go and move on."

"Why didn't you?"

"I've watched every wretched moment of your life, Lanyard Everett. Cheating, killing, trading in misery. Seems you've done your very best to be a disappointment."

"At least I did something right," Lanyard mumbled.

"You gave up!" Bauer shouted, startling him out of his self-pity. "I sniffed you out, plucked you out of a short and wretched life because you had promise. Potential. You can't walk away from what you are."

"I never asked you to save me!" Lanyard cried. "You did me no favour at all. I wish I'd never known this, known any of it!"

This was more or less word for word what he'd said by that old campfire, one last spit of hatred before a boy picked up a rock.

Silence, and the men nursed their tea, sharing the memory of a hundred similar disagreements. It hadn't been the smoothest of apprenticeships. A coal spat then, and Lanyard stirred from his reverie. A dozen flies tracked about in the sweat on his back, drawn to his map of wounds.

"I've seen you dabble at your trade, boy. Killing the odd witch, stomping on the things that have no business being here. Good."

"It's kill or be killed," Lanyard said. "I'm no Jesusman, not now, not ever."

"Stop being so weak!" Bauer barked. "I sent many people to the other side, Lanyard, and they were all down there waiting for me. I beat them all, again, and then I beat anyone who looked at me funny. What's your excuse?"

"How did you..." Lanyard pointed to Bauer as he struggled to frame the question. For a split second, Bauer's features swam around on his face in the waxy manner of a witch. His cheek sagged slightly as if he'd just had a stroke. The change was hard to spot, but Bauer slumped and seemed to cave in on himself, like a candle slowly burning away into nothing.

"Found a way out, I did. Clawed my way up out of death and convinced the man in charge to send me back, even if only for a short time. My work," he pointed at Lanyard, "isn't done."

"You're wasting your time," Lanyard said. "Piss off and leave me alone."

"I did all this for you, you damn knucklehead. Your education was never completed. Now, I don't have very long, so clean yourself up and put these on."

Bauer handed Lanyard a clean shirt and a pair of jeans.

"Things are about to get nasty, boy. The world needs a Jesusman and you're the only option."

Lanyard soon understood Bauer's hold over the witches; each of them was branded with the mark of the Jesus, a simple B + N that most of them tried to hide and shift around to some unobtrusive part of their waxy skin.

"A witch is just a Jesusman gone bad, much like yourself," Bauer said. "Easy enough to remind them of their old loyalties."

The old man's skin was taking on the texture of an orange peel. He was leaving little dribbles of himself as he walked around, faint smears of wax in the dust. This loan body of Bauer's was crumbling fast.

"The bossman is watching, Lanyard, so get it right," he said. "It was himself who sent me back, after I tracked him down and hollered at him some."

"The Jesus?"

"Enough with the semantics." Bauer grizzled as his face clenched. "The quick version is this. Certain folks have woken up who shouldn't have, and an old argument is about to turn the Now into a cinder. You will stop this."

Lanyard resented the return to his lessons, until Bauer knocked sense into him with a swift right hook. Ears ringing, Lanyard paid attention, and once he was past that first moment of his old fears, he was glad for the learning. He'd spent years with half a lesson in his head, not enough to deal with the wrong kind of visitor to the Now. Lanyard grumbled and dragged his feet, but he was secretly glad to round out what little he knew.

He finally learnt the greater marks of unmaking: a grid of names and sigils scratched into the earth. As he copied each one, Bauer scrubbed it out, and when he'd finished, Bauer made him write out the whole lot from memory.

"No, no, no!" the old man bellowed, cuffing Lanyard across the ears. "Do you think Papa Lucy is going to wait patiently while you remember how to write these? He'll sing the life out of you and then piss on your sorry corpse."

For practice, Bauer wiped the Jesus mark from one of his bound witches, and it leapt for Lanyard with hunger in its eyes. Lanyard sent the twisted monster to its death with nothing but word and a mark. His master nodded, offering a rare smile of approval.

"That gun was borne by the Jesusmen for almost three hundred years," Bauer said. "My father carried it before me and his before that. You killed me for it. So, where the hell is it?"

"Crooked folk took it," Lanyard mumbled.

"You got stupid is what I'm hearing," Bauer said. "Oh well, can't send you in with your bare hands and a smile. Come on."

The growing witch nest sat on the edge of the salt flat facing out onto the Waste. It was a marker for the boundary of the safe lands, a lighthouse for anyone unfortunate enough to be out there wandering.

Not that a witch's home is any safer than dying on the salt, Lanyard thought.

The two Jesusmen entered the nest, which was nearly completed. As they passed by the industrious witches, the ache in Lanyard's bones grew. He felt the murderous urge with all of the old fears. Years ago, he'd been tortured by a witch in the Greygulf, and his hatred of their kind smouldered still.

"I'm letting them finish this because you will find it useful," Bauer said. "Sad, misguided bastards. They started off on the right path, and then they got hooked on all that Before-Time junk that doesn't bleedthrough right. Electronics, televisions, and what-not."

They reached the centre of the nest, where all the power cables and fixtures led. Here was what Lanyard had been sensing—a tear in the world veil little bigger than a window. The edges were unbound and flickering, razor sharp.

"Quicker than the shadow roads. With this, they can just reach through to any of the realms, pluck out whatever they want. Stupid little sparrows. You, come here and work this thing."

One of the witches put down its tools and slid across the floor in its graceful, greasy manner. The waxy man looked at the pair of them with barely disguised resentment and rubbed at the Jesus brand on the back of its hand.

"My boy needs kit. Guns and bombs and anything else he wants. Bring it all over."

Giving mutinous whisperings to its fellows, the witch worked the controls, feeding more power into the device. It looked like a moonshine still hooked up to a tableful of gadgets, computer parts, and a cracked television. It was half science, half sorcery. Lanyard felt an agonising tickle as the witch opened a tear directly into the Before and pushed its waxy limb through into that dead world.

Without full power, the witch's capacity to search the Before was limited, but the creature stumbled across a small cache of weapons, a gun-rack in somebody's home. It plucked out a pair of pistols, a long rifle, even a wickedly sharp bowie knife.

"Now, watch carefully," Bauer said as he showed Lanyard the making of the marks and what phrases to write with the etching tool. It took them many painstaking hours but soon the guns were marked with pictures and words in the same way as the old shotgun had been, making them much more than just weapons. Lanyard marked the knife himself, and Bauer judged it a success.

"I sure hope you get to tickle Bertha's ribs with this," Bauer said, turning the knife over in his disintegrating hands. "What a rotten bitch."

"This is Turtwurdigan," Bauer said, throwing the cloth back over the chattering glass and silencing it. "Taursi spirit, here long before we were. Going by the tellings of the old Jesusmen, she was the greatest of our allies back in the war. Mad as a meat hook, though."

Mere days later, Bauer was almost completely gone, a runny candle spreading out, his trunk sinking into the goopy mess. Only his shoulders, neck, and head remained coherent.

The witches lurked around the light of the campfire watching carefully, waiting for the old man to pass. Lanyard wondered how long the protection would last and whether their loyalties would continue once Bauer passed over into his final death.

Lanyard had spent years angry at his master, and under the weight of his guilt, he'd never mourned the man. Now that Bauer was dying his second death, Lanyard realised how much this man had loved him. He had clawed his way out of death just to give him what he needed to do his job.

Of course, they never spoke of love. Nothing but gruff instructions from the master, and sarcasm and sulking from the student. The old man was tough and still demanded everything from the scrawny boy he'd saved.

"You get to that big bleedthrough, that Waking City," Bauer demanded, his face starting to run. "Hitch a ride with a spiky native, nick a bike, but whatever you do, you get there quick."

"What am I meant to do, then?" Lanyard asked.

"Kill 'em all," the drooping man burbled. Then he finally spoke to Lanyard about Sad Plain, about what he needed to do.

Swallowing a little, Lanyard put the last fragment of Turtwurdigan into his new satchel, handling it like a hot coal.

He knelt by his master's side, keeping watch as the man crumbled until only a face peered out of a wax puddle.

"One more thing, boy," Bauer whispered, and Lanyard leaned in closer.

"You should be ashamed of yourself running away from this lot. Finish the job."

Then Bauer was gone, his strange second life at an end. Lanyard heard the quiet creep of witch feet, the static of their thoughts as they closed in on him. He knew then that Bauer was repaying like with like, that the marks binding the witches had just expired.

No kindness from the old man, no words of forgiveness or inspiration, nothing but a kick in the arse, and the hope of a violent and lonely death.

Then, the rush, the low howl as a score of hungry witches came for him. The sleek iron snouts of his pistols cleared leather. Lanyard Everett stood firm against his enemy, calling up mark and word while his holy guns barked vengeance.

PART THREE

— THE FAMILY —

— 13 —

I t's easier to think of the realms as if they're a deck of cards," Papa Lucy said. "Or a sandwich."

A small group of students lounged around in his solar. The apprentice sorcerers were recruited into Lucy's latest great idea: the Academy. Lucy paced the room as a series of icons floated above his head, each picture representing one of the known realms.

"Most of the realms can be reached. Difficult, but not impossible." He boomed the same loud voice he used indoors or out, whether wenching or hosting the Moot. He gave the impression of transparency, though he kept more secrets than anyone. Everything about the man was lurid, a calculated distraction. He could lie—had lied—but you would love him while he did it to you and make excuses for him even as he robbed you.

Sol, who was not yet the Boneman, liked to sit in on these classes if he was in the neighbourhood. It felt good to finally have another group of young sorcerers on the rise. He longed for the time when they would master their art and when they could have a vibrant academia, a legacy.

Most of all, the brothers missed their fallen comrades, the friends and rivals who'd perished in the Crossing. A sorcerer's life was a lonely one, and their cadre of five was stagnating of late.

Hesus was the grit in the oyster, of course, but the less said about him the better.

It was a long cry from the Collegia, that marvellous sky-city orbiting the world of Before. Here, they'd brought in anyone with a dribble of talent: riverboys and reavers, beggars and shepherds. The process was frustrating to Sol, who likened it to teaching a remedial class, but Lucy made himself a willing mentor to these accidental sorcerers. It was he who coaxed out their first awkward magics.

"These are the Prime Realms, habitable by men," Lucy said, "such as Before and Now." He rearranged the symbols above him, an elaborate planetarium, and Sol smiled. He'd taught a few classes himself and found it just as easy to scratch out marks in the dirt with a stick.

"Prime Realms connect via the Greygulf, and if you can tear a hole in a world veil, you can step from one to another as often as you like." This was said lightly, of course, before the full consequences were known.

"Above the Greygulf, it's rumoured that there's another realm, the Overhaeven. Certain energies can be detected in all of the realms, but we've not been able to find the source. A mystery, even in the Before."

Sol had wrestled with the Overhaeven theory for a full year, but he'd given up when Bertha came along. It seemed more profitable to shift his studies to the Underfog, even if necromancy was the sorcerer's equivalent of taking up a trade. Good money in it, back before the breaking of the old world. Before their great escape.

"The Greygulf rests on top of the Aum, the reflecting realm. Entered through mirrors and shadow. Most useful for long-distance communication, but I wouldn't want to linger there long," Lucy said with a shudder. "Terribly empty place."

"Below all of this is the Underfog," and here Lucy raised the lower-most image, a landscape of mist riddled with standing figures.

"Here is where the resonance of life ends up and the dead hold court," Lucy said. He had their full attention as he discarded the other icons and stretched out the image of the Underfog like a mural.

"It's very dangerous to visit the Underfog. We still don't know much about it. I figure a man's ancestors are best left alone. There's time enough to talk with them when you're dead." That was all he would say about the land of lost souls.

The Academy was a great distraction, and Sol watched Lucy pour three decades of his long life into the institution. The apprentices became journeymen and then learned enough that they passed muster, though they fell far short of the standards of Before.

Barely fit to mop the floors of the Collegia, this lot, thought Sol.

Eventually, this average cabal of magicians grew in hubris and their greed overtook their awe. They tried to seize Papa Lucy, to prise out the rest of his secrets. Lucy destroyed them all in a single horrific night and never taught sorcery again.

Papa Lucy was the most powerful of the surviving sorcerers and was certainly one of the leading lights back in the Before. Even he had visited the Underfog only twice, the last time on the strength of an old rumour.

Lucy's path took him through the now-tamed Greygulf, past the industry of the Hesusmen as they ferried the remnants of Before through to Now. They bowed to him of course, but Hesus was their true master. There was something odd about their movements, almost furtive. He briefly inspected the works and spoke with a somewhat nervous Neville, appointed by Hesus as steward and custodian of the Greygulf.

Something's not right about Neville, Lucy thought and decided to investigate later. He'd had enough of politics for some time. He had abandoned the Moot mid-session and vanished from his home the next day.

Let Sol deal with buttons and bicycles. I've got places to be.

Casting about on the shadow roads, Lucy found a likely place and dropped through into the Aum. There he spent almost a year assaulting the gates to the Underfog.

Weakened and maddened from his sojourn in the dark Aum, Lucy slipped into the Underfog, the only living being to walk the land of the dead. This place was the only visible aspect of the afterlife, the gutter where the final residues of life lingered for a while. Where a soul went after that, no one knew, and none returned from whatever lay beyond the Underfog.

Tall grass, acres of reed, vast stretches of burnt stubble—the geography of the Underfog was far from fixed. Lucy fought through cities of thorn and swam through rice paddies where nothing grew.

Demons walked in the mist, the spirits of creatures that defied explanation. If theory was right, other worlds touched onto the Greygulf, worlds uninhabitable by men, or where the world veil was too thick to pierce. But everything ended up here. These unapproachable worlds could be studied by proxy in the Underfog, their dead inhabitants quizzed.

Lucy did not come for academia's sake. He had nothing to prove when packs of malicious revenants came for him. He sent them on to their final rest and combed the mist asking only one question:

"Where is the Cruik?"

It took every magical device he'd saved from the Collegia days just to survive his journey. He siphoned every lick of power out of the rings, wands, and brooches he'd stolen, and still it wasn't enough. Sometimes, he caught a flicker of movement in the corner of his eyes, only to realise it was a hairs-width sliver of his own soul stepping away from his body and fading into the mist.

Not once did he doubt himself, not even when a dread beast wounded him grievously.

Bertha and the others rarely crossed his mind, but he often thought of Sol. The thought of his earnest brother drove him on more than his ambition did. If he was ever going to return to face Sol's clucking, poe-faced sanctimony, he sure as hell wanted something to show for it.

The Cruik was his current obsession, but if what he guessed was true, it was the means to a most magnificent end. Every wrong thing he'd done, everyone he'd screwed over, all of it would be washed away with his greatest act of magic.

"It will be worth all this spooky bullshit," Lucy barked, scaring off a family of spectres.

On the fifth year of his search, he spent a month with the Half-Buried, a monastic order that had found a way to permanently reside in the Underfog. Mummified with oils only found here, the souls were half buried in the dark brown soil, their top halves bound to a brace, free to talk and sing amongst themselves, to share wisdom with their visitors.

This repository of knowledge was astounding, but it didn't interest Lucy. He asked for the whereabouts of the Cruik. At first the Half-Buried tried to put him off and persuade him to go back to his own world.

"Find a woman, walk in the sunlight," they whispered. "Forget the Cruik. It is beyond you."

Papa Lucy was furious that they dared to deny him. He pressed them further, visiting all manner of torment upon the Half-Buried...but they only answered him in vagaries or omission. When he began work on a great and terrifying magic—the means to uproot the entire order and force them on to their final doom— one of the monks broke.

"There is one last shore, at the furthest edge of the Underfog. There you will find the Cruik, lingering on the edge of Death itself."

The journey to the boundary of life was a long and perilous one, and it took him almost ten more years to reach the desolate beach. Time enough for the Underfog to bleach his soul and drive him half mad.

The shore was a litter of grit and shattered stone, waves of black water smashing at it relentlessly. The ocean beyond was the deepest black that reached to the sky, curving up until it brushed against the sepia heavens above.

"So this is death," Lucy said. The draw of the water was almost irresistible. He longed to strip off his clothes and leap into the dark foam, to let the water take his cares and pains away.

He frowned as he made the marks of clarity and warding, and the morbid urge passed. As his senses returned to him, he saw the fat tendril of the black water questing towards him, brushing against the rocks like a worm. Another mark and a word of unmaking, and Death's tendril collapsed, soaking the stones beneath it.

Lucy walked on, searching, calling upon the true sight, even scanning that wretched place with a pair of binoculars. All the while Death called to him.

Finally, he saw his prize in the distance—a skinny shape that barely stood out against the fury of the black ocean.

The Cruik. A hooked staff, resting on the tip of a pointed stone at a perfect vertical. It was so close to the breaking waves that the deadly spray washed against it. Lucy saw several of the reaching tendrils dancing around in the water...but they held back, as if afraid.

Papa Lucy approached the Cruik. He was so fixed on the staff that he slipped in the shale and cut his knee badly. Limping on, he stood before the curved pole, marvelling at its simple elegance, his eyes drawn to the proportions of the staff, the turn of the shepherd's hook.

Shuffling forward, his skin burned from where the deadly spray touched it, but he paid this no mind. He licked his lips and reached out for the object of his long search.

"It's perfect," he breathed.

When Papa Lucy stumbled back into Crosspoint, wasted and filthy, almost twenty years had passed. He greeted people in the street as if he'd never left, and returned to his house.

He evicted the factor who'd seized it ten years ago for non-payment of debts. Swearing everything from a bloodied nose to an injunction, the man fell silent when he saw the sorcerer's dead stare, his grip upon that disturbing hook. The factor left with no further argument after uprooting his extended family from every wing of the manse. In their haste, they left nearly everything behind. Lucy ferried their belongings out into the courtyard with invisible hands.

Sol stepped out of a far door just as his brother set fire to the lot. He took in the wear on Lucy's face, the first signs of grey hair above his temples. Most of all he noticed the way his brother lovingly caressed the shepherd's crook by his side.

"You're getting old," he teased. Lucy gripped the staff tighter as he scowled.

"My house stinks like merchant. Why did you let some cabbage seller take my house?"

"No one knew where you were, Lucy, and you left a lot of bills behind. The Moot gave your estate to that man. The law is law." Sol watched the bonfire for a long moment, disturbed by the mad glint in his brother's eyes.

"There'll be trouble," the younger brother continued, but Lucy scoffed, tipping another flask of grain fuel onto the fire.

"Laws are nothing," the prodigal magician said. "All this squabbling over coin, over politics? We've forgotten who we are, brother, what we are capable of."

"You passed beyond my sight," Sol said softly. "We all thought you were dead."

"I've seen death," Lucy said. "It's nothing. Just water and darkness."

As gaudy furnishings and the beloved toys of the factor's children blazed, the brothers stood in companionable silence. This brutal eviction was not the worst thing Lucy had done, and Sol loved him so much that he would overlook almost anything and make excuses even as his brother pissed in the punchbowl.

He stole a glance at Lucy's new staff and could feel the gravity of the thing. The way the light touched it made it look too real, more *present* than anything had a right to be. Their shadows were firm, but the dark line running away from the staff was wavering, indistinct.

"I do not like the look of your walking stick, brother," Sol said.

"This is the Cruik," Lucy said by way of explanation and added nothing further. They'd both heard the rumours back in the world of Before of a construct that held powers beyond reckoning, the means to unlock all of the realms. A construct that would mould its bearer into something approaching a god. Many sorcerers had braved the Greygulf hunting for the Cruik in all of the Prime Realms. None had returned.

Sol felt the tickling whisper as the spirit within the staff reached out to him, tested his defences. Then the brute force withdrew. It was as if it had found him...wanting.

"Do you know what you are doing, Lucy?" Sol asked. "Take it back to where you found it. That thing is dangerous."

"Not as dangerous as me," Papa Lucy said, and in the intimate company of his brother, his mask of bonhomie slipped. He regarded the Cruik with a grim satisfaction, and Sol felt afraid.

This was a long time ago, before they'd raised temples to themselves, before the madness of Sad Plain. In those days, Hesus only opposed Lucy in the Moot, John Leicester still called himself friend, and Turtwurdigan slumbered in the ground.

Today, a monster led a dead horse along a track, once a patrol route for the Riders of Cruik, now overgrown and forgotten. Papa Lucy swam in his mirror, cackling and driving the Boneman onwards.

"C'mon, Sol," Lucy laughed. "I'm dying to drop in on the old lady. I wonder how Bertha's been keeping herself."

The Boneman gritted his teeth and urged the skeleton horse onwards. Some worrisome cracks were beginning to appear on the horse's long thigh bones—the first sign that his servant was failing.

"Just a little longer, friend," he whispered, and the horse picked up the pace. The Boneman didn't relish the idea of carrying all of his baggage or the treasures Lucy looted from his own crypt. Besides, the mirror was too cumbersome to lug across the countryside.

Lucy thought he knew where Bertha had gone, but he delighted in keeping his brother in suspense, indicating the paths he should take without enlightening him in regards to the destination. They hid once from a drover and his dogs, watching from within a tall stand of mushrooms as the drover bullied his sheep towards their miserable fodder.

"Look at us, frightened of a bloody shepherd," Lucy chuckled. "Time was I'd have had him peeled and dancing with nothing but a word."

"Be quiet," the Boneman said. If they were discovered, more might come, and he knew he couldn't move fast enough to avoid the birds and bikes in a fevered hunt for a monster.

They made a quiet camp that night, somewhere just north of the boundary between the Overland and the Riverland. The Boneman didn't risk a fire, even though he shivered. At least he was spared the sight of his dinner running into his stomach and through his gizzards. He could not help but peek at the workings of his new body, and for once was grateful to eat in the dark.

"Clever girl!" Lucy exclaimed. His mirror was propped against the skull of the disassembled horse. "She did it! She went and got it!"

"What do you mean?"

"My little pigeon, my mirror friend. She's got the Cruik! A new Rider!"

"What?" the Boneman said. "You didn't destroy the Cruik?"

Lucy just laughed.

"It's evil," the Boneman said sadly. "Those poor fools never knew what they rode under."

"I tell them some pretty lies, and they enlist willingly enough. I never forced anybody to take up the Cruik."

"You were mad to form your little army of monsters, and you're doubly damned for bringing some poor girl into it."

"Turns out there's still a Jesusman." Lucy muttered in the dark glass. "Figured my champion could use a helping hand."

"The Cruik will twist her inside out," the Boneman said, holding the mirror by the edges and wanting to shake it. "We should have buried it underneath a thousand tonnes of stone. It nearly killed you, Lucy!"

"Seems you didn't hear me, Sol," Lucy said. "A Jesusman is out there and free. Even after all the pogroms, everything I did to wipe out that foul tribe, somebody is still bearing *his* mark."

"Let it go," the Boneman sighed. "Hesus is gone. We won, brother. Why even bother with some hold out fanatic?"

"It only takes one," Lucy said bitterly. "I want that bastard dead."

They came to the tangled forests of the Riverland. The old patrol route had been almost obliterated by time and the marching undergrowth. The dead horse plodded onwards, occasionally shedding a sliver of bone. The fractures were getting worse. A wide crack had appeared across the skeleton's nose.

I should let it pass over. This is cruel, the Boneman thought, but he kept the horse skeleton together, urged it onwards even as the sorcery ate away at it. It reminded him in many ways of his favourite horse, a placid beast from the days when the horses bred true. Horse riding had been a pleasant escape from the grinding reality of government. His animal had demanded nothing more than food and kindness.

The native vegetation of the rainforests was alien yet beautiful in its own way. Towering trees grappled overhead strangling each other in the slowest of duels. Small creatures held court in the undergrowth, and the Boneman called out a pair of sleek grass-eaters for his own supper, stilling their hearts with a murmur.

"That could be poisonous," Lucy called out from the glass. "No point carking it over your tucker."

"I'll take the chance," the Boneman said as he filleted out the oil sacs and spurs. None of the beasts they'd brought over from the Before could graze on the native forage, and bush-meat was a dicey proposition at best.

It seemed somehow just that the Now was winning the fight against settlement, pushing away the farms and wiping away the scars of the canals. The Boneman wondered if they'd been right to tamper with this world so much.

It was easier to clear a field for cattle than it was to butcher local stock, and while initially friendly, the Taursi were quick to retaliate when the settlers hunted in their traditional grounds.

When he'd made laws and directed the public works, the man who'd been Sol Papagallo had fallen into expediency more than once. Clear that field. Move on that tribe of Taursi. Kill off any two-headed calves and keep it quiet.

He'd been too eager to force the human way onto this strange new world. The early settlers were fast to break everything that didn't accommodate the ways they'd been relearning, empty-minded farmers with a few tools and no memories from the Crossing.

"We should have done the whole thing differently," the Boneman said mournfully, skewering the creatures on a stick. Soon the flesh was sizzling over hot coals. It gave off the confusing waft of roasted chestnuts.

"Alright, we need to talk about appearances," Lucy said, his image made demonic by the reflection of the cookfire. "We're going to need to lurk about in the river towns and find ourselves a boat. Can't have you walking around looking like someone's dead nanna."

"I've got the wig and the makeup," the Boneman said. "I'll get by."

"No, you bloody well won't," Lucy said. "Look."

A humid rain began to fall, pattering against the glass of the mirror. The Boneman felt the moisture wash down his face and understood what Lucy was saying. His makeup would run in minutes, exposing him as an unnatural freak, unhuman.

And in the Riverland, it rained constantly.

"You're going to need some illusions. Bend the light, trick the eye," Lucy said. "I know it was never your strongest suit, but perhaps I can help."

Lucy's disembodied head thrust against the skin of the mirror, pushing as far out of the Aum as he could manage, and he spoke the words of form and light, named one thing as another. The Boneman felt the faint tickle as the magic washed over his flesh.

He looked down to see his arm covered with skin, perfect down to every mole and hair.

Then the false skin swam, slid off his limbs, became mist and then nothing. Lucy growled in frustration.

"I can't do anything in here," the mirror man moaned. "All I can do is whisper in people's ears and piss around with visions. Okay, watch carefully."

A breath of fog against the glass, and Lucy carefully scratched out a series of marks with an invisible finger. The Boneman recognised the marks for binding, a series of instructions for colour and tone, and, strangely enough, the sigil for iron.

"Now follow this carefully. It's just like doing a dot painting," Lucy said. "Not as quick as the way I'd do it, but you should be able to manage."

The Boneman worked slowly, pausing only once to turn the meat on the spit. Repeating Lucy's words and marks, he slowly painted sorcerous colour onto his fingertips, working downwards until he'd covered all of his hands with an imagined flesh. Using the whore's hand mirror, he worked on his face, slowly daubing in his pores and freckles. Finally, the marks of iron and permanence.

"Why iron?" he asked Lucy, shaky and exhausted. He was still a weak sorcerer, unused to magic after his long sleep.

"Your hands just became a weapon," Lucy said. "Plus, no one will be able to shoot you in the face. I'd recommend doing the same for your groin. You never know."

— 14 —

It took several days to colour in the horse, and the Boneman worked during rest stops for several hours each evening. He disassembled the skeleton at night, and if anyone were to happen on his camp, they would have seen a handsome young man crooning into the severed limbs of some poor animal.

"Are we going to Mawson?" the Boneman said as he worked on each thread of mane. The work was exhausting and particular, and he was beginning to remember why he'd left the illusions to Lucy.

"Too big," Lucy said. "Your little patch-up job isn't perfect, and I'd hate for the bailiffs to pull us up at the dock."

"Too big? Mawson's just a handful of slap shacks around the peat diggings," the Boneman said. "Perfect place for us."

"Brother, you have been asleep for a long time," Lucy laughed. "Trust me, Cape Baun is much safer."

The old Riders' path petered off some days ago, and the Boneman was pleased to emerge from the thick belt of rainforest. He found the going much easier across the abandoned farms, skirting ruined settlements where he'd once cut official ribbons or met with petitioners unable to travel to the Moot.

This far from the Niven, there was nothing to keep people chained to the land, and all they saw were the shacks of loners and outlaws who preyed on the tradeway between Mawson and Slanely. The Boneman quickly crossed the main road, not wanting to test his illusion just yet. They slogged across a boggy marsh. He hated every minute of it.

He spotted the beginnings of a new town set on a rise, a circle of stonework, the shell of a town hall. It had been abandoned as a bad idea, with most of the stonework already carted away by the locals.

"We stop here," the Boneman said, exhausted to his core. The horse was almost complete, but he could not think straight, let alone polish the illusion. He let the skeleton fall with a clatter, a pile of fresh-looking limbs, the brown eyes in its face still gazing on him warmly.

He was just lighting the fire when he heard the distant crack of a rifle with the answering pop of pistols. Lucy insisted on watching, so the Boneman picked up the mirror and sat on top of the half-finished wall.

The sun was setting upon a scene of anarchy. A group of bailiffs were surrounded on the tradeway, an army of highwaymen firing upon them from all sides. A buggy was burning, and birds darted back and forth, scratching at each other like giant roosters.

"Lucky we missed that," Lucy said. "Say what you will of my Riders, they'd have made short work of those scum."

"And then bled the wretches for your damn staff," the Boneman said. "That's not justice."

Lucy merely chuckled, watching intently as the forces of order were butchered. Soon it was dusk, and the burning vehicle lit the night. Figures danced around it, and the distant strains of drunken singing reached their small camp.

"This is the world we have made, brother," the Boneman said, sliding down from the low wall with a groan. His muscles were locked up. He staggered over to their fire, carefully tending it so the flames did not climb too high. He lay down beside it and was asleep in seconds.

He dreamt of that night at Sad Plain, the moment when their little family made common cause against an old friend. Lucy was at the forefront, a changed man hurling unimaginable magics at the foe. An ancient city destroyed just to prove a point, and then the mad chaos as Hesus unleashed his disciples who were twisted from their time in the Greygulf.

John Leicester fell, and climbed into stone, and never came out.

The Cruik was taxing Lucy's considerable willpower, despite the brass demons he'd bound it with. He didn't have the strength to finish Hesus and used the last inch of his life force to push their old friend into the Greygulf and bind him there.

It took the battle at Sad Plain for Sol to finally beg Bertha for help, but she went to Lucy—a final betrayal. Already the Mother of Glass had poisoned her mind, and she crooned wordlessly. She regarded Sol with a vacant stare as she cradled his wounded brother.

The Cruik lay just beyond Lucy's outstretched fingers, and only now did it call to Sol, begged him to pick it up. It promised him the strength to defeat this enemy, to set things right. To fix the damage his brother had done and to undo the effects of his world-shattering pride.

He looked at the powerful construct for a long moment, then took a step towards it. Then he saw the shrivelled body of his brother and the mad gibbering of Bertha. He turned away from the staff, ignored its pleas and threats.

At the end of that terrible day, only Sol stood, alone amongst the dead and fallen, treading through a landscape of shattered glass. He looked up into the terrible face of Turtwurdigan and woke in a cold sweat.

Cape Baun was smaller than the Boneman remembered. The whaling town had once been a bustling place, with ranks of scarred ships offloading their catch. If you wanted to go to the islands, some captains were willing to brave the sharks and eels for the right price.

Now, the whalers were long gone. The only ship in sight was a rotting hulk in dry dock. Small boats dotted the still bay like a scattering of leaves. Fishermen were unwilling to slip beyond Lady Bertha's broad chain. The Boneman smiled when he looked upon her old work; he remembered the day she gave Cape Baun a sliver of safety.

"This year, the sharks took five of my ships, one of them inside the breakwater," Bertha said. He pictured her as the too-serious darling of the Collegia, the rich girl who'd walked away from everything to follow Lucy's venture. "It's not much, but it's better than nothing."

I miss you, the Boneman thought, smiling sadly. It was better to remember her that way, not as the vacant creature from Sad Plain or the unhinged harridan eaten away by the Cruik.

"Sol! Point me at the docks," Lucy said from the horse, stirring the Boneman from his reverie. He unwrapped the frame and panned the mirror to take in the whole town. The Boneman took care to linger on the empty docks and crumbling warehouses that he'd personally written into the town plan, the houses crumbled into ruin and left where they'd fallen. The broken hulks of ships, the hulls stripped for housing and firewood.

No barbarians here. Just economics and despair.

"Well, shit on this," Lucy said. "We need a boat."

"Where is Bertha?" the Boneman asked directly.

"She had a place," Lucy finally admitted, looking towards the sea. "Out there."

"Oh." The Boneman felt the twinge of an old wound, fought the bitterness back. He was surprised by the rawness of this emotion, given what had happened since that old betrayal. The land of his memories was a much different place, where his friends were all alive and whole with honest ambitions as they carved out a new world with their own powers, within their own limitations.

It didn't seem worth chewing over that old injury, given the grind of time and everything that had occurred since Sad Plain. Despite everything, despite his own addictions and shortcomings, Papa Lucy had come through for him in the end and tried to make things right in his own ham-fisted way.

"Chin up, old boy," Lucy said. "You were a good sport then. Be a good sport now."

Half-starved dogs followed their passage through the rotting outskirts of the town, the cheap weatherboard homes were no match for time and the coastal weather. The Boneman led the illusory horse through the rubbish strewn streets, towards the fragment of housing that bore signs of shoddy maintenance, smoke curling from the chimneys. Only the barest crescent of homes remained, twenty or so dwellings facing the dock.

Cape Baun had been a grand proposal, a place from which to launch naval expeditions to search for new lands. The Boneman had put his plans before the Moot, and he'd allowed for a population of up to ten thousand, which was a conservative estimate.

Now there were no stevedores, no captains, no doomed ships loaded with surveyors and settlers. A fishing village huddled inside the corpse of one of the largest settlements in the Now.

The Boneman felt eerie wandering through the outer ruins. Civic buildings had gone to rot, pulled apart for building materials. Parks were overgrown with native scrub, and the streets themselves were buried beneath a few centuries of dirt and neglect.

Sol was surprised how much he mourned the failure of his great plan.

"There, that place looks like a taverna," Lucy piped up. "Quickly now. We've gotta get a boat, even if it's full of leaks."

The thought of Turtwurdigan lent speed to his feet. The Boneman pushed away the feral dogs with a simple mark, sending them whimpering into the ruins. Man, horse, and mirror emerging from the old town surprised the handful of people fixing a net beneath their sagging porch.

If this was Cape Baun's taverna, it was a sorry one, a place of sack windows and outer decking stained with the grease of a thousand fish.

"You've got a horse," one of them said, a lank haired boy with several teeth missing. The fishing folk stood, net forgotten.

"I'm after a boat," the Boneman said nervously. The fishermen ignored him, stepping forward slowly. They hadn't drawn their sharp fish knives yet, but they could be on him in moments.

"The Selector's daughter nicked off with that horse," the boy said, pointing to a wanted poster tacked to the wall, the purple image of a girl. "Big reward."

"That's not true," the Boneman said. "This is my horse."

"Only one horse left in all of the Now, and that's him." An older man grunted. "Bucephalus, the Last True Horse. Where's the girl?"

They stepped forward, but before they could seize him, the Boneman leapt onto the dead horse's back and willed it to run. The skeleton galloped away, and the Boneman clung to its spine as best he could. He felt a pinch as the shifting vertebrae snagged his inner thigh.

The villagers gave chase for a short distance, and one of them threw a stone. When the horse outstripped them, they stopped in the street to stare until they passed from sight.

"You could have told me that all the horses were extinct," the Boneman said furiously.

"I don't take notice of the details," Lucy said from the mirror. "That was always your thing."

The Boneman found the Temple in the ruins of old Cape Baun, one of the first holy sites they had raised to themselves. His portico was still dedicated to Lord Sol the Goodface, the religious "handle" he'd used in the years before the Boneman persona defined his legacy. The sepulchre offered up the bones of many a drowned sailor, unfortunates knifed in the dark, and every kind of death a port town offered.

Lucy laughed with wicked delight as his brother raised the dead, when once he'd scolded Sol for working in the corpse arts. Sol had pursued the career as a way to fund his marriage, dissuaded from Overhaeven studies by Lucy, who'd gone after his fancy with unusual venom. Even then he'd continued gibing and undermining, but this was his standard volume of scorn.

The corpse arts had never been a particular passion for Sol Papagallo. It was mostly a second choice driven by circumstance and discouragement.

I wonder why Lucy pushed me away from Overhaeven studies? the Boneman thought.

Now the Boneman led a shambling group of corpses through the streets. He had reminded the green-tinged bones of how they were connected and how they should move as a body. He'd been respectful as always, gently laying out the corpses for his work.

"I didn't want to wake them," the Boneman said through gritted teeth. "But we need that boat."

"If you do something well, just do it." Lucy chuckled.

Just before dusk, they made their reappearance by the taverna. The Boneman had unravelled the horse's fictitious flesh and rode the crumbling skeleton into view, his own shirt completely unbuttoned to reveal his hideous innards.

The villagers took one look at the walking dead and fled for their lives. The screaming fisherfolk took to their boats and paddled madly for the breakwater. Cape Baun emptied in less than a minute.

"Damn it," the Boneman muttered. "They took all the fishing boats. There's nothing left."

There was a sudden cracking sound, and the horse lurched to one side. The thick femur was split in half and another rib fell. The horse shuddered, barely held together by necromancy.

"Oh, my sweet horse, you poor old thing," he said soothingly and climbed down from the skeleton. "What have I done to you?"

Swiftly removing the mirror and all his belongings, he sang the life out of the dead horse and let it finally fall into bones and dust. With a gesture and a word, he let the former residents of Cape Baun pass back over. The corpses fell as their spirits returned to the Underfog.

"Trust you to let the help leave work early," Lucy mocked.

"You have no sense of gravitas," the Boneman replied. "It's right to treat servants with respect."

"Absolute rubbish. They've chosen their station in life."

"They're not even alive. I don't think your rational egoism argument applies to the undead," said Sol.

"We are the gods of this world and you quibble about these skeletons?"

"Please, just be quiet."

"Are you—you're burying that dead horse? Why?" asked Lucy.

"Because it deserves to be treated well."

"At least use magic to do it. You are a Papagallo and you disgrace the family name whenever you touch a shovel."

Despite Lucy's exasperation, the Boneman took the time to bury the horse in a bare vegetable garden. He laid the skull down on top of the jumbled bones and patted the soil down firmly. He could still see the reflection of the horse as it had been in life: a beautiful beast.

"Are we done here?" Lucy asked.

"I cannot believe you let the horses die out," the Boneman finally said. "You've done a lot of crummy things, but there's a new one for your list."

He sat with the mirror on the dockside watching the sun set across that murderous sea. The Boneman was frustrated that this long journey had come to a dead end.

"I'm going to have to face Turtwurdigan alone," he said. "With an idiot in a mirror for company."

"Don't give up, Sol. We'll steal a boat in Mawson," Lucy said. "It'll have to be a riverboat, but it might make it."

The Boneman was about to remind him of the thirty-foot eels when he caught sight of the shark-scarred hulk, decades removed from the water. He laughed out loud, relieved.

"Our kind hosts did leave us a boat. I can fix it."

"That old wreck? We'd be better off swimming."

The Boneman called back his army of bodies, grumbling and frustrated by their brief rest in the Underfog. He spotted the bloated body of a shark snagged on the outer edge of the breakwater. It took almost a hundred dead pairs of hands to haul the enormous predator over the rocks, but then it was over and simple enough to push the corpse through the water where the world's last necromancer could use it.

It took two full days for the Boneman to repair the whaling ship. He peeled great slabs of flesh and skin from the shark, wedded them to gaps in the hull, and tricked the mouldering flesh into joining with the wood. The bones of the shark helped to shore up the weak spots, and soon the dead townsfolk were hauling the ship out of dry dock and launching the refitted monstrosity.

"Safest boat I've ever sailed on!" the Boneman exulted. Attached in place of the rudder was the dead shark's tail, thrashing around to drive the ship forwards.

"This is just disgusting," Lucy said. "I used to have a fleet of nice boats up at the lake. Good ones, too."

"Beggars can't be choosers," the Boneman said, and with a simple gesture, he dropped Bertha's harbour chain to the ocean floor.

—◄●►—

The shark-ship lurched forward, the great sweep of the rotting tail obeying the Boneman's commands in only the most literal of manners. Spending many moments with his eyes fixed to the scatter of islands before them, Sol did his best to fight off the nausea.

To the far right, he could just make out the fuzz of the delta, an almost permanent miasma where the Niven spilled into the sea. A growing metropolis peered above the mangroves, dominated by a Before-Time skyscraper.

"Mawson got big," he said. It looked to be double the size of Crosspoint and spreading.

The bizarre ship was in the open sea for less than an hour when trouble struck. The Boneman did his best to stop all the leaks, but the boat was incredibly old and the shark skin halfway to rotten. He gave up the bailing bucket and spent the rest of the voyage cranking the Archimedes screw.

Between his efforts to keep the shark-ship afloat and command the thrashing tail, he didn't notice the swarm of eels keeping pace with the ship and trying to decide if it was food or not. Their simple minds went with "food."

The boat began to rock. One of the sea-snakes threw itself at the ship and crunched the deck rail into splinters with foot-long fangs before slipping back into the churning water.

"Ah, the sailing life," Lucy warbled, whistling a jaunty maritime tune.

Using his electric torch to examine the hold, the Boneman spotted a dozen new leaks. As the planks bent underneath the assault of the eels, he abandoned the primitive water pump. Braving the deck, he sat cross-legged by the mast. The ship lurched and began to list. The Boneman watched the water nervously and wondered how long the ship had before it broke apart. Casting out his mind, he searched through the life that surrounded them.

It was a shock to suddenly perceive the scale of life in the ocean. His mind's eye reeled before the inhospitable soup around them, crammed to the brim with enormous monsters. He sensed the eels circling the ship, pummelling the hull, tearing confusedly at the shark flesh.

"Won't work," Lucy said. "Eels are cunning things. Too smart for you or me to possess."

"I don't want an eel," the Boneman said. Frowning with concentration, he found what he was looking for then put the right insinuation into his target's mind. He called it forward, gently, then let the animal's instincts do the rest.

The water around the boat bubbled with movement, with the ink of spilled blood. After many moments, the rocking of the boat ceased and all was quiet.

"What happened? Let me see," Lucy said. A long shadow passed across the surface of his mirror, then another. A forest of pink trunks emerged from the sea, rising above the ship before snatching it up. Chitin-crusted limbs wrapped completely around the ship.

The Boneman met the enormous eye of their saviour, an alien orb set in a wall of interlocking plates. It regarded him dully. He fought off the sudden panic and impressed the creature with the notion of swimming toward the islands before them.

The dripping brush of its mouth was above the waterline now, a broad gash ringed with smaller tentacles that was capable of swallowing the ship whole. He repeated the telepathic instruction, hoping that the sea monster wouldn't be confused by the shark parts of their vessel. He wasn't sure, but he thought this creature preyed on the killer fish.

The ship began to glide through the water, moving sideways now as the sea monster tightened its grip. The hold was almost completely full of water, and big chunks of the ship had washed away, leaving a wooden trail that smaller monsters snapped at.

"Which way?" the Boneman yelled into the mirror as he squinted into the spray. Lucy bobbed around unable to find a point of reference.

"Small island," he said. "Rocky plateau, trees, beautiful sand."

The Boneman tried not to think about what had happened on that *beautiful sand* and did his best to chart the islands by prodding at the monster's simple mind. Once, he caught a glimpse of a large island riddled with rude dwellings and people running inland as the sea monster came within sight of their shores.

There were rocks bare of life and other islets that seemed habitable, but none of them matched Lucy's description. Finally, he saw the island and its distinctive ridge that could only be the hiding place of Lady Bertha.

The colossal sea creature placed the broken ship gently onto that perfect shore and then slipped away, a forest of thick tentacles sinking back beneath the waves.

"That's it. No more seafood for me," Lucy said quietly.

— 15 —

The Boneman clambered awkwardly down a rope with Lucy's mirror lashed to his back. He fell to the sand and moved quickly out of the shadow of the ship. A plank fell, and he flinched. The crustacean had been less than gentle, and the hull was riddled with cracks. The whaler would never sail again.

The beach was littered with broken wood, and some of his supplies began to wash up in the foam. Most of it was waterlogged and useless. A handful of Lucy's treasures glittered in the sunlight, and the mirror man insisted that his brother gather it all, broken or not.

"That's my backgammon set. Look, you remember this, my valedictorian plaque from the Collegia. Quickly now, we're not leaving these for the crabs."

As he worked, the Boneman was conscious of the thick treeline over his shoulder with the almost impenetrable undergrowth. Strange animals gave voice in that rainforest: a burbling hiss like a kettle boiling dry, answered by a rapid clicking from somewhere up in the canopy. Something was on the hunt. An agonised screech, and he felt the tickle in his mind as a small life was snuffed out.

Shading his eyes against the sun, he searched the island for any sign of habitation, any hint of Bertha. From here, the island looked untouched by man, but choked by an alien jungle of multi-coloured trees. The underbrush was dominated by sweating tubers half again as tall as he was.

"Let me see it," Lucy said. The Boneman pointed the mirror on his back towards the jungle.

"Yes, definitely the right place. She's let things go a bit, but we're here. Her beachhouse is round the other side."

"She had a *beachhouse*?" the Boneman said, but Lucy kept his own counsel.

"No, you don't get to ignore this. Tell me about the beachhouse."

"Stop making so much out of ancient history. I brought us here for the right reasons."

"She is my wife."

"Ex-wife."

The Boneman trudged along the ribbon of beach, eventually kicking off his boots and letting his see-through toes sink into the sand. The island was perhaps three miles across, and the plateau overlooked everything. The summit was as straight as a razor.

Finally, he rounded a headland and came upon the crumbling relic of a dock. A handful of shipwrecks were scattered around the calm bay. An old road, nearly reclaimed by the jungle, led into the island's interior.

With an ear to the cacophony of the bush, the Boneman grimaced as he pulled an old revolver out of his belt. He'd found it in a fishing hut in Cape Baun and he didn't know if it would fire or not.

The last time he'd held a firearm was back at the Collegia, a day at the gun range with John Leicester and Hesus. *That was a little over seven hundred years ago*, he calculated. He'd never liked guns and always relied upon his mastery of the magical arts in a tight spot. Now he was the master of nothing but bones and dust. He gripped the pistol gratefully.

The Boneman trod carefully through the gloom, the light swallowed by the canopy, watching everywhere as he advanced along the cracked asphalt. He felt a hundred sets of eyes upon him, meat eaters from species not discovered yet. He pushed away as many of the beasts as he could, but many of the animals shook off his invisible touch and crowded closer. A python curled around a branch overhead but watched him pass with its own alien bemusement, unwilling to stir from the beam of sunlight it had found.

Then the road came into a clearing and the Boneman stopped still, his heart beating rapidly. Even though it was almost completely embraced by the jungle, the large manse nestled into the side of the hill, its crumbled roof flush with the lip of the plateau.

It was a perfect replica of their old house.

"Sol, you might want to move," Lucy said. The Boneman looked behind to see the bulk of a great shape slowly creeping forward, a pair of hungry eyes and the shifting of at least a dozen legs. His weak attempts at repulsing the beast did nothing, so he ran, huffing as the road wound up the steep hill at the island's centre.

Passing the ruins of an outer terrace, he felt the boundary and saw a set of old marks etched into the paving stones. The big animal kept its distance from this invisible fence while it snarled at the Boneman from the depths of the jungle. With shaky hands, he slid the gun back into his waistband and sat for a long moment on the mildewed steps.

The gardens were overgrown now, but he recognised the layout, down to the banks of shattered terrariums and curving gravel walks. He'd taken a turn at amateur sculpting when life in the Moot got too stressful, and he recognised his own efforts at art, blasted and featureless by the passage of time.

This wasn't a replica. Bertha had used the Cruik to bring this building over from the heights of Langenfell, down to the last brick. He'd left with good grace, but this was needless, a twisting of the knife.

"You spiteful bitch," he whispered as he walked into the ruins of his own house.

"Careful now," Lucy said. "I know things got weird for a while there, but don't say anything we all might regret."

"Shut up," the Boneman said with a ragged edge to his voice. "You knew what she did. You've been here!"

He stalked into the atrium, horrified at the sight of his ruined furnishings, the slime encrusted tepidarium, the shattered mosaic floors. The aviary had been torn apart, the great holes in the wire mesh spoke of violence and anger. Everywhere was filth and neglect, pointless vandalism.

It was bad enough that she'd left him. Left him for *Lucy*. This was a new level of heartbreak though. This had been a home built with love, back when they were young and brave. Then she had stolen it for lust and hidden the history of their marriage on this island while he'd been broken and grieving.

She could have built any structure with the power of the Cruik, but she had chosen to live in this shell of their broken love.

He searched every wing of the manse, but the building was empty and every sign indicated a long abandonment. It had been many years since Bertha raged through these halls, a vibrant woman reduced to an animal shell. Finally, the Boneman sat down in the ruin of his solar, gaining some satisfaction in laying Lucy's mirror face down on the floor.

"Very funny," his brother mumbled.

He cast out his mind once more, hoping to find a sign of her, any clue to her whereabouts. He felt the presence of the animals in the nearby jungle held at bay by the house's enchanted perimeter, but there was something else. He turned his attentions downwards where he felt the faintest glimmer of life.

Excited, he gathered up the mirror and strapped it to his back. Searching through the vaults and basements, he found the opening in a far corner of the ruined wine cellar, earth and paving stones scattered as if by giant mice. A waist-high tunnel curved downwards into the hill.

The Boneman switched on the electric torch and began to crawl. In one place where the tunnel was choked with tree roots, he spent many uncomfortable minutes forcing his way through them. Rocks dug into his ribs as he blunted his knife on the woody tendrils.

Soon the tunnel emerged into a larger chamber where the walls and floor were fused glass. The Boneman slid out of the grimy hole and gazed around with wonder at the fluted ceiling, daylight and fresh air entering the cave from a series of well-placed skylights.

"Taursi," he said, admiring the tall glass spires. Above his head spread an elaborate structure that was paper-thin in places. He recognised the whorls of memory-glass and felt the presence of generation upon generation of alien thought captured in the glass. A cathedral, a library, and a museum all in one. The art of casting this glass had been lost to the natives long before the settlers had arrived, and a complete installation was rare indeed.

Much could be learnt here, he realised, touching the nearest spire. It glowed a rose-pink under his hand, and he felt the gibbering of its captive dead, eager to rush forward with their teachings. The Taursi spirits had difficulty meshing with his mind, and he lifted his hand quickly. His head was already twinging with pain. The voices fell into sullen silence, denied the chance to impart their wisdom.

Once more the Boneman thought of Sad Plain and the guilt at what had been lost. Of what they had done. Some of the blame fell on Hesus, but the Boneman was just as culpable, following Papa Lucy into his madness. Into vengeance.

"Well, I didn't know this stuff was down here," Lucy said.

Then the creatures rushed in. The Boneman heard the shrieking, saw the pasty white of their flesh. Mad Millies, Bertha's foot soldiers. Where once they had been the stern vanguard of the

Family force, here they had fallen into the same madness as their mistress. Their tunics were in rags, and the stink was incredible.

"Back!" he shouted as one hissed in his face, darting forward with foul claws. Panicked, he squeezed the trigger. The revolver cracked once, punching a hole into the woman's chest.

The gunshot reverberated against the crystals and glass of the ceiling, which emitted a painful high pitch. The rest of the Millies scattered, clutching their ears as they stole away to their hidey-holes and crevices. Soon, the chamber was empty.

"I'm sorry," the Boneman said to the dying Millie, who looked up at him with confusion and perhaps a crumb of recognition. The Cruik had touched all of Bertha's women, granting life far beyond their years. But one look at the woman's dead animal stare proved to the Boneman that he'd always been right.

The cost was far too high.

As the woman's spirit passed into the Underfog, he felt the wind in that holy cavern move and heard the heavy tread behind him. The Boneman turned to see an enormous creature bearing down on him. It was eight feet of ropy muscle, a body wreathed in a foul mat of hair, eyes that swam with madness and a primal fury.

His gun wavered. The Boneman held his fire.

Bertha fell upon him like a bear. She knocked him down and slammed his head into the glassy floor. His vision swam with stars as she tore at his flesh, screeching like a banshee.

The Boneman felt the mirror crack underneath him and heard Lucy cursing frantically. Still he did not fire. But when that hateful face descended towards his, its rotten teeth gnashing, he raised his pistol butt and struck Bertha square in the temple. She fell across him, dazed. He pushed her aside then straddled her sour-smelling body and hammered at her face with the pistol butt, sending her into unconsciousness.

Breathing heavily, the Boneman looked down at what was left of his wife and shivered.

He tore his shirt into strips and used them to hog tie Bertha, hand and foot. She slumped across the floor where she'd fallen, a bruise spreading purple across half of her face.

"She always thought you had a temper," Lucy said. His mirror was cracked in three places, but the large shards still sat within the frame. Smaller images of his face floated in each piece.

"Be quiet," the Boneman said. He watched Bertha closely, shocked by her appearance. The Cruik's influence lingered, expanding her over the centuries into a gangling beast with hands a twist of claws and feet like big thorny slabs. At some stage she must have dispensed with clothes altogether, and only the mat of hair gave her any modesty, a wild tangle growing untended for hundreds of years.

He remembered the young girl with the quick mind, the slender dancer, and he wanted to weep. Despite everything, despite the betrayals and the cruel grindstone of time, the man called Sol still held a sliver of love in his heart.

He still remembered seeing them together in the Moot, Lucy and Bertha, as she appeared in public carrying the Cruik on his behalf. When she'd met Sol's eyes, there was nothing in them but lust and the pinched look of an addict.

Was it the Cruik that broke our marriage? Was she tempted by that power or did it happen afterwards?

When Lucy had first appeared with the staff, Bertha had expressed the same concerns Sol did. It was too powerful, barely in Lucy's control, sinister in its origins. A few years later, she was clutching to both the staff and the fool who claimed it as his own.

"We are perfect," Bertha had told John Leicester and Hesus, glassy-eyed and smiling.

The giant Bertha on the floor stirred, howling in pain and confusion. She strained against her bonds, her face knotted with effort. But the Boneman had soaked his makeshift ropes in the cave's spring, and even with her unnatural strength, the wet fibres proved impossible to rip.

Finally, she gave up and stared at him in sullen defeat, grinding at her teeth and muttering. The Boneman remembered her sorceries. She'd been his equal in power and in some areas his master. There was a time when a simple rope would never have bound the Lady Bertha.

He regretted the loss of his own power, even though he'd never been much of a healer. It might have taken him extra effort, but he'd have been able to lead her back to sanity past the darkness and fog in her mind.

Raising a hand to rest on her forehead, he retreated when she snapped her teeth at him, snarling like a cornered dog. It broke his heart to see what she'd become, and he couldn't feel much anger towards her. The theft of his house was a small injury now, a punk move from a forgotten life.

"Look at us," he said to Lucy. "Three monsters in a cave. What am I meant to do now?"

"Fix Bertha's mind. Get me out of this mirror. Kill Turtwurdigan. Really, Sol, you make too much of your problems."

"For once, Lucy, you're actually right," the Boneman said.

Leaving the mirror man alone with his monstrous wife, he took a walk to gather his thoughts and contemplate his next move. The Boneman explored the entire complex, and not once did he need his electric torch. The Taursi had honeycombed the plateau with caves and galleries, carefully channelling in light and air through glass-lined tubes, in places buffed to a mirror shine.

Did she realise exactly where she was planting her love-nest? he wondered, passing through a cave of glowing spires of neat ranks of glass taller than he was. They were the same as the lonely pillars found throughout the land, but these examples were preserved better and untouched by weather and the elements. They had been shaped into the vaguest suggestion of a hominid form, a trunk of crystal with the nubs of limbs and the bob of a head.

A breath of wind passed through from somewhere below. The fluting wind pipes gave a faint musical note or something like a distant set of whispers.

As the Boneman travelled through the abandoned structure, he heard the sounds of movement and felt the presence of the Mad Millies as they followed him. Perhaps twenty of them remained, the smallest fragment of Bertha's terrifying army, once an immortal force to rival the Riders of Cruik.

They made no move to approach him. Perhaps they were scared of his gun or of the way he had defeated their mistress. Smiling at the timidity of Bertha's creatures, he continued his search. He was elated to unearth a cache of star-glass and a handful of spearheads. The hafts of the spears had long since rotted away, and he understood that this temple was incredibly old. It had stood on this island long before the time of people.

Again, a long mournful note, and something like distant muttering. The sound sent a shiver along the Boneman's arms, and he headed toward it, going deep into the bowels of the mesa.

Following a wide gallery inlaid with star-glass, he came to a tall set of double doors, twin panes of smoky glass that were about thirty feet in height. The Taursi had no written language, nothing even approaching pictograms, but the doors were engraved with many strange images, eye-twisting shapes that were incomprehensible, a continuous arc of something that might have been writing.

Overhaeven marks. No one had been able to interpret the tongue, and most serious scholars thought the occasional relic to be a hoax or the doings of some lost tribe. Only Hesus and a handful of his colleagues were game enough to suggest the obvious: that these were the leavings of aliens, of gods.

One of the repeated themes in this frieze was the depiction of an object that might have been the Cruik, had it been a twisting serpent with a thousand feet. It did battle with a rank of terrifying beings, each one a cloud of hands and eyes. Then it hid from these foes and finally slid into a hole, defeated. Words and curses followed it into infamy or perhaps exile.

Thin lattice-work peppered the glass doors, clever whistles and flutes that caught the wind. This was the source of the strange sound, and this close, it was a cacophony. The Boneman looked on the mad scene and knew that this door was something beyond even Taursi hands, an artefact of true alien beauty.

"Who made this?" he whispered.

He felt Bertha's ragged servants hesitate and fall back. Whatever was on the other side of this doorway terrified them.

The Boneman laid one hand on that perfectly smooth glass and pushed. The door swung open silently, effortlessly, and he stepped through the gap. He was in a cathedral of stone and glass, immense in size. Crosspoint would have fit into this single chamber with room to spare. From the ceiling far above, countless glass stalactites dangled, humming with a resonance that made his teeth ache. The Boneman stood on a slender crystal bridge. Warm winds buffeted him from below. When he chanced a look over the side, vertigo sent him scrabbling backwards.

Honeycomb fluting ran down as far as he could see, and further still. If he fell from this bridge, he might never stop falling, not until he reached the hot core of this world.

The footbridge terminated at an island of sorts, a platform supported on that flimsy lattice. The path was barely wide enough for two people to stand abreast. He shuffled forward, resisting the urge to drop to his knees and crawl.

His hands dripped with sweat as he had images of skidding off into that terrifying drop. Slowly, he edged forward, and with his heart pounding, he climbed over the lip and stood on the island at the temple's heart.

A pair of crystalline Taursi stood as an honour guard with their spears crossing overhead. Passing between them, the Boneman shivered. The spiny creatures had transformed into glass; these were not carvings. The vaguest suggestion of their innards could still be seen, and the outline of their bones slowly melted away. There was just enough gristle and meat for him to glean the echoes of these warriors' lives, and what he saw was nonsensical. They had lived a mixture of a physical life and as abstracts, those rarely glimpsed symbols the Collegia had observed gyrating around in the Overhaeven.

The Taursi are from the Overhaeven?

The glass-bound Taursi glowed gently with captured sunlight. Suddenly, the fallen spires littered across the Now made a lot of sense.

Is this what awaits me? he wondered, glancing down at his own bones, wondering if they too would fade.

In the centre of the island stood a quartz hoop, a semi-circle almost twenty feet in diameter. It was flanked by the ruins of similar stone bands, structures that had shattered long ago, leaving only jags and jumbled stone to show where they had once stood.

In the middle of that surviving frame was an image like a painting that was crystal clear. Examining every side of this structure, the Boneman saw nothing but space, and from the far side, it was simply a hoop of empty stone that framed the bridge and the doors.

His heart quickened as he stepped around to stand in front of the stone band. His hand passed through the world veil with no resistance. A portal, then, a doorway that led through to a landscape of mercury and silver. The winding road of shadow led away on the far side.

The Boneman looked into the Greygulf, and wept with joy.

16

Well, I'm glad you've given up on all that Overhaeven stuff," Lucy said, fixing Sol's tie. "No future in studying it. Certainly no money."

This was the closest Lucy ever came to praising his new career as a necromancer. Sol suffered his brother's last-minute adjustments with good grace, knowing that Lucy was just as nervous as he was. Once more, he tried to fight down Sol's errant cowlick with the hair gel, but he soon gave it up as a lost cause.

"You must be hung like a rogue elephant," Lucy said. "Damned if I know what that girl sees in you."

"Me neither," Sol admitted with a grin. The brothers waited in the empty registry. The celebrant quietly asked where all the guests were, and Lucy deftly changed the subject. Sol spent a quiet moment enjoying the view of the world below, the magnificence of the Collegia's orbit taking his mind away from the butterflies in his stomach.

"She's here," Lucy whispered, and he turned to see Baertha in a simple white dress, smiling shyly through her veil. John Leicester held her arm, grinning broadly as he led her down the aisle. *A true friend, to stand in at such a time.* The celebrant fumbled with the music controls, and a subdued bridal theme preceded their walk to the front dais.

John gave Baertha to Sol, with hearty handshakes all round. Blood might have been thicker than water, but her entire family had condemned this wedding. It was good friends today or it was nothing.

"You look beautiful," Sol said tenderly, and Baertha sniffed back a tear as she clutched his arm. The celebrant stopped mid-ceremony to check on her welfare, but she waved away his concern and insisted he continue.

At the end of that brief rite, Sol Papagallo and Baertha Hann were husband and wife. He felt shabby in his rented clothes, embarrassed that he could not afford the wedding that Baertha deserved, but her sunbeam smile melted these concerns away.

The Hanns were an influential family, captains of industry and long-time patrons of the Collegia. None of the invited guests had come to the wedding, out of prudence if nothing else. Sol was sad for his new wife, but understood this. Still, it pleased him to see one man lingering in the back row, openly defying the boycott.

"It's so good to see you," Sol said, embracing his old professor and one of his dearest friends.

"Wouldn't have missed it for the world," Hesus said.

The Boneman found a way to bring Bertha back, a sorcery known only to the dead Taursi. It felt like the memory-glass was twisting his mind to the breaking point, but he persevered. He gleaned the symbols, and the words that he needed were a guttural sound that felt wrong when pronounced by his human tongue.

It was Turtwurdigan who had struck Bertha mindless, so it was somehow fitting that these obedient spirits offered up the key to her ailment. The memory-glass served any who called upon it, even though the Boneman was technically an enemy.

He droned the words, contorting his hands into positions that human hands weren't meant to assume. Bertha lay twisting and groaning in the spot where she'd been felled, surrounded by a circle of star-glass, the spearheads placed at the cardinal points.

The spell was taxing him to the limit, but somehow he found the power moving through him, bypassing his burnt-out wiring, following some radical new pathway. He'd never known the Taursi to exhibit signs of sorcery. Using their method felt like stepping back into journeyman shoes, wrestling with a power that he barely understood.

Turtwurdigan had pillaged Bertha's mind in the crudest of ways, a battlefield sorcery that was more strength than subtlety. Now that the Boneman had the means to survey the damage, it was quite easy to see just what had been done to her at Sad Plain.

Her scarred frontal lobes were a map to the other Realms, and it was not difficult to track down her errant mind. Parts of her ego and superego were still floating around in the Aum, while the greater part of her subconscious had been scattered in the Underfog, her thoughts dancing with the demons and ghosts. Much of her essence had passed over death's final shore, leaving great holes in her mind. These parts were lost forever, and the Boneman had to work around these gaps, clumsily stitching everything back together.

When clarity returned to her eyes, the Boneman was there to see it. Shaking, he fell to his knees, and the tenuous thread of the magic slipped away from him. He felt hollow.

"Sol," she said and then slipped into shock, all other words failing her.

Bertha lay in catatonia for days, breathing shallowly, staring up at some point in the ceiling. She had taken water, but any food he gave her lay in her mouth like a foreign idea. He gave up for fear of choking her.

Rummaging through the ruin of his house, he gathered a stack of mouldering rugs and blankets and a rusty pair of scissors. Once he had sharpened the scissors on a stone, he snipped away at her hair. He was forced to cut down almost to her scalp. She'd worn her bridal braids to the very end, even as she stood by Lucy's side on Sad Plain. Bertha had been proud of her hair, and it felt almost criminal to shear away her womanhood like this.

Her mane was riddled with spider nests, tangles of captured food and waste, and centuries of neglect. It all had to go. The Boneman took an armload of the clippings to the garden and burnt them. He retreated from the stink.

She was too heavy for him to lift, so he bathed her on the cave floor, using rags and an ancient bar of soap to sponge away the filth. Once, he had longed to touch her just one more time, to relive the early days when their arguments could be eased that way, hard words giving way to love and laughter.

Now, he had his wish, for all the good it did any of them. He scrubbed away the grime, washed the cobwebs and mud from her sour skin. Bertha's blank face was a coat of crusts and scabs. It took an hour to clean the gunk out of her eyes, and her ears were another nightmare of wax and infestation. The bruises he'd landed on her were purple and black, and one of her eyes was puffy, almost completely shut.

His blades were useless when he tried to pare back the yellowed talons on her hands and feet that had grown too thick to trim.

Something that might have been a sacrificial vessel served as his wash bucket, and he emptied the glass bowl several times. Each load of spring water turned black within minutes.

When he'd finished, she lay on the old rug, skin scrubbed pink. The Cruik had robbed Bertha of her petite dancer's frame, twisting her into something less than a person. Her limbs were out of proportion, as if she'd been turned on a rack, and her face was pinched and long. The curves he'd mooned over in their Collegia days were almost erased, replaced by slabs of hard muscle, a sleek form that reminded him more of a greyhound than the woman he'd married.

The Boneman's amateur hair cut gave emphasis to her pointed skull. He swallowed, confronted with the depth of the change and her unwilling departure from humanity.

"Your old lady really let herself go, Sol." Lucy laughed. The Boneman resisted the urge to kick the mirror, covering it with the filthy washcloth instead.

He turned to see Bertha regarding him, half-raised on one elbow. She shivered and drew an old blanket over her nudity.

"How long?" she asked in a croaky voice.

"A long time," he said. His mind raced. There had been a million things he'd wanted to say to her. It felt like a hundred lifetimes ago. Accusations, pleas for reconciliation, words of apology.

Here, at the end of all things, he couldn't think of a single thing to say to her.

"You found me," she whispered. "You came."

He nodded and knelt down by her side. He patted her shoulder awkwardly, but held back, unsure if he should hold her or if he could even stomach any intimacy with this monster.

"Come closer," she said. "Let me see your face."

He leaned down until he was close to her broad mouth, and she raised her claws to his cheeks and his nose.

"Not this. Your real face."

She pinched her claws tightly and pulled, whispering gently as she snagged the sorcerous skin and yanked it like a thread. The illusion unravelled, revealing his skull and the visible tangle of his vertebrae and jawbone.

Bertha undid his cloak and pushed the fabric aside, exposing the ribcage, the shivering organs, and everything that was his second body.

"Look at us," she said, wheezing and sobbing, somewhere between laughter and tears. "Look at what we are now."

Lady Bertha and the Boneman stood in the crystal room looking into the portal. Something was also blocking her access to the world veil, and she could not open a far-door. This was their only way off the island.

In her fugue state, she'd kept a little of her sorcery, but the relevant mind-muscles had atrophied from centuries of disuse. The best she could manage was to craft a crude dress using her magic to break the jungle plants down into hemp. She wrapped the cloth around her like a sheath of coarse felt, holding everything in place with a weak mark of binding.

If they found trouble in the Greygulf, magic would be no help. The Boneman checked the bullets in the gun. He studied Bertha's impressive new frame and felt some comfort when he considered her claws and remembered the ease with which she'd thrown him across the room.

"We go quickly, in and back again," he said, gesturing to the portal. "Hesus might be in there watching for us."

"Where is John Leicester?" Bertha asked. "We could use his guns and his soldier-magic."

"John went over, after the battle. He's with Hesus now."

"Oh."

Lucy protested as they brought his mirror close to the portal. He'd been remarkably quiet since the return of Bertha, a rare moment of wisdom given the history between them all. Bad blood held in check by the gravity of their situation.

He'd be mad to say one word to her, the Boneman thought. *With her temper, she might stamp his mirror into dust.*

As peaceful as it was, it was very awkward. Bertha was pensive, perhaps due to the return of her memories. The reunion of these sorcerers had been a long time coming, and now they were acting like strangers.

If we start remembering we're family, it's going to end in blood.

"Leave me here," Lucy begged, his three images dancing around in the broken mirror. "If you bring the Aum into the Greygulf, this whole thing will shatter into powder. I'll be done for."

"Your prison is just a window, not the Aum itself," the Boneman said. "C'mon Lucy, you taught me that. You'll be fine."

Bertha and Sol stepped through the portal, cradling the mirror between them. A sensation ran across the Boneman's face like walking through a wall of still water, and then they stood in the Greygulf, their feet upon a cracked and abandoned shadow road.

"What happened here?" Bertha whispered.

Fires burned across that nitrate geography, fat columns of smoke punctuating the skyline. A distant bustle of figures lingered around a tear in the world veil, their shouts and screeching cries faint in the distance.

Sol and Bertha travelled the shadow road for many long minutes taking in the desolation around them. The last time the Boneman had visited, the Crossing was in full swing, an orderly progression of goods shifting over from Before to Now.

This time the industry of Hesus and his followers had given way to something else. Instead of the dangerous wilderness they'd braved in the Crossing, the Greygulf was a desolate wasteland, a land of slag pits and ashes.

"They've picked everything clean," he said.

The Boneman heard a sound nearby, a snuffling far beneath them. Laying down by the lip of the shadow road, the Boneman inched forward to peer over the side and down to the silver ground.

What was left of a man shuffled forward, a great bulk of white flesh almost the size of an elephant. Impossibly long arms stretched through the world veil, and the other ends could be faintly seen dragging through some forsaken Prime Realm.

"It's fishing," Bertha said. They watched in horror as it plucked out a cow and fed the animal into the broad fold of its mouth. The Boneman remembered the disciples of Hesus, twisted from their frequent work in the Greygulf, and realised he was looking at the end result.

He saw crude rips throughout the world veil where the misshapen figures plundered the other worlds. Lucy's noble venture, the escape and the taming of this world between worlds, all had come unstuck. Now the custodians were the monsters, and the Boneman felt the thinness of the world veil, the damage caused by all the looting.

Above the old terminus of Neville, a boil pulsated in the magnesium sky, a sore that threatened to burst. Whatever realm lay on the far side, it was forcing its way through the weakened world veil and into the Now. A violent and permanent connection would soon be joining two of the Realms, creating a gateway from one world to another.

He made note of the location, as did Lucy.

"Let's get out of here," the Boneman said with a shudder. "Quickly now."

They crept along the shadow road making for the safety of the portal. The glass in Lucy's mirror began to bulge and struggled to rise from the frame to break free.

"It's Hesus!" Lucy said, a touch of hysteria in his voice. "He comes!"

Husband and wife stumbled back into the Now, almost dropping the mirror in their haste. Nothing followed them through, but on the other side of the portal was a great shadow with no observable source. It flickered across the silver hills testing the old shadow road, then hunted elsewhere when it lost the trail.

It was the outline of a human hand, enormous in proportion and moving with speed and grace, a vast squid of shadow. Just when the Boneman thought they were safe, the creature reappeared, rushing at them, slamming into the portal. In the split second before the impact, the Boneman caught a glimpse of a ragged hole in the centre of that palm, and a white legend beneath this. It read "BEFORE" in letters taller than a man.

The shadow hand could not pass through, but the stone hoop snapped in half. The image of the Greygulf winked out and vanished altogether.

Hesus had seen them, and set his first attack against the Family the next day. Something scared the Mad Millies out of their rude nests and hiding places, and as a single gibbering force they burst into that vast chamber of glass. Every last woman leapt into the gleaming abyss at a full run. The Boneman felt the moment that their miserable lives were snuffed out, bones breaking as they bounced from the crystal spans, plummeting into the depths of the earth.

They were scared of this room, he thought to himself, looking over the edge. *What called them in? What made them do that?*

He knew the answer.

The second attack came in the Boneman's old laboratory, now cleared of detritus. On a bench lay Lucy's new body, a rough replica of clay that was fortified with animal bones and looted Taursi glass. They'd only been able to find the skull of some jungle cat, but it would have to serve.

They were going to free Papa Lucy from the mirror by plucking his essence out of the Aum.

The Boneman was attempting another form of Taursi magic gathered from the memory-glass in the temple below the house.

The long-dead Taursi magicians had not crafted a loan body since time unknown, but their spirits still knew the art.

It was exhausting work learning the alien magic on the fly. This was their third attempt at a receptacle for Lucy's spirit. The remnants of the last two bodies were swept into a corner, a mixture of clay shards and burnt flesh.

Bertha was trying to gently pry out the broken mirror shards with some old tweezers, her misshapen hands causing more frustration than success.

"Let me do that for you," the Boneman said.

"I was once *your* teacher! Do you think me so useless?"

"That's not what I meant. Your hands—we just need to be very careful with that mirror."

"Yeah, watch those dirty great paws," Lucy chimed in.

"Shut up! Sol, if we had any sense we'd drop this bastard into the pit."

"We need him, Bertha! We are all in great danger!"

"Sol—" Bertha began, and then the mirror suddenly shattered, a cloud of slivers erupting from the frame and up into her face. Bertha staggered away from the bench, bloodied and gasping.

"I saw him, I saw," she babbled. He set to work with the tweezers picking the sharp glass out of her face and hands. Thankfully none of the glass was lodged in her eyes.

"What did you see?"

"In the mirror, it was the hand. Hesus! He got Lucy, and then he saw me. He came for me!"

The skeleton man held the twisted woman for a long moment, and they cried together. They were broken by time, misshapen and lost, and now an old enemy had taken Lucy. They were no longer Baertha and Sol and they were somewhere far beyond love, but grief took them in readily enough.

Mustering his courage, the Boneman knelt down and gathered up the pieces of Lucy's mirror. He felt old then, defeated. *If Lucy can fall, we're all finished. Turtwurdigan wins.*

We'll never leave this island.

Then, he saw it. A piece of mirror no bigger than his thumb, a sliver from the top corner. Within it, turning and dazed, was the battered face of Papa Lucy.

"He lives," he said, astonished. "Lucy's alive!"

Jarred out of her sorrow, Bertha took the shard and snapped it in half with her strong hands. She slid the two shards into the clay face, in place of the eyes, and drew the mud down, sealing them in under a crude pair of eyelids.

The next part of the procedure was taxing, an old blood rite designed for a different species. Using his knife, Sol pressed marks into every inch of the mud form, a bird-claw scatter that resembled the marks from the glass doors. Overhaeven marks, three symbols carved in a repeated pattern. He slavishly printed this into every inch of the mud body, not understanding the meaning of what he wrote.

Bertha smeared her own blood all over the clay, rubbing her opened wrist up and down the limbs, then soaking the face until crimson pools forming over the false eyes. The Boneman droned on, head thrumming, Taursi words falling from his tongue with difficulty.

The clay grew warm and then hot. The trail of Bertha's blood sizzled. The dummy's damp flesh had dried out within minutes. Deep cracks ran all over the torso and up and down the limbs. They brought out new clay and water to work it, with more blood to maintain the sorcery. The strange marks needed constant attention because the pattern was frequently interrupted by the sluice of clay and blood. Even their sweat obliterated the occasional sigil.

They worked for days, lighting fires to work through the night. Bertha learnt enough of the rite to give her husband a rest. The Boneman took turns slashing his skin to sprinkle his own strange life fluids onto the loan body.

He pressed on through the doubt and exhaustion. Would the magic fail? Would it kill them all? Would a loan body made to Taursi design reject the essence of a human?

Their stock of fresh water was running low, and he didn't know if he could leave Bertha for long enough to fetch more. She teetered weakly over Lucy's intended body, droning on and digging her claws into the clay belly, hoping for some reaction.

The Boneman soaked a cloth in the bottom of their water pail and ran it across the crumbling clay on the carved man's face. He worked at the facial features, kneading the nose into shape. He felt a twitching underneath his hands. Something moved under that layer of clay.

"The knife! Quick!"

Working delicately, he slid the blade into the corner of one eye and drew the steel across. The lids separated then blinked. Beneath them lay a perfectly formed eye. It swivelled about, staring, its iris shrinking from the streaming sunlight.

"It worked, Bertha," the Boneman cried. He freed the other eye, opened the clay nostrils and the plain slit of the mouth. Papa Lucy took a breath, and then another.

17

Hard days are coming," Lucy said to the others. "People don't believe us, and they're all going to die. So forget them."

The five sorcerers held counsel in a rented room, down on the planet's surface. Baertha's family had chivvied and driven them out of the Collegia, a concerted campaign backed by all of their funds and influence. The Hanns threatened to cut off many endowments and scholarships and threatened the High Council with political embarrassment and legal injunctions. They even found a way to end the tenures of Hesus and John Leicester out of nothing but spite.

"It is not fair what my family has done to you!" Baertha protested. "If you were up at the Collegia, you could get someone to listen to our proposal."

"We lost that battle," John said. "We're fighting a bigger war anyway."

The Papagallo brothers had given up on fighting the might of the Hanns. A newer problem had arisen, nothing less than the world ending. Neither science nor sorcery had the answer. Nothing had the power to avert the inevitable—apocalypse, the imminent extinction of humanity. And only a handful of days remained to address it.

Worldwide, the power stations were overheating and could not be shutdown. Every street corner had one, a golden glass tower that powered everything from homes to transport. The larger stations powered industries and kept orbiting sky-cities like the Collegia from crashing down to earth.

These stations gathered magical energy from the Overhaeven, that misunderstood and distant realm. For centuries it had been a safe power source that freed up the world to pursue arts, culture, and sorcery. Now, it was their doom, glowing merrily across the globe.

Every attempt to tamper with the power network was speeding up the meltdown. There were no optimistic predictions, and as near as anyone could calculate, it would melt the entire planet's mantle into slag. No survivors.

Sol had seen Lucy spending hours at the power stations around the city, face pressed against the golden glass, pouring his own magic into that stored within each station. Whatever he tried to do didn't work, and he'd already pivoted to another plan.

While billions wasted their final hours watching for the first signs of the end, these five outcasts worked around the clock. Lucy had stumbled across the solution—one that the Collegia was ignoring—even in those last panicked days. A great exodus. A crossing.

He'd found humanity a new home.

"I have my concerns," Hesus said. "We don't know enough about the Greygulf to cross it safely."

"Yes, it will be brutal," Lucy said, a kind hand on Hesus's shoulder. "Perhaps deadly. I'm hoping your new recruits will help the people cross safely."

"Don't forget the sheep," Sol said. "Cattle, horses, dogs, pigs, chickens. We need a viable livestock population."

"Ever the practical one, my brother. Perhaps you could raise some of the dead to become our farmhands," Lucy said. He was met with laughter from the others. Sol took it in good nature. His was a working man's industry after all.

"So Lucy, how did you find this place?" Baertha asked.

"Luck, really. The other Realm is lining up with ours, briefly. It can support life. The rest is up to us."

"About that. The two worlds don't quite mesh up," John Leicester said, aligning two sheets of tracing paper. "I've sent through probes, but they don't all match. See, the patterns are all wrong."

A clear map of their present continent showed the topography and the locations of towns and cities. The other map was bare, with only the hint of a coastline, a mountain range, the tentative sketchings of a watercourse. The world veil was thick, and details were hard to come by.

Five probes were sent through the Greygulf, but the results were scattered. The destination points came out as a tangle in the destination world.

"There's no point in doing this, not if people will starve in the wilderness." Lucy thundered. "We need machines, food, resources. I don't care how the goods come over, but find a way."

"It's going to be hard to bring things over once we make the crossing," John admitted. "But I've found a way to locate population centres and make it easier to bleed the items through."

He dumped a handful of photos on the maps, several shots of war memorials, obelisks, stone plinths, and slouch-hatted warriors in stone and bronze, holding eternal vigil.

"One in every town," the soldier mage said with a smile. "I've got my people out there now marking as many of these as they can get to. Get a fix on one of these statues from the other world, and you've hit paydirt. Then, it's just a matter of reeling everything in."

He mimed the action of a fishing rod frantically bringing in the big one. The sorcerers chuckled.

"Lest we forget," Baertha said with the flash of a smile, putting aside the photos. They quickly moved onto other matters. The logistics of this venture were staggering. There was no time to waste on pleasantries, not when millions of lives were at stake.

Papa Lucy looked like he'd been baked in a kiln. Steam rose out through the cracks in his casing of mud. Working frantically, Lady Bertha and the Boneman chiselled him loose and peeled away chunks of earth.

Lucy shook, bouncing on the bench like a landed fish. His new skin was burnt in places, angry marks that mirrored the etchings from the broken mud case. As the Boneman shook his brother by the shoulders and called out his name, the eye-twisting sigils began to fade, leaving him with the fresh skin of a newborn.

Bertha dashed the last of their water across Lucy's face and he sat bolt upright, gasping, staring at nothing. They wrapped him in rags, massaged his perfect limbs, and slowly brought him out of the shock.

The second birth of Papa Lucy was a success.

He didn't say anything that first day, but he took their water and food willingly and stood when he had the strength. He tested the new body by walking all over the ruined house and the temple beneath, his young man's legs managing all of the stairs with no effort.

The Boneman looked upon his brother and felt the old jealousies returning, the feeling that Papa Lucy led a charmed life. In his new body, Lucy could have passed for twenty, a man in the first flush of his youth. His face was young, unlined, the same handsome features that dropped countless knickers in his salad days.

The Boneman turned to see Bertha contemplating Lucy's new body, her own monstrous face unreadable.

"It's just not fair," she finally said, looking down at her twisted hands. Sol patted her taloned paws with his own monstrous hand then watched as she wrapped her fat fingers around the visible interplay of his small bones.

"I'm sorry, Sol," she said. They watched from a distance as Papa Lucy attempted calisthenics in the garden, nude and grinning.

"I've waited hundreds of years to hear you say that," the Boneman said, and smiled his sad skeleton smile.

"I could blame the Cruik, blame you—hell, I could even blame him," she said, nodding towards the laughing sorcerer. "But it was me. I was always in here, even when things went crazy, when—when it happened. I did it."

"It's okay," the Boneman said. "It doesn't matter anymore."

They sat in a comfortable silence and kept a peaceful vigil on the front stoop of their first house. If the Boneman kept his eyes closed, he found that pretending came a lot easier, the fantasy that they were still young, a beautiful couple with nothing but potential and promise ahead of them.

Then he opened his eyes to realise they were two monsters huddled in a ruin with their marriage as dead as the old world. And they remained in the service of the greatest monster of all.

Later, Lucy joined their simple dinner at the newly built table with a smile. He'd been gone for hours, wandering somewhere beyond his brother's sorcerous gaze. He offered no explanation as to his whereabouts.

"Here, try this," the Boneman said, knowing better than to ask his brother anything when he had that look in his eye. Lucy picked at a plate of native greens, boiled and pulped into something approaching food, dosed with as much salt as they could find in the storerooms. It tasted nasty, but it wasn't poisonous.

The Boneman had learnt some new tricks from the memory-glass and had used them to join fallen branches into furnishings. He had moulded the separate pieces together into a new whole, flattening bundles of sticks into planks. The joins were stronger than anything a nail or dovetail joint could provide, and he was proud of the results.

"You're planning on staying?" Lucy scoffed, looking at the house. Bertha and Sol had spent hours cleaning the rooms, fixing the windows and doors where possible. The curtains were crudely ensorcelled hemp similar to their clothes.

"We can't leave," the Boneman said. "The boat's broken and the portal to the Greygulf is beyond fixing. We're stuck."

"Might as well get comfortable while we wait for Turtwurdigan to kill us," Bertha said morosely, crunching down on the charred flesh of some dead animal. Lucy smirked as he pushed his crudely fired plate away.

"No imagination, either of you," Lucy said. "We're not stuck here, and damned if I'm going to sit around and watch you play house." Lucy stood up and unravelled his hemp toga. Beneath this he wore a t-shirt and denim jeans, clean and new. His feet were clad in a comfortable pair of sneakers, and a shining pistol hung from his belt.

"We're leaving. Now."

Sol and Bertha stared at him in shock, their rude meals forgotten as Papa Lucy opened a far-door.

"Hesus has changed. He's something else now," Lucy said. He led the way through the far-door, and in one instant they left the distant island to set foot on the mainland. The three sorcerers stood on the scar of the original Crossing overlooking the slums of Crosspoint.

"But I fought him just the same, beat him too," Lucy continued. "Sent his stupid shadow-hand limping out of the Aum. Believe me, I knocked some truths out of that old fraud."

By witchlight he showed them how to defeat the barrier that kept them from piercing the world veil. From his prison in the Greygulf, Hesus had done his best to keep his old enemies trapped in the Now, constructing a powerful ward that had taken him hundreds of years to complete. The block was keyed to them specifically and almost impossible to untangle.

Papa Lucy didn't know impossible.

"I'm disappointed in you both," he said, forcing open the obstruction when they both pleaded exhaustion, amused at their inability to crack the ward. "It took me less than a day to break his little spell. You've had weeks and you didn't even try."

"What happens now?" the Boneman asked, feeling the presence of the world veil once more. He'd greatly missed the convenience of the Greygulf, the skin that he could tear with his mind, opening doorways to other places.

"I'm taking back my town," Lucy said, his hands on his hips as he considered the walls of Crosspoint. "That's what happens now."

Lucy tried the direct approach by standing before the closed gates, yelling at the guard, and demanding that they fetch the Overseer. Papa Lucy insisted that Crosspoint be turned over to its rightful owner: himself. The guards sent him away with a shower of stones and insults, laughing at his solemn vow that, yes, he was Papa Lucy returned from death.

"I don't know why you thought that would work," the Boneman said, cloaked by Lucy in an illusionary skin. He took his brother by the elbow and led him away before he could unleash the marks of death and fire upon his tormentors.

A far-door would let the sorcerers into the city, but this was not the return Lucy wanted by sneaking in like a robber. He wanted his grand entrance. He wanted to see the capitulation of the local ruler. The Boneman simply could not talk him out of it.

Papa Lucy had made up his mind.

"If I had the Cruik here, I'd smash that gate in and sweep them all from the battlements," Lucy said through gritted teeth. His hand clenched as if gripping the shaft of his absent staff. The Boneman frowned.

"The Cruik is bad news. Call back that poor girl of yours, your Rider, and we'll find a way to destroy the damn thing. It's time to let it go, Lucy."

"Do not speak to me about the Cruik." Lucy scowled. "You don't know."

They rejoined Bertha at their vigil point and made plans to take back the town. The Boneman spent hours at the old cemetery crooning at the dead and raising the corpses from the earth. He gave them false life and motion, and then led this shuffling force towards the open caravanserai.

"No killing," the Boneman warned, as the first screams were heard. The phalanx of mobile corpses had been seen.

"I can't promise that, brother. We'll do what we must."

Once more he was bound to his brother with a mixture of love, self-hatred, and fear as he followed him into another bad decision. He could rationalise his brother's behaviour in a hundred different ways and still come up with no real answers.

If you weren't scared of Turtwurdigan, would you still be here with him?

It wasn't a question he was prepared to answer, not even to himself.

Chaos, shouting, and curses arose as the carousers and night scum found the walking dead in their midst. The Boneman's shambling servants seized guns. Mounted on stolen birds and buggies, they broke open the slave pens and freed the prisoners, adding to the chaos. The dead were fearless and constant as they shrugged off the weapons of the caravanserai guards and dragged down the living with their bony hands.

Lucy plucked men from the panicked crowd and broke down their will with nothing but a gaze and a mark. With their minds captured, he set these slaves to defending the sorcerers from the disorganised resistance.

Bertha stalked through the canvas alleys, knocking down any who raised arms against her, calling the women out of hiding. She sought out those with the coal of madness within and fanned this ember into a full flame. She sang to them, lured them to her cause, and her new force came creeping out through the fires and chaos. Drunkards and whores, fortune-tellers and slaves, all were now Mad Millies—furious and fearless berserkers with the strength of three men.

An expeditionary force of bailiffs came from the town to quell the sudden outburst of violence in the caravanserai. The lawmen were surprised and scattered, quickly overrun by the mouldering undead. Any survivors were mowed down under the dead-eyed calm of Lucy's gunmen.

The same guards who'd mocked Papa Lucy fled in terror as the gates were assaulted by a horde of madmen and monsters. They brought gunpowder forward, while the undead made a neat pyramid of fuel canisters at the door's base. Lucy laid out the fuse himself.

"I want you to remember that I asked them nicely," Lucy told the Boneman, then set a match to the charge. They ran for cover as the night erupted into flame and noise. The thick beams of the gate ruptured.

It took many hours of bloody fighting, and the barracks held out for some time. It pained the Boneman to see his old house burning, an entire wing crumbling under the explosion when a munitions dump went up.

Using far-doors to coordinate the fighting, the sorcerers made light work of the town defenders. Shortly after dawn, the Overseer offered the surrender of the town. Papa Lucy accepted the corpulent official's surrender, and then put a bullet into his face just to prove the point.

"We go north," Papa Lucy said. He slouched on the Overseer's ridiculous throne, which he found hilarious. He drummed a tattoo on the imposing armrests with his fingers.

"Why?" Bertha said. A tailor fussed over her terrifying body, nervously dropping pins and measuring tapes. She wanted a good set of clothes, but nothing fit her misshapen body. Even the biggest men's clothes were too small for her.

The Boneman did not blame the tailor for his nerves. It wasn't every day that your customers were murderous conquerors, let alone ancient gods returned from legend. It made all of the Boneman's interactions tiresome and he was thankful at least for his false face.

Imagine how hard this would go if they could really see me, he thought wearily.

"There's something that I want up there, up in the Waste," Lucy told Bertha. "Turtwurdigan knows, and Hesus knows too. But I'm smarter than all of them." He tapped on his temple like a madman and refused to tell them any more than that.

The Boneman sat behind a small table below the throne, and as usual, he took care of the details. It fell to him to meet with the terrified representatives of the conquered townsfolk and listen to their fawning and tentative attempts at furthering their own interests. He took inventory of items within the town, gathering everything that Lucy had asked him to find.

"You know that the far-doors don't work out there," he warned his brother, continuing to work through supper. "If you want to bring an army into the Waste, it'll need to make its own way."

"So get me bikes and birds, all of that stuff," Lucy said, waving a hand to indicate that the subject was already boring him.

"No, you don't get to do that," the Boneman said, throwing down his pencil with exasperation. "If you want my help, you tell me what we're up against."

"Nothing to worry about. My little Rider is on her way, and she'll get there before anyone else. She bears the Cruik, Sol, and the Cruik works for me."

"Hardly," the Boneman sighed. "What's in the Waste? Stop talking in circles."

"A Waking City," Papa Lucy said. "A second chance."

A week after the Family strode out of legend and took back Crosspoint by force, the sorcerers left. Lucy installed a puppet leader and allowed his brother to make a handful of cosmetic changes to the laws and governance. The Boneman insisted on reviving the Moot, an authority to conduct fair elections in their absence.

"No more politics," Lucy grumbled. "Let the merchants and bean counters sort it out. I just want a veto and to be bloody well left alone."

A great force set north following the pilgrim's road. The Boneman had rounded up every working vehicle, every bird, camel, and lizard. Crosspoint was emptied on the word of the gods. Coin-riders were pressed into service, and the handful of remaining merchants were coerced into funding the expedition.

"There'll be an uprising," the Boneman warned, but Lucy simply did not care. He kept looking north with impatience writ large on his face. Something else, too. There was a disturbing light in his eyes that might have been hunger or lust.

Papa Lucy had his army, thousands strong with engines sending up a column of dust and exhaust smoke. Mad Millies shrieked and hollered, clutching to the sides of buggies driven by the undead. Ranks of Lucy's mind-slaves kept the conscripts in line by riding the perimeter on motorbikes and watching for deserters through their elsewhere eyes.

This had better be worth it, the Boneman thought. Only the fear of Turtwurdigan kept him silent. If they wanted to survive the return of this old enemy, they needed every gun. He rode in a shuddering convertible next to his brother, his skeleton exposed to the light of day. As Lucy saw it expedient to travel openly, he had taken away the Boneman's false skin to "remind these folks of what we are." He had even convinced Bertha to shuck her new dresses and wear a horrible outfit of leather and metal.

We're meant to be the good guys.

A handful of shadow-roads brushed against the Waste, but the ways were old and the path too dangerous. The sorcerers might survive the short-cut through the Greygulf, but it would strike their forces dumb and strip their minds, leaving them helpless.

So they went the long way, a rumbling horde thousands strong. Crooked mobs fled before the dust and the rumble of engines. They passed many empty holdings, torched and abandoned. Word had got out about the devastation at Crosspoint, of Papa Lucy's peculiar brand of mercy.

Lucy seemed to relish his newest incarnation as a feudal warlord. The convertible had been the pride and joy of the dead Overseer, a rusty sedan with fat tailfins and cracked leather seats. Lucy revved the engine constantly, heedless of how much fuel it was burning.

The sorcerer wore a leather jacket and sunglasses, his hair slicked back with gel. A big pile of guns slid around on the back seat, and he occasionally fired a round into the air, whooping through a megaphone as he fish tailed the car up and down the column.

"No point sneaking in," Papa Lucy confided to his brother. He smoked a kennelweed pipe, lounging back against the deep seats and steering the car with only his sorcery. "Gotta let 'em know we're coming."

— 18 —

The Collegia lurched, a sickening spectacle captured by the last of the journalists still filming. The world watched in shock as the university fell out of the sky, the magic that fixed it in orbit sputtering and finally failing altogether. The glorious sky-city was nothing now but an enormous hunk of glass and cement, a meteor that struck the eastern seaboard like a fist.

After two cities were wiped from the map, the orbital hotels and luxury resorts began to drop, fiery bombs raining from above. The last structure to fall was the Hann-Slatter Observation Platform, a flimsy structure set at the upper limits of orbital sorcery. The handful of Overhaeven researchers burned up on re-entry, leaving nothing but dust to signal the end of humanity's hold on the sky.

The end was here.

Lucy was Luciano Papagallo then. His face ran with sweat as he pushed his will against the rubbery world veil. The Greygulf was tantalisingly close, but nobody had ever attempted to open such a large door. Only the occasional sorcerer had the strength to breach that terrifying boundary between all the Realms.

Lucy intended to open a passage for thousands of people, most of them non-sorcerers. It was madness, an impossible bending of the physics of space and time. It was pure Lucy.

His dearest friends joined the assault. A handful of Collegia sorcerers added their strength, defectors who'd left the fruitless talks to cast in their lot with the disgraced Papagallos. In those final days, Lucy had been everywhere talking to the press, bothering politicians, speaking at rallies. Soon, the Hanns could not contain him any longer.

He was determined to be heard, and now he had a movement behind him, enough resources to attempt this mad action. It was a desperate roll of the dice, but also a chance where there was none.

The air began to feel like jelly. Every movement took a gargantuan effort. The sun shivered and fractured, black lines webbing on its surface. It slowed, then became still, dim and fading. Sol felt the magic begin to fail then, and the sorcerers started dropping dead as their bodies collapsed under the strain of this last great undertaking.

An hour, perhaps less, and it would all be over. Humanity had bled this world dry, and now it was shrugging them off like a bad idea.

"Wait," Sol gasped, holding the spirits of these dead sorcerers back, preventing them from slipping through the world veil. The spirits of the newly dead wailed, denied their release.

"We need more," he told John Leicester, who nodded mournfully. Leicester understood what was required. He stalked through the panicked crowd, gun chattering as he slew their panicked followers. The soldier-mage worked to a ruthless calculation, murdering one from each family, focussing on the old and the weak.

"Enough," Sol gasped and let the restless spirits go. They rushed forward in one mass, their essences hitting the world veil together. The thick skin between the worlds shivered then gave way as these dead wriggled through, seeking a path into the Underfog and eventually Death.

"Yes!" Lucy said through gritted teeth. He used this momentum to force open his own doorway in the universe. A great ragged wound in the world veil opened onto a landscape of silver and dusk. The Greygulf. Lucy took a moment to shore up the edges of this portal, and then he was through, fires blazing as he battled with the guardians of that alien Realm.

Helping a dazed Baertha to her feet, Sol joined the panicked throng, nodding when saw Hesus nearby. His old professor led the small rearguard of failed students and journeymen sorcerers. Overhaeven theorists, mostly. Hesus had found others in the last few months, volunteers who responded well to his tests and exercises.

They called themselves the Hesusmen, and at first this group was an endless source of amusement for Lucy. Now, these people held firm and kept their calm as the bubble of safety shrank. They got the last of the people through and kept order as the livestock and supplies were funnelled into the sorcerous gate.

"Go, Sol," Hesus called out, even as the outer edges of the rearguard collapsed, twitching and choking as their bodies betrayed them. "Don't wait, just go."

Then there was the lunacy that was their trek through the Greygulf. Demons prowled those strange roads, pouncing on the unwary. Creatures that were all teeth and eyes feasted on the terrified fugitives. There was murder in that dim world, but Lucy led from the front, driving away the darkness with fire and pushing through to their new home.

On later reflection, Sol realised this was the only noble act of Lucy's long and sordid life. Of course, Lucy milked it for all he was worth.

A contingent met Papa Lucy's horde before the gates of Hislott Springs, first of the Inland towns. A trio of Family priests grovelled in the red dust, and a sweating dignitary offered him the mayoral chain, a twist of car badges and other bleedthrough gewgaws.

Word had gotten ahead, even though they had felled every telegraph line they came across. Half the town fled for their lives, while the remainder gambled on the Family's mercy.

"Well, this is more like it," Lucy said, shrugging into the symbol of office. "This means no one has to die."

He walked back to his car, then paused. He turned on his heel and pointed to the priests.

"Except for them," he told his blank-eyed followers, who stepped forward with blades and shooters drawn. The clerics begged and wailed and called upon Papa Lucy's mercy. One of them broke and ran. They died just the same. The old ruler of Hislott Springs looked on this blood price in mute terror. He agreed rapidly when Lucy told him it was a bargain.

"Burn the temples and shrines," he told Bertha. After a moment of indecision, she sent her Millies through the open gate, her chattering madwomen pushing past the terrified townsfolk.

"What? Don't look at me like that, Sol," Lucy scolded. "I'm rethinking our religious aspirations, is all."

"I thought the Family rote was supposed to be our legacy," the Boneman said. "Precepts and edicts, in case the laws ever failed."

"We're warlords now," Lucy said. "People won't respect piety and handwringing."

"So disband the temples. Killing priests! It makes you—I don't even know what you are anymore."

"You read that scripture. They twisted our words."

"I thought you liked being a god."

Lucy gave no answer except an infuriating smile. A tendril of smoke climbed above the walls, and then the awful cries, a chorus of animal screeching as the Millies murdered someone.

The Boneman oversaw the reprovisioning of their forces as they emptied the larders of Hislott Springs to starvation levels and seized a brace of birds. It would all be needed, every last crumb. Anyone fit to point a gun was press-ganged into the sprawling army and squeezed into the trucks and buggies.

Lucy gave the mayoral chain to the first person he saw, a young boy he swore into office at gunpoint. The law books were brought to him for inspection, and after a quick rifle through the pages he burned the lot, already bored by the process of annexing a friendly town.

"Goodbye then," he told the frightened townsfolk through his megaphone. "Be good."

The army rolled out, pushing north for Sad Plain. The old ruler of Hislott Plains jogged behind the convertible, naked and chained. Only the Boneman's insistence that they spare the man gave Lucy pause. He laughed and set the man loose three miles down the road.

"If you can't see why this is hilarious, I just feel sorry for you," Lucy said.

Begging off from travel in the convertible, the Boneman claimed the need to perform maintenance sorcery on his undead cadre. A lie, since they'd walk until the sorcery ground their bones into powder. He breathed a sigh of relief as Lucy roared off into the distance, fat wheels kicking up a shower of dust and small stones.

Flagging down Bertha's truck, Sol climbed up into the flat-bed. His wife lounged against the back of the cab, her stylised dominatrix uniform slightly ridiculous when viewed this close. The outfit that Lucy had designed for her showed off the Cruik's ruinous touch to full effect, her scars and twisted flesh on full view.

The Boneman travelled nude at his brother's request, and he understood why. Lucy needed monsters for generals and terror for a flag. It was all a grand statement, the end result of a carefully considered plan.

"Lucy's gone too far," he said quietly, clutching the side panels as the truck bounced along the track. Bertha nodded.

"We need him, Sol," she said. "Any army we can get, any way he can get it."

"Expedience is no excuse," the Boneman started, and then drew up short. The small army they'd taken to Sad Plain made little difference. Riders, Mad Millies, John's stone soldiers, all of them had been swept aside when Turtwurdigan woke.

He shivered and wished for an army twice the size. When he remembered the Mother of Glass and her fiery kiss, he found that he could overlook Lucy's methods.

Bethel was an atrocity.

As Papa Lucy's horde approached, the faithful came out in force with pilgrims and local missionaries lining the tradeway for almost a mile. The town existed to service visitors to Sad Plain, and the imminent appearance of the Family, gone for so long, brought out the makings of a grand procession. Those who were on pilgrimage counted themselves extra lucky; they'd come to look upon the holy site, and the gods themselves were paying them a visit.

The huddle of shacks and wayhouses was decked out with bunting, the richest wayhouses bringing out their finest strings of Taursi glass, shining stars that tinkled in the faint breeze. Pilgrims smiled expectantly as the convoy neared, while some gibbered and wailed. Every order of religious mania was on display. Some spilled blood onto the road, while others left scripture books and pamphlets across the tradeway, the better for the gods to walk upon.

As the first vehicle approached, replica Cruiks were held up high. Rose petals rained on the tradeway for the Lady Bertha. These were imported from the Riverland at great cost, but the pilgrims dumped them heedlessly, packet after packet, the air soon filling with petals and dust.

"I can see her!" someone said, and the maddest of Bertha's acolytes whipped themselves with wire whisks, drawing blood and flies.

"The Papa! The Papa is here!" somebody else screamed, and a car emerged from the dust. It was a thundering Before-Time machine, riding low to the ground, all fins and rust. Standing in the front of the car, one foot on the steering wheel, a man grinned, resting a big gun across his shoulders.

"Papa Lucy!" the pilgrims screamed. Their god smiled broadly at this fervent treatment. Then he levelled the gun and squeezed the trigger.

The screams of ecstasy became cries of agony, the keening of lost seagulls as the wounded and terrified ran for their lives. Lucy drove forward patiently, taking care to strafe both sides of the tradeway. He signalled his followers to chase runners into the desert and finish everybody off.

Nobody survived the Family's first visit to Bethel. When they left, there was nothing left of the place but the blackened scars where buildings had once stood, and the tradeway that made for Sad Plain like an arrow.

After Bethel, none of the soldiers were game to test the patience of the slick sorcerer. Desertions stopped entirely, even as the suicides climbed. But death did not release them from service. The recently deceased were hauled back from the Underfog, their bewildered spirits tucked back into their cold bodies. The Boneman insisted that they rise, take up their guns and spears, and keep on walking.

"You're still on the books," he'd say mournfully, patting the reanimated soldiers on the shoulder. "Sorry."

It taxed him to raise so many, but soon the murdered pilgrims lurched along behind the main body of the army, weapons pressed into their dead hands. Lucy enjoyed the irony of these pilgrims honouring their vows of "undying service," and overrode his brother's objections.

Less than a day's travel brought them to the holiest site in the Family faith, the location of that ancient and most terrible battle. It had been an empty city once, a place of glass and light, an oddity in a world where the inhabitants were nomads and did not build anything beyond the rudest of structures.

The Boneman remembered the day that Hesus stood in Lucy's way, denying him passage and defying the warrant for his arrest. Unable to best his old friend with sorcery, Lucy used the Cruik to break the nameless city out of spite and frustration. The glass fell for miles, raining down upon Hesus. Thousands were sliced into ribbon, including John Leicester.

Then, Turtwurdigan woke.

The Boneman couldn't look upon this glittering prairie without terror seizing his heart. He wanted to cry, he wanted to throw up. He'd walked into this place a man and left it a charred and broken monster.

Bertha placed a heavy paw on his shoulder and squeezed gently. She shook slightly, the memory of her wounds no less than his.

Lucy bade the horde to stop at the very edge of Sad Plain, not wanting to risk their wheels on that carpet of shattered glass. Not even the lizards would enter. It was folly to walk in. The thickest boots would be shredded within the first mile.

Nothing to see in there, the Boneman thought. *It's just a wreck now, the place where someone finally told Lucy that he couldn't do something.*

Papa Lucy stood on the hood of the convertible, and the megaphone gave a little squeal as he brought his voice to most of the army. Others repeated his words or guessed at what their new leader was saying.

If the conscripts could not hear his address, they pretended they could, shuddering whenever his blank-faced servants drifted through the ranks.

"Thanks for coming, friends," Lucy said, his face flush with bonhomie. "Can you hear me down the back?"

A general murmur rose matched by the moans of the undead and the cackles of the Mad Millies. Lucy laughed. The Lady Bertha and the Boneman stood next to the car on display for the troops.

Lucy spoke. "Now, you're probably wondering why we stopped here. It's a bit out of our way, but I wanted you folks to see this place."

He gestured at the field of sharp glass, interrupted only by the occasional jag of a shattered column, the low remains of walls poking out of the sea of shining wreckage. Thousands of tonnes of broken glass, left where it had fallen. If there were treasures here, they were inaccessible.

Papa Lucy's ultimate display of sour grapes.

"This wasn't always called Sad Plain. I gave it that name after what happened here. It used to be an old city, a beautiful place of glass and mystery. Natives had a name for it, and it stood for thousands of years."

More silence. Lucy looked across the petrified gathering, as if watching for raised hands and questions. Nobody living and sane made a peep or even dared to cough.

"I broke that city, just to prove a point. And I'd do it again," he said, looking evenly at Bertha and his brother.

This is for our benefit, the Boneman realised. *He doesn't need to address the troops. He just doesn't care.*

"We're going to cross the Waste now, boys and girls. I can't promise that all of you will get there in one piece, but life would be boring if it was safe, right?"

Bertha shifted restlessly, scratched at the bristle on her shaven scalp. The Boneman looked down at the complex interplay of his body, at the body that Turtwurdigan had cursed him with. He was committed to this course of action. He was as culpable as his brother the tyrant.

"There's a Waking City, right on the edge of all things. An amazing place, towers of glass and steel. All sorts of goodies that could make a smart man rich. But here's the thing: I've been rich. It doesn't make you happy. And there's no point preserving these fragile places just because they're old. This here," he said, once more indicating the ancient scene of destruction, "*this* is progress. It's a beautiful thing."

Papa Lucy climbed down from the car, patting Bertha with familiarity. Then he wrapped an arm around his brother and leaned in close. A young rake embracing a monster, immortal brothers from a long dead world. And the Boneman felt his distrust melt away and knew that he'd follow this maniac to the literal ends of the earth.

"We're going to cross the Waste and find this Waking City. And when we do, we're going to destroy it."

That night was a reconciliation of sorts. Lady Bertha and the Boneman coupled under starlight, their strange new bodies coming together in frustration and perhaps fear. But the rhythm was wrong, and their love too wounded to kindle anything approaching warmth. It was a big mistake.

They stared up at the carpet of stars, dissatisfied, emptier than when they'd sought each other out.

"Lucy's not telling us everything," the Boneman said.

Bertha said nothing, her eyes were dark reflections of the guttering campfire. She hitched the blanket up higher, cutting him out, shielding her broken body from his eyes.

"Doesn't this bother you?" he pressed her.

"Of course it bothers me," she snapped. "We're going to die out there."

Lucy had been gone for hours, stepping through the world veil without explanation. His excursions into the Greygulf were a nightly thing now, and he always went alone. Only now did the Boneman feel safe enough to tryst with the remains of his wife. He didn't know what he feared worse—discovery or the inevitable mockery. Perhaps Lucy would even find it fitting. Monsters seeking out their own kind.

"I need to know something. About the time when you—when Lucy—"

"What?" she said, voice low and wary. An old argument lay just beneath the surface, one that neither was ready to resurrect. The Boneman bit back his accusations and sought calm.

"Did Lucy tell you anything about the glass city? What it was before Sad Plain?"

"Oh," she said, with something approaching relief. "He told me some things, but I was confused. The Cruik was already deep in— in here." She tapped her temple.

"Lucy never told me the reasons behind the arrest warrant, he just waved his damned stick and demanded my obedience. And Hesus—we were his oldest friends. He did his best to kill us!"

The Boneman looked up at the stars, an old bitterness gripping his soul. There'd been no words between the brothers on that fateful day, no discussion beyond the reading of the warrant. War was a foregone conclusion.

"I used to adore that man, Baertha. I still don't know why they quarrelled. Why did Hesus stop Lucy from entering the glass city?"

"Because Lucy found out that the whole place was a gateway," she whispered. "Hesus started a war to make sure it stayed shut."

— INTERLUDE —

Fos Carpidian was almost seventy years old now, and his mind was slowly failing with each passing season. These autumn years ate at his memories like locusts, but he remembered the day he met Turtwurdigan with complete clarity.

Fos was born into a time of poverty, and the faithful hadn't sniffed out a bleedthrough since long before his birth. Times were tough for the nomadic followers of Leicester-We-Forget, and Fos's earliest memories were of hunger.

The townsfolk scorned them and called them statue-lovers or worse. Leicesterites were refused entry into the towns, forced to beg for scraps at the gate, drifting throughout the holdings and wayhouses in the search for work. Fos spent his formative years in an overcrowded tent, beaten by the other urchins whenever they stopped at a caravanserai.

He first saw the glass demon on his eighth birthday. The faithful met in the Inland at a grand gathering of all the families. They'd braved the crooked men and the dangers of the Drift, but enough of the elders were here now to hold quorum.

Fos was brought out with the other children, one from each of the old families. They were paraded around a ring of Leicesters, these portable gods allowed to inspect the candidates. The old words were said, a prayer from the old Before-world that spoke of memory and finding. Of sacrifice, and the blood of the brave spilled to protect the whole of the tribe.

A group of men pulled apart a stone cairn with crowbars and chisels, breaking away the mortar. A bronzed Leicester marked this place, set aside with great reverence as they tore the shrine apart.

A slouch-hatted priest plucked an old tobacco tin from the base of the cairn, and the others took care not to stand too close. The first child was called forward, a little boy of perhaps five.

Face painted pure and thick, the minister leant in close and put one hand on the boy's shoulder. The boy was shaking, blinking back his tears.

The minister said something quietly. The boy shook his head and made to run. A man from his family held the boy still, perhaps his father or an uncle. The priest leant in again with the tobacco tin, and the boy trembled, a wet patch spreading on his shorts.

The priest opened the tin. Something within the box burnt with an impossible light, like they'd trapped a sliver of the sun. The boy stared at the glass fragment, transfixed, his small mind overcome. He began to rave and scream, frothing at the mouth, legs and arms kicking.

Only the headsman's axe silenced the awful screams. They painted the family's Leicester with the boy's lifeblood. A weeping woman was already chiselling his name into the holy list, "IN MEMORIAM."

The next child was brought forward, a girl just shy of her teens, knock-kneed and weeping. Again, the glass drove a child mad, and she was given to Leicester-We-Forget.

Then it was time for the Carpidians to offer up their own. Fos was pushed forward, weeping and protesting. It took two of his uncles to hold him still, to pry open the eyes that he squeezed tight. The men looked away as the box was opened.

Fos looked upon the glass shard nestled inside the beaten-up tin. Every facet of the crystal drank deeply of the sunlight and reflected it tenfold. It was painful to look upon, but he felt it then, the strange probing at his mind, the feeling that a stranger was inside his skull ripping at his thoughts.

"Obey! Obey Turtwurdigan!" it demanded, and young Fos nodded his head rapidly, whimpered that yes, of course he would obey. The glass seemed pleased by this, and the pain subsided. At Turtwurdigan's urging, Fos plucked the glass from the tin, the glow of the shard bleeding out of his little fist.

He stood, and the congregation murmured with amazement. He ignored this commotion, seeing another overlay to the world he'd always known. Everywhere, pillars of light reached to the heavens, thin and broad, near and far.

The demon that called itself Turtwurdigan begged Fos Carpidian to search these locations for something that it needed. He promised to do this. As the creature retreated from his mind, the glass splinter dimmed and he gently replaced it in the box.

"That way." He pointed with unwavering accuracy towards the nearest bleedthrough. For the first time in over a decade, a statue was found, a Leicester of exceeding purity.

The presence of Turtwurdigan seemed to bring everything through much faster and cleaner than the wild bleedthroughs folks sometimes stumbled across. A fragment of an old neighbourhood bled through into the Now, the melted buildings containing enough treasure to feed the entire tribe for weeks.

Fos led his people to many riches, and then Turtwurdigan showed him the biggest bleedthrough yet—an entire town pushing at the boundary of this world, about to burst like an ugly boil.

The folk of Carmel owned this land. A family of miners grown rich on tin, they'd come here in the hope that the plateau contained metal ore. Firm believers in Papa Lucy, they were known for turning away the Leicesterites. It was decided by the elders that this fledgling town must be taken by force.

Many of the Leicesterite faithful died in the siege, but soon Carmel's flimsy walls fell. The town was theirs. Fos watched as his uncles torched buildings, raped, and murdered.

Within a week, the bailiffs came from Crosspoint demanding the blood price, prepared to massacre the heretics over this slaughter. The lawmen arrived to see a bleedthrough field beyond reckoning and the tribe hauling countless riches out of the warped ruins.

The blood price was met with interest, and the proper bribes were paid to the Overseer, who assured his colleagues in the other towns that this annexation of Carmel was legal and just. Word got out about the riches just laying around Carmel, and the riverlords sent an army to seize the Leicesterites' wealth. They were met with a large force of fresh coin-riders and a wall three times as thick as the one the faithful had toppled.

Times were good for many years until the bores in the plateau ran dry. The water barons crept north with greed in their eyes, and they murdered the town slowly.

Turtwurdigan scorned Fos Carpidian, demanding that his servant ride out and seek a distant bleedthrough on the furthest edges of the Waste. It had finally located the one thing it had been hunting for. It insisted that Fos make good on their original bargain.

By then, Fos was an old man, less than fervent and comforted by the thickness of his walls. The crooked mobs of the Inland were more numerous than ever, and he was scared to venture anywhere beyond a day's ride.

The spirit in the glass cursed the man and finally refused to show him anything else. Turtwurdigan lay silent and morose for almost thirty years, and then Tilly came along, the final fruit of Fos Carpidian's withered loins.

—◖●◗—

In his old age, Fos dreamt once more of the stone man on Sad Plain, a white Leicester moving like a living man, stone limbs swinging as he waded through the carpet of broken glass. He'd dreamt of this almost every night since Turtwurdigan claimed him, with only the oblivion of drink granting him a dreamless sleep.

In the dream, the Leicester-We-Forget was encased in marble flesh, intangible proof that Fos's religion was true and his god was real. Only the stone god could safely explore that razor-sharp ruin, and it picked through the glass piles for months. The living statue worked both day and night, fossicking for something small, one piece of glass amongst a million others.

People came and begged him to stop, calling to him from the edge of the ruin. The burnt skeleton of the Boneman, who called him friend and pleaded for reason. Bertha the madwoman, who came only to curse and throw handfuls of glass.

Finally, Papa Lucy stood on Sad Plain, demanding that Leicester-We-Forget abandon this disobedience and return to his service. The white statue ignored the head of the Family and continued to sift through the ruins.

Papa Lucy disowned him, publicly and loudly, and declared John Leicester's servants to be heretics and outlaws. Then the terrible sorcerer-god hurled many magics at his former ally. He used the Cruik to scour the plain with great waves of loose glass, and even ordered a squad of riflemen to shoot him dead. But the Leicester's stone skin was impervious to these attacks, and soon Papa Lucy grew tired of this. He opened a magical door and left without a backwards glance.

Leicester-We-Forget continued his search, and one day the god held aloft a glass shard that shone gloriously: the final fragment of something beautiful and broken. Turtwurdigan.

Then, a flicker of images as the god entrusted this relic to his own faithful. Fos saw the faces of his ancestors, dozens of them, passing Turtwurdigan through the generations, until its internment under rock and stone.

Fos awoke from this frequent dream to the grumbling of his old bones, every muscle aching as he climbed out of his bedroll. Once more he looked on the hopeless scene and watched as his people hacked away at the rocks, trying to clear a path.

Almost every part of his plan had worked with precision. The water barons were still reeling from the surprise attack. Now, the faithful had enough water for a year or two, enough to sink wells and bores at their journey's end.

Tilly was the latest Carpidian to pass Turtwurdigan's test, and she led the way to their salvation at a new home. She could only describe it as a "Waking City," but her description of the light-pillar confirmed his faith in her path.

A bleedthrough beyond anything they'd ever witnessed. Wealth beyond reckoning.

Lanyard Everett was a minor problem, but Carpidian had already sent a squad of gunmen to stalk him into the Waste, waiting for Spence's signal. An ambush awaited the crooked folk. The outlaw may have guaranteed Tilly's safety, but she held a treasure map in her head. More importantly, she was Carpidian's only daughter, and he'd bargained her away like a goat.

"Should never have made a deal with a Jesusman," he grumbled and limped over to inspect the works. Despairing at the lack of progress, he shook his head.

His plan did not take into account the manoeuvring of a water tanker through the narrow defiles of the outer Ranges. They'd made it a mile in before the lizard snagged it on a tight corner and wedged the metal cylinder into place.

"We fill up everything," Fos shouted. "All the bottles, containers, hell, every piss-pan and tea set."

A mournful procession waited by the valves, lugging away as much water as they could carry, drinking themselves sick, and even bathing in that gurgling flow. Fos looked at the stuck tanker for many long moments, considering what he'd given up to steal this much water, the sheer waste of leaving it behind.

He'd given up his daughter for this.

"Strike the valves," he said bitterly. "Empty the whole damn thing."

For a few brief moments, a gushing creek flowed down that bone-dry gully, the flood scaring the Rangewyrms and small rodents out of hiding. Just as quickly, the sun resumed its work. Within the hour, the cracked clay was as dry as it had ever been.

The homeless Leicesterites entered the Waste, a convoy of handcarts and bird-drawn wagons hundreds strong. Almost immediately one of the outriders spotted Spence Carpidian's marker, scattered and broken. The crooked folk had made sure they wouldn't be followed.

"Where do we go, Fos?" someone asked, but he couldn't answer. As they set up camp, they faced the enormity of the unbroken landscape ahead of them.

Tilly could be anywhere in that, he thought. *If we wander around blind, we're gonna die out here.*

One of the lads brought Fos his favourite chair, and he sat on the edge of the camp, facing toward the razor-straight horizon. Clearing his mind, he tried to reach out the way he had in his youth when Turtwurdigan had favoured him.

There seemed to be the flicker of something strange, but it wasn't a pillar of light. The sun got into his eyes and made them water. Whatever gift the Taursi spirit had given him, it had taken it away when he fell from grace.

A shout went up. A group of riders were coming out of the Waste, faint dots throwing up a dust trail. Those with guns knelt in a ragged line, but were relieved when they recognised their own people. It was the posse of gunmen sent to murder Lanyard Everett.

"Been riding around out here for days, bossman. There's no trail," one of them reported. "The dust just shifts around out here, doesn't hold anything. They could be anywhere."

"Keep looking," Fos demanded. "Find my little girl."

"Where's the water?" one of the men demanded, but Fos would not say. With mutinous rumblings, the men shared out what fuel they had. The camp grudgingly parted with a handful of supplies for the posse.

"We'll never see them again," someone muttered within his earshot, and Fos privately agreed. They were all as good as dead, no matter what he did.

Then a flicker of movement, a reflection on the horizon, a pin-prick of light running from the horizon to the sky. Fos blinked and rubbed his rheumy eyes, wondering if they were playing tricks. There it was again.

For the first time in many years, Fos Carpidian had a religious epiphany.

"Bring out the statue," he hollered from his chair. "And someone find me an axe. A sharp one."

PART FOUR

— THE WAKING CITY —

— 19 —

T illy could still feel the whispers of Turtwurdigan, faint but true. She didn't need the glass to point the way and offered the direction without resistance. To defy the crooked women was to invite another beating.

She could see the Waking City before them, like a giant bonfire blazing on the horizon. The land was starting to look funny, as if the earth had forgotten how to be ground and was close to giving up and floating into the sky. Little hills rose and just as quickly sank back into the flatness, or burst like giant pimples, sending a scatter of earth and stone high into the air.

The Waste got stranger by the mile. The further they travelled from the settled lands, the more the sun misbehaved. Sometimes Tilly saw strange creatures standing in the distance, collections of limbs and heads that just watched them pass by.

It felt like they were the only island of normality, a bird and a rattling motorbike tearing across that nowhere land. She sat on the riding harness behind Dogwyfe. Her escape attempts had ceased the moment Slopkettle threatened to skin her feet down to the bone.

Every day the crooked women grew agitated, squabbling bitterly over minor things. Even Gog felt the tension, snapping at

Dogwyfe whenever she fed him and drawing blood more than once. Slopkettle became obsessed with a grease spot on her hands and scrubbed at it with more of their drinking water than was necessary.

The flenser couldn't clean it off. If anything, her attentions spread the grime across both her palms, grey stains reaching almost to her wrists. Convinced her motorcycle was leaking oil somewhere, she insisted they halt for about three hours while she stripped the bike down to parts and rebuilt it.

Dogwyfe spent most of these elastic days muttering to herself, reliving past injustices under her breath. The scarred woman yanked on her old braid until it seemed she would rip it out her scalp. Tilly kept absolutely still, fearing to provoke Dogwyfe into another swift back-hander.

Gog often glared back at his mistress with an evil eye, and the crooked woman spent a lot of time rapping him over the beak with the lead-weight knout. Tilly remembered the way the bird had ripped apart her uncle, so she kept completely still whenever he looked at her.

Some days into the Waste, Dogwyfe finally taught the bird to say his own name, and he repeated it ad nauseam with endless enthusiasm.

"Gog! Gog Gog!" he boomed in the middle of the night, startling them all out of their sleep. On the third night that he woke them, Slopkettle went for the bird with blades drawn. Dogwyfe drove her off with the whip, taking a bloody strip from the flenser's forearm. Gog looked down on this interplay with a gleam in his eyes, croaking with mirth.

From then on the two women eyed each other murderously, and Tilly knew that only the promise of riches held off further violence.

This Waste madness hadn't taken a hold in Tilly's mind, but she was very scared and spoke only when one of her captors barked at her. She silently mouthed prayers to Leicester-We-Forget, praying that the white warrior would come and free her from captivity. She entertained notions of Father coming to her salvation with Lanyard the Jesusman at his side, the outlaw holding a smoking shotgun in one hand, and raising Turtwurdigan on high, calling on the spirit's power.

He's going to rescue me, she thought fervently, remembering the toy horse and the rough honesty of the man. *He'll get out of his chains and then he'll come and save me, because he promised.*

Then the girl slumped in the saddle, her head bowed as reality sank in. Lanyard Everett was dead now, black-tongued and shrivelled by the sun. Her father was lost, her people wandering. They'd never survive this eerie place.

No one was coming, and when the crooked women had their loot, they would slice her up for their greypot. Tilly faced her fate with detachment. Her final prayer was one of vengeance offered to any god who would listen.

I hope this awful place destroys these women, Tilly Carpidian thought coldly. *I hope they never even see the Waking City.*

Another nightmare: this time the memory of Nona Joan splashing around in the sacrificial trough. Tilly's grandmother fought against her young hands, bucking and fighting for breath, going back on her promise to die quietly.

"Hold her down!" her father screamed, watching his old mother drown. Tilly cried as she pushed Nona's head back under the water. She looked up and saw the lust in the eyes of her neighbours, the joy with which they welcomed yet another sacrifice.

Held aloft by the priest, Turtwurdigan caught the light then shone in her eyes. She'd been chosen, the first in a long long time. Tilly gritted her teeth and got on with the job. Nona always said she was a good, practical girl.

"I love you, Nona," she said as the thrashing slowed and stopped.

Tilly woke, limbs stiff as she rose from the sack that served as her blanket. Gog had quietly killed an intruder sometime during the night, a nightmare of black tentacles and translucent wings. The bird watched her warily as it ripped into the corpse, munching with relish.

As Gog turned slightly to get at more meat, Tilly saw the latest horror and felt her stomach rebel. Dogwyfe sat slightly forward of the saddle clutching her bird's neck like a zealous mother. Her face was pressed against the bird's flesh. When Tilly looked closely, she couldn't tell where the woman ended and the bird began.

Their flesh was melted together in a seamless join.

Then Dogwyfe opened her eyes and looked at Tilly with animal rage. The warped birdwoman worked her mouth noiselessly, frustrated by the loss of her voice.

Gog dropped his meal then looked at her askance. The bird's muscles bunched, and Tilly took a step backwards, wondering if this awful mutant was about to leap up and tear her to pieces in this lonely place.

"Girl," the Gog-thing said in a booming voice. "Stay."

Tilly stayed.

She looked to where Slopkettle slumbered on the back of her bike and realised no help would be coming from that quarter. From the thighs down, the flenser's legs were fused with the machine, and her snores were the quiet rumbles of the motorcycle's engine.

Gog trotted toward her after his feast then knelt before her. What was left of Dogwyfe blinked furiously, unable to frame whatever it was she wished to say.

"Ride," the bird burbled. "Now."

Tilly climbed into the harness, noting how the wicker frame felt more like bone, the blankets something closer to fur. She wondered if she would end the day as part of this creature, a girl-tumour growing on a bird's back.

Nestled in the middle of the birdwoman's back was an oblong of canvas and rope that had been rejected by this new form, snagged on a bony outgrowth. Lanyard's shotgun! Tilly carefully reached for it, sliding it onto her lap. When she fashioned one of the ropes into a strap and slung the bundle over her shoulder, Dogwyfe did not seem to notice.

A shame he ran out of bullets for this, she thought, with the image of herself blowing off Dogwyfe's disturbing head. The gun was too precious to leave behind, and she held onto it like a talisman against the hope that the brutal man would fulfil his promise.

He might need it.

Slopkettle pulled alongside the bird, a creature of flesh and steel, her right hand now fused to the throttle. The bikewoman snarled a wordless query at her, her voice a whining motor. Arm trembling, Tilly pointed in the direction of the bleedthrough, and the plaintive note ceased.

The two changelings abandoned their campsite, left all their belongings and supplies to be swallowed up by the wilderness. The bird-thing and the bikewoman burnt a tireless trail across the Waste. They refused to pause to let Tilly relieve herself. She wondered if they had the ability to remember the reason for their journey. She puzzled over what drove them onwards.

What use do these freaks have for treasure?

She noticed more changes over the day, like how Dogwyfe pushed further into Gog's neck. Her face was rising towards the base of the bird's skull. Slopkettle seemed to relish her new life as a machine, her face resting in the centre of the handlebars, chest and belly slowly sinking into the fuel tank.

The sun dropped from the Waste sky with its usual brute finality, and only then did the mutated women halt and allow the girl to rest. The Gog-thing watched over her intently, while

Slopkettle slowly circled the campsite on guard. Her headlights pierced the perfect darkness, scattering the handful of curious predators drawn by Tilly's smell.

She woke to see that Dogwyfe had taken over the bird entirely. Her face stretched out over the bird's own, scarred cheeks wrapped around the base of the bird's beak. A pair of long arms now dangled from the animal's chest, marked with familiar tattoos. A thick braid of wiry hair cascaded down from the bony crest.

Slopkettle was still racing around the campsite, but now the bike-thing resembled a person-shape with spinning wheels for feet. Her chest was a throbbing engine and her arms were a mixture of steering forks and handlebars.

Oversized knives and sharpened wrenches hung from a fan belt, an imitation of her old bandolier. Above this, the flenser's grimy face was framed in a helmet of pipes and fuel lines.

The plaintive notes of engine sounds came again from Slopkettle, followed by Dogwyfe's demand for "Place. Where." Tilly pointed in the direction.

They reached the site of the bleedthrough on the third day. This part of the Waste was as unremarkable as the rest of it, but Tilly felt an enormous pressure here and could almost hear the slow groan as two worlds rubbed together. All around her Turtwurdigan's marker glowed, painting the Waste golden from the earth to the sky.

"Here," she told Dogwyfe, who slowed to a trot and then stopped, chest heaving. The birdwoman regarded Tilly with suspicion along the length of her beak. Her forward facing eyes weren't sitting quite right on the bird's head, and this new creature seemed myopic.

"I mean it. The bleedthrough is here."

Slopkettle skated alongside, engine purring, and asked Dogwyfe a question in her new machine tongue. The birdwoman hissed back, scratching at the ground like a chicken. Tilly watched anxiously as she clutched the horny ridges where the riding frame had been.

Then she saw it. The ground stretched out to a point, elastic and pliable, but eventually it snapped underneath the pressure. Sliding out of the earth like a tooth, a white figure rose, perfect in every way.

A Leicester. Tilly watched in awe as the land birthed a god. The white warrior supported by an enormous cenotaph: LEST WE FORGET, it began. It listed hundreds and hundreds of names. Honoured sacrifices.

Tilly had spent her entire life in Carmel, the city of statues, but never had she seen such a perfect example of the Leicester-We-Forget. It was twice the height of a normal man, and its features were not marred or warped. It was perfect down to the last button on its shirt. Tilly slid out of the saddle, unnoticed by Dogwyfe as she made for the cenotaph. The monstrous women ignored her, quailing and muttering in the face of this miracle.

Turtwurdigan had led her true, shown her the way to the Waking City. Tilly felt the rumbling of the earth as the bleedthrough began. Kneeling on the lower steps of the marble shrine she wept, praying and burbling and shaken to her core.

Through a cloud of marble dust, she looked up to see the Leicester moving, stone imbued with the motion of flesh. The marble soldier inched downwards, using the ornamental carvings on the bottom pillar as finger and toe holds.

"My lord," Tilly whispered, rising and backing away with fear. The Leicester regarded her impassively, a stone spider that crept towards her, towards the ground.

The earth shook as a forest of glass and steel arose, every angle perfect, every windowpane clear and bright, structures of impossible size, great buildings that loomed far overhead and made her dizzy to look upon.

A city, awoken.

She heard the screech of Dogwyfe and the stuttering roar of Slopkettle. Tilly looked down to see her captors run, pursued by dozens of Leicesters. Even now, more statues rose from the split in the earth, leaping down from their plinths and hefting their stone guns.

One moment, the plain of salt was flat, uninterrupted. Then a twist of shadow, a vertical slit parting just far enough for a Taursi to slip through. It stood there for a long moment, one foot still resting on the shadow-road until it decided that none were watching.

The spiny creature walked along the edges of the salt flat, piercing the thick crust with its spear. Frogs slumbered underneath the salt, fat with water as they lay waiting for the once-in-a-decade rains.

On the shore of that dead sea, the witch's nest smouldered, half-melted and sagging. The wind was slowly driving the witch-stink away, and the Taursi decided it was once again a safe place to hunt. Curiosity drove it close to the wreckage of the camp, and it picked through the site, as all Taursi did when the invaders gave up on a place or were driven out.

The Taursi turned over smouldering tin with its spearhead, sniffing at the burnt flesh of a dead witch. There was bread here and a tin of flour. Putting these into its basket, the creature searched for more items to trade for grog.

The Taursi's bushcraft was good, but the fires dulled its senses, and it didn't smell the man hiding underneath the charred pile of blankets and rubble. Bursting out of the mound, Lanyard leapt onto the native and beat it senseless with his rifle stock.

He bound its hands together up to the elbow, making sure that the glass-glands on its forearm faced inwards. Lanyard had worked for the groggers and slavers so he knew all of the natives' tricks. The creature woke with a start then tried to run, but the leather hobble pitched it snout-first into the dust.

"Cut that out," Lanyard barked. "I caught you fair and square, so don't try nicking off."

The Taursi honked mournfully as it tried to wriggle out of its bonds. It leapt around the campsite, ungainly and confused, knocking over rubbish and causing an absolute racket. It hissed at him and brewed glass, but did nothing more than cut itself. Finally, it sank back against the side of the burnt nest, its quills settling as it watched its captor.

"You're done. Good." Lanyard gave the native a belt of bleed-through grog, which it lapped at gratefully, snout buried deep into the neck of the bottle.

"Might not have to kill you, or sell you. I'll make a deal with you, young lad," and Lanyard knew enough from his time as a slaver to name it as a young buck, a hunter without a tribe or a mate. No one would know its whereabouts, and they both knew this.

"I know about the other world, the grey one. The one between the others. Take me to the shadow-roads, and then I'll let you go."

The Taursi's eyes went wide, and it shook its head with terror. Lanyard gave the native a ringing back-hander and raised his fist to give it another. The Taursi whimpered and yammered in its own tongue, but it would not speak of the Greygulf or surrender the secrets of its kind.

Lanyard sighed. Bauer didn't have the time to teach him how to open the world veil, a discipline that required years of study, not the brief window of time Bauer's reprieve from death allowed. Once again, Lanyard's tuition as a Jesusman fell short of the task.

"Look," he said, popping open his shirt to reveal the Jesus tattoo. "I've been in there. Jesusman. I just need you to open the way. Do it, and I'll let you go."

It took an hour of cajoling and threatening, and more grog than he was prepared to give away, but Lanyard finally convinced the Taursi to open the shadow-road. Gripping it firmly by the elbow, he led it to the doorway where the tracks of the dead witches led to an unremarkable patch of ground.

"No funny business," he warned. "I'm coming in there with you."

Once more they stood inside the puckering doorway, standing on the winding silver band that was the shadow-road. Lanyard leaned over the side, retching and heaving as his stomach seemed to eject every meal he'd ever eaten.

When he stood up, he found the Taursi shuffling forward, attempting the slowest ever escape. It clung to the edge of the road as if working up the courage to jump and shatter its body on the silver soil far below.

"Don't be bloody stupid," he said. "Get up."

As they crept along, he kept watch for witches, but the shadow-roads seemed much quieter than the last time he'd been here. Nothing foraged on the plains below. All of the witches were elsewhere, as if drawn away by a summons.

"Trouble," he muttered to the Taursi, who looked at him fearfully. Indicating it to continue, Lanyard urged the creature across the nightmare landscape. The shadow-road brought them to the tall spire of Neville, the terminus of the shadow-roads.

Overhead an enormous bleedthrough was ready to pierce the world veil. The bulge pressed against another fold in the cosmic skin, wearing a way through. Soon it would burst like a boil, passing straight into the Now. A perfect bleedthrough of incredible size, shining with a strange golden light.

A line of shadow stretched across the silver sky, as if the sphere ran with a hair-line crack. It was a reflection of something in the Now, but Lanyard could not guess what it meant. The black line reached towards the bleedthrough, the end curled and waving about like a hair in the wind.

"More treasure in there than a man could ever spend," Lanyard said, pointing upwards. The Taursi honked quietly, terrified by the spectacle. It yammered at Lanyard, trying to tell him something about the imminent bleedthrough. It didn't know the man-tongue and could not accurately communicate its fears.

"I don't understand a bloody word of your language, mate," he said. "Got no idea what you're trying to say."

The Taursi gave up and shuffled forward as fast as the hobble would allow. After what seemed like hours on the shadow-roads, they stole into the lair of Neville. Lanyard watched carefully, wary of the gluttonous master of the house.

He needn't have bothered. Neville lay dead on the distant floor, his immense body crushed beneath a bombardment of bleed-through junk. Fridgerators and chunks of stone had been used with aerial precision, shattering his arms, grinding his head into jelly. Lanyard thought he could see marks graven into the items, enchantments rendering them effective against witch flesh.

They were Jesusman marks, the same as the ones on his guns. He frowned, puzzled at this development. Was this a revolution amongst the witches? Or was it the Jesus himself, the master taking revenge on his wayward servants?

Either way, Lanyard decided to get out of there as fast as he possibly could.

"That one," he said, pointing to another shadow-road with certainty. He did not know how he knew it was the correct way; there were dozens of roads in the terminus, like a tangle of silver string that met in the middle. But they followed it all the same, and

Lanyard had no doubt. This was the path back into the Waste, to the place where he'd been taken.

It could have been minutes or hours, but Neville's house was now a distant mark somewhere near the restless horizon. Out of the eerie quiet, a hollow booming sound ran through the Greygulf as if someone had struck an enormous kettle drum. Thunder without lightning, and the bleedthrough lurched across the sky on the verge of pushing through the world veil. The path beneath them shook.

A worrying crack developed on one edge of the shadow-road, and a large chunk of the silver pavement fell to the distant ground. Without a word, Lanyard quickly cut through the Taursi's hobble. Pulling the native to its feet, he urged it to run. The native soon outstripped the human, loping along on its back-bent legs.

Lanyard ran until his sides ached, each breath an agony. Across the landscape, he saw a distant shadow-road give way and collapse. The tremors snapped a great span and sent it tumbling to the ground, columns and all.

Ahead, he heard an excited honking and saw daylight. The Taursi had reached the end of the path and was holding open the doorway for him. It beckoned him to hurry with its bound arms.

"Wait," he gasped, and a final tremor sent him to his knees, almost to the lip of the elevated pathway. He pushed himself away from the precipice, shaking at the nearness of his escape. Rising, limping, he leapt through the doorway, gagging and retching as the shift between worlds worked its usual misery on his insides.

"You waited for me," he managed to say. Without another word, Lanyard slit the Taursi's bonds and watched as the creature brewed up a batch of sharp glass, finely weighted and ready for throwing.

The creature finished its work, quills settling and dimming to a dull red as the heat dissipated. It quickly snorted up a drift of loose sand to line its second stomach for future glass firing.

Lanyard scanned the Waste, featureless in every direction. Behind him, the distant shape of the bottle-tree, the place where Slopkettle had chained him and left him for dead.

Ahead, the Waking City. Tilly Carpidian needed him, and a promise was a promise.

The Taursi honked excitedly when Lanyard brought out the shard of Turtwurdigan from his satchel. He unwrapped it from the cloth and fed it a trickle of sunlight to glean the direction to Tilly. He fought against its seductive pull. The Jesusman looked up from his interrogation of the glass to see the Taursi bowed in worship, claws spread as it pressed its face into the earth.

"I guess you're coming too," he told the native, and when he set off on the correct path, it leapt up to follow.

20

The big Leicester carried Tilly on its shoulders, jostling her around roughly as it lurched along the street. Behind followed the bestial roars of Dogwyfe and Slopkettle, knocking over the other bleedthrough statues and pushing through their ranks.

The Leicesters came to her aid, wordless and plodding. Perhaps they recognised one of the faithful or they were compelled to guard the weak from monsters. Perhaps they had a different doom in mind for her.

Either way, a reprieve.

Slopkettle and Dogwyfe had spent the last few hours lurking on the edges of the Waking City, terrified, but hunger defeated cowardice. The mutant women were far from human, but now that they'd seen their untold wealth, their blasted minds remembered the girl and remembered the joys of a bubbling greypot.

"Quick! She's coming," Tilly told the stone soldier. It didn't speak to her but regarded her with that vigilant stare, its expression fixed. She looked back to see a knot of smaller bronze soldiers beating at Dogwyfe with their false rifles. The birdwoman simply barrelled through them, scattering statues like leaves.

The Jesusman's gun strained against Tilly's back, a useless hunk of iron without any shells. But she wouldn't leave it behind. To give up on it meant giving up on Lanyard, and if she did that she might as well climb into the greypot herself.

Slopkettle roared, an echoing whine that bounced against the glass canyons. Tilly clung tightly to her saviour, ducking as a large jag of metal whistled past her head. The flenser was fashioning knives out of her new flesh, shards of steel that she hurled through the air with reckless abandon.

"We need to get above them. Off the streets," she said, pointing through the ranked buildings up to their dizzying heights. The big statue nodded once and plodded forward. Its marble feet sank into the pliable earth, but it made the most of the bleedthrough, sticking to the occasional cement footpath, jumping onto patches of fused asphalt where the Before-Time roads once ran.

"Girl!" she heard Dogwyfe shout. Tilly turned to see the mutant grinding a soldier into the earth with her claws, plucking stone men from her back and hurling them into the buildings on either side. Statues fell into old storefronts, still marked with the names of the merchants and pictures of goods Tilly didn't recognise.

The Leicesters bounced from the plate-glass windows, and Tilly watched in disbelief as the statues stood up and chased after the changlings. The glass wasn't scratched, though it should have shattered into a thousand pieces.

"What is this place?" she whispered, as her rescuer reached the side of a brick building that was half the height of the skyscrapers around it. The Leicester stretched out to its fullest height and snagged a ladder with its fingertips. He slid down the steel rungs. Tilly saw that a rickety iron stair ran to the top of the building.

The folks of Before had elevator boxes. Something like this would be for emergencies only, especially if it was located on the outside of the building.

The roar of Slopkettle was closer now. Shaking, Tilly climbed up the statue's arm, hauling herself up and onto the ladder. When the statue made to follow, the steel frame groaned and a support bracket began to pull away from the wall.

The big Leicester stepped back and pointed upwards with some urgency, glaring at her with the same stoic expression. Tilly did not need to be told twice. She climbed up the ladder as quickly as possible. When she reached the staircase, the statue seized the ladder and gave it a twist, snapping the metal frame and then letting it drop to the ground.

With the heavy shotgun bouncing against her back, Tilly climbed towards the heavens, muscles straining as she cleared flight after flight. She made the mistake of looking down, and the iron grating of the steps seemed flimsy with the ground a distant place. If she slipped over the rails, she would splatter like a bug.

Slopkettle was below, wrestling with the big Leicester statue. Steel met stone as the two monsters traded blows. Dogwyfe was leaping up against the building trying to grab the bottom of the fire stair. A vast horde of statues below mobbed the pair and tried to stop them.

Closer to the roof now, Tilly spotted her reflection in the glass across the street, and she looked like a tiny termite scaling its nest. Suddenly, the whole staircase lurched, nearly shaking her from the handrails. Dogwyfe had finally clawed onto the fire stair and was climbing up the outside of it, yelping excitedly and crying for "Meat!"

Everything shook, and Tilly cried out as she tried to keep her footing on the stairs. She heard the squealing of metal as the brackets strained under the weight of the bird. The lower half of the staircase pulled free of the building and the wobbling frame fell onto Slopkettle and the crowd of statues directly beneath. Plummeting to the earth, Dogwyfe scattered soldiers like they were skittles. She limped away, yowling with pain and frustration.

Tilly continued her ascent. When she reached the safety of the roof, she shook with relief, adrenaline souring in her stomach. She took in the majestic view from her eyrie and a smile spread across her face.

The Taursi showed Lanyard the secret way of travelling, the one they used for places where the shadow-roads did not run. Cradling Lanyard in his arms like a giant baby, the spiky native moved forward at a blur, his quills spread out to their full extent. Lanyard felt a great heat come from the creature and saw his clothes start to singe wherever they touched the Taursi's skin.

The landscape before them blurred, and Lanyard felt the world veil shift just a little, as if pinched together by an enormous finger and thumb. With its claw, the Taursi made a ragged tear in the veil just big enough for the two of them.

The Taursi took a league-long stride and then another. Lanyard gritted his teeth against the searing heat and ignored the sweat that ran into his eyes. He needed to do this.

Eventually the Taursi indicated that it was tired, and it set him down. It snuffled at the earth with its snout. Lanyard saw beads of hot glass dripping from its quills and understood how much this magic taxed the creature.

"Enough," he said. "We can walk awhile."

This far into the Waste, it seemed like they had left most of the freaks and mind-traps behind. They only met with a weatherboard slap shack, which kept pace with them for an hour or two. It never moved when looked at directly, but the building slowly closed in, circling them like a predator. Finally, it stood in their path, door yawning open like a mouth. Within, he heard the scratchy sound of a record player, dead voices warbling a forlorn tune.

"Piss off," Lanyard said as he put bullets through each of the windows. The Jesus-marked guns caused it pain, and it howled at them, until the door slammed shut and cut its cry short. Lanyard raised his hand to sketch out a mark of unmaking, but the boards started to give and the whole structure collapsed in on itself.

"Have to burn it, just to make sure," he said, digging into his pockets for a match. The Taursi honked mournfully at the jumble of rotting wood.

Lanyard called a rest as he burned the predator house into ash. The directionless sun seemed at its highest, and he drew the chattering glass out of his satchel. Turtwurdigan drank deeply of the sunlight and showed Lanyard the bleedthrough. The beacon was a broad column of golden light now less than a day away.

"Hesusman," the old spirit whispered. "Friend of old."

He felt his head turning, as if in the grip of a powerful hand. Once more, he looked across the Waste, southwards to the settler lands. A smoking column beckoned to him, marking the antithesis of the Waking City. Sad Plain.

"No," he said and threw the cloth back over the glass. His hands shook with the effort of resistance. Only when he buried the glass deep into his satchel did he regain a mastery over his own thoughts.

Tricky bugger, Lanyard mused. *What's it playing at? There's nothing at Sad Plain, nothing but broken glass and bullshit.*

"Oh, get up," he said as he nudged the Taursi with his boot. Once more the native lay in supplication, mumbling whatever passed for a prayer to those people.

"You wanna carry it?" He offered the satchel to the spiky beast. The young buck retreated in horror, honking and holding up his hands.

"Settle down, mate. Just pulling your leg."

Lanyard set a billy over the embers of the house and boiled a pot of tea. He felt the same light-headed tingle of old, the first idle squirt of adrenaline. He knew in his bones that a killing time approached. The little ritual with the tea calmed him, and only here at the end of things did he realise that this was Bauer's habit, one he'd been aping for years.

Soon, he would have to stand tall, an inadequate man in a lonely place. Monsters were coming and perhaps gods. It was up to him to stop them all and save a kid who needed him.

Perhaps he wouldn't measure up. He might panic at the sight of his foe. The marks and words might jumble in his mind. He remembered fighting by Bauer's side, hands shaking and useless, bullets missing more often than not. A scared boy who tried to murder his way out of that life.

You could run, he thought. *This doesn't have to be your problem. Bauer doesn't own you. No one does.*

Live your last few days in peace. Find a woman and a bottle, see out the world's end in style.

The pot boiled. The Taursi tried the tea but spat it out in disgust. When Lanyard offered the native a cigarette, he accepted, wheezing and slobbering over it. Smoke curled out of his snout and his dark eyes seemed glazed.

"Nothing like a smoke and a good cuppa tea," Lanyard said, idly poking at the fire. "Life's pretty nasty, but if you can sneak in a smoke and a brew, you're doing okay."

The last of the Jesusmen looked over his kit. He stripped and cleaned the gleaming guns. When he held his hands out level, they did not shake. Dead calm. He thought of Tilly alone with the crooked women and felt shame that he'd ever brought his foul gang to her gate. It was up to him to fix this.

Spread out along the top of a fossilised bus, Lanyard adjusted the telescope. As he panned across the Waking City he whistled softly. The Jesusman observed the cluster of shining buildings, massive structures that made the Selector's Tower look like a slap shack.

"Look at that. Fos told the truth," Lanyard called out. The Taursi squatted in the shade of the half-buried vehicle, visibly scared at the sight of the enormous bleedthrough.

Like a garden of glass, the city slowly grew, one storey at a time. Around them the Waste trembled with a series of small aftershocks Lanyard felt deep in his joints. Perhaps this sinister land was wounded by such a large intrusion. Acres were displaced as the city pushed into the Now.

There was movement, and Lanyard twitched the far-glass left and right trying to find what walked in this mass of buildings and bizarre monuments. There. A white shape flicked into view, joined by another. Soon, a pack of white shapes ran those glass gullies, hundreds of them swarming and on the hunt.

"Witches," he said, his blood running cold. Then, he realised he wasn't feeling that typical dread down to his bone marrow, the famed witch-sniffing skills of the Jesusman. These were something else. Leicesters that moved like men, statues given life. He shuddered and hoped Carpidian's slouch-hat marked him as a friend.

He passed across that shimmering phalanx of skyscrapers punctuated by lesser buildings of brownstone and brick. Everything had bled through with perfection down to the street signs and traffic lights. A man with a crowbar and a sack would walk away from the Waking City with riches untold.

Then he saw her, and all thoughts of loot fled from his mind. At the edge of an apartment rooftop, a small figure sat, her mousy fuzz of hair tangled by the wind.

"Tilly!" he said, laughing with relief. He wasn't too late. The girl was safe for now, but when he saw the running battle underneath her high seat, his heart froze.

Two enormous creatures rushed at her building, battering at the doors and windows, throwing off the soldier statues that sought to pin them down. They were freaks from the Waste, twisted creatures that might have been human once.

A moment later, he realised just who they were. With a curse he snapped the telescope shut and reached for his rifle. Sliding down the gritty bus roof, he landed lightly and stalked towards the city with purpose.

"Don't stop," he warned the Taursi. Blinking against a sudden shift in the light, he kept his feet as the land itself lurched. Tonnes of loose dust drifted earthward, a dry mist that got into his eyes and made him cough.

He ran as he fought the sucking grasp of the pliant earth and pushed against the hills that rose and fell like little waves. Finally, he passed an unseen border, the outskirts of the bleedthrough. All of the lunacy ceased here, and even the sun moved the way it was meant to on this side of the line.

"Quickly now," he called to the Taursi. "Hell if I'm staying out there."

Lanyard's companion stepped into the outer edge of the Waking City, quills clicking together as he shivered with fright. He honked quietly, pointing a claw to the glass city with increasing frustration and insistence.

"Can you draw?" Lanyard said. "I don't understand a bloody word."

At the creature's blank look, Lanyard knelt with a sigh, tracing a finger through the dirt. Nodding with understanding, the spiky giant joined him on the ground. The concept seemed foreign to the creature, but eventually it drew a long scratch with a curling end. A snake or something with a hook on one end.

"Grook," the Taursi said, pointing at this mark, then back out into the Waste. It repeated the word but gave up in a sullen huff when the man couldn't grasp its message.

"Enough of that, I'll work it out later." Waving him forward, Lanyard kept low, using doorways and scattered vehicles for cover.

Everywhere the wealth of another world. He ignored it, worried only for Tilly.

If I can keep just this one promise, I'll be free of a million broken ones, he reasoned. *Poor kid shouldn't be caught up in this mess.*

Reaching a corner, he saw a bronze statue hurtle past him, arms wheeling. It landed in a bus shelter that crumpled like tissue paper.

A familiar howl, so close that it made his heart quicken. He peered around the corner and saw the thing that had once been Dogwyfe, a terrifying marriage between human and bird. Leicesters swamped her, and she lay about with an animal fury, snapping stone heads and knocking statues over with the cruel talons on her feet.

Slopkettle was something else entirely, and Lanyard shivered when he saw his old lover. A blend of steel and flesh, she ignored the statues that climbed all over her as she tried to kick in the main doors with a spinning tyre that was now her foot.

"Time to strike my colours," he told the nervous Taursi. He unbuttoned his shirt with an odd calm, revealing the Jesus tattoo to the world. Lanyard stepped around the corner, and walking coolly towards the melee, he fired a single round into the air.

Everything stopped. The living statues ceased their silent offensive and slowly advanced towards him, regarding him impassively. Lanyard looked warily at the crowd. He hoped that the combination of slouch hat and Jesus ink would mark him as a friend.

Bauer best be right on that front, he thought as he chambered another round into the ensorcelled rifle. The statues paused, unsure, and then Dogwyfe burst through their ranks, howling for Lanyard's blood. She bore down on him with lightning speed. He drew a bead on the twisted freak and noted in that last moment how the Waste had turned her into a perfect instrument of death.

He pulled the trigger, the rifle bucking in his arms, and then he stepped aside at the last possible moment, unflinching in the face of this flailing monstrosity. The tip of one claw snagged his hat, and then Dogwyfe slid past him, bloodied and screaming. He loaded another bullet and shot it into her face as she rose. Incredibly, she staggered towards him, oblivious to the ruinous holes in her chest and face.

Lanyard's Taursi ally honked, and what was left of the riding bird in Dogwyfe flinched at the sound. Wild birds feared the natives, their bridles and swift hands. Brewing up a handful of throwing glass, the Taursi filled the air with the sharp jags. Lanyard lined up his gun between the dazed Dogwyfe's eyes. One more thunderclap of gunfire and the ruined woman fell stone cold dead.

Then an engine roared, and Slopkettle slammed into Lanyard. He felt a rib crack beneath her steel fists and he toppled to the ground like a cloth doll.

Lanyard struggled to rise, cursing his stupidity. She'd come from an unexpected direction after circling the block, the chatter of her engine heart misleading in the narrow streets.

Coughing and wincing as the broken bones scraped around in his insides, Lanyard got to his knees. He could only watch as the bike-woman ran down the unfortunate Taursi, who cried out in fear and tried to run. The young buck threw glass and then scratched at the monster, curling up in a ball as she made pass after pass, grinding him into paste.

"Poor bugger." Lanyard gasped.

He looked for his enchanted rifle, only to see Slopkettle across the street, examining it with a sour look on her face. Slopkettle broke apart the gun with her chrome hands. With no effort, she split the stock and twisted the iron barrel crooked. She looked at him with the same scorn he remembered, but the only insult to pass her mouth was the mosquito whine of her motor, followed by a tiny trickle of blue smoke.

He'd kissed those lips. They were dark and grey now. Oil leaked from hoses that the statues had yanked loose, and she was wreathed with exhaust smoke, every inch of her frame dented and battered. One of her tyre-feet was flat, riddled with Taursi quills.

With a squeal of spinning rubber, she came for him, her gait lurching and uneven. It was all that Lanyard could do to lift one of his pistols and empty an entire clip into what was left of her face.

It was enough.

21

I 've got a theory about the Waste," Lucy said, drinking from a jam jar full of crème de menthe. He offered it to his brother, who waved away the frothy green liquid.

"Suit yourself. As I was saying, we knew this world had troubles when we picked it. Half-finished really, a nice spot in the middle to plant our refugees, but the edges weren't quite done."

He slouched in his usurper's throne, brought all the way from Crosspoint. A trio of slack-eyed children waved paper fans, trying in vain to drive the heat out of the tent. Another mind-slave brought him a map and unrolled it on the table. Lucy indicated that Bertha and the Boneman join him.

"If Turtwurdigan was the one who made this land, she should have left it a bit longer in the oven. Was she that stupid? I don't think so."

The Boneman recognised the map. It was one of the earliest surveys of the Now, drawn by John Leicester and himself, a vellum document crumbling around the edges. The ink had turned to sepia, very faint and hard to read. The Boneman gauged the document to be over three hundred years old.

Lucy planted his jam-jar in the centre of the map, leaving a sickly green ring on top of Crosspoint. The Boneman winced but said nothing. Lucy fished out another map from a pile on the table and laid it next to the historic document.

"See? The outer Range is slowly shifting," he said. "All of those mountains and foothills have moved south, over one hundred miles since we planted the flag. Three hundred more years and Price will be swallowed up by the Waste, maybe Peddler's Creek too."

Bertha gave up hovering over the table and settled her body across the rugs, nursing a jug of Riverland wine. The Boneman thought she was glorious, a savage beauty. She'd survived the depredations of the Cruik, and the slow grind of time had remade her inhuman, a mistress of lunatics. A goddess, in fact now as well as in name. He felt awe in her presence, perhaps a little fear.

Above all, he still felt love for his wife, and it grew by the day. They were broken, but they were alive and finally reunited. He could get past the infidelity, their recent failed attempt at connecting. After everything, they were alive.

Surely, the rest will work itself out?

"This tells me one thing," Lucy said, drawing in the Range's movement on the old map. "The world we are in was only ever meant to be a temporary one. The Waste is a mechanism built into the Now, a way to wipe things clean."

"That can't be right," the Boneman muttered, looking over the map, but realised the truth of things and saw the slow advance.

"In a few thousand years, this whole place will be blank. Wet clay ready for the next god who wants to have a turn. C'mon Sol, don't tell me you never noticed this. You know I'm right."

Lucy leaned in close to the Boneman and gave a weary grin.

"This world is an Overhaeven playground, nothing more. Sol, the gods are very real, and what's left of the human race is in danger."

The Boneman felt a moment of doubt, his transparent hands resting on the map beside his brother's. What if Lucy had a different motivation, the actual desire to save this world and the people in it?

Sad Plain was a gateway, he reminded himself. *So is the Waking City.*

Lucy is using us.

"It's no coincidence that this bleedthrough is happening on the furthest edge of the Waste, where the very fabric of this Realm is raw and pliable. Turtwurdigan is up to something rotten, and Hesus has been helping her."

The Boneman remembered his burning flesh, and swallowed nervously. Only Lucy could save them from the Mother of Glass. He was in this distasteful business to the bitter end, clutching his brother's coattails and praying that fortune would favour this bold maniac.

The Boneman knew he couldn't face Turtwurdigan on his own.

"There might be another Realm, somewhere safe we could go," Bertha offered. "Maybe we should just leave."

"Oh, don't worry," Lucy said. "I plan to."

The Waste worked its cruel magic on Lucy's army. Each mile changed the coin-riders in some small way, until almost every hour somebody became a growth on a camel or crawled into the engines of their machines and replaced them with enormous fleshy hearts, exposed and throbbing. Some of the conscripts simply took a step and crumbled into dust, their shadows freed and leaping southwards across the plain. Others went to sleep as people, only to meet the dawn as stone.

The Boneman wandered the camps offering what succour he could. He'd learned many Taursi magics from the memory-glass on Bertha's island, and sometimes he could ease or reverse the early cases.

"I didn't mean for that to happen to your uncle," he finally blurted. The girl looked pained, but blinked away a tear and met Lanyard's gaze with courage.

"Uncle Spence was a bad man."

"I'm just sorry you had to see that."

Tilly nodded.

"We're probably both going to die today," he continued, regarding his injury with something approaching calm. "Just being honest. Least I stopped those horrid bitches before they could get you."

"Why did you help me?" Tilly asked. "You've got your treasure now."

Lanyard said nothing.

"You're hurt because of me."

"No. This is not your fault," Lanyard said. "You're just a kid, and we took that from you. Didn't sit right with me."

He remembered another kid, this one not much older than the girl. Still wearing a noose around his neck, one end severed by a bullet, coughing and wheezing as an old fool gave him water.

"That's a nice lanyard you're wearing," Bauer had said, the day he both saved and damned a boy without a proper name.

"I'm not some stupid kid, mister."

"Never said you were stupid."

More wind, the shifting of stone feet. Lanyard felt the words bubble up, a confessional that leapt from his lips. He'd hidden the truth his whole life, but it felt so easy handing the burden to this girl. The words poured out.

"I... I lied to you. Back on the bridge."

"I know."

"I'm a Jesusman."

Tilly said nothing but lifted a heavy bundle from her shoulders and pressed it into his hands. Snapping a string, Lanyard peeled back the canvas to see Bauer's old gun. He smiled at the familiar curve of the stock.

Struggling against the grinding pain of his injury, Lanyard spent a while exploring the bleedthrough city. He noted the landmarks, places where vehicles formed bottlenecks on the street. The rooftops offered an excellent field of fire, but he didn't like the idea of being trapped in a building. Street fighting, then, if it came to that.

The Leicesters followed them everywhere, a silent band of body-guards. They seemed protective of their human guests but could not communicate in any way. Lanyard didn't understand their mobility and supposed that they were guardians, bound to the city in some way.

Most of the Waking City was a perfect bleedthrough, frozen in the exact moment the Before fell. Entire blocks full of Before goods, cupboards full of food. It would take years to gather up everything and cart it across the Waste to the land of people. Assuming you could find a caravan mad enough to make the journey.

The glass towers were something else altogether. Perhaps fifty of them, great monoliths that dominated the skyline and dwarfed the lesser buildings. As he watched, they stopped growing, one final aftershock shaking the street slightly. The towers reflected the sunlight more brilliantly than glass had any right to do.

When Lanyard held his hand against a shopfront window, he felt a faint hum, as if the skyscraper contained a multitude of bees. The glass was hot. None of the doors opened, and the door frames seemed set in place as if fused together. Each building was seamless, closed in, as if in imitation of the original structure. He yanked on a door handle as hard as he could, and the doors did not even jiggle a little.

One final test. A big gamble, but he had to know if Bauer was right. His heart hammering, Lanyard drew a pistol and fired at a ground-level window point blank. The bullet ricocheted, winging past his ear. He rubbed at the glass with amazement that the point of impact wasn't scratched.

"Good," he said. "We don't want these to open. That's how the world ends."

It pained Lanyard to move too far, so he called a rest. He and Tilly shared the last of the food from his satchel and sat on a car marked "POLICE."

"These were the bailiffs, the lawmen," Lanyard explained. "Back in the Before."

He used a crowbar to lever open the trunk of the car by snapping the lock. Tilly helped him pull out the lawman's shotgun and a box of shells. She plucked out a vest, body armour for bullets, but when Lanyard tried to strap it on, the armour pressed against the metal shard anchored in his flesh. Crying out in agony, he shrugged off the heavy vest and left it on the ground for all the good it would do him.

They experimented with strapping Lanyard's wound, but the pressure of the cloth strip caused him excruciating pain. He took a slug of booze, and another when the pain began to spread. Tilly stared glumly into the distance.

"My uncle was a physician," she said. "He might have been able to help with that."

"No doubt he could," Lanyard said. "If he was smart, he wouldn't help someone like me."

"He would help anyone. Even a faithless or a criminal. He said to live in service however you can. That is what is right."

"That's nice. The world doesn't work that way."

"Liar," she scoffed. "You're a helper too. My Nona Joan said the Jesusmen saved people. They fought the monsters."

"The Jesusmen changed," Lanyard said. "My master was a good man, but stupid. The family business wasn't going well, but he signed up for it anyway."

He pulled out one of the pistols to check the clip and safety. Tilly took it from him, wide-eyed and running her finger along the etchings, Jesus marks from barrel to tip. He gave her a quick instruction in its use, and between them they peppered the nearest street sign with bullets.

"My master never had his own kids, so he took me under his wing. I caught up with him the other day, had a good old chin-wag. Told me a bit about our mate here." Lanyard put the cloth bundle onto the hood of the car and unwrapped Turtwurdigan for a quick moment, long enough to catch its chatter and bullying. The spirit fell back silence when the cloth descended.

"Seems your mob and my mob were friends, secret chums back in the old war," Lanyard continued. "Good old John Leicester found this glass afterwards and thought it might help the Jesus out of a jam. The heart of Turtwurdigan."

Once more he felt the pull towards Sad Plain, but Bauer had explained this for what it was. The spirit in the glass shard was powerful, but it had the faculties and patience of a child. Turtwurdigan was an alien intelligence, blustering and grandiose, confused from centuries of captivity.

Quite simply, it didn't know what it wanted. All it needed was a guiding hand, someone to correctly interpret its one desire.

Turtwurdigan didn't want him to visit Sad Plain, and in its roundabout way, it only wanted to draw his attention to that ruin. It needed the bearer of the glass to mark this location and form a bridge between the two places.

Bauer's instructions were simple. Lanyard was meant to summon a broken guardian and hold the fort until it arrived. Anything else was the world's end. He could not fail.

Working up the courage, Lanyard whipped the glass fragment out of the cloth and held it up high. He did not fight the pull; he let his body become a conduit to this ground, a flesh lodestone to guide in something that was broken and lost.

Behind him, a set of double doors flew open, and Tilly raced onto the street, stone escort crowding close to her. He shouted at her to get back inside, but she ignored this to join him at the barricade.

"Get off the streets, you stupid girl!" He growled, but she remained there, a stubborn expression on her young face. He smiled despite himself when he saw a little girl stoic in the face of this thunderous death.

The lizard was close enough that he didn't need the telescope to see it. It darted from side to side, smashing into the buildings on the city outskirts, shaking off stone men like fleas. Leicesters lost their grip and fell, and whoever drove the lizard onward hurled down the statues as they tried to board the pagoda. Pieces of shattered marble rained to the ground, heads and limbs torn from the Leicesters.

"I got a feeling that's just the appetizer," Lanyard said. "Are you scared?"

She nodded once.

"Me too."

He felt the girl's fingers lace through his own, and without another word they waited for the first of Papa Lucy's creatures to meet them.

— 22 —

The lizard bounced along the street like an excited puppy, crunching cars underfoot. Lanyard stood nervously behind the final barricade. He wondered if the bank of trucks and buses would slow down the enormous monster.

It was barely two blocks away when another wave of Leicesters swung out of a side street. It wheeled on the spot, infuriated as the statues hammered it with marble guns and drove their blunt bayonets into its flesh.

Lanyard could see the driver now, a young woman perhaps half again the age of Tilly. She howled with anger, hunched over the controls of a weird machine gun.

Lanyard was close enough now to realise the extent of that mutation. It was more of a gland than a gun, a boil erupting from the lizard's back. The woman swept the gun across the attacking Leicesters, and a hail of bone and rock flew out of the spinning aperture, breaking the first row of soldiers into dust and shattered pieces.

In all the excitement, neither woman nor lizard noticed Tilly running low behind the row of cars. She sparked a cigarette lighter in one hand, trying desperately to summon a flame.

"C'mon," Lanyard urged. He was useless at this distance. He checked the action on Bauer's old shotgun and felt for the extra rounds in his pocket. He was ready.

Tilly finally sparked a flame and set it to the very end of the bedsheet then ran as the fire crept along towards the gas tank of a van. She hid behind a flight of steps the way Lanyard told her to, but in her haste, she knocked over a rubbish bin that sent the iron lid ringing.

The lizard turned at the sound, and its cruel eyes fixed on the little girl, her back to the wall. Thick ropes of drool fell from its metal fangs, and it ran for her, hissing and swift, climbing over the wall of cars.

Then the van erupted into a ball of flame and flying steel, the explosion almost directly underneath the giant. With an ear-piercing shriek, the lizard ran around in circles, batting at cars in its confusion, blindly seeking its attacker. A mess of guts dangled from a hole in its belly, and most of a car door was deeply embedded in its rear leg.

Above, the woman was trying to climb back into the pagoda, one hand hooked onto the fleshy railing. The gun hung limp in its harness with a dribble of bone falling from its tip.

Lanyard was over the barricade and running, shotgun primed. He couldn't see Tilly in all the smoke and feared the worst. The lizard stood between him and the burning wreckage, regarding him with rage. It snapped at him as if he were a fly, but the holy shotgun barked once, then twice. Blinded, the creature staggered backward. Cracks appeared in its face as the enchantments in the old gun told true.

As it crumbled it continued to stalk him, sniffing him out with bloody nostrils. Lanyard dropped the shotgun and swept his pistol up and out. He sent a tight cluster of bullets into the lizard's chest, and the corruption spread rapidly. As he loaded another clip with shaking hands, the monster fell apart, its flesh falling from its concrete bones, bubbling and hissing as the sun rendered it down to nothing.

"Tilly?" he called out, scooping up his shotgun. He ejected the smoking shells, but as he reached for fresh rounds, the young woman climbed out of the wreckage and came for him calmly.

She was beautiful, with the olive tan of a Riverlander. The woman wore crumpled travel wear and held out her empty hands. Lanyard hesitated as he snapped the breech shut with only one round chambered.

"Stop," he said, unwilling to shoot an unarmed woman. "No closer."

The woman smiled. Just as Lanyard realised that her healthy tan was actually a wood-grain skin, she struck. He fired the big gun but the strange woman was faster, her arm stretching out to an impossible length to bat the gun aside.

The woman's hand turned into a woody tentacle, circling the barrel of the gun like a treeroot grown. The symbols on the gun seemed to burn her, but she smiled against the pain, wrenching the gun out of his grip.

She cast it aside with a clatter and stepped closer. Lanyard drew his pistol but the woman seized his wrists in her warped hands and shook the weapon from his grip. Her wooden arms stretched out like warm toffee, and she held him up effortlessly. She drew his arms apart, and he cried out in pain as she gently teased out his limbs as far as they would go.

"Jesusman," she said, smiling sweetly with wooden lips. "I've been looking for you."

It felt like she was about to pull his arms out of their sockets, and his pierced stomach burnt with a renewed agony. She licked her lips, and slowly her tongue crept forward, a sharp root tip that rested against his eyeball.

"I'm only going to ask you once, Lanyard of Hesus. Where is the talking glass? Where is Turtwurdigan?"

"Die in a fire, you wooden bitch."

The monstrous woman looked at him with disappointment. As he braced himself, the tongue-root moved away from his eyeball to slowly wrap itself around his throat like a garrotte. A first gentle squeeze cut off all his air, with the promise of enough strength to snap his neck.

"I can smell the Mother of Glass, Jesusman. She's close."

Her wooden tongue withdrew from his throat, and he drew in a ragged breath. She poked into his pockets then smiled in triumph as she drew out the rag containing Turtwurdigan. She brought it towards her mouth with relish.

Then a gunshot. The woman keened with pain and dropped the glass. She cast Lanyard aside, then wheeled to face this new threat. The wooden creature loped towards Tilly Carpidian, who held her gun steady and drove another Jesus-marked round into the devil that ran at her.

The creature staggered, and Lanyard could see daylight through the hole in its belly. The magic spread, but something within the creature fought off the marks of unmaking and began to close the hole. It limped forward, wooden arms reaching for the young girl.

"Tilly, no." Lanyard wheezed. His pistol was underneath a car, the shotgun somewhere behind the dead lizard. Only one choice. Despite every step like a knife in his side, he dragged himself forward. Another shot from Tilly, this one a fluke head shot, and the creature was down on one knee, struggling to hold itself together.

Still those murderous arms crept, the deadly tendrils mere feet from the terrified girl. Gritting his teeth, Lanyard jogged forward, gasping with the movement.

He drew his bowie knife. As the woman embraced Tilly, he stepped behind her and drew the blade across her throat, driving it deep into the bark.

She gurgled, her arms falling limp as the life ran out of her. It was sap that ran over Lanyard's hands, not blood. He pushed the bizarre creature to the ground and stabbed again and again in the area where he thought her heart might be.

The etchings in the blade held true, and soon the woman was still. The tentacles withdrew and reformed into arms. Lanyard watched, amazed as the corpse shrank, limbs and head becoming narrower until only a brass-shod staff lay before him, one end curved into a shepherd's hook.

As Jenny looked down on her body and watched herself die, she felt a strange detachment. She sensed the horror of her violent murder, but her last living thought was one of defeat. Her holy quest had failed. The Jesusman had been in her clutches but she'd failed Papa Lucy.

Nothing would save her father now. She had let down her end of the bargain, and the god had no reason to spare Horace Rider from the riverlung. These living concerns were replaced by a sense of peace as she let the cares of the world wash away from her soul. She and her father would be together soon, the last of the Riders, reunited in the land of the dead.

A way began to open for her, an invisible door to elsewhere. Her soul took an eager step towards release, but something seemed to catch her foot and to hold her back.

She looked down to see the Cruik curled around her ankle and watched in horror as she was drawn away from the release of death and into the staff itself. The last she saw of the world was the Jesusman's face splattered with her life fluids, and then she was walking in the sunlit palace.

She trod the familiar halls, barely noticing when the big doors closed behind her with a finality. The other guests greeted her enthusiastically, and she had the vague feeling that she had passed some rite of passage, that she belonged here. She smiled, and it didn't matter that her mouth was just a slit in a featureless mask, her eyes pinholes.

There were many games and parties held in the house, and Jenny found herself welcome in every room, barred from no one and nothing. As she took a turn at croquet, a passing thought came to her. There had been a man by that fountain, a friendly man with a dog. He'd given her guidance the last time she visited, stern words but well meant.

The fountain bubbled away peacefully, but there was no man. She shrugged away the thought. It was a big house and perhaps he was walking his dog in one of the other gardens.

A shade lurked in the colonnades that watched as the newest guest began to lose her identity and sense of self. He knew that soon she wouldn't know her name and that one distant day the games and merriments would stop for her too. There would be nothing left for her but the shady corners of the house, and then oblivion.

The shadow man took a brief walk with what remained of his dog, and then the thought passed. He was content to be here, to stand in this corner. Everything was perfect.

"My Rider is dead," Lucy said suddenly, pushing away a terrified barber. "She's dead, Sol!"

The sorcerer hammered against the hood of his convertible, shaving cream dripping from his head. He shook with fury and cursed the heavens. Booting the low stool as hard as he could, Lucy called up a mark of fire that rendered the chair into flame and ash before it could touch the ground.

The Boneman came running to do his best to limit the damage as Papa Lucy raged, destroying the camp around him. Despite his effort to contain his brother's destructive energies, a lick of lightning escaped from Lucy's mouth. It danced across the car, shocking the life from the unfortunate barber as he ran for safety.

"That Jesusman killed Jenny," Lucy said, wild-eyed and panting. "He killed her, and now he has the Cruik."

"He's there already? In the Waking City?"

"When I fought Hesus in the Aum, I shook a handful of secrets out of him. Look." Lucy made a mark on the Boneman's forehead that sent him into a vision of the Waking City. Lucy's war camp disappeared and there was nothing but a blank spot in the Waste, the suggestion of something just beneath the surface pushing through the world veil. Marking that spot was a naked man inked with the marks of Hesus. Bloody and grinning, the Jesusman brandished Turtwurdigan's heart like a trophy.

Reeling, the Boneman fell to his knees. The vision faded. It was no wonder Lucy hadn't shared this with him yet. If Hesus had scried the truth of the future, victory was anything but certain.

Once more he stood in the presence of his brother, who had regained some of his composure. Lucy was emptying a can of hair spray into his new mohawk and teasing the hair up into a garish fan.

"I pressed the Rider as hard as I could, but that bloody Jesusman got to the Waking City first," Lucy said, applying a can of hair colouring. "We're up against it now."

"He won't take the Cruik. He can't," the Boneman said calmly. "Not in the way you think."

"What do you mean, he can't?" Lucy said. "It's right in bloody front of him. He just has to pick it up."

"You'll want him to," the Boneman said. "The moment he touches that staff, he is yours, heart and soul. The Cruik serves you."

A lie. He'd been there when Lucy bound the staff with brass and blood, but the Boneman had seen enough to know that the Cruik only served itself.

Whatever it took to keep Lucy on target, he would say it. Just that small glimpse of Turtwurdigan's remains had been enough to twist his gut. He remembered that bright light, and then the heat, the burning...

"Yes," Lucy said, finally cracking a smile. "That would be nice and ironic. One of *his* serving me."

Whipping out his megaphone, Lucy chivvied his monstrous army into motion, driving around the camp and delivering choice insults. Few of the conscripts were close to humanity but they rose grumbling from their rest, a vast force of mutants and gibbering machine-things.

Before them lay more trackless Waste, but the Boneman felt the pull of the gaping hole in the world veil that lay just beyond the horizon. Less than a day away.

He fought down the bubble of fear, the knowledge that Turtwurdigan was waiting for them. She'd robbed him of his body and was coming back to finish the job. It was time to put the spirit that slept in the glass down for good.

"Let's go, brother," Lucy said as he pulled up next to the Boneman. The door opened by itself, and the mohawked sorcerer patted the bench seat with a wide grin. "We've got nothing to worry about."

Lanyard stepped back with a curse when the woody corpse melted into a shepherd's staff. He'd seen a lot of weird stuff since swearing oath to Bauer, but the sight of that hooked pole gave him the shivers. He nudged it carefully with his boot, but his murderous enemy was just a walking stick now.

Then, he found himself admiring the craftsmanship of the staff and the elegant curve of the hook drew his eye. The brass hoops drew in the sunlight, and the whole thing seemed warm and clean, like it would be pleasant to the touch...

"Lanyard!" Tilly cried, appearing at his side and clutching his reaching arm. "Don't. It's not right. Leave it."

"Piss off." He snarled and shook her loose. He blinked as she held her gun to his head and took his eyes from the staff long enough to see her frightened face. The Carpidian girl desperately pulled Lanyard to one side.

"It's the Cruik," she shouted, slapping him across the face. "It belongs to Papa Lucy."

This news registered in his foggy mind. He'd seldom had time for the mummery and nonsense of the Family religion and had but a passing familiarity with their rite and trappings. But just like everyone else, he'd heard some of the folklore surrounding Papa Lucy's magical staff.

"That's what your Taursi friend was scared of," Tilly babbled. "The Grook. He meant to say Cruik. Papa Lucy sent that to kill us. Lanyard, please!"

He pushed the girl aside, all the pain in his body forgotten as he reached for the Cruik. It whispered to him and showed him what he might achieve if only he would stoop down and pick up the sorcerer's weapon.

The Cruik could heal his broken body. With it he could hurl those cars at his enemies, sweep down the very buildings on their advance. Fire, power, the ability to live forever, it could all be his. Hadn't Bauer abandoned him to die here? Where was Jesus when his final warrior needed him?

Lanyard could rely only on himself and the tools at his disposal. His Jesus guns were all well and good, but with this staff at his command? It was the ultimate weapon.

The Cruik was perfect.

"Yes," Lanyard said and reached for the staff, smiling. Then, a gunshot. Lanyard felt a searing pain in his leg. He saw the spreading patch of blood on his thigh and fell to the ground. Tilly stood over him with her pistol smoking. Now the gun was aimed at his heart.

"I'll do it," she said through her tears. "I'll kill you."

The agony of this new wound brought him back to full awareness. The seductive lure of the Cruik was an annoying mutter in the back of his mind. He dragged himself away, leaving a worrying blood trail in his wake.

The Cruik lay in the middle of the road where he'd left it, whispering, promising many things. He traced a mark of warding in the air, and the corruptive influence of Lucy's staff faded into background noise.

"You're a good girl, Tilly," Lanyard mumbled. "Good shot too."

"Father let me shoot at bottles," she said as she put the gun into the front pocket of her smock.

Using his belt to stem the blood flow, Lanyard jabbed the bowie knife into his wounded leg, screaming as he dug around searching for the bullet. He flicked it loose, and it fell to the tarmac with a clinking sound.

"I deserved that," he gasped. "If I do it again, give me another."

"You won't live to pull out a second bullet," Tilly said. She used a road flare from the lawman's car to heat up the knife. She cauterised his wound, and there was nothing left to say, just the screams that fought through his clenched teeth and the hissing of his flesh as it cooked.

— 23 —

The Waking City was before them, a skyline of golden towers that rose above the Waste. The Boneman thought it was beautiful and terrible, a shining fragment of something that belonged in the old world. But of course it was much more than a bleedthrough.

Where does your little gateway lead, Lucy? he pondered. *What other world are you leaving me for?*

Though Papa Lucy itched to advance, the Boneman begged him to pause and insisted that his undead troops required maintenance before they could advance on the city. Papa Lucy settled down to play backgammon with something that used to be a buggy, but now resembled a fleshy ball of arms and wheels.

"Be quick about it," Lucy said as he rolled the dice.

By far the largest contingent of the Family's army were the risen corpses at the Boneman's command that were formed into neat squares. He walked through their ranks barely noticing the putrid stench of rot. Waving away a cloud of flies, he looked over the mouldering soldiers and made pretence of investigating his own sorcery. The magic that kept these bodies walking would hold true until he released it. He held thousands of souls hostage, denying every one of them the peace of the Underfog.

"I'm sorry about this," he told the nearest revenant, a coin-rider turning to rot. The dead man stared at him dully. The Boneman sensed the resentment of his trapped spirit.

The bones were starting to shiver and splinter. The Waste was quickening his necromancy's corruption. Some of the corpse soldiers had turned the way of the living, merging with vehicles and stone. A cluster of skeletons had formed into something approaching a giant horse, comprised of at least fifteen bodies.

The Boneman tolerated this ungainly structure, thinking wistfully of his own horses. It seemed a sycophantic move by his underlings to raise his pity.

"Just a little further," he told his servants, patting the dead gunman on the shoulder. "We're almost done. You'll be released soon."

He was little better than Lucy, he realised. At least his brother's mind-slaves were still alive.

At that moment he was tempted to undo all of his magic, to release every single dead warrior into the peace of death. Faced by rank upon rank of dead faces, he was sickened by the depths of his dependence on his brother.

Is there anything I won't do for that prick? he thought.

"What are you doing?" Bertha said, stomping over with a coterie of madwomen in tow. She wore a set of thick iron plates of armour for the imminent assault. "We need to take down Turtwurdigan. Right now. Have you lost your nerve, Sol?"

"I wanted to talk to you," he said. "Without him around."

In the camp, Lucy raised his fists in triumph, pleased with the results of his game. His opponent rumbled and belched out a cloud of exhaust, limbs slumping with dejection. They might not have very long.

"I'm scared, Baertha," he said. "But I'm no coward. Turtwurdigan can't live, not after what she did to us. We finish this today."

"Why are we stopping here then?" Bertha said. "Let's get on with this."

"Listen," he said, laying a hand on her monstrous forearm. Their broken bodies were grotesque enough, but as their flesh touched, it proved that humanity was a distant memory. Bertha flinched and drew away.

"Please," he said. "What happens after Lucy opens his gate and abandons us forever? There's nothing here for him."

"You're brothers."

"There's nothing here for him," the Boneman repeated.

"Our little family is finished, Sol," Bertha said with a sigh. "If we survive this day, if our business is finally done, it's—it's probably right that we go our separate ways. It's been a long time coming."

"We've only got each other now," the Boneman said softly. "Please, I want to give it one more try. Baertha, I love you."

A tear suddenly leaked across her broken face, and Bertha struck like a snake, knocked him over with a swipe of her claws. Coughing up dust, he struggled to rise and watched as his monstrous wife stormed away.

"What's the point of forever if you're alone?" he called out, but she did not stop.

Fos was busy with the axe. The remaining Leicester statue stood vigil over the sacrifice, every inch of marble daubed with blood. Most went willingly, and only one man broke and ran. He died with a dozen bullets in his back.

"Better a clean death here, one in service of your god," Fos thundered. "Make your peace. It's time."

Mothers, babies, the old, all went to Leicester-We-Forget to take up a seat in his bloody hall. Fos made a neat stack of the heads. He let one of his nephews take over the axe work when his old arms grew too tired to lift the hatchet.

The sun began to set on that butchery. Fos took the axe and gave his nephew over to the Leicester-We-Forget. The boy met his death without so much as a whimper. A final peace, and now it was his turn.

Fos Carpidian stood alone surrounded by his dead kin. Kneeling at the base of the statue, he calmly hefted a pistol and held it to his temple.

After taking a moment to collect himself, the old man pulled the trigger. His final thoughts of Tilly were cut short by the crack of the gun. His brains painted the stone plinth.

Then, nothing but the silence of the dead.

The sun drew towards the horizon and the blood dried. Scavengers came out of the Range to feast on the stacked bodies. But they scattered in terror when the impossible happened. The bloody statue moved like a man, climbing down from the plinth and walking through the corpses with a heavy but careful tread.

With every step it grew, the stone frame pulsing with a terrible force, drawing mass and life from a distant place. The red statue was soon twice a man's height, and still it was growing, the marble tunic cracking and reforming over and over.

The Leicester swept its impassive gaze across the sacrifices as if mourning those it once knew. Hefting its stone rifle, the bloody warrior opened a doorway to somewhere else and stepped through into a golden light.

Tilly pulled a tarpaulin over the Cruik taking care not to touch it. The girl carefully rolled the staff into a bundle and bound it tight with a roll of duct tape.

Broken and weary, Lanyard sat with his back to a car, the bright glass of Turtwurdigan resting in his palm. He had nothing to fear from the spirit now. As it fed from the sunlight, its bizarre rantings seemed to comfort him.

It tests her, the glass said. *Fallen fools promise much.*

Tilly paused for a long moment halfway through winding the tape around the bundle. The girl frowned, moved her lips silently. Shook her head. Snapping out of the trance state, she rapidly finished her work and threw the wrapped Cruik to the ground in disgust.

"Kid's stronger than me," Lanyard told the spirit in the glass. "Ten years old and she sees through its bullshit. Not me."

Tilly dragged the bundle towards the barricade, and the Leicesters covered the staff with bleedthrough junk. Finally, a row of heaving statues overturned a truck onto the pile. Whoever wanted the Cruik would have a hell of a time pulling it out from underneath all of that.

The Papa comes! Turtwurdigan interrupted, a moment of clarity amid its constant raving. *The Family comes!*

With a twisting pain in his guts and the gunshot wound throbbing, Lanyard slowly drew himself up and onto his feet. Drawing out the telescope, he watched as thousands of twisted figures emerged from the Waste, a terrifying host that filled the sky with dust.

Papa Lucy's horde were making straight for him and the golden towers behind his junk wall. Sensing the intruders, the remaining Leicesters drew into a ragged line, with Tilly's big marble friend at the centre. Barely fifty of the stone guardians remained. Lanyard wondered if they would be able to slow down the assault.

He knew then that he was facing his death and living his final moments. Despite Bauer's intervention, despite his courage in taking up the most lost of all causes, there was nothing he could do to stop the world from ending. His entire journey was a farce.

"What am I meant to do?" Lanyard shouted, shaking Turtwurdigan as if that would provoke an answer. "How am I meant to stop an army? How do I kill a god?"

Be strong, Hesusman. A fast wind blows.

Using farsight, the Boneman spotted the Jesusman. He cut a pathetic figure, a wasted man staggering around behind a hasty barricade. If this was the last of Hesus's disciples, Lucy had little to fear. A young girl stood beside him. He briefly wondered if this was the man's daughter or his slave.

Before the Jesusman's junk wall he recognised a handful of John Leicester's soldier animates, leftovers from the old war. It seemed strange that these constructs would be guarding the Waking City. He had thought John's servants had all been wiped out during the pogrom.

Turtwurdigan was nowhere in sight. Not yet.

Behind this feeble defence, dozens of enormous sky-fingers painted the horizon with glass and gold. The Waking City. His brother's gate.

"Come on! Don't tell me John's here too," Lucy scoffed, peering through farsight eyes. "He obviously wasn't listening when I told him he was a dead man."

"He's already dead, Lucy," the Boneman said. "You saw how he went into the stone. Too deep."

"Good thing I brought some dynamite," Lucy said. Brow furrowing for an instant, he silently sent out his orders, and small groups of his mind-slaves raced about, scaring the monstrous vanguard into a semblance of order. Bertha and her psychotic warriors were in the first wave just behind the most Waste-twisted of the troops.

If Turtwurdigan showed herself, the Boneman was expected to send in the dead. In death they were weak, but their sheer weight of numbers would turn any battle, and fire did little harm to bare bones. That he knew, from bitter experience. He was the general of a silent reserve, his soldiers rotting and fly-blown.

Bertha met his eyes briefly over the press of troops, but she turned away. He'd been kidding himself. Baertha Hann was long gone and their marriage centuries dead. All that was left of his wife was a monster that loomed above the lesser creatures. He felt the anguish as the final cord connecting them fell away, the finality of her gesture obvious.

After tomorrow, if they lived, he would never see her again.

"We shouldn't go in that way," the Boneman told his brother, fighting off the dull ache in his chest. "All of the Jesusman's defences are in that narrow corridor. If we circle the city, we can reach the towers from the other side. It won't take us an hour."

"Sol, you're a boring man and that's a boring suggestion, even for you." Lucy dismissed the plan entirely, and the Boneman saw how his brother favoured one mad charge. Lucy was unable to do any differently, given that someone dared to stand in his way.

That's not to say that Papa Lucy was stupid. He certainly understood the fine art of delegation.

"Lady Bertha, be a dear and fetch me that Jesusman," Lucy said through the megaphone. "Do whatever you want with John's garden gnomes."

She nodded, snarling and baring a jagged row of teeth. Someone set a hand-cranked klaxon into a strident warble, followed by the tooting of a hundred car horns. An angry hum, the redline revving of coin-riders now grafted onto their machines.

Then the rush. The surge of broken beings thundered into the Waking City, straight into the funnel of barriers and roadblocks, into whatever traps the Jesusman had laid for them.

"I tell you, Sol, it's funny where ambition can take you," Lucy said matter-of-factly, a mad light dancing in his eyes. "Could you have imagined this? Back in the old world, you'd never have thought we'd end up here, today. You, all bones and misery, and your missus an actual ogre. Me, I'm still as handsome as ever."

He ruffled his mohawk playfully. Ahead, the shouts of the vanguard, a spatter of gunfire. Then Bertha's car was lost in the dust, and the Boneman's heart fell.

"Now, we're lording it over this broken arse of a world. All the pompous shits who doubted us are dead. The Collegia became a smoking crater, and under our watch, the human race fell to cannibalism and scavenging. An amazing life, and we saw it all. And now...now we get to see *this*."

The sorcerer pointed grandly to the golden towers that shined so brightly they were difficult to look upon.

"I ask you, Sol Papagallo, could you have ever imagined this moment?"

"Not in a million years," the Boneman said softly.

"That's because you have no imagination. I've looked on this scene every single day, my brother, every miserable day of my existence. And when this moment arrived, I always knew exactly what I would need to do."

"Do what?"

"Trust me, Sol. It's gonna rock your world."

Bertha leaned out of the speeding buggy, her personal chariot now a hybrid of undead flesh and scavenged mechanics. One of John's stone soldiers reached for her, and she swung an iron pipe with precision, snapping its marble head clean off.

Her mutated buggy slammed into a cluster of bronze men, scattering them in all directions. The fleshy engine chattered and then died. Bertha saw a bronze rifle lodged, bayonet first, into what passed for the vehicle's heart.

As she struggled to extricate herself from the buckled vehicle, a large marble soldier came for her, half again the size of its comrades. It slammed the butt of its rifle into her face, and again.

She lay trapped, fighting off the stars and the spinning darkness that beckoned.

"No!" She growled and brought up the iron pipe, blocking the stone gun. Swiping downwards, she snapped the false gun in half. Fighting like a cornered dog, she sent the statue reeling backwards with a web of cracks spreading across its broken face.

Finally, she pushed the bent frame aside, the metal tubing squealing and then snapping before her strength. Rising above the melee, Lady Bertha climbed out of the wreckage gripping the iron pipe in her ham fist.

The big Leicester came for her. With a snarl, she broke off the hand that reached for her. When the jagged stump came around in a haymaker, she wrenched the arm clean off.

The other fist rang against her armour plating. The statue pinned her to the car and drove its broken head into her nose. Stone fingers closed around her throat.

Fighting for breath, she reached up and snapped the statue's head and broke its arm off at the shoulder. The hand continued to choke the life out of her, and she slowly plucked at the marble digits, twisting them off one by one.

"Stop trying to kill me." She gasped as she wrenched off the statue's legs like drumsticks. The disembodied limbs continued flexing as they kicked at her. She remembered fighting these animates during the first pogrom, enforcing Lucy's shit-fit in the months after John Leicester turned rogue. None of them had given her this much trouble. Only after she had stripped it down to a torso did the Leicester grow still.

Around her the advance was bogged down, her loping mutants held back by a stern-faced wall of stone and bronze. Mad Millies darted through gaps in the melee, but their knives and guns had little effect on their stone enemies.

The Jesusman had set wards, spray-painted marks of unmaking and warding that flared. Her soldiers fell. They reformed into their constituent parts and died from shock. But the marks were crude, and it was child's play for her to undo the worst of them to allow more of her people to advance.

Every Leicester that fell took a dozen of her vanguard with it, and their strange corpses piled high. Those Millies who had crude bombs or grenades from Before hurled them at the statue line, blowing up friend as often as foe.

"Enough of this," Bertha said. Then she felt a tickle in her soul that stopped her in midstep.

The Cruik was nearby, close enough to call to her. The Jesusman had tricked it into captivity, bound and hidden behind his little wall. The Cruik promised her strength, promised to serve her exclusively. It had been so long since she'd touched the staff, and the long-forgotten absence seized her body and soul. She ached for the Cruik, she needed it.

Gasping, sweat washing across her bloody face, she remembered the moment that Lucy came for her with similar promises on his smiling lips. Then, the touch of the staff as they lay together in her husband's bed, the thrill as its power caressed her. Started to change her body.

"You'll be perfect," Lucy had told her. The first of many comfortable lies. Bertha felt anger then, an old jealousy she'd forgotten in the long night of her madness, pacing and mindless in the ruin of love's home.

The Cruik was hers.

A handful of the mutant machines broke through the line and made for the final barricades where the Jesusman stood between them and the golden towers. Bertha saw the buggy-things roar forward screeching and smoking. Part of the car wall exploded, burying her forces in metal and rubble. Then the popping of gunfire, two guns coughing lead at the survivors.

"Forward!" she yelled. "Break these damn things!"

Shouldering a wounded bird-thing out of the way, Bertha pushed into the front of the line, battering a bronze soldier into a flattened mess. Another Leicester reached for her, and she sent its marble head flying.

In every stern visage, she imagined Sol's face and found that this helped. Her own face bloodied, her armour plate hanging by one remaining strap, Lady Bertha fought on and fought through. It cost them hundreds of dead, but she didn't mourn a single one of her soldiers. That was what Sol was for. Every soldier that fell in Papa Lucy's service would fight again, and again, until they were dust.

The last of the Leicester animates lay broken, severed limbs twitching. Now, nothing stood between her and the Jesusman but a wall of junk and whatever crude booby traps he'd managed to assemble.

The Cruik called to her, begged her, promised itself.

Looking over her shoulder, Bertha felt reassured. Sol's walking graveyard stood ready, plus the rest of Lucy's warped army. Hesus's final servant was about to make a pointless last stand.

Then I'll be free, she thought. *Free of that charming bastard and his mope-faced little brother.*

I'll take the Cruik, and they'll never see me again.

"You lot, go in and get the Jesusman," she told a group of bike-wheeled camels. "Alive."

She drew the mark for farsight with one talon then drank in the terrified faces of the Jesusman and the girl at his side. They cradled their Jesus-marked guns as they watched the approach without a word. A smile crept across Bertha's ravaged face, and it was a terrible thing.

Then she felt it. A push from elsewhere, the sense that something was stepping through from a distant place.

Even as her monsters leapt forward, the world veil tore right there in the middle of the street. A golden far-door eclipsed the towers behind it, the other side so bright that it pained her to look at it.

An enormous Leicester stepped out of the gap, a tower of stone that stood three times the height of a man, with every inch of the stone soldier stained a deep crimson. The asphalt cracked beneath its heavy tread. Behind it, hundreds of figures spilled from the sorcerous gate, gleaming in the otherworldly light.

Then the far-door winked closed. Bertha saw the red giant stand above a host of Taursi, but these were not the rude prisoners that died one drink at a time. These were clad in glass breastplates, their limbs sheathed with shining bracers. Quills spread and glowing white hot, the creatures drew shining blades from within themselves through apertures in their transparent armour.

On each breastplate, a sigil glowed with a soft light. Bertha recognised the sign that was scrawled over and over Papa Lucy's clay body as she and Sol brought him back into life.

These strange Taursi bore the mark of the Overhaeven. They were exactly the same as the ones she'd fought at Sad Plain.

"No," she said with a tremor. Her troops quailed before the giant, and some of them openly turned and fled. The red Leicester stepped forward, swinging its sculptured rifle like a scythe. It scattered the first rank of Bertha's force and stomped on a bird-thing mad enough to attack it, crushing it into paste.

The Taursi charged honking and leaping, and filled the air with glass and death. When the shards struck flesh, it was like the breaking of a miniature sun, a bright flash of light as it burnt the enemy from within.

Those that held fast against this terrifying onslaught answered with gunfire, but the glass armour of the Taursi held against this offensive, often taking two or three bullets before cracking.

Swatting aside deserters and anyone who stood in her way, Bertha pushed through the packed lines of her freaks on her way towards her ruined buggy. Leaning inside, she plucked out an enormous rifle. Near as Sol could figure, it had been an elephant gun in the Before. They'd removed the trigger guard to fit her misshapen hands.

Before the Collegia had fallen from the sky—before she'd married into poverty and infamy—Baertha Hann had spent many weekends hunting on the family estates. She hadn't forgotten a trick.

Climbing onto the top of the wreck, Bertha rained bullets onto this force of Taursi, each round punching through their armour as if it were paper. The rifle gave a mighty kick, but she was big enough to ignore the recoil.

Even as she worked the massive gun, Bertha spoke the words of madness and fear, sending marks flying into the press of battle. Some of the Taursi staggered and shook their heads as they fought an internal battle. Others broke and fled, or laid into friend and foe alike.

When she'd given the Taursi enough grief, she turned her attention to the giant Leicester. Her bullets knocked big divots out of its face and neck, and she sent a cluster of rounds into its stone heart. It continued to stride through her soldiers, carving a bloody path towards her.

"Baertha," it boomed, broad mouth open and stone lips flexing. Its features moved slowly and shifted subtly. Stern eyes gave way to a friendlier cast, hard cheeks filling out, moulding into a round face wrinkled with laugh lines. She remembered seeing that face in a chapel, smiling and hopeful as he gave her to another man. In later times, he'd smiled less and frowned more. He kept his own counsel when once he'd roared with laughter, loved, and fought with passion for the things that mattered.

Now that familiar face hung with sorrow, grief tinged with anger.

"John?" she whispered.

A shadow fell across her face as her old friend raised his rifle.

— 24 —

J ohn bloody Leicester," Lucy said, shaking his head. "Of all
the dead shits to make an appearance. Oh well. Let's go kill
him."
 The Boneman stood up in the moving convertible, shading
his eyes against the flashes of light and using his farsight to
penetrate the smoke from the burning vehicles. He boggled at
the sight of Taursi bearing Overhaeven marks and fighting with a
glass-magic he'd never seen the likes of.

None of this was as concerning as the sudden reappearance
of an old ally, a friend he'd thought long dead. He watched with
sickened fascination as John Leicester stalked through the chaos
and straddled Bertha's buggy with his tree trunk legs.

Bertha stood frozen before her fate, her gun forgotten as the
stone man loomed above her. Sol saw their lips moving as the old
friends spoke to each other with brief words.

In a final moment as Bertha stood hypnotised by terror, John
raised a stone rifle the size of a telegraph pole. Then the gun butt
fell with a dreadful blow that shook the buggy. When the giant
soldier turned away to take the slaughter elsewhere, Lady Bertha
wasn't moving.

The Boneman fell back into his seat and grief gripped his chest, a bubble that rose up into his throat and burst. He howled with sorrow and shook as tears leaked across his ruined face.

"Plenty more fish in the sea, buddy," Lucy said cheerfully.

"She's dead, you horrid fuck," the Boneman sobbed. "My wife is dead."

"Hey, take it out on the bad guy, Sol. Just trying to lighten the moment."

Blinded by tears, the Boneman summoned his thousands of mobile corpses and sent them teetering into the Jesusman's funnel of death. Then he made them run, pushing them faster still, heedless of the damage it did to their fragile bodies. They passed around the roaring convertible, a tide of bone and rot that swept into the Waking City. Dozens of the corpse soldiers were consumed by the magic and crumbled, then were trod underfoot by the thousands following behind.

"That's the spirit!" Lucy shouted, leaning hard on the car horn. "Give 'em hell."

Papa Lucy drove into the madness at full tilt, knocking aside friend and foe alike. The street was like a field of stars gone nova as the strange Taursi glass magic burned away Lucy's front ranks. But these bright flares were slowing. The Taursi had used up nearly all of their mysterious weaponry, and now the Waste-twisted freaks began to drag them down.

Above this battle strode the red giant, batting aside any who came within reach. It was John Leicester recast into the image of a First Soldier. *The sad fixations of a wannabe warrior carried out to their conclusion*, the Boneman thought. He remembered the rain of shards on Sad Plain and the moment that John's life bled out, when he abandoned flesh for stone.

He'd been a traitor then. And John Leicester continued his treachery. The Boneman saw the buckled wreck of Bertha's buggy and the flashes of her prone body as Lucy's maddened beasts wheeled past striking into the Taursi's flank.

"Where have you been hiding, John?" the Boneman shouted, grief stricken. He snatched up a gun from the arsenal in the backseat and clumsily emptied a clip into the red titan.

Stone chips fell from the bullet holes, which had no more effect on the giant than a cloud of biting gnats. Propping a rocket-propelled grenade launcher over the windshield, Lucy sent the missile spiralling towards John's chest. It struck with a cloud of fire and smoke, the explosion knocking the giant back a step. Thick sheets of stone rained on the melee below, crushing mutant and Taursi alike.

That got John Leicester's attention.

"Quick, get me another grenade. From that box there," Lucy said, shouting impatiently as John Leicester came to meet them. His great stone boots beat a path towards their fishtailing car.

"Oh damn it," Lucy said, kicking open his door and rolling free. The Boneman barely had the sense to follow a moment before the stone rifle fell. John staved in the front half of the car. The old motor gave a final death rattle, while John's next blow remodelled the passenger compartment into pressed tin.

"That bastard wrecked my ride!" Lucy shouted, face flushed with anger. The Boneman fell prone as the enormous rifle came around on the backswing, a stone tree trunk that swung mere inches above his head.

"This way!" Lucy said, dragging his brother to his feet. They ran through the press of battle. Lucy called up fire marks on his own troops and burned them to ash when they blocked his passage. As John slowly turned and raised his gore-streaked rifle, the mohawked sorcerer set a blinding sigil on his eyes.

Those great stone lids fell closed and fought to re-open. John Leicester staggered around, blindly crashing into the buildings on either side. The giant shattered rows of windows as he lashed out impotently.

A glass-clad Taursi reached for the Papagallo brothers, raising a shard of mundane glass in one hand. The Boneman snapped its alien vertebrae with a word. He saw a knot of resistance, perhaps a dozen of these creatures surrounded by Lucy's mind-slaves. The Taursi fought a brutal last stand with spur and claw, dropping foes with animal fury.

"Leave them," Lucy ordered, and they pushed through the battle, heading for the final barricade. Bodies lay everywhere, scattered by the flaming wrecks of cars turned into bombs. The Boneman saw the last Jesusman and his child helper unleashing small-arms fire as a camel-faced man and a bird-thing scaled their wall of cars.

Behind this flimsy defence, mere blocks away, the first of the golden towers stood. The Waking City was humming with potential. Lucy's gateway, his golden prize, was within reach.

"Gonna kill that Jesusman nice and slow," Lucy began but stopped in his tracks, eyes staring vacantly. He reached out a hand, fingers curled into an invisible grip.

"It's here," he whispered, smiling with rapture. "It's here and it's mine."

The Boneman felt the incredible attraction between two powerful forces and heard the echoes of a familiar whisper. The Cruik, long denied its chosen puppet, was so close now that the last of Lucy's defences crumbled. There were no Riders to foist this awful weapon onto, no deputies to bear his awful burden. Hands shaking, Lucy reached for the Cruik, willingly.

Nearby, a truck broke apart into shards of metal and a geyser of junk spewed into the air. The Boneman saw a parcel fall, its canvas wrap blistering with an incredible heat and pouring from it as dust. Clean and shining, the Cruik drifted into Papa Lucy's hands.

"Lucy," the Boneman began but faltered when he saw the vacant smile on his brother's face, the loving way he caressed the staff in his hands. There was nothing human in his eyes now, nothing but a cold reptile stare that considered the Boneman.

"Put the Cruik aside," the Boneman begged. "Please, Lucy, you're in great danger."

A bloodied Taursi came running. Papa Lucy twitched the Cruik in its direction and the spiky warrior blazed with an intense light. Not even ash remained. In the afterimage of this magic, the Boneman saw faint ghosts slowly failing, images of the warrior retracing its steps. The Cruik was killing the warrior several seconds into the past, just to prove it could.

"Stop your bleating, Sol," Lucy said coldly. "The only thing dangerous here is *me*."

Emitting a roar that sounded like two stones rubbing together, John Leicester came for them, his eyes now open to slits as Lucy's binding mark began to fail. In his haste, the giant trod the last of the Taursi into the dust as it lumbered to finish off his old friends.

Lucy held the Cruik like a lance, jabbing it towards the approaching giant. An invisible fist slammed into John's chest. The giant staggered, dropped to one knee, cracks spider webbed across the stylised tunic as big chunks of stone fell.

"Stop, Lucy," John Leicester said, sad and beaten. He stood up on shaking limbs and took another step forward. Lucy laughed as he swung the hooked staff like a sword. An invisible blade cut clean through the giant's right knee, severing the lower leg. John teetered and fell with a loud groan, his impact shattering an outline into the asphalt. The cracks continued to worm through his body and limbs as he rapidly fell apart.

"John, you know I have to kill you now," Lucy said, standing before the soldier's enormous face. The giant made to rise but the effort cost him too much. With one hand still obeying, John tried to swat Papa Lucy like a fly, but the sorcerer held the Cruik aloft, fending off John's furious blows like rain from an invisible umbrella.

John gave up and sank to the ground with resignation. He looked at his old master with stone calm. The goat on the altar, passive before the knife.

"Deserter. Traitor!" Lucy crowed. "Feel like explaining yourself?"

John said nothing.

"I've got a confession to make, John. I always envied your golf swing," Lucy said. He swung the Cruik at John's cheek. The boulder of red stone split from the broken body and sailed through the air. John Leicester's head struck the side of a building and fell to the ground in a shower of glass and broken cement.

"Fore!" Lucy called, following through like a pro. He looked back to see his brother weeping.

"What? He killed your bloody wife, Sol, so you can cut out that doe-eyed sanctimony, thank you very much."

The battle was over, the city's mysterious defenders dead to the last. What remained of Lucy's warped army regrouped before him, all machine-farts and nervous bird-warbles. They'd all seen the power of the Cruik firsthand, and none were game to test Papa Lucy's temper.

"Well, that was pretty straightforward," Lucy told the army, his voice amplified by the staff. "Wait here, you bunch of weirdos. I've got some stuff to do."

The Boneman considered the last Jesusman, half dead and pale behind his flimsy barricade. Lucy threw the man a friendly wave as he walked casually towards his post with the Cruik across his shoulders.

A wind began to blow.

"It's Papa Lucy," Tilly said, shaking with hysteria. "He killed the Leicester-We-Forget. He's coming!"

Lanyard opened the shotgun and pulled out the empty shells with a strange calm. He fed two more rounds into the big gun and then made sure his pistol was full. Tilly fed shells into the policeman's shotgun then laid this on the car hood before him.

"The last of the Jesusmen. And I thought I was a relic," Lucy called out, standing before their wall with a smirk. With the Cruik across his shoulders, the sorcerer hooked his arms over the staff as if he were a farmhand in friendly conversation with a neighbour.

Lanyard Everett raised the shotgun and emptied both barrels into Papa Lucy's chest. He snatched up the lawman's unmarked gun and emptied that too. Tilly joined in, white-faced and pistol blazing. But an invisible buffer turned the gunfire aside.

The Cruik flexed as if in pleasure, more a wooden serpent than a staff. Lanyard felt sick. He contemplated putting a bullet through his and the girl's heads before the sorcerer could introduce them to his favourite toy.

"Cut that out," Lucy said with a cold smile, unfazed by the attempt on his life. "I don't blame you for trying, but...seriously?"

Funnelled by the closely packed buildings, a draft ran along the road. Lanyard felt the wind rise and saw the dust and debris kick along the road. Resisting the urge to reach for his telescope, he made a point of calmly reloading the guns.

"That's it? No begging, no final defiance? I gotta tell you, Mr. Lanyard Everett, you're turning this into an anticlimax."

"Nice haircut, dickhead."

Papa Lucy displayed a benevolent smile that didn't reach his eyes.

"I've broken everything that your master ever owned, every scrap of Hesus's legacy," Papa Lucy said. "I gave him a good licking recently. Even went into the Greygulf and wiped out his turncoat servants. There's no help coming for you, Jesusman."

"Piss off," Lanyard said, holding Bauer's gun ready. He threw a handful of marks at the mohawked god and muttered every word of the old sorceries that Bauer had ever shown him. Lucy blinked at this attempt, waving the sigils away like flies. The marks burned out, their potential soured and undone.

"I fought magical duels in the Collegia." Papa Lucy laughed. "I defeated the finest sorcerers in the Before. You're just embarrassing yourself."

The wind kicked up approaching a hurricane gust. Lanyard felt a burning in his pocket and drew Turtwurdigan into the light. He juggled the glass like a hot coal until it rose from his hand to leap across the city. A tiny star in flight.

"You're fucked now," Lanyard said with a wide grin.

Papa Lucy saw a shining tornado pour into the city, chewing up everything before it. Taller than the city, that terrifying funnel destroyed entire buildings with ease. All of Sad Plain had arrived, down to the last sliver of glass.

"I'll deal with you two later." Papa Lucy snarled as he held the Cruik tightly. He tapped the car hood and pointed the hook of the staff at Lanyard's throat. "Don't go anywhere."

"Wouldn't miss this," Lanyard said around a cigarette, struggling to light a match in the wind. "Not every day you get to see a god die."

When Lucy came running, the Boneman felt dread rush through his body. It was only when he heard the first screams behind him that he dared to look.

A funnel of glass spun and scoured its way toward them, grinding Lucy's army into pulp. It was Sad Plain all over again, the ruins of the city rising against Papa Lucy and his allies.

Overhead, a point of light flew, a glowing sun that dove into the heart of the storm. Turtwurdigan's heart. Great flashes of lightning flickered in the centre of the tornado. The twister formed limbs, a rough man-shape that towered above the buildings.

Then the wind stopped as suddenly as it had arrived. Glass shards hung suspended in perfect sequence, each touching the other. This gargantuan being took one shining step, and its body tinkled with a brain-twisting melody, an alien music that got into his head and made him question his sanity.

Marks fell from it like snow as bright alien sigils. Where these symbols touched the living, they brought madness or catatonia.

The face, that horrid face! A snout swinging freely, eyes a sunken hell of mirrors and reflected light. He'd seen that face in his dreams, awoke from a thousand nightmares where he remembered the singular attention of those eyes.

When the transformation was complete, the being resembled a Taursi rendered as a hundred-foot sculpture. Deep in its innards, its heart glowed with a white heat, a furnace that slowly baked everything within a mile of it.

Turtwurdigan.

The Boneman stood numb, even when Lucy shook him and said something. His brother gave up in disgust, racing off to fight the Mother of Glass by himself.

"Lucy!" the Boneman cried. Turtwurdigan stood tall, her glass quills spread, glowing brighter than the sun's heart. The glass shards that formed her chest folded inwards, a shining iris that drew light into the demon's heart.

Then she emitted a beam of light so powerful that it burned everything it touched. When Turtwurdigan turned that radiant sword against Lucy's forces, his freaks died by the dozens. The beam left nothing but spots of grease and clouds of ash drifting across the ground.

The Boneman froze. All of his art, new and relearned…all of it fled from his mind as his greatest fear approached him.

He stood helpless as Turtwurdigan returned him to the flame. His agony was an exquisite thing as his rebuilt flesh melted from his bones. She focused the sun-ray on him for several moments, perhaps remembering him from the old days. Remembering her defeat at his blackened hands.

This time, I die, the Boneman thought. *My bones to dust, and then I am released once and for all.*

Then the fires passed from him as she moved across the ravaged street for further mayhem.

But the Boneman still stood. Once more, he lived. His mastery over death was not an easy thing to overcome.

In a state of shock, he examined his blackened skeleton. A distant part of him noticed how it still smouldered, the delicate interplay of bones, all still joined, and his limbs moved the way they were meant to.

"You can't kill me," he sobbed hysterically, some scrap of spirit serving as a tongue. "You can't!"

Knots of their soldiers attempted escape by scaling the blockages in the side streets. Turtwurdigan let no one escape and set buildings blazing on every street.

The Boneman fell to the ground, clutching his bony knees against his rib cage. Once he'd been the saviour, but this time he could only stare as Papa Lucy faced Turtwurdigan alone.

The ray of light came down upon his brother, but Lucy held the Cruik on high as he met the attack with an unseen force from the staff. The flames flowed around the sorcerer but they warped and melted only the road. Lucy gave the staff a deft twist and pulled something downwards.

It was the heart of Turtwurdigan, shining and burning. Lucy pulled it forth, fought the glass body as it stretched out and attempted to reclaim its centre.

Finally, the heart snapped free, and tonnes of glass fell, littering the Waking City as it once littered Sad Plain. The shards rained down upon Lucy's protective shield. He stood safely as the heart of Turtwurdigan lay at his feet.

Then he slammed down the Cruik, cracking the heart like a nut.

"You only get the one body, Sol. I had a hell of a time growing you that first one."

The Boneman tottered along behind his victorious brother, and they were the only two to walk away from that charnel house. Thousands dead, and now only the Jesusman stood between Lucy and the golden towers. The dying man and the girl had abandoned their barricade. Lanyard Everett was slumped against the tower itself, gun across his lap.

"Why spare the Jesusman?" the Boneman said shakily. "Why did you let him live through all that?"

"I wanna make that son of a bitch hurt," Lucy said. "I was expecting more. A Jesusman? He's barely a sorcerer. But he won't die easily, no. He'll see the end of this and then he's gonna burn."

The very word made the Boneman's smoking bones ache, but the skeleton followed his master faithfully.

They walked up to the abandoned barricade. Lucy threw the cars and trucks aside with a simple wave of the Cruik. The brothers approached the towers, and now the Boneman could feel the potential contained in the structures, the great stores of energy filling each one to the brim.

Something about this bleedthrough felt wrong, and the spirited defence of this place was unexplained. Why John Leicester? Why the strange Taursi? There'd been power stores in the Before but nothing on this scale. Lucy had obviously found a gateway into another Realm, a direct path that didn't require the Greygulf. He needed to access this energy to open the way.

Even with the Cruik, he wasn't sure that Lucy could survive the attempt.

"Turtwurdigan's finally dead," the Boneman said. "We're safe. We can go now."

"Oh, I'm going," Lucy said. "And I want you to come, too, you walking xylophone. We're checking out of this dump."

The Jesusman tried to hold himself up as the sorcerers approached, but he slid halfway down the glass tower. The girl helped to push him upright. Her face was drawn with fear, and her pistol was aimed at Lucy's heart.

Lucy twitched the Cruik and sent the girl tumbling across the ground. She flopped across the cement like a ragdoll, and when she stopped rolling she did not move. The Boneman took one shuffling step towards her, mortified, but Lucy held him back with a raised finger.

"The girl, I don't care about. But the Jesusman, he and I are going to have a little chat."

Lanyard the Jesusman stared at them groggily, his face grey and slick with sweat. He raised the enchanted shotgun, but the end of it wavered. The weight of the weapon finally proved too much for the man to bear. Lucy laughed.

"Mister, you couldn't guard a bowl of milk from a cat," Lucy said. "I'm guessing the standards for Jesusman recruitment have fallen in recent years."

"Get stuffed," Lanyard whispered.

"I had a friend called Hesus once," Lucy continued. "Smart man in many ways, but he asked too many questions. Why bring all the refugees to this shithole, when there were so many better worlds to settle? Why the Cruik? Why such an interest in the Taursi relics?"

Papa Lucy leaned in close, his nose almost touching the Jesusman's. The broken man struggled to raise his great gun, but Lucy gently pushed it to one side and shook his head as if disappointed.

"I'll tell you why. This place? It's a gateway, something my little brother has probably guessed...but there's more. Turns out that there's direct access between this world and the kingdom above."

The Boneman reeled with shock. The Taursi marks, the Taursi temple beneath Bertha's island hideaway. It all made sense now.

"So enjoy the show, Jesusman. Before you die—and you *will* die—I want you to see this. Watch what you failed to stop me from doing."

"Don't do this, Lucy," the Boneman said. Everything, the evacuation, the old war, all of this was in service of Papa Lucy's true ambition. Those who'd died today—even Bertha—all of these were acceptable losses.

Luciano Papagallo always got his way.

"We're going to Overhaeven, Sol. Today, we war with the gods."

He raised the Cruik, touching the hook end of the staff against the hot glass of the tower. The sinister construct writhed, pushed against that humming glow. Lucy gasped with pleasure, his eyes half-closed with orgasmic bliss.

The Boneman witnessed a black line spread out from the point of contact, a wriggling fault in the glass itself. It pushed forward, spiralling around the tower like a tangling root. At the forefront of that perfect curve was the questing face of something that didn't belong in this world.

But it certainly belonged in the Overhaeven. The Boneman saw the bristle of limbs as the Cruik's shadow gripped the golden tower. In that other world, a black serpent walked on a thousand feet.

The Cruik wanted to go home.

"I need more time," Lucy said, the first beads of sweat appearing on his forehead. "Help me, Sol."

The Boneman rested his skeletal hands on his brother's shoulders, added what he could to Lucy's struggle. He reeled with the strain but felt the immense forces at play here. The Cruik was drawing a massive amount of energy from the towers to fuel its assault on the boundaries of reality. All of this was being grounded through Lucy.

It took enormous strength of will for the Boneman to resist this load, even on the periphery of the sorcery. How Lucy was able to keep his body from drifting apart on an atomic level, the Boneman could not guess.

The Cruik writhed and fed and grew, but only so much. Lucy withdrew it slightly, the staff remaining attached to the tower by a thick rope of shadow. He undid the magic holding the brass cladding onto the staff, setting these lesser demons free. Long ago he'd bound these forms to the Cruik in an attempt to control it, but now they were holding the entity back and limiting its potential.

After Lucy hurled the brass hoops to the ground, the released demons fled from the Waking City. They grew shining wings and howled with fear.

"They're coming," Lucy said. "Be ready, my brother."

The tower hummed. The golden light within flickered as the naked Cruik strangled it. The other towers behind it suffered the same malaise, and the black tendrils climbed them as the Cruik somehow multiplied its assault.

The glass swam with shapes, as if it were a golden aquarium filled with all wonder of creatures from an amber sea. Vast beasts that were a forest of eyes and hands appeared, pushed against the glass from the far side. In vain they fought to limit the spread of the Cruik.

The shadow hook lashed about, and where it caught the alien beings, they shrivelled and faded, falling back into the amber murk.

"Well, lookie there, Sol," Lucy said. "Wave hi to Hesus."

One of the defenders was a pair of giant hands, twin squids that coasted about in that mysterious aether. They were marked with Hesus's old tattoos of the words BEFORE and NOW and pierced with the same ragged holes that Lucy had inflicted upon their owner during the battle of Sad Plain.

"We'll be seeing you real soon, old buddy." Lucy crowed.

Something swift and strong knocked Lucy and the Boneman to the ground.

Rising from the concrete, the Boneman saw Bertha straddling his prone brother, her bloodied and twisted hands closed around his throat. Her armour lay shattered, and her body was irreparably broken, but his wife still lived.

"The Cruik is mine." Bertha howled. "Give me the Cruik."

His hands gripping the staff tightly, Lucy raised it and drew out a curling ribbon of darkness from the tower. An offering. Bertha released him as she reached for the Cruik as if entranced.

Lucy jabbed the staff deep into her belly like a spear. She howled in disbelief, and the Boneman cried out in despair as he watched her body shrivel, her essence drawn into the Cruik. In moments, she was a dried husk, then dust that fell to the ground.

"It's all yours," Lucy said to Bertha's drifting remains.

Fuelled by the dead woman's essence, the shadow-Cruik continued to grow. The towers were now almost completely wreathed in those black threads. The Overhaeven defenders beat against this constriction, but fell by the hundreds. The flesh of this dark serpent burned them like acid.

The golden towers began to flex as the Cruik drew its coils tight. Much more of this assault and the glass skin would rupture. Papa Lucy would have his gateway into Overhaeven.

"What have you done?" the Boneman shouted. "You killed her!"

"She was already dead, Sol," Lucy said through gritted teeth. He hauled on the Cruik as if landing the world's biggest fish. As the coils tightened more, he laughed in triumph.

"They're all dead, baby brother. Her, the Jesusfool there, every single person between here and the sea. They're all about to burn."

The Boneman saw the first cracks appear in the glass and felt the pulsing energy as the crumbling world veil gave way to the Overhaeven. He saw the meaning of Lucy's words. When that gateway opened, the Now would be burnt to a cinder. A whole world in flames. Papa Lucy thought nothing of this.

"We'll be gods, Sol. The usurpers of the Overhaeven. What price is a world when the universe can be ours?"

Before the Boneman, Lanyard Everett struggled to rise and lifted his gun. Even at the end of things, despite the futility of his actions, the Jesusman continued his duty. Lucy laughed as he froze the man in place with a word.

"I will pave our way to glory with every single one of their pointless lives. And do you know what?" Lucy raved. "Tomorrow you'll thank me."

"I thank you now, brother," the Boneman said, advancing slowly towards Lucy. "Thank you for showing me what you really are. Thank you for bringing me to your moment of triumph."

In sleeping, the Boneman had lost his art, but this one thing remained to him. Death was his, and in this strange second life, the sorcerer could still hear the whisper of life that ran in bones.

He stood next to his brother, behind the corrosive protection that the Cruik offered. Reaching forward as if offering to take the load of energy, the Boneman laid his hands around Lucy's forearms and reached in through the skin for the bone.

As Lucy cried out in shock, he plucked the bones free and cast them aside. Everything from the elbow to the fingertips tore from the flesh. Two trees of bone that instantly reverted into the animal remains they truly were, substitutes that were baked into clay. As Lucy's false bones fell apart and struck the ground, they shivered into dust.

Lucy howled with pain and anguish. His arms were now floppy bags of skin that could not hold onto the Cruik or even draw upon a single sorcerous mark. The staff clattered to the ground, and Papa Lucy ran.

The Cruik's shadow whipped about, drawn back towards the abandoned staff like an unravelling thread. It fought to keep its purchase on the Overhaeven, but the remaining spirits pried the hook loose with their ghost fingers.

Hesus was there at the last, his great fists battering the Cruik's shadow-self, driving it out of the tower. With its last ounce of strength, the staff stood up on its end, the hook quivering with rage. Finally, it was spent and stood in a sullen defeat. The Boneman tipped over the Cruik with the point of a bony finger, and the wooden staff clinked against the cement.

Hysterical with bags of skin flopping from his elbows, Lucy ran about mindlessly, crazed and scared. He froze when he heard the low bubble of laughter behind him. He turned to see the cold stare of the dying Jesusman, now standing on unsteady feet. Then, there was nothing left to Lucy's world but the double infinity of the shotgun barrels.

Lanyard Everett pulled the trigger and turned Papa Lucy's head into a bloody mist.

— EPILOGUE —

The Boneman spoke to Lanyard's ravaged insides. He drew out the jagged sliver, sealed up the holes in the man's intestines. In moments, he made the broken ribs line up correctly and knit, then saw to it that the flesh would mend clean. He mixed his own magic with the best of the Taursi's sorcery, deftly sketching out Overhaeven marks on the man's skin.

"You turned against your own," the Jesusman said to the charred skeleton. "I understand what that's like."

"Oh, you do?" The Boneman continued his ministrations. Although his scrap of silvery tongue clearly unnerved the man, the Jesusman made a point of looking at the skeleton's face when he talked.

Lanyard watched as the corpse worked sorcery upon his broken guts. "You had to do it." He winced as muscle shifted back into place. It was far from a painless procedure. "If someone acts like a bad dog, you gotta put 'em down."

"It was nothing like that," the Boneman said, but he wondered if this was true. He helped the man climb to his feet, a dead hand gripping a living one.

Tilly still lay on her side, her mousy hair protruding from a bundle of blankets and rugs. The sorcerer searched her for any lasting damage, but she fared no worse than if she'd taken a bad tumble from a horse. She was still unconscious but was breathing easily. She just needed rest.

"Kid's resilient," Lanyard said from his side. The Boneman nodded.

They took a walk through the ruins of the Woken City. The battle had levelled nearly half of the magnificent bleedthrough, and the fires burned out of control now. Almost one quarter of the city lay buried beneath razor-sharp glass, a shining snowfield to mark the final resting place of Turtwurdigan. It was a valiant ending for such a strange creature, defending Overhaeven from the Cruik and its favoured slave.

"So, what happens now?" Lanyard asked. The Boneman shrugged, his collarbones lifting and falling. As the pair poked through the aftermath of the slaughter, the Boneman eased the suffering of the occasional twisted survivor into death.

The Jesusman assisted here. His marked guns delivered a swift mercy to the lingering mutants. When his bullets were spent, he tried to send the dead over with his knife, but more often than not it proved too difficult to cut through machine veins and engine hearts, so it was up to the Boneman to sing these ones to a gentle sleep.

They came across the severed head of John Leicester half-buried in rubble. To their surprise he was still conscious, eyes blinking, stone lips gently moving.

"I am sorry, Sol." The broken head rumbled. The Boneman nodded, gently patting the statue's cheek with his blackened finger-bones.

These three survivors held council and talked until the sun sank below the city's horizon and slid across the Waste. They paused only to carry Tilly down to where the red face of her god lay buried. Lanyard lit a fire to warm them as they talked into the night. The Boneman sat as far away from the flames as possible, frightened by the orange licks.

"What we called the Now is actually a prison," John Leicester was saying, "and Turtwurdigan was the warden."

He explained the hierarchy of Overhaeven. The Taursi were servants, something like the angels of the old belief. Whenever one of these servants fell from grace, the criminal's entire bloodline was condemned and sent into exile under the watchful gaze of the Mother of Glass.

These criminals were stripped of all but the crudest of glass-work and allowed only the run of this world and certain aspects of the Greygulf. When the mountain range finally met the sea and this world was at an end, Overhaeven had decreed that their sentences would have been served.

"Lucy broke into a prison," the Boneman said, and then his absent lungs flexed with laughter, tears running from his all-too-human eyes. A broad smile spread across the statue's face, and he laughed, too, sounding like a rockfall.

The stone head and the burnt skeleton talked long into the night, reminiscing over ancient memories, friendships, and enmities that were centuries dead.

"Never heard of this Overhaeven place," Lanyard mumbled later, poking at the fire with a stick. "Seems to me that if there was all this going on somewhere else, old bones here would have known about it."

"There was a political decision long ago," John rumbled. "After each Prime Realm was created, Overhaeven was not to interfere with it. They withdrew and left the facets of creation unfold as they would. No engagement whatsoever, for good or ill."

"Well, that went well," the Boneman said, remembering the sudden death of the Before. The fire crackled, and they watched as the Jesusman cooked a looted tin of beans on the coals.

"After Sad Plain, Hesus and I were admitted into Overhaeven," John said. "On probate. Because we defended its borders against our own, we were to be the guardians of this world. Your jailers."

"Why did you stand against my brother? Why guard the borders of some alien race?"

"Hesus learnt the truth. Lucy destroyed the Before. He used the power stations to fuel his first assault on Overhaeven, knowing it would destroy our old world."

The fire crackled, and the Boneman bowed his head as this final truth struck home. Lucy had destroyed the Before, even as he acted like its saviour.

"And here I was thinking that we'd won at Sad Plain," the Boneman mused. "The Family won nothing but a jail cell, didn't it?"

"The gods wanted you dead, Sol. Be thankful for the centuries you had, lording over this dust bowl. The punishments of Overhaeven, you—you don't want to know."

The next morning, they fetched a car to tow the stone head back to the golden towers. Wrapped in ropes and chains, the red stone scratched deeply into the asphalt.

At the base of the nearest tower, Lanyard and the Boneman used levers and rollers to move the stone closer to the glowing glass. This was John Leicester's only exit from Now, and he was needed back at his post.

"I'm sorry I didn't get here sooner," John said. "Hesus and I petitioned our superiors for leave to stop Lucy. They take a long time to make a decision."

"Bureaucrats," Lanyard muttered, straining at a crowbar while the stone shifted another few inches.

"When Lucy summoned this gateway into the Now, I bent the rules a little. I told Turtwurdigan where to guide what remained of my faithful. I'm in disgrace now, if you must know."

He said the word with some emphasis, revealing that staying in a state of grace was very important when it came to Overhaeven.

"Wait a minute," the Boneman said. *"Lucy* brought the Waking City here? He did this?"

"He did a lot of things while he was stuck in the Aum. Your brother was using you, Sol. I'm sorry."

Lanyard withdrew for a cigarette, letting the two old friends make their goodbyes. After they had a long talk, the Boneman waved him back over, and they rolled the stone head into the glass. The skin of the Overhaeven parted to accept one of its own.

Tilly woke that afternoon, aching and bruised. Blinking wearily, she saw Lanyard sitting across a cookfire from the Boneman. The girl panicked as she fumbled in her blankets for the gun the Jesusman had gifted to her.

"Be easy. We're just talking," the Boneman said, his blackened skull turning towards her. She shivered and felt pinned in place by those sad brown eyes.

"It's okay, Tilly, he's a—" and here Lanyard paused, unsure of what Papa Lucy's immortal brother actually was now.

"A friend. If you wish," the moving skeleton said.

Warily, Tilly joined their parley, and it was then that the Boneman made his offer. He told the pair what would be expected of them now. Lanyard left the decision to Tilly, who nodded after a long moment of thought. She shook the dead man's hand solemnly.

Only then did she cry.

The Boneman built a pyre for his brother, a great stack of furniture and doors, anything that would burn. He wept as he built it and cursed his inability to build a grand marker like the cairn of bone Lucy had left for him.

Lanyard helped the Boneman haul the canvas roll containing the mortal remains of Papa Lucy and set the bundle on top of the bonfire. Already the flesh was returning to clay, Lucy's borrowed parts reverted to their true forms. Silty water ran from the ends of his improvised shroud, dark with blood.

"He deserves more," Sol cried, cringing when Lanyard brought a flaming taper forward. He retreated, and though fearful of the impending blaze, was unable to look away.

"No, Boneman. You deserved more." Lanyard grunted and then he set the pyre alight. Tilly waited by the sorcerer's side and held his bony hand as he watched his brother burn.

Later, the trio stood around the Cruik. Lanyard nudged it carefully with his boot, but the staff was still. Its promises were subdued, listless murmurs that barely registered in his mind.

"You sure about this?" he asked the Boneman, who picked up the staff in his bony hand and leaned heavily on it.

"There's nothing to fear if you're the master of your own house," the sorcerer said, tapping the side of his skull with a finger. "It's just a stick now."

He opened a far-door, a portal of purest night. The fleshless sorcerer regarded the man and the girl, then spread his jaw wide in what might have passed for a smile.

"Humanity is a fine thing, and worth saving," he said. "I'll see you soon, Jesusman."

"Good luck, Boneman," Lanyard said.

"Please. Call me Sol." And with that, the last of the Family stepped through the gateway and was gone.

In the moment of his murder, Papa Lucy fell out of his loan body with shock. He was nothing but a soul now, an essence that shone with a slowly fading light. He fought the forces pulling at him. He stood firm as a doorway opened and sought to draw him into the Underfog to his final death. He knew enough of necromancy to resist this temptation and cast about for a place to hide his spirit—a mirror. Or perhaps a body with a weak mind that he could expel and seize for his own.

As he cast his eye upon the Jesusman's girl, he felt a second impulse, more disturbing than the draw of death. Before he could escape, a black tendril snatched at his foot and drew him away from the Underfog and into the Cruik.

The entity shivered with glee, gobbling him up with relish. In sympathy with the Cruik, Lucy experienced his own consumption from its perspective. He knew that he represented the most fulfilling meal of its ancient existence.

He stood in the sunlit palace, a false house modelled after his own. This was no accident. He'd designed this prison himself, a golden cage to lull the Cruik's many victims into dumb obedience.

Papa Lucy had bound the Cruik and sent it away when it had nearly mastered him despite this. He had fed it a thousand others, distracted it with its cadre of willing victims, the Riders. Still the Cruik came for him at the end. It claimed a lifetime of favours owed.

Behind him, the golden doors closed. Lucy stood in the courtyard surrounded by blank-faced souls, each of whom he'd doomed to this end. Their friendly games came to an end now. They hefted croquet mallets and grasped whittling knives drawn in anger.

Before him wearing the shape of her earlier life stood Baertha Papagallo. All traces of the Lady Bertha were gone, and her frame was once more that of the demure magician from a dead world, the ballerina's body that had drawn Sol to chase a bride above his station.

Although her face was washed out, he could just make out the shape of her eyes, the full lips that were slowly fading into a narrow slit.

Baertha snarled and drew a fireplace poker from behind her skirts. All of the prisoners were similarly armed, their placid existence riled into rebellion by this new champion.

"Here is the one who imprisoned you!" she shouted. "Papa Lucy gave you to the Cruik. Look where his lies have brought him!"

"Come now," Lucy said, holding his hands up and regarding the circle of hostile prisoners closing around him. "Go back to your badminton and let the grown-ups talk."

The other souls fell back from this command. They struggled to overcome Lucy's iron will but failed. Baertha hefted the iron poker, trembling slightly. He smiled at her and advanced slowly. Her arm fell, and as he gently ran a finger across her wrists, the poker fell from her grip. It rang against the flagstones, a note of defeat that made Lucy smile.

"Baertha dear, you really must relax," Lucy said. "This is your home now, but I must be on my way. Do be sure the other guests are comfortable during their stay."

Baertha fought to resist Lucy's charms and frowned as he massaged her temples. He smiled at her with utmost confidence. She wandered away to play at boules, confused and blinking.

Lucy turned his attention to the outer doors. That was when the girl leapt upon him and drove a knife deep into his guts. He felt it grate against his ribs and the cold flow of his soul-stuff leaking from the wound.

It was possible to die a second death.

"You lied, you lied," the girl sobbed, driving the knife in again. "You were never going to save my father."

Shocked and gasping with pain, he recognised Jenny, last of the Riders of Cruik. She led a force of the most wasted souls, the oldest prisoners. One of them held a dog at bay, a low shape coughing up a ragged sound like barking or the distant memory of the sound.

There was little left of these revenants, just shadow-stuff and the faintest sense of self. They ignored his commands, broke his spirit-body with shadowy fists and feet. Flailing, trying to fight free, he saw the depths of the dark colonnades and knew what fate awaited him should his soul perish inside of the Cruik.

He sketched out a mark with one trembling finger, and then another. The souls fell back with howls of pain, and Jenny Rider writhed like a landed fish, her back arched and her feet drumming.

Papa Lucy rose then jerked out the knife from his side. Hands shaking, he dropped it to the ground.

"Just for that, I'm taking away your cucumber sandwiches," Lucy said. Snuffing out a handful of the trapped souls, he forged the leftover souls into a great silver battering ram that he used to force open the doors. He left the Cruik's house with a spring in his step, even as the walls shook and a distant voice howled with rage.

Elated with his escape, he did not notice when another slipped out of that false house and followed him into freedom.

Sol Papagallo passed into the Aum and found a likely spot to enter the Underfog. Where it had once taken Lucy almost a year to force his way through, Sol took a much gentler approach. He asked for permission to enter the lands of the dead.

A way opened for him and his passage was marked. He would not be permitted to linger for long, unless he cared to stay forever. He thanked his unseen hosts, recognising them now as the opposites of the lords of Overhaeven.

"As above, so below," he marvelled. At its height, the Collegia had known so much, while also managing to know next to nothing. His professors in necromancy had never guessed at this hierarchy. Sol smiled as he felt a flicker of the old excitement. Once this task was complete, his education could begin anew.

He walked the shifting roads of the Underfog, asking the way from those who lingered in this final land. Some of these spirits turned and fled, more from the sight of the Cruik than any fear of his appearance. Skeletal shapes were common down here.

Lucy had left signs, of course. Communities of the dead lay ravaged and twisted, or set to war or mischief by his twisted whims. Scars remained from Lucy's many attempts to exit the Underfog, but each time he had been rebuffed, pushed a little further onwards.

Sol followed, respecting the lords of death and paying tribute when asked. Secret ways were opened to him, paths that sped his passage across the dead kingdoms. Where it had taken his brother a decade to first cross the Underfog, Sol followed in mere weeks.

He was not surprised to find Lucy on the final boundary of death itself. What was left of his brother's soul stood on that lonely beach, shivering before the black waves that crashed against the shale.

The silvery stuff that was his brother's soul had been badly treated. He wore the scars of knife wounds, and one of his arms hung at a strange angle, broken in at least two places. His hair hung in patches.

It was possible to die twice. The second death was absolute, a trip into that undiscovered country beyond the black sea.

Even now Lucy was attempting to escape. A loan body stood ready, a scarecrow of beach stones stacked into a rough man-shape glued together with the last of his magic. The veil between Underfog and Aum was heavily scratched, but so far Lucy had been unable to force a way through.

Only the greatest force of will kept Papa Lucy from walking into the dark ocean. The sorcerer clung to existence tenaciously, even as death drew him in by inches.

"Sol." Lucy sobbed. "You came."

The skeletal sorcerer maintained a safe distance, resting on the Cruik. The staff squirmed a little at the sight of its former puppet, but Sol stilled it with a twitch of his wrist.

"Quickly, brother," Lucy said. "I don't have much time. Give me the Cruik."

"No," Sol said.

"No? You kill me and then this? After all I've done for you."

"What you have done? This...this you *deserve*, my brother. John and I spoke, and he told me a lot of things. How you brought about the doom of Before. Used the power stations to fuel your first assault on Overhaeven. That was news to me."

"So what?" Lucy scoffed, his face suddenly drawn and pale as his feet slipped another inch across the slick rocks. "I'd do it again. It nearly worked. I would have brought you with me. We were almost gods, Sol. Gods!"

"You've killed an entire world, Lucy! You've lied with every breath in your body and hurt everyone who ever cared about you. What makes you think you have the right to live?"

Papa Lucy opened his mouth, but all of his glib responses and clever words fell away. He simply could not answer his brother's question. They stood in a long silence, death's waves almost deafening as they lashed the coast mercilessly.

"But you are my brother," Sol said. "I will help you."

"Yes," Lucy said, a tear of gratitude sliding down his grey spirit-face. "Thank you, thank you Sol."

Sol stepped forward, carefully navigating the cracked shoreline. His bony feet had trouble getting purchase on the slippery stones, and death reached for him greedily.

"Quick, give it to me." Lucy reached for the staff. A wave broke, and this time the spray struck him. He howled in anguish as the substance of his soul began to melt away.

Keeping low, gripping a stone as tightly as he could, Sol reached out with the Cruik, the staff quivering as Lucy's hand got closer to it.

Then Sol jammed the Cruik into his brother's solar plexus. Lucy fell backwards, arms wheeling as he sought to keep upright. His eyes were wide with terror as the obsidian waves closed around him.

Sol stood on the edge of death as Papa Lucy screamed. He watched as his brother's mad thrashing slowed and then finally stopped. Lucy's head sank beneath the dark water, and then he was finally dead.

"Someone acts like a bad dog, you gotta put 'em down," Sol said mournfully. He held the Cruik in his skeletal hand for a long moment, considering something, and then he cast the staff into the water too.

It flopped around like a frightened eel, magnesium flashes painting the dark beach as thousands of souls were suddenly released from captivity. Then the Cruik bobbed away like driftwood, until a barrage of waves folded it out of sight.

Sol turned around and began the long trek towards the lands of the living.

When Lanyard finally got to loot the Waking City, he took no joy from it. The man poked through the intact buildings, always with a worried eye to the golden towers.

One full day, John Leicester had promised them. Then the glass towers would sink back into the earth, dragging the lesser buildings through in their wake. When the lords of Overhaeven reversed Papa Lucy's ambitious bleedthrough, anyone caught filling their pockets would be killed.

At his heels, Tilly pushed a wheelbarrow loaded high with everything they would need. But there were no books here, no music discs. Lanyard gathered bullets, provisions for travel, food in tins and packets. Clothes that would wear well on the road, for himself and for the Carpidian girl.

He took a carton of cigarettes, and Tilly took a pile of gaudy jewellery. When he raised his eyebrows, she said, "For trading, stupid." Lanyard held in a smile when the girl wore everything at once, slim arms loaded with the jangling wealth of a dead world.

Tilly wore her father's slouch hat now. Her eyes were red-rimmed from crying. Before he had made the offer, the Boneman delivered John Leicester's message, words from her father now seated in his bloody hall.

There'd be no searching for Fos Carpidian in the Waste, no hope of finding anyone. Her whole family was dead by their own hand. Tilly tried to tell Lanyard about the rite of sacrifice, how her people served a bloody but fair god, but here the words failed her.

"Leave it," Lanyard said. "Leicester released you from his service. You're mine now."

The Jesusman and his new prentice stood at the edge of the Waste, a smouldering and broken city behind them. The glass towers began to shudder, the light within them failing. The buildings in the centre of the city began a rumbling descent as a cloud of dust spread outwards.

"Time to go," he said. He deftly sketched out the marks that Sol the Boneman had taught him. The Jesusmen had been using an old method for centuries, a roundabout sorcery deemed good enough for those who served Hesus.

The last of the Overhaeven sigils hung in the air for a long moment, and then the doorway opened. The Greygulf lay on the other side, a buckled shadow-road that was solid enough to stand on.

Lanyard had learned that these hidden ways were far from set. The next trick was to call the shadow-roads to you wherever you were. Something else his predecessors had never figured out.

"C'mon, girl," and with that he stepped out of the Now and into the world between worlds. Tilly Carpidian followed. She kept her mind—the only qualification needed for her new career.

When he'd finished throwing up his breakfast, Lanyard got to his feet. Tilly's education as a Jesusman began here in the

Greygulf. He explained the Realms, the ways that connected them, and the sinister creatures that crept from world to world preying on the innocent.

"That's what Sol was worried about," Lanyard said. "See there? After all the damage Lucy caused, the world veil is as thin as tissue paper. Anything could step through that and find a way into our world. Nasty things, hungry for flesh or worse."

Tilly nodded and rested her hand against the pistol on her hip. Lanyard smiled grimly.

"Good. Now step quickly, the bossman is watching," he said, pointing up to the silver heavens. A giant pair of hands fluttered across the sky. His skin crawling with fear and awe, Lanyard nodded at Hesus.

"Let's go be Jesusmen," he said and led his prentice into a new and most violent life.

— AUTHOR'S NOTE —

I t feels surreal to be writing this, almost a decade to the day since I finished writing the first draft of Papa Lucy and the Boneman. This book has been on a long and weird road since the start, and there were times when I was almost convinced that the story was cursed, that I should abandon it and work on something a bit more accessible. Being a literary cross-genre piece made the path to publication damn hard, but I'm glad it came through in the same bizarre glory as the short stories I'd earlier written in the same setting. For the eagle-eyed collector the stories of Lanyard the last Jesusman originally appeared in Aurealis Magazine in the early 2000s/late noughties.

No writer is an island, and I am eternally grateful to everyone who has backed me in this endeavour. My beta readers, numerous writer friends who kept my spirits up, Arts SA for funding the production of the first draft, my agent Angel Belsey (you will always have this victory!) and Outland Entertainment for finally giving it a great home. Above all else, my family, who have adopted this writer and kept him from going completely feral.

Lanyard will return in volume 2 of the series, THE DAWN KING, and I promise you, it's going to be a wild ride.

Meanwhile, keep watch for things that don't belong. Try not to lose your mind when you pass from one place to another. Know that an enemy is always watching, licking its chops, ready to step into your world and lay a waxy hand upon you...

From the Before to the Now,
Jason Fischer
Adelaide, Australia

— ABOUT THE AUTHOR —

Jason Fischer is a writer who lives near Adelaide, South Australia. He has won the Colin Thiele Literature Scholarship, an Aurealis Award and the Writers of the Future Contest. In Jason's jack-of-all-trades writing career he has worked on comics, apps, television, short stories, novellas and novels. Jason also facilitates writing workshops, is an enthusiastic mentor, and loves anything to do with the written or spoken word.

Jason is also the founder and CEO of Spectrum Writing, a service that teaches professional writing skills to people on the Autism Spectrum.

He plays a LOT of Dungeons and Dragons, has a passion for godawful puns, and is known to sing karaoke until the small hours.